CRIMES

and the People Who Commit Them

Fiction with Conviction by the Guy who Did the Time

CRIMES

and the People Who Commit Them

Fiction with Conviction by the Guy who Did the Time

Phil Lippert

Fresh Ink Group

Guntersville

Crimes and the People Who Commit Them
Fiction With Conviction by the Guy Who Did the Time

Copyright © 2021
by Phil Lippert
All rights reserved

Fresh Ink Group
An Imprint of:
The Fresh Ink Group, LLC
1021 Blount Avenue, #931
Guntersville, AL 35976
Email: info@FreshInkGroup.com
FreshInkGroup.com

Edition 1.0   2021

Book design by Amit Dey / FIG
Cover design by Stephen Geez / FIG
Associate publisher Lauren A. Smith / FIG

Cataloging-in-Publication Recommendations:
FIC050000 / FICTION / Crime
FIC029000 / FICTION / Short Stories (single author)
FIC062000 / FICTION / Noir

Library of Congress Control Number: 2021902718

ISBN-13: 978-1-947893-12-2   Papercover
ISBN-13: 978-1-947893-14-6   Hardcover
ISBN-13: 978-1-947893-25-2   Ebooks

Dedicated to Cynthia Joelle Lippert

You inspire me.

Table of Contents

Preface

ippert was thrown into the bowels of the Michigan Department of Corrections as a 17-year-old adolescent. He remained entrenched in a world of malfeasance for the next 42 years.

With astonishing honesty, he reveals the raw details of what a life of incarceration looks like from the inside. His observations of human behavior and stellar ability to tell a story reveal the courage and resilience of a man who has survived horrifying and savage injustice. These are stories of miscreants and corrupt institutions. They are tales of men who have made poor choices and suffered grave consequences.

His tales of the criminal counter-culture are sometimes tragic, but often humorous and redemptive; through it all, he displays a sly sense of humor and the quiet wisdom of a man who is, ultimately, a survivor. Lippert's journey has been one of an unrequited longing for freedom. This book is a resonant journey through the geography of a resilient soul.

Ellen Lord,
Behavioral Health Therapist & Poet.

Acknowledgements

I met Sister Pat Schnapp in 1998, and immediately had a sense that this was someone who would impact my life. She encouraged me to write and when I did, she insisted that I write better, providing the advice and direction necessary to accomplish that. She gathered up a collection of my short stories and produced my first book, *God Bless America: Stories by Some Guy in the Joint,* which she then convinced the administration of Siena Heights University to use as a textbook. Sister Pat was a driving force in bringing this book into being. To the extent that I am a writer, it is because Sister would have it no other way. I could not be more grateful or humbled by the friendship that has developed over the years and countless hours she has spent advocating on my behalf. Thank you, Sister.

I am indebted to so many people for so many kindnesses and opportunities that were pieces of the puzzle that ultimately became this book; acknowledging them all just isn't doable. I remain grateful to Lee Lewis of Words+Design for bringing *God Bless America* into being, which was an essential stepping stone to *Crimes and The People Who Commit Them.* Writing this book would not have been possible without the support and feedback of my lovely wife, Cynthia, always available with insights and critiques only another writer can provide. Special thanks to Josh and Maggie Mae Compton, along with the entire Compton clan, who welcomed me into their family and an environment conducive to creativity. I am blessed to have two families.

I would never have survived the last few years without the wise counsel of Ellen Lord, who helped smooth out bumpy patches, shed light into dark places, and forced monsters back into their closets. A poet extraordinaire and a dear friend, Ellen's support has been invaluable.

My family went deeply into debt over the decades shoveling money to lawyers who made big promises and ultimately accomplished absolutely nothing. Early in 2016, retired Michigan State Police Commander Ken Anderson brought my story to the attention of Morning Sun editor Rick Mills. That exchange led to a series of articles that ultimately led to my release. Absent that conversation and what grew out of it, I would remain incarcerated today. Heartfelt thanks to Commander Anderson and Rick Mills.

It turns out that publishing a book is a big job, and very much a group effort. My contribution—writing the stories—was the easy part. Those who work their magic behind the scenes are unsung heroes, and have my sincere gratitude. None of this would have come to be without the expertise and infinite patience of Stephen Geez, founding member and publisher at Fresh Ink Group, and the invaluable input of Fresh Ink Group producer and editor Beem Weeks. Thank you, guys, and thanks to Anik, our cover artist, and to associate publisher Lauren "Wearer-of-Many-Hats" Smith.

(Articles written by Rick Mills are available at *www.TheMorningSun. com.*)

Introduction

Rick Mills
MediaNews Group

*P*hil Lippert lives on a river these days.

I like that from a practical standpoint, but I love the symbolism—a notion of flowing water, of life moving on, and of peace and tranquility.

This book you are holding will give you a peek at Phil's life, his core values, his sense of humor, wry observations of other humans of all ilks, and lessons learned in 42 years of incarceration.

How he got there is the story of a one-time prostitute who was renowned for her multiple affairs and became smitten with the teenage Lippert, a schoolmate of her own children, and gifted him with sex and drugs and a car to drive.

One evening, smoking marijuana with his high school wrestling coach, a recon marine recently returned from Vietnam, Phil divulged that his girlfriend was pressuring him to find a hit man to eliminate her husband. The coach responded, "I'd jump at the chance." After being paid one hundred dollars for the task, he did just that. The murder was accomplished two weeks later.

Both men were arrested within two months, and Lippert was sentenced to life in prison fourteen working days after his arrest for his role in the crime.

It would be forty years later before I met Phil. He didn't trust me. I wasn't sure I trusted him. We quickly got past that. He and his family shared every report, every newspaper article, every document and review from the Department of Corrections and Parole Board. Approaching age 63, Phil was a man out of place, a kind and caring individual who took developmentally disabled prisoners under his wing, who often protected the vulnerable from predators, who trained dogs for police work and worked many years in prison hospital units. And he read. He spent hours every day living in books from the prison library.

"I know this may sound weird," he once told me, "given my history, but I am not a violent person. I have never been in a fight. I have never twisted someone's arm around their back and made them say, "Uncle.""

A series I wrote and published in the *Morning Sun* newspaper may have helped win parole for Lippert, who has been out of prison at this writing for four years, after successfully completing the mandates of his parole.

Since that time, we have become friends. My wife and I stood with them as Phil married his lovely bride, Cynthia. He's visited my family and I his. We are friends.

Phil brings compassion, keen observations, 42 years of seeing things the rest of us can only imagine, and a great talent for writing to this book, and to all of his short stories.

I hope you enjoy them...

Dude

My name is "Dude." I am a country boy and known as a bit of a cowboy, which is an uncommon background in prison. This name was hung on me decades ago, long before everyone was going around saying, *"Hey dude...."* It seems a silly nickname now, but that is what I am known as and is too late to change it now. I used to work over in the Hospital Annex. As far as I am concerned, I lucked out and landed the best job in the institution. Who knew? I've had a pretty good run, actually.

That is all winding down and the era that shaped my reality is now is very much an anachronism. I don't know how it all shot past me so fast—the decades, the generations—but suddenly I am an old burnout, a has-been ready for Boot Hill. Such is life.

The tales contained herein all took place at SPSM—State Prison of Southern Michigan—at Jackson. Jackson Prison has stood for many years, since before Michigan was a state, as the largest walled prison in the world. Forget the prisons you have seen on TV; Jackson was a village enclosed by brick walls—five thousand inmates on fifty-seven acres, and an infrastructure as complex as any you will find anywhere.

There were several full-size baseball fields and a football field on the big yard—the "back 40"—a dozen or so factories and several different rec yards. The area between Health Care Annex and the chow hall was called Peckerwood Park, and was primarily frequented by white guys and an ideal spot to smoke dope.

Over from there, the corner where Three Block meets Four Block, was an area known as Casino Royale—which featured three dozen tables used for gambling; poker, blackjack, keno, tunk, and the all-time favorite, skin, were played every yard period with enormous amounts of money changing hands every hour. There was a tacit agreement between those who operated these games and the yard cops—as long as there was no violence at your table, you were good to go.

Put a bunch of guys together and there will be gambling. Case closed, dot the i's and cross the t's. This was brought home a few years back when, in response to violence, a new warden declared that he would crack down on gambling and remove that scourge from the institution. It became illegal to play cards on the yard; there were horrendous penalties for being caught with dice or betting slips. Those activities faded away, and were replaced by such things as—Hey man, see those two pigeons on the Control Center roof? *I'll bet you five cigarettes that the one on the left flies away first...*There were a hundred variations that theme.

So much has changed over the years that when I try to tell these new guys how it was in the old days, they laugh it off. Never could there have been such a system in Michigan....

At some point many years ago, our state's highest court determined that *Yes, indeed, women may work inside of men's prisons.*

A lot of guys, old heads like me, especially, were appalled by the notion. Women supervising showers and other more personal moments of the daily routine? Women shouting orders and pushing guys around? *Please, no!* A large number of those female employees went to work in the Hospital building.

What was known as *The Hospital* addressed all health care needs. It was Sick Call, First Aid, ICU—which housed critical care patients—and long-term geriatric care. Inmates did all the work. Hard to believe now, but when I started as an Inmate Nurse, we not only did all manner of inpatient care, inmate nurses also did blood draws, sutures, all of the x-rays and lab work. All learned OJT. It worked. When women started working in the hospital, pretty much all the inmates on that assignment were fired and most of the staff hired to replace them were female. Instead of paying inmates sixty-five cents a day, the State hired RN's, PA's, Lab Techs, X-Ray Technicians and other professionals to do their jobs. At a million times the cost. Your tax dollars at work.

In those days, every department had at least one inmate clerk and for all intents and purposes, clerks ran the institution. Want a specific job? Give the Classification clerk three cartons of Lucky Strikes. Would you like a certificate for your parole board interview proving that you have attended A.A. for the last four years? See the appropriate clerk. There are a couple dozen clerks who are the real movers and shakers; those jobs are coveted and pretty much impossible to get. There are clerks in this facility who have been in their jobs for decades.

Sick Call has always been a major part of the daily routine. Send in a sick call request and next morning you have a pass to talk to a male nurse to discuss your ailment. It's a triage sort of thing. It usually doesn't get more involved than handing out something for athlete's foot or sniffles. Anything more serious gets referred to a doctor. It is not uncommon for a couple hundred guys to show up for Sick Call.

As part of the on-going effort to keep distance between inmates and female employees, the Activities Building became the Hospital Annex. Sick Call takes place there five mornings a week. Since there is no female staff involved, there is a job there for an inmate worker. When my position in the Hospital was dissolved, my supervisor got me this job. I clean up and generally make myself useful. I was unenthused at first and was thinking of applying to the license plate factory. What a mistake that would have been.

There is an officer who comes to work every morning and does nothing but sit at a desk near the front door of this building. He "works" about two hours every morning. Come through the door and he will take your pass; when you leave he will sign it and give it back. The rest of the day, he does cross-word puzzles, talks on the phone and looks at girlie magazines. Good work if you can get it.

Claude is a very large man, and not what you would call an over-achiever. The current state of affairs works well for both of us. I come to work in the morning and usually drop off a couple bear claws or other munchies at the desk, and sometimes a magazine or two. We spend a few minutes analyzing whatever sporting event was televised last night and ignore each other for the rest of the day. Sick call lasts a couple hours, after that we both do our own thing. My thing often is to sit by myself and enjoy an interlude of quiet. What an extravagance. You can be in jail for many years and never know a moment of privacy or quiet.

Once I realized what a sweet deal I had here, I put a lot of thought into making it work for me. The possibilities were endless. For exam-ple, there is a room in the back filled with long-forgotten items—a stack of old floor tiles, a one-wheel wheel chair, broken furniture. You know the kind of room. I had some five-gallon buckets in there I used to brew some pretty nice hooch. I could have gone crazy and made ten times as much but I have learned a few lessons over the years. As the Buddha so wisely said, *all things in moderation*. Having my operation found out would have meant immediate termination. I always had various items of contraband stashed around the place, but again, I didn't go crazy with it.

The recipe for hooch is simple. Pretty much anything will ferment. You can use potatoes, tomatoes, Brussels Sprouts, corn, whatever. I have known guys who fermented such things prunes, onions, jalapenos, with a resulting concoction every bit as unpleasant as you might think.

I had a good connection in the kitchen, though, so I kept it simple and stuck with fruit. Toss it all into a bucket with sugar, add water and let nature take its course. For yeast to start it off, drop in a soda cracker. A few days later—presto-changeo—you got yourself some wine.

The big problem with this production is the smell. Fermenting fruit smells to high-heaven, and usually when a guy gets busted with some, it is the smell that gave him away. Consequently, a lot of guys making it get nervous and drink it before it reaches its peak. An imma-ture wine is weak and very sweet. You can drink enough to get a buzz, but you will probably get sick and have a horrendous headache. Who needs that?

My brew was stashed away in a safe place, with the smell vented out a window. I could let it sit long enough to become strong as Ajax and sharp as rubbing alcohol. It was highly sought-after. I marketed my product in bread bags I got from a guy who works in the bakery. I'd measure out twelve ounces with my favorite coffee cup, tie a knot in the top, and there you go. Two dollars a bag and that's a great deal. I let my clientele know when some was ready, and anyone interested (who am I kidding? *Everyone* was interested) signed up for sick call, where we made the transaction.

Like I said, I could have sold much, much more than I did, but that was never my thing. I dealt only with guys I knew to be absolutely trustworthy.

I made some money, but beyond that, most of my stuff went for barter. The guy who smuggled fruit and sugar from the kitchen got some, the bakery guy got some; there were a couple of old-timers I'd just give some to pretty regularly. I knew a guy who handled impressive amounts of marijuana. We did a lot of trading back and forth.

My thing worked for as long as it did because I always kept it low key. So many of these guys are show-boats and want nothing in life so much as to be seen as Mr. Big. I always thought of them as lightning rods. As long as they were occupying the cops' attention, I could slip and slide beneath the radar.

Everything I did was designed to promote my one true passion in life: I want to hear your story. I don't want to hear any boo-hoo, poor me tales; I'm not interested in *ain't it a shame?* or the absurd, grandiose lies so many guys tell about where they have been and what they once had. Some guys are idiots and talking to them isn't worth wading through the b.s. they bring with them. I have no time for guys who are full-time predators, always on the lookout for someone to rip off or otherwise victimize. When I say someone is "okay with me," it means that he lives his life the best way he can without taking advantage of anyone or creating grief in order to get ahead. I don't care what a guy did to get here; all that matters is who and what he is in this reality. If you can function as a decent human being in this mad house, you are okay with me.

If there is a real story to you, though—if you have had unique experiences or are just plain *interesting*, I am all ears. It probably sounds like I'm just nosey, but people who know me will verify that it's not like that. I'm not "all up in yo bidness" as the bros say. I am truly interested. I believe the adage that there is a novel in everyone. I want to hear yours. I don't repeat what I hear; I don't gossip. I don't judge. I just want to hear your story. I'll tell you mine in return, if you wish. Tell me where you have been and what you did there and paint me a picture with it. Most people, you may be surprised to learn, are happy to do just that.

Over the years, a lot of guys have trusted me enough to reveal things they have never spoken out loud before. Sometimes the process was excruciating for them. I never took that lightly. Now, as my days on this earth are winding down, it seems a shame that those stories be lost. I have procured a typewriter and set to work preserving what I can of them. The following collection represents a few of my favorites, tales I have either received permission to repeat, or are the stories of guys beyond caring at this point.

One of my challenges here has been to transform much of the dialog into language that doesn't alienate the reader in the first paragraph. The dialect spoken in prison is pretty rough. It consists of ever-evolving slang and massive doses of profanity. To actually present much of it verbatim would not only risk leaving the reader confused, but also offended. I've done my best to clean it up, but for the sake of verisimilitude, a few of *those words* were included. This is particularly true in *A Canticle for Frank*. Even though the language is considerably watered down, it may still be a bit much for more sensitive eyes. Fair warning.

Please contact me with any questions, comments, whatever, using the contact button on my Member Page at https://freshinkgroup.com/author/phillippert/.

A Canticle for Frank

Most of my peers have engaged in a wholesale slaughter of their brain cells from an early age. These guys live hard lives, develop serious health issues in their forties and die young. Drugs, alcohol, cigarettes, the effects of violence in all its many and varied forms, and just hedonism in general take a toll. You don't run into a lot of rocket scientists on the yard. There are guys who are into physical fitness, but most of them love to get high as much anyone else. They might get healthier, but they don't get much smarter.

I know Frank from way back. I always thought of him as an intellectual, although in a more normal environment he might just be a regular guy. (I honestly don't know. It has been so long since I was anywhere normal.) I always liked Frank because I could get a conversation that wasn't profanity laced, and had to do with matters outside of the small number of topics that dominate conversation in this corner of paradise. Frank has an impressive vocabulary, but he wasn't all show-offy about it. The man read voraciously and over the years has absorbed a lot.

Frank was fascinated with the world, and couldn't wait to travel and see it all. Not as a tourist, but one of those guys you see in documentaries. He had a subscription to National Geographic magazine and devoured every issue. Frank wanted to paddle a canoe along the Amazon River, start to finish, and could tell you what such a trip would entail, the distance of the river, the kind of fish you could catch along the way, the different people you would meet. He didn't just fantasize about things he hoped to do, he did serious research and absorbed as much information as he could garner. He wrote letters to college professors and people he had read about, asking them questions about their travels, and looking for advice about moving around in danger-ous parts of the world. He was fascinated with different cultures and the way people lived in other places, and hoped to visit each continent and see the most obscure places on each.

When Frank was finally paroled a few years ago, I wished him well and thought of him as one of those rare individuals I would never see again. I was surprised and disappointed to hear that he was back, slightly more than four years after I watched him walk out that gate. Not only that, but that he was now a bug (psychiatric head case) and generally not doing well at all. When I tracked him down, he was sitting on a ledge behind the kitchen. It was a hot August day, but Frank was dressed in blue jeans and a flannel shirt, with a jacket over that. He was sitting with his arms wrapped around himself and sort of rocking forward and back, hunched over like he was freezing, and obviously lost in his thoughts. I spoke from a distance of several feet, to announce my approach. It is never a good idea of startle one of these guys.

"Oh, hey Dude," he said distractedly. "I don't know how many people I killed." He continued, "My conscience is clear, but sometimes I wonder." He continued rocking. "It was just so cold. You don't even know, man. You never been cold like that."

As a conversation opener, that was somewhat different, and I admit to being caught a little short. I decided to be nonchalant and pulled up a milk crate to sit on. "Never thought of you as the homicidal maniac type," I ventured in a casual manner.

"It wasn't like that," he said quietly. "My toes mostly. I never knew the human body could register than kind of pain. From the cold. My feet didn't go numb, they just *hurt*. From the cold. Each toe was an individual agony. Like someone went down the line with a ball-peen hammer. Then all that running. You don't know, man."

"So tell me, Frank. Start at the beginning. I'm all ears."

"Is that what you think, Dude?" he hissed, suddenly furious. "I'm just some freaking idiot on the yard, and you're going to sweet-talk me into telling you something about the Taliban? I got news for you, Man, I ain't the one." Frank was suddenly standing over me, fists bunched. I was at what you could call an extreme tactical disadvantage.

Frank was on the verge of throwing a serious punch and from our vantage points, I reckoned I couldn't avoid catching it just above my left ear. Neither of us needed that. "Easy Frank. This is me. Remember how we used to walk this yard and talk about those places you were going to visit? You told me about those people in the South Pacific who built a wooden replica of an old airplane to lure other planes in, like you do with duck decoys or whatever. "

"The cargo cults," Frank said, suddenly relaxed and sitting back down. "The best thing that ever happened to them was World War II. American planes stopped over a couple times on their island and they went bananas over the stuff the Americans gave them. Canned food, candy, metal tools; they were blown away that such wonderful things existed. They were still living in a stone age culture and thought those guys flying in with all those extraordinary things were gods. After the planes were gone, they built a replica so the gods flying over would be attracted. They put in landing strips and built a reproduction of the compound Americans had established there. The one English word they all knew was *cargo*."

Frank went quiet and continued rocking. I remained silent and after a couple minutes, he picked it back up. "Never made it to the Pacific, Dude. Went the other way. Where it is cold." I asked him where that was and he said, "Up in the mountains, where people kill each other, man. Just because it is so freaking cold. Dude, it was *so cold*." Frank shook his head and rocked. We sat quietly for a while, and the announcement came that yard was over. I helped Frank to his feet, and asked him if he needed anything. He looked at me as though surprised to find me there, and was obviously annoyed by my presence. "The fuck would I need?" he asked belligerently and turned away. I watched Frank walk, and it was obvious that his feet pained him. It was sad to see the state he was in. There was obviously a story here, though, and I knew I wouldn't rest until I had heard it.

Over the next few days, I asked a couple of the old heads what they knew about Frank's story and nobody knew much. This guy B-Lo who works in the psych ward told me that Frank had been extradited from Russia "or some damn where over there" and was held in Federal custody for a while. Apparently, people from several different agencies had wrung his story out of him and they weren't gentle about it. No telling what he went through with them. He had obviously been down a rough road. I gave a lot of thought to how to get him comfortable enough to talk to me about it.

Several days later, I sat down next to Frank on a bench in the west yard and lit a joint. He was quietly rocking, lost in his thoughts. He accepted the joint and took a big hit. "I think this will help my feet," he said quietly.

"Always been good for mine," I told him.

Frank was annoyed. "Don't do that. Don't get all patronizing and shit because I am fucked up in the head." He was smoking the joint, but I had gotten off on to a bad start.

"That's just me being my smart-ass self, Frank. There is no disrespect in that. You know how I do. We walked down a lot of miles on this yard back in the day. You ever known me to not have a wise crack for any occasion?"

"True that," he finally said. "It was ugly, Dude. There are some real monsters walking around here," Frank said, gesturing around us, "but they are light weights. I was up there living with creatures who were pure evil. They didn't care if they didn't eat, they didn't care if they were in pain. They literally lived and breathed for the opportunity to kill and inflict grief. You think the DOC doesn't give a fuck about you? You have no concept of people who don't give a fuck about you." Frank was suddenly trembling and on his feet, rage blazing in his eyes. "You think it's a joke, Man? You think you could go through all that and be superman or something?" He was shouting now, "You dumbass motherfuckers got *no idea*." And then, quietly, "You all think you're so tough." Frank jammed his hands into his coat pockets and stormed off. It was obviously an effort on his part to move fast due to the pain in his feet.

That went well, I said to myself, more intrigued than ever.

I kept Frank in my thoughts but life's little dramas kept coming my way and I had other matters to occupy my attention. One of them had to do with some knucklehead friends of my friend Doc. The long and short of it was that one of these goofballs, call him Jerry, swallowed a bunch of balloons filled with heroin out in the visiting room one day last week. Nothing unusual about that. The problem was that they had been inside him for several days now and he was getting nervous. He hadn't been able to bring them back up immediately after the visit, and hadn't been able to pass them out the other way since. Doc asked me to grab a bunch of laxatives from the dispensary, which I didn't mind doing.

Two days later he told me nothing had happened—and this was a massive laxative dose we're talking about here—and Jerry was not only worried about the balloons, but was in extreme discomfort from the log jam. Doc asked me for an enema kit, and that I couldn't do. Way outside the area I can move freely in. Finally he asked about a pair of rubber gloves and a length of that rubber tubing they use to tie off your arm for a blood draw. That was do-able. I didn't ask any questions.

Meanwhile, I learned from another guy that Jerry's girlfriend was sweating bullets over this scenario. Should it all end badly, it would not take any real fancy police work to trace the whole magilla back to her. She called the balloon manufacturer and spoke with someone in customer service. Apparently, that person was very matter-of-fact about the whole conversation and was able to anticipate most of her questions. She was far from being the first to call with such inquiries. Turns out, different colored balloons decompose at different rates in the human gut. Yellow ones, for example, will give out in five days. The red ones are tougher and will hold out for a very impressive nine days. Other colors fall within that span. This information surfaced on day four.

Doc cobbled together a short piece of eighth-inch PVC, a large heavy-duty garbage bag and the rubber tube he got from me into a horror show of an enema bag. Posting look outs in strategic locations, he slid into Jerry's cell and told him to assume the position. Doc mixed a whole bottle of baby oil, a bottle of liquid soap and several mystery ingredients with three gallons of warm water in that bag and plugged it in, as it were. I will spare you the graphic details—you are missing a colorful story, believe me—and just bottom-line this by saying the procedure was a roaring success.

All this was just another day-in-the-life story, really. What was interesting to me was that all of the balloons were actually white at this point, their color having been bleached out by stomach acids and such. Two of them burst open on the way out from the rough and tumble way they came into the world.

Doc scooped up four of the intact ones for his trouble, swished them around in a coffee jar with soapy water and within minutes had them sold for more money than I will see in the next six months. Life in the big house.

Watching this lunacy play out over a period of several days and playing a peripheral role in it kept me occupied and I left the Frank question to simmer for the duration.

B-Lo told me that they were working on adjusting Frank's meds so he could be more functional and live with his anger issues. The problem was that the feds had pumped an entire pharmacopeia through his system and there were all kinds of complications connected with that. Especially since they wouldn't release any specifics about it.

When I saw Frank again, he was sipping a cup of coffee, staring off into the distance. He was still dressed against that chill that was deep inside him. Handing him a lit joint, I sat and said, "You know what Frank? I once knew a guy who ate live June bugs. He said they tasted like Copenhagen. The chaw, not the city."

After a long pause, speaking in a neutral voice and still staring off, Frank replied," You know what, man? I used to know a guy who was utterly full of shit. His name was Dude. The smart-ass, not the cowboy."

"Touché Franklin!" I congratulated him, "Touché! I knew the old Frankalony was still in there." I really was delighted. This looked like progress. I told him the Jerry story and he commented that Doc was good people. "The best," I agreed sincerely. Frank seemed better, but would only speak in response to what was said to him. We made some small talk, and I finally ventured, "I know you been through hard times, man. If there is anything I can do...you know that, right?"

"Yeah, yeah, yeah," Frank said tiredly.

I spent the next few minutes talking about the time I met B.B. King in a bar in Austin, which is kind of a neat story, especially if you are a blues fan, which me and Frank both are. Frank was with me, but he still wasn't feeling talky. "Just tell me what country you were in, man," I tried. Something in Frank's demeanor suddenly changed, hard to describe. It was like he had switched to anger mode, but just didn't have the energy to embrace it. After several false starts, he sighed, "I don't even know, man. *Over there*. Over in that God-forsaken part of the world where abso- lutely everything is for shit. People fight and kill each other because they wish they were dead, and they are so pissed off about it they just want to take someone else with them. When you are over there, being dead seems like the most wonderful thing in the world."

"Heard somewhere that you may have been in Russia," I offered as casually as possible. That broke the *one-too-many* rule. Frank stood. "You don't know shit about Russians," he spat out, finally connecting with his anger. "You think that was fun and games over there? He stood and this time I stood with him. "Frank, come on," I said. "Don't you know I'm your friend?"

Frank was enraged. "Then where were you when I needed you?" he screamed. Where were you when I was frozen and starving and going insane from the pain in my toes? Where were you when I was living that nightmare? I destroyed my soul, man! What kind of friend are you? Where were you when I *needed* a friend?" Frank was breathing hard and looking slightly unhinged.

"I was right here, Frank, where I was when I met you, where I was when I sent you home," I said quietly. "Otherwise, I would have been there for you. Like I'm here for you now."

Without speaking or acknowledging my presence in any way, as though he had forgotten I was there, Frank wandered away in his slow, unsteady way. I let him go. That was enough for one day.

This Jerry character was a real piece of work. He always had a scam going. The heroin thing worked out the same way most of them did. Generally speaking, he was fairly well thought of and guys liked him well enough. Something that was always a great puzzlement to me. I thought of him as the sleaziest white boy I ever knew. A text-book sociopath, he was reasonably intelligent, could be charming when it suited him, and was an adept manipulator. He was also a dope fiend.

In my unique position around here, hearing everybody's stories eventually, I could by this time just about fill a book with this cut-throat's exploits. I don't want to give him that much ink, though, so I will just offer up this beauty, to give you an idea of the kind of sweethearts you can run into in this bizarre little world.

Back in the old days, you were allowed to attend the funerals of family members. You had to pay the day's wages of the two officers who escorted you, plus all costs of transportation, etc. You attended the funeral, and in some cases, the graveside ceremony. At this time, Jerry was receiving regular visits from his mother, who was his only family. She regularly deposited money in his account and made sure he didn't go without too much. I'm giving you the Readers Digest

Condensed Version here—Jerry arranged for his mother to be murdered. Some ass-clown friend of his was going out on parole and they arranged for him to kill Jerry's mom so he could go to the funeral. This sack of crap would show up with a gun, drop both of the officers and Jerry would escape.

First part of the plan worked like a charm. This idiot went over and killed the mom…and then got busted an hour later. Jerry got his funeral, but it was anti-climatic. The story was all over the yard. Someone asked Jerry what his mom did to make him want to kill her. He just shrugged it off and said that he actually had always liked the old girl…it just worked out better for him—in theory at least—for her to get dead. I have never liked that guy.

The next time I saw Frank I gave him a pair of these really thick wool socks that would keep your feet toasty on a trudge across the tundra. I didn't ask any questions, but Frank knows me and the asking wasn't necessary. We sat quietly for a while, making small talk, and finally Frank let go a deep sigh. "I only had an eighteen-month parole, Dude. That ain't shit. I needed that much time just to get my head straight and save up some money. Ford was hiring then and I had no problem getting a great job first week I was out. I lived in a rented room and lived as cheaply as possible. Day I discharged from parole I had a passport. I had booked my flight way ahead, so my flight to New Delhi was about what you would expect to pay to get from here to L.A.

"India, man. I was living the dream. I can't begin to describe it. It's another world, I can tell you that. I'd be here from now 'til Christmas telling you about things I saw, food I ate, people I met. India is so far out. Just every day walking-around reality, Dude. I mean, there was a guy, a street vendor, who stood out on the sidewalk with a pair of pointy scissors, and he would trim your nose and ear hairs for a penny. And people lined up.

I'm talking about people in business suits, carrying brief cases, on their way to work, would stop, on the sidewalk, people passing by, and give this guy a penny to snip their nose hairs. Nobody thought any-thing of it. All kinds of stuff that was just so foreign. I loved it.

It was so hot sometimes, you would think you were in a kiln, but man, it was beautiful. I can't begin to tell you. My plan was to travel the world, but every day in India was such a great adventure I realized I could spend years right where I was without it ever getting stale. That pretty much became my plan.

I ended up living in a slum village on the edge of Calcutta. Not because I had to, but for the experience; to get next to the people. This little world, Dude, people lived in shacks made out of any material they could salvage. They would just add a room to the last house in row. Your neighbor's wall might be made of chicken wire with chunks of cardboard wired into it for privacy, and you come along and add a space to that; your enclosure might an old shower curtain and some baling wire. Whatever you can scrounge up. And that's your home. Whole families lived like that, generation after generation. And they were the lucky ones. There were families who had gone generations without ever sleeping under cover. You cannot even imagine the kind of poverty millions of people live in. To me it was an adventure, to them the only reality they had ever known. Pick up any one of them and drop them into the worst prison in America, and they would think they died and went to heaven. That's not hyperbole—a big word, I know, look it up—I mean that literally. Three meals a day? Medical and dental? Shoes on your feet. And *socks*? I'm not kidding, Dude, that would be such a dream for these people, they couldn't even embrace the concept.

I can tell you from that experience, Dude, people are people. There were folks there who were starving and would share their last crust of bread with you. There was also no shortage of people who would cut your heart out and roast it over an open fire if they could get away with it. Everything in between. I was surprised at how many had regular jobs they went to every day, but earned pennies and could never hope for anything better in life than what they had.

One day this kid comes to me with an Amex Gold Card that had been stolen from a tourist that day and wanted me to do something with it. I asked him why he didn't do something with it himself. He looked at me like I was an idiot and asked if I really thought he could pass for Blaine O'Shaunessy. I told him probably not.

I got cleaned up, dug out my best clothes, and me and this kid went shopping. Vendors we visited did not ask for ID. I was obviously a Westerner, the card cleared and they were happy with that. We ended up with tons of groceries and all kinds of things that were important to people living in abject poverty. Ultimately, I kept very little for myself. I sent this kid home with a wagon load of stuff and it quickly became apparent that several dozen people benefited from it. Pretty cool."

At that point I was paged over the yard speakers to report to my assignment and had to go. I said some encouraging words to Frank and headed out. I got to the Health Care Annex to find a guy bleeding profusely from a slice across his forehead. His whole face was covered in blood, which was dripping off his chin. There were two slightly frantic officers standing there, a little green around the gills, looking like they were about to wet their pants.

The story that came out was that this guy was sitting at a card table and someone had come up behind him with a very sharp knife and tried to slice his throat open with it. I knew this guy from the yard, they called him Shy—short for Chi-Town—an okay guy as far as I was concerned, but the kind of guy who was likely to get his throat cut eventually.

A lot of guys don't like Shy, but he is alright with me. He is an interesting guy, about six feet tall, muscular, with an enormous red afro. You don't see that 'fro very often, but when you do, I can tell you, it is impressive. Most of the time he kept it braided up in these long, fat braids that I always thought made for a pretty cool look. Shy was loud and sometimes a bit obnoxious, but he wasn't looking to victimize anybody. He did his own thing, and if you didn't like it, he didn't care.

Anyway, Shy was alert enough that he understood what was coming his way and tried to drop down and get away from the blade. In the end, the slice started next to his left eye, went across that, over the bridge of his nose and on across his forehead. The cops told me that they had brought him over, but all the medical personnel were either on break or off on tending to an emergency somewhere and they didn't know what to do so they called me. I told them relax, I got this.

I laid Shy on his back on an examination table and went to work getting him cleaned up. I put a stack of 4 x 4 gauze pads on his forehead where the deepest part of the cut was and wrapped an Ace bandage around them for pressure to staunch the bleeding, and just stuck white tape over the rest of the cuts to stop the blood flow until I could get him stitched up. Back in the old days, inmate nurses did sutures. Shy asked me what it looked like and I told him that as such things go, I see worse on a regular basis. "A few stitches and you'll be back in action on no time", I assured him.

Shy told me that he thought he had something in his left eye; he said it stung like crazy and asked me to take a look. I noticed that he had kept that eye scrunched tightly shut the whole time. I pried the lids open with my thumb and fore finger and it took a moment to realize what I was looking at—which was the inside of his eyeball. The knife had sliced it in half. Imagine slicing a grape in two and lifting the top of it up. You get the idea. Shy asked me what it looked like. I told him, "It looks like you will be going downtown, Big Guy." At that moment the captain arrived and asked me for my assessment of the situation.

I told him, "This man needs to see an ER physician *immediately*. He needs way more attention than we can give him here." The captain motioned me off to the side, out of ear-shot of Chi-Town and listened to my explanation. He immediately called the Control Center and said he needed transport to the hospital downtown pronto. I've watched this scenario unfold a number of times over the years and I have been angered and appalled at how long it takes from the time such a call is placed until he guy is actually out the gate and headed to the ER. In this case, for reasons unknown, it happened fairly quickly. I was impressed.

Chi Town was likewise impressed. "You the man, Dude," he said, slightly awed. "You make shit *happen* around here. Guys bleed to death waiting for a ride downtown. You speak, and the place starts *jumpin'*. You my new hero, Dude."

"Keep that to yourself," I told him, "we don't want people to start taking." Shy was giving me way too much credit. Sometimes things work, mostly they don't. Believe me, the fact that things fell into place for him on this thing had nothing to do with me. Still, Shy heard me tell the captain he needed to go down town, and downtown he went. Shy was the kind of guy, I knew my prowess would be broadcast far and wide.

It was three or four days later before I saw Frank again. He was wearing his arctic socks. When I noticed, he explained, "Obviously, my toes are not freezing now, but they hurt. They are sensitive to the touch and it is painful when shoes and socks rub against them. These socks add a lot of padding, and that helps. So, thanks for the socks, Dude."

I shrugged, "Glad you like them," I said. "So how you doing generally?"

"How *you* doing, Dude?" Frank was in a sour mood, but that seemed to be as good as it was going to get. "Know how many times a day someone asks me how I'm doing?"

"No, I don't," I said, matching his tone. "Tell me. How many times a day does someone ask you how you're doing?"

"Too fuckin' many, that's how many."

"You have my sympathy," I said. "You know how many times a day someone lets me know they don't give a rat's ass how I am doing?"

"That's because you are such an asshole," Frank opined. "That's why I have always hated you."

"I've always hated you back, Frank," I responded. "I should have stuck a screw driver in the side of your head a long time ago."

"You should have jumped off a bridge a long time ago, and then I wouldn't have had to carry you all these years," he said

"*You* carried me?" I asked incredulously.

"I only let you hang out because I felt sorry for you. We both know, it wasn't for me, these yard sharks would have eaten you alive long ago."

It went on in this vein for a while. This is what passes for friendly banter where I live. A lot is said between the lines. You get it or you don't. When it finally wound down, Frank picked up where he had left off, "There are a thousand great stories from my days in that slum.

A sociologist could go crazy just studying how people live like that and make it work. I mean, on three sides of you, people are living their lives and somehow, they make it work. In most cases, all that is between you and your neighbors is cardboard or some kind of flimsy scrap material, but you adjust your reality to where you don't hear their sounds or see them through the cracks. Your space is yours and people respect the boundaries. If your neighbor wants to talk to you, he could say, *"Hey Dude, what's up?"* without raising his voice, but that would be rude. If he wants to speak to you, he goes outside and comes to your front door. Just like neighbors do anywhere in the world. So many things about that life were fascinating, but I'll admit, it got old living like that.

I found a little place to rent in what passed as a pretty decent neighborhood and moved without leaving a forward. There were people around me I had begun to care about, but I didn't need any of that.

Let me tell you something else without going too far afield here. People hear *Calcutta*, and all they can imagine is the scene from movies or whatever of a city with masses of beggars and lepers and starving

children with flies crawling in their nostrils. Calcutta has all that, to
be sure, but there is a beautiful city there, Dude. Pisses me off when
people say disparaging things about Calcutta. The city is right on the
Hooghly River, which makes it not only the oldest seaport in the state
of East Bengal, but the only riverine port as well. It is the cultural, and
economic and educational center of East India. They have a stock
exchange.

There are over ten million people in Calcutta, Dude; way too much
poverty, it's too hot, and pollution is out of control, but I love that city.
I love the museums, and the theater, and the concerts; the *history*, man.

I had liked living in the slum, but that was a little too much reality for me. Sleeping on the ground in my little shack, the smells, no
plumbing. There was way too much disease. I compromised on getting a funky little place that was just a few steps up the social ladder
from the slum. Mr. Ford had paid me real well, but had to make this
money last. I was like Scrooge McDuck. It hurt me to let go of a
nickel. So now I am living in a tiny apartment in downtown Calcutta
and I knew this wouldn't last long. I stood out, and was swarmed by
beggars whenever I stepped outside. It is true that the worst thing
you can do is give them something. When I say *swarmed,* I mean
being mobbed like a rock star. It's no joke. I had people grabbing
at me, begging me in desperation for a penny, anything. They were
utterly pitiful, Dude, but my sympathy wore out fairly quickly. They
were shoving their diseased children in my face, *please help save my
child's life!!!* It was just too much.

After a week or so living there, the kid who had brought me the
gold card showed up at my door. I didn't even ask how he had found
me. A westerner who lived in the slums? Yeah, I blended. He said there
were some friends of his wanted to meet me. I told him I wasn't interested, but he was persistent. The thing we had done with the credit
card was a very big deal. I hadn't thought much of it, but that haul
fed a lot of people. One of the things we bought was a small water
pump that ultimately improved the standard of living for a number

of people in the slum. On and on. Word of my "bigness" circulated and people just wanted to say thank you. I told him to relay that I said "you're welcome," closed the door. Several hours later, I stepped out the door and stumbled over this kid sitting there on the door step. "We go now," he said and led the way.

"Oh, why not?" I thought. "I'm here for the adventure."

We ended up in a dark club a few blocks from my apartment. There were six guys there, maybe early twenties, well dressed, throwing money around like showboats and gangsters anywhere in the world. One of them introduced himself as Naveen and poured me a glass of Dom, establishing himself as the Alpha. It took a while for me to relax, but these guys were cool and the champagne was good. The inner circle of this clique appeared to be Naveen and the five guys with him, Amit, Mahesh, Raj, Kumar, and Alok.

There was a lot of joking around, there were women—beautiful women, Dude—don't get me started on the women—hanging all over us. The party revolved around our table—champagne never stopped flowing, good food never stopped coming. There was coke, hashish—they don't really smoke weed, but hash is common. I was high as a witch doctor and felt like we had all be friends for years. It was a great time.

You been high before, Dude, you how it is. Anything can be funny. With these guys, *everything* was funny. I never laughed so much in my life. A big part of it was—and they didn't have a clue—I was laughing *at* them. They obviously learned how to be gangsters from watching American television shows and movies. They mimicked *Scarface*, and *The Sopranos*, and all the *Godfather* movies. Raj did his damnest to talk like Bogart. On top of that, they tried to use as much American slang as they could and were constantly getting it wrong. It was hysterical sometimes. My favorite was when Kumar was going for the expression *tore up from the floor up*, to describe how stoned he was, said, "I am tearing the floor up."

In the same conversation, Alok made reference to the Richard Gere in the Movie, *A Woman Who Is Pretty*. All in that lilting accent they have. I loved it.

Even so, you know, Dude, that kind of thing, it's never been my trip. Sure, I'll cop a buzz now and again, but I'm not about flashy clothes and night clubs and jewelry and that whole bling scene. But—I don't know, I just really enjoyed that night. It was fun, and I really hadn't let off any steam since I got out of the joint. Next day that kid came for me again, said it was time for brunch and the others were waiting for me. Do you know how odd it is to hear a Calcutta street kid use a word like "brunch?"

Anyway, from our conversation the night before, I understood that it was as simple as them needing a white guy, a westerner—one with criminal inclinations—to be part of their circle. They had had one—a Brit—who was no longer around. I couldn't get the story on what happened to him, but hey, he was in the life. People come up missing, don't they?

This brunch, I have thought about it a lot, because this is where the wheels came off. This is where I meandered down the wrong path in life. Why did I go? They made me feel important, that's why. The night before, that whole trip at the night club, I felt like I was clever; I felt like the woman crawling all over me really were bananas about me. I felt like I was *That Guy*.

What the fuck, Dude? That has *never* been my thing. But these guys, they were *cool*. They were cool in a way that was new to me, and I dug it. I felt like I was hot shit. Embarrasses me to admit it, but there you go."

At that point, Chi-Town walked up on us, with a patch over one eye. "Dude, thank you, man. You are one righteous white boy. I gotta say it, you alright, man. I owe you. Big time." In saying this he was shaking my hand and giving me a bro-hug. I was a little confused.

"Shy, what's up?" I said. "Obviously, I *am* the coolest white guy on the yard, but all I did was apply a pressure bandage. Basic first aid. You don't owe me, man."

"Fuck that, Dude. You made them hunkies carry my black ass downtown; anybody else would have let me bleed to death. They fittin' me for a glass eye—ain't that a bitch?—but I'll be in the hole when it comes in. I got bidness to take care of. I just wanted to give you this." He shook my hand again, and this time there was a folded piece of paper in his palm. I accepted it and before I could say anything or even look at it, Shy was already walking away from me.

I told Frank the story about how Shy got cut up and lost his eye. Frank was unsympathetic, "I used to lock near that guy in 4 Block," he said. "He never shut up. Whenever he wasn't talking loud—all that jive-ass shit those guys talk all day long—he had his radio blasting at a hundred thousand decibels. It was never quiet. Forget about catching a nap or reading a book. I used to dream about somebody cutting his throat. Surprised it took so long for someone to get around to it."

I shrugged, "There is subject to be some blowback over this. Shy may talk shit, but he ain't no punk."

"Blah, blah, blah," Frank mumbled. I could see he was a little stressed out so I asked him if he wanted to grab a table and push a game of chess. "What I want," he said, standing, "is to get away from you for a while." He walked away without another word.

Returning to my cell, I kicked off my shoes, got my stinger out of its hiding place and made a cup of instant coffee. I tuned my radio in to a jazz station out of Detroit. Just chillin'.

When I was sure I was unobserved, I slid my hand in my pocket and pulled out the square of paper Shy had slipped me. I unfolded it to discover it was a one-hundred-dollar bill.

As a *thank you*, as show of respect, this was huge. Apparently Shy really did believe that I had saved his life. A way-overblown perception on his part, but I wasn't going to argue. This was an enormous wind-fall for me.

Green money in the joint has great value. The going price at that time for a twenty was about $32.00 in script—prison money. There were guys all over who would happily give you seventy-five in script for a fifty-dollar bill. A C-note could fetch $175.00. My friend Dutch had a thing going with this cop in 7-Block who was bringing him in all kinds of contraband, mostly marijuana, and, of course, the cop would only take green money for it. Dutch was always on the look-out for green. It was usually available, but hundred dollar bills weren't that common.

I was thinking I might sell it outright, or I might buy me a big, fat, juicy bag of pot and sell joints for a while. Double the money I could make just selling that c-note and get high a few times in the process. Good old Shy.

This was a very old-school gesture on Shy's part. In his mind, he owed me. In our world, a man doesn't walk around indebted to some-one else. These youngsters around here today, they don't know any-thing about that kind of thinking. Don't let me get started on that.

Frank saw me coming a few days later as I approached him on the west yard. You have to understand, Jackson isn't like those prisons you see on television, where guys come out of the cell block and there is one big yard they hang out in. Jackson is the largest walled prison in the world. It is more a small city with a wall around it than anything else. There are several different yard areas. What is officially designated as "West Yard" is known to inmates and staff alike as "Peckerwood Park," because for reasons way too involved to go into here, this is predominately a white-guy area. There is always a smell of marijuana smoke in the air in Peckerwood Park. Anyway, Frank saw me coming and rolled his eyes, "I'm not going to get a moment's peace from you, am I?"

"Frank," I began seriously, "The last conversation we had before you left here, you told me about this project where people went over and worked in a leprosarium in Northern Thailand. You went from working with lepers to doing a gangster trip in freaking Calcutta, and you think what? I'm just going to forget about hearing the rest of that story? You think that, you really are nutso. Have you met me?"

He heaved a huge sigh and continued; he knew it was true, he had me hooked and nothing would keep me from hearing this story. "What you are getting here is the condensed version, Dude. Living in the slum, hooking with this this crew, all the rest of it—I could spend days telling you about it. There are a dozen novels in it. Every day there could have been a movie. Every day I met some far-out people and had extraordinary experiences. I could spend hour after hour just describing things—the sounds in the air—it is never quiet—the food, the smells, the people, what it was like to just walk around. This is one of the oldest cultures in the world.

America is two hundred years old, Dude. People in India had art and music and a written language five *thousand* years ago. All of your senses are overwhelmed just walking around trying to absorb it."

"And you decided to become a gangster," I observed flatly.

"That surprises you? Imagine how I feel. Even at the time, I was thinking, *this ain't none of me, what am I doing?*" Frank shrugged. "For some reason, at that time, it seemed like the way to go, what can I tell you?

I'm going to really, really fast-forward this because there are parts of this period of my life nobody will ever hear about. Some of it, I'm not proud of. Nothing in your bag of tricks will pry it out of me. Take what I give you here, Dude, and be happy with it. If you try to get more than I want to give, I will shut down completely." I could tell he meant that.

Frank knew that I seriously wanted to hear his story—this kind of thing is what I live for—so he knew that was a heavy threat. I assured him I would not push for details, and that if I asked a question that was out of bounds, all he had to do is say so and I would drop it. "Dude," he said," Listen, all that stuff, that's not even the story. I'm just trying to get you point where I ended up in Afghanistan, up in the mountains killing people." Suddenly the emergency siren started up, and we had to split. This siren is extremely loud, ear-piercing, and not to be ignored. This is one of the most no-nonsense times in the joint. You can't mess around—when that siren goes off, you need to get where you are supposed to be. Period.

After I was locked in, my neighbor, Jimmy, asked me had I heard what happened, meaning what had set off the alarm. I told him I had no idea. I was surprised and intrigued when Frank had mentioned hooking up with a crew over there; I was beside myself with this talk of killing people in Afghanistan. He had mentioned that before, but I chalked it up to general raving. I hadn't seen that one coming. I was mulling all that over and it hadn't even occurred to me to wonder about that big deal emergency was about. I was just annoyed that it had broken up the story-telling.

Jimmy asked me did I know a guy they called Crawl Dog. "Tatted-up gang guy, works in the garment factory," he said. That rang a bell. I think he was an artist. I told Jimmy I knew who he was. "Hope he wasn't a friend of yours," he said. "That guy just got butchered over in the gym. It wasn't pretty."

"Well," I said philosophically, "Crawl Dog fucked up." What can I say? If someone decides to touch you up like that, chances are you brought it on yourself. Things like that don't happen at random. This was just every day stuff, though, and I was a little surprised Jimmy found it conversation-worthy, until he went on to explain that he had been there and had watched it come down. That makes a difference. You witness something like that, it's a big deal. I had Frank's story on my mind, though, and wasn't really listening to Jimmy's account of the incident until he said, "Guy that did it had red braids and a patch over one eye."

I had taken the hundred dollar bill I got from Shy and rolled it up as tightly as I could. I wrapped that a few times in plastic wrap from the kitchen and slid it down into a tube of toothpaste. Green money, especially in large denominations, is major contraband. Not only will you lose it if it is found, there can be serious consequences to getting caught with it. Some cops will just take it and nothing more is said. Some fancy themselves real police and feel duty-bound to make a big deal out of it. Under no circumstances will you ever see it again.

I met Dutch in the weight pit. I was carrying a small bag with my shaving gear, toothbrush and toothpaste, and a few other personal hygiene items. I had a story ready for if I was stopped and questioned about it. Dutch slid me a small paper bag with a three Cup-A-Soups in it.

He told me I'd really like the chicken. I set my cosmetics bag down and let the toothpaste fall out. Dutch scooped up the toothpaste, nodded, and walked away, slipping it into his coat pocket. I knew without looking that it would be impossible to tell that the chicken soup had been tampered with. Dutch is a pro. I also knew that when I opened it up later on there would be a nice, fat bag of marijuana in it. From it,

I would roll one hundred two-dollar joints for sale and barter on the yard. What was left over would be for my personal use. This was going to work out well for me.

"These Indian guys I hooked up with, Dude—they were bad people. That wasn't apparent in the beginning. They were fun, loved to laugh, and seemed to be just regular guys who happened to have a lot of disposable cash. I assumed they had a hustle going, maybe drugs, maybe something more sophisticated. I was right and wrong at the same time. As it turned out, their money came from a dozen different operations. They owned a string of prostitutes.

They handled stolen credit cards, they moved dope, at different times massive amounts of counterfeit money passed through their hands. They were criminals, and didn't let any opportunity for a buck slide past them.

The really nasty stuff wasn't revealed to me until I was committed. In the beginning, all I saw of it was the credit cards and funny money, some of the gambling operation. Later on, I had some involvement with the gambling. This went on for a period of maybe three months. It was mind-boggling, Dude. Those months shot by in a blur. I was constantly high, always partying, always laughing. I never went to bed without several beautiful women for company. They were always just *there*. I was living a life of utter hedonism, and feeling pretty good about it.

Then I started seeing things that bothered me a lot. People being victimized who shouldn't have been. Families living on the edge of starvation having what little they owned taken from them. People being seriously hurt when it wasn't necessary. Don't ask for details. This is the part I will not talk about. Even being stoned, I was aware enough of what I was a part of that I didn't feel good at all about it. I just didn't know how to get out. These guys would leave a whole family utterly devastated, and forget about it ten minutes later.

I just said I didn't know how to get out. The correct response is to ask, "why not just walk away? Get on a plane?" The honest answer is, 'I don't know.' I kept having that conversation with myself, but it would end up being qualified with, *just as soon as...or I'm going to leave right after...once I have this amount of money...*I swear to God, Dude, I just don't know. So much of it I didn't like and felt bad about. But the rest...Dude: the women, having my pockets stuffed full of money, being high all the time, having the best of everything—that was new, believe me—the whole package. I didn't recognize myself. None of this had ever been a part of my thinking. For some reason, I just couldn't break away.

Maybe nine or ten months into this, right when I was really feeling sick about hooking up with this bunch, we had an important pow-wow. An opportunity had come our way to pick up a plane load of opium directly from the growers for just pennies on the kilo. Everyone in the crew was putting up hard cash to pay for the plane, pilot, and crew. Arrangements were being made to get it processed into heroin. We would all be millionaires.

One of us needed to go along to keep an eye on our investment. That person would get an equal share of the final product without having to put up any cash. None of the rest wanted that job; I'm pretty sure any one of them would have opted out entirely if going had been a requirement. For me it was a golden opportunity. This is the kind of thing I had in mind when I started out. Not international drug-smuggling, to be sure, just doing edgy and outrageous shit. What a story I would have to tell when it was over! I also hoped it was my chance to break free of these guys and get on with my life. I told myself that if I saw an opportunity to just wander off, I was gone.

It all came together almost overnight. Early one morning, Naveen was driving me to an air strip about two hours north of the city. I was spacy and sleepy, having partied hard the night before, and running on just a couple hours of sleep. We were drinking this Indian coffee that is so strong, I'm not kidding you, a spoon could just about stand up straight in it. Suddenly we are at this air field and Naveen is pushing me up the ramp. The crew is rushing me because this whole undertaking is illegal.

I noticed that the plane was full of wooden crates, but before I could inquire about them, the engines began revving up. I felt a little frantic, "Hey, Naveen," I shouted, "What do I do? How do I pay for this dope? We haven't talked about any of this!" He told me that the money was in those crates, and what was there to talk about? Load the dope on board and hurry home. Keep an eye on things so we don't get off-ripped." And then we were in the air.

There was a pilot and co-pilot, and two crew members. None of them were friendly, but one guy spoke English well enough and filled in the gaps for me. He had lived in Vancouver for several years and had become fairly well Westernized. His name was Scout—a nickname he took from an old John Wayne movie he had seen and thought was cool. Scout filled me in on the details nobody had bothered mention—most significantly that the reason we were getting such a good deal on the opium was that we were bartering for military weaponry. This was a win-win for my guys because several people had been killed in the acquisition of this hardware, and it was impossible to put any of it on the market anywhere near home. "Your very good friends," Scout inquired dryly, "this fact they withheld?" I nodded. "What you need to know," Scout continued, "is that if you get caught with a plane full of opium, you will be put to death very quickly. If you get caught with a plane load of weapons, you will die slowly and wish it was quick."

Scout gave me an insulated flight suit, explaining that the cabin would get cold before too long. Naturally, it was raggedy and didn't fit well, but as predicted, the temperatures dropped, and I was glad to have it. It turned out to be a very long, very uncomfortable and very boring flight. The plane's engines were roaring way above my comfort level. The flight was bumpy and there was no place to sit, except the floor, which was cold, and filthy with oil and grime. Among other things, I wished I knew what I was doing. How many guys are in the joint right now because they were always stoned, living in a little fantasy world, and jumped into something that stood little or no chance of success? I was sent on this trip so these guys wouldn't just fly off somewhere with our cargo, but how did my being there stop them? I'm pretty sure no one on this plane would have a problem slinging me out a cargo hatch at 30,000 feet.

"Before I forget again," Frank said, interrupting himself, "Can you get me a stinger? Up there where I live, I can't get shit." I told Frank no sweat, I'd have it the next time I saw him. A stinger is a home-made device used for boiling water, and is a necessity in Jackson.

To make one, you cut the cord off of any electrical appliance when nobody is watching, and bare about two inches of the cut ends of the wires. Wrap each around the end of a piece of metal—a broken-off spoon handle works famously. I like to use a piece of an old toothbrush to keep the two metal parts separated, and then wrap them all together with thread, or dental floss. Submerge this in water and plug it in; a few minutes later, you have hot water. Fix a cup of joe, a Ramen Noodle, whatever.

"I'll be happy to have it," Frank said. "Anyway, I was shoring myself up with the idea that if everything came off without a hitch, this will have been a really, really cool experience. Not to mention, highly lucrative. Right at that moment a string of Christmas tree lights lit up long the inside of the fuselage, some cherry pie splattered against one of the crates and the noise level raised significantly. That was how my mind processed initially anyway. That string of bright lights was actually bullet holes in the wall of the fuselage, and the cherry pie was the other crewman's brains. I have been in a few highly-charged spots over the years, Dude. It is fascinating what zips through your mind. I was looking at this guy's head splatter, and thought, *This is a classic wrong place/wrong time scenario.* Then I felt the plane descending at an angle and rate of speed that obviously spelled trouble, and no wise-ass one-liners came to mind.

The crates were tightly strapped down; I saw Scout squeezing himself under a strap and that seemed like a good idea. I followed suit. We hit hard. From there it was a carnival ride. We were sliding downhill, and spinning at the same time. The wings snapped off from hitting boulders and the hillside. I was aware of the dead guy's body, and several other loose objects slamming around like dice in a cup. If we hadn't been strapped down, Scout and I would never have survived. As it was, this was a rough trip down the hill side.

It took a minute to get my senses back when we finally stopped. Scout was about his business. He immediately got free, and pried open a crate of AK-47's, and another of ammo clips. He tossed me a rifle, and found a couple backpacks and we commenced to loading them up. There was no conversation, but it was understood that we needed to get away from this plane as immediately as possible. The pilot and copilot were dead. We squeezed out through a sprung hatch and set off into the mountains. Scout struck me as the ideal kind of guy to be with in this scenario; on my own, I would have been through. I was hoping he really did know his stuff. This was already more adventure than I had in mind.

I didn't even know what country we were in. I knew from what Scout had said that we were planning to fly over Pakistan, but did we get that far? Were we still in India? Was this Afghanistan? Were we in Iraq? Freaking Russia? All there was for reference was rocks and snow. It was cold out there, Dude, and I was not dressed for it. We were heading uphill, trying to walk where we would leave the least footprints, following the sun. At some points, the snow was knee deep, but mostly it was just cold. We stepped on rocks as much as possible. Scout seemed to have a plan. He wasn't talkative. I was hoping he knew of a town or some such where we could get out of the weather. I was running a sleep deficit, hadn't eaten recently and, as I said, was under dressed. We were at a high altitude and my entire body was one huge mass of aches and pains from rough landing we had just endured. After a short time, I was puffing for breath and desperately needed to stop. Stopping meant getting left behind though, and that was all I needed to know to dig deep and find the strength to keep going. I seriously *did not* want to be lost up there on my own.

"We had trudged along for what seemed a long time but was probably less than an hour when the quiet was ripped open by a burst of machine gun fire just up ahead of us. At this point I was utterly miserable. My fingers and toes were frozen, I was feeling weak, I was starving and really, really worried about where all this was going. Now this loud crack of gunfire.

"I stopped and looked up to see about a dozen very hard-looking dudes with long beards and rifles pointed right at us. Scout dropped his gun and I followed suit. In all this time, we had not spoken. Now Scout spoke out the side of his mouth, '*Do what I do. Don't talk, don't ever let anyone know you are American.*' That was everything I needed to know."

At that point, we were interrupted by my friend Kool Aid and his entourage. He had won some big bucks from the gambling outfit I am a part of and stopped by to razz me about finally breaking my bank. I told him that was chicken scratch, I throw away more money than that every week so I don't have to be bothered counting it. Talking smack is the biggest part of conversation around here. It was all good. I like Kool Aid. This guy is called Kool Aid because his last name sounds very much like that. In a world where there are more nick names and aliases than regular names, *Kool Aid* was a natural for him. Kool aid is a pretty decent guy and a natural athlete. That he moved around these days with an entourage points to how silly things can get in this little world.

Sports are a big deal around here. Guys play basketball and hand-ball year-round, of course, and other team sports during the appropriate seasons. Kool Aid played baseball and even guys who have no interest in baseball came out to watch his games. He really was amazing. Naturally, where there are sports, there is gambling. There were actually a couple of really good teams this year and as the season wore on, the amounts of money being shuffled around by guys like us who were running tickets was staggering. I'm glad I don't handle the money in the operation I am a part of. You can get robbed, and it is never done gently. Anyway, so much money is being bet at this point, inevitably, someone put out a contract to get Kool Aid off the field. Nothing extreme, any broken bone will do. The plan had been to bet big money on the other team and then take Kool Aid out of the picture at the last minute. Word of that surfaced, now Kool Aid can't move without being surrounded by body guards. And so it goes.

After making a sincere effort to engage Frank and make him part of the conversation—Kool Aid really is good people—those guys moved on and then it was just Frank and me again. I was about to jump out of my skin wanting to hear what happened next, but knew I had to go easy. I ended up talking about the time I was hitch-hiking through the Louisiana boon docks and ended up sitting in a van smoking pot with Freddie Fender and his band. He hadn't had his first hit yet, but having spent a lot of time in Texas and across the south—and seeking out live music wherever I was—I was already a bit of a fan. The guys in the band didn't like me being there, but Freddie was cool. They were stuck with me because they had pot and no papers, and I had papers and no pot. The only deal I would make for my papers is that they let me smoke with them. We sat quietly for a while, then I risked prodding Frank a bit. "So what happened when the guys with the beards and rifles confronted you in the mountains?" I asked.

Frank started talking in a monotone, staring at the ground, "Scout put his hands on top of his head. I put my hands on top of my head. Four of the bearded guys approached. The rest hung back, keeping their weapons pointed straight at us. None of them looked like they were bluffing.

"I think at that point we were still alive only because they were curious and wanted some answers. Everything about these guys suggested that they were very hard-core individuals. I was scared, Dude. I'm not kidding, this whole situation was extremely intimidating and I was way out of my element. You can't imagine how desperately I wished I wasn't there.

"I immediately thought of these guys as The Fighters. That is how they remained in my mind for the duration. The Fighters. Once they reached us, the leader of this group said something to Scout in a language I had never heard spoken before. Scout replied and they went back and forth. Meanwhile, my fingers were freezing in the mountain air. My arms were aching from being held up over my head. Since there was a conversation going, I felt like we were getting along well enough that I could relax somewhat...and I was wrong.

As soon as I started to let my arms down just a bit, I was face-down in the snow with a boot on the back of my head. I didn't even know there was anybody behind me. I was aware that nobody was laughing or jeering me. These guys were grim. They weren't a happy band of lovable rogues. These guys were the real deal, and my face was being pressed down so hard that I was really worried I might not survive this. The cold on my face became excruciating. After a very long time, I was jerked to my feet by my hair and stood blinking stupidly.

"'Come on, then'," Scout said, and then we were jogging along the side of the mountain with these guys. After a few minutes, I said, "Talk to me, man." I was going crazy trying to cipher out what was going on.

"Scout looked over at me and shook his head. We jogged on. Maybe ten minutes later, I don't know what had changed, but he moved closer to me and said that we were still alive because he had convinced them we were believers in their cause and had brought the plane load of guns and ammunition to them as a gift and that we were there to join them in their fight. He told me to remember that I was Canadian, if anybody asked. He said that was only marginally better than American, but I wasn't smart enough to pull off anything trickier than that.

"What *is* their cause"? I asked Scout.

"'Who the fuck knows?'" he responded.

"'Where are we?'" I asked him. He turned his head and looked me in the eye, "'Who the fuck knows?'" he repeated." I started to ask another question, and he told me, "Save your breath." That sounded like good advice, so I took it.

"I have no way of knowing how long we jogged along, but eventually we reached a clearing where there were about a dozen other fighters. I stopped and looked around and that was it. We were suddenly forgotten. It was like we were invisible. I sidled up to Scout and started to speak. He cut me off with, "'You cannot count on me to wet-nurse you,'" Scout replied. "These people don't like me any more than they like you."

"'Then we are in this together,'" I said. 'We both want to get back to civilization. You know a lot more than I do about what is going on. Talk to me, man.'

"After a very long pause, Scout shrugged, and said, 'These guys are resistance fighters.'

"The Russians are invading their country and they don't like it. What you see is what you get. Look around you. Now you know as much as I do. Survival means playing these guys along until there is a chance to get away and get back to wherever. If you do something stupid, I will drop you like a hot rock. Nobody here speaks English, so you should be okay. If you complain about anything or show pain in any way, they will know you are a pussy, and you will probably be left to die somewhere'".

"'They actually believe that we came up here, dressed like we are, to join them and live like *this*?'" I asked incredulously.

"Mostly they don't care," Scout replied. "As far as they are concerned, we will never leave here alive. We will eventually die fighting with them, or they will kill us because they decide we are not what we claim. In the meantime, they have two more fighters.'"

"'They probably won't have many questions. Actions speak louder than words. They will watch what we do. Do *not*, under any circumstances, acknowledge pain or suffering. Do not admit to being American. Do you understand?'"

"'Scout,'" I said, "'Where do they sleep? Are we going to get to eat?'" I was worried.

"Scout shook his head, "'You are worrying about the wrong things','" he said. "'Worry about staying alive.' "

"'I am,'" I told him. "In order to do that, I need food and sleep. I need to get warm."

"Don't let any of that show," Scout advised. "Act like this is what you are used to; this is what you flew half way around the world for. Eat when they eat. Go indoors when they do. Don't be excited about any creature comforts."

We stood looking around for a while and finally a couple of those guys came over and started talking to Scout in that weird language. It was obvious that a good part of the conversation was about me. They seemed to have trouble with the story Scout was giving them, but as we spoke, others were filing into camp carrying weapons salvaged from the crashed plane. All attention was drawn to the haul. "We're in," he told me. "Now all you have to do is blend."

"That means we do what we have to do to survive until there is a chance to move on." A short time later, we headed out, hiking single-file along a faintly marked trail winding up the mountain side. We waked for a long time and I have never been more miserable in my life.

I was physically exhausted. I desperately needed sleep and hadn't eaten an actual meal in the last few days. I was cold and my feet and hands were frozen. Add to that the aching muscles and throbbing bruises caused by the plane crash. It was too much. I knew that if I dropped in my tracks, nobody would bother to notice and I would lay there and die. Probably should have. ,

I can't tell you how long we marched. Somewhere along the way, I noticed that the wind had picked up and that just added another element of discomfort to what was already an agony.

It all ended at a solid rock wall high up in whatever mountain range this was, just as the sun was setting. Everyone was moving over against the side of the mountain, and I noticed one guy drop and roll and disappear. There was a crack in the rocks and a passageway right there at ground level. There was an order to it all. I was the last to enter, right after Scout.

All I can say for the cave we were in is that we were out of the wind. It was dark and very cold. One small fire was burning and over it was what looked like a five-gallon bucket with some kind of soup in it. The fire didn't do much to warm the cave, but it did fill the air with smoke. In the same order we entered the cave, fighters got a cup and scooped up some soup.

There weren't enough cups to go around. When the first ones in finished slurping theirs down, they set their cups down by the fire and wandered off. The next guys picked them up and used them. Nobody was impatient about waiting. So it went. Eventually Scout and I were the only ones who hadn't eaten. I was surprised to find that when I dipped my cup in, there was enough left to fill it up. Probably a sixteen-ounce cup, the soup was meaty and fairly thick. And hot. No idea what it was comprised of, but it felt good to have something hot in my stomach. There wasn't much conversation. Guys were finding places to curl up and sleep. Scout and I found a place to lay down and, awful as I felt, I fell asleep almost immediately.

The next day we just sat around the cave. It was dark, cold, uncomfortable, and very boring. I dozed on and off, but was in pain from the plane crash and the cold in my toes and fingers. I wanted to talk to scout about finding a way out of here but he was obviously as unhappy as I was, and anything I could have said would have been superfluous. I just did what everyone around me did and waited for something to happen. If you had any idea how absolutely rotten I felt during this time, and add to it mind-numbing boredom, you would wonder how I managed to sleep at all. The truth is, I slept quite a bit during this time. It was low-grade sleep, just barely unconscious, snoozing in fits and starts, often waking up to grim reality. I couldn't imagine a way out of all this. We ate twice most days. Usually soup, always thick with vegetables. Sometimes a big glop of rice or couscous.

On day four, we were roused out of the cave and Scout and I were issued rifles; everyone was given a chunk of tar to chew. I call it tar, because I don't know what it was. Certainly opium was involved; it killed the pain, but opium will put you to sleep. This was a stimulant. To say it tasted nasty is to engage in understatement. Following Scout's sage advice, though, I did what everyone else did and chewed my chunk of this nasty crap. We were all given a hot cup of strong tea, and then were out into the world and jogging down a path in the snow. I just concentrated on following the guy in front of me.

I could tell I was under the influence of some kind of drug, but that didn't make the running any easier. Not at first, anyway. My survival, quite literally, depended on keeping up with those around me. I put forth a 100% effort, and after a while mastered the technique of letting the mind float and putting the body on automatic pilot.

I used to be a runner, Dude. I have a pretty good feel for what is a seven-minute mile, what is a nine-minute jog, whatever. Depending on the terrain, I'd say we fluctuated between and ten-minute mile and a nine, sometimes eleven or more on the steeper slopes. This went on for a while. Just sailing along. We finally came to a stop, and with sign language and hissing, I was made to understand that we should crouch down behind a large boulder. Which we did. And waited. And waited. Scout gave me a comprehensive crash course on how to operate an AK-47. It took about thirty seconds: *Put the clip in like this, point, and shoot. Repeat as necessary,* was basically it. After a while, without a word, Scout scurried off to crouch behind his own boulder.

I was dozing off when the sound of a diesel engine awakened me; several large trucks bearing Soviet markings loudly rambled by. Suddenly, our guys were emptying their machine guns into these trucks. There were soldiers jumping out of the trucks and making it to safety behind rocks and trees. They started shooting back.

I was petrified, Dude. I mean, what path have you wandered down in life when you set out to make a dope run and find yourself in the mountains of nowhere, exchanging machine gun fire with the Soviet military? There I was, and it was terrifying. You just don't know. I was crouched down behind this boulder, and suddenly a rock flew through the air and cracked me in the middle of my back. I looked around and saw Scout, motioning to me to get involved, and I understood that I wasn't holding up my end. I lifted my AK-47 and emptied out a clip on the direction of the truck.

That wasn't so hard, so I popped that clip out and slapped another one in. The Russians who had run for cover were quickly surrounded and cut down. And then it was over. When the last shot was fired, everyone came out and started collecting the Russian weapons.

Then they were going through their pockets and dragging duffle bags and boxes out of the trucks. Scout nudged me with an elbow and motioned to a dead Russian in front of us, "There are your warm boots, my friend. Better to grab them before someone else does." I was horrified. But he was right. I'll spare you the moral dilemma I experienced and just bottom-line it: My feet were painfully cold, and that Russian had no further need of his boots. Once I got the boots off, I noticed that he had some pretty warm-looking socks on too. I left him there barefoot. Scout had a good eye—the boots fit nicely. It was hard to find a coat that wasn't soaked in blood, but I did find something that was marginally better than what I had.

Suddenly there as the sound of a helicopter and the fighters sprinted down the path single file. We hadn't gone far before I heard the loudest gunfire ever. We were running under the cover of the trees and rock outcroppings and whatever; that gun-ship was chopping up the real estate. They knew we were down there somewhere. We got away and it was another long jog back to our cave.

When we got back, guys who had scavenged cigarettes smoked them, everyone got another cup of tea, and a chunk of some kind of meat, and that was it. Lights out. I slept like the dead until mid-morning the next day. My feet were marginally warmer, I should say somewhat less cold, but I was no less miserable. A few hours after I woke up everyone was given a hot breakfast, which proved to be the one meal we had that day. Scout sat down beside me and said I had basically done okay, in terms of keeping up and not whining. "You must be more involved with the fighting, though. These guys were too occupied to really keep an eye on you this time, but you must show more. Do you know the expression, *If you are not with us, you are against us?* That applies here. You can be one of two things in this life: In or Out. This is a choice you will be pleased to make for yourself. It simply will not do to have them chose for you."

The weaponry and some of the crates looted the night before were stacked up in front of our cave and sometime during the afternoon a group of fighters I hadn't seen before arrived and carted them off. Later on, some others arrived with food and other provisions. I had a sense of a network of these guys all over the mountains, shuffling things around to where they were most needed. That told me that we were a part of something much larger, probably operating as a cell system. Whatever, the delivery of groceries did not appear to be on a specific schedule, but there seemed to always be chow. I was a little surprised by this, given how prehistoric everything else was. Now I realize they had no choice: the cold, the physical activity, nobody could possibly survive on less than we were getting. I was still hungry most of the time. During the hungriest times, raids against Russian convoys were, for me, a trip to McDonalds. A good ambush could net enough food that everyone got a good meal. Sometimes there was no more than a bite or two scavenged from a corpse's backpack or pocket. Occasionally one of the fighters would bring down some woodland creature and that would go into the pot. To them, food was fuel and therefore necessary, but the idea of not being hungry most of the time was way outside of their experience or concern. None of the basic creature comforts meant anything.

A couple hours after sundown—it was completely dark in the cave—someone pressed a chunk of tar into my palm, and I immediately began chewing it. Nasty as it was, it erased hunger pangs. And then we were out jogging under the starlight. As before, I concentrated on keeping up with the guy ahead of me. The mental separation of mind and body came more naturally this time and I felt like I was just peacefully floating along watching my body glide along this trail. Eventually we stopped and set an ambush, just like before.

This time I was much closer to the road. The first truck to come along was a Soviet troop transport. This truck was the size of a semi, Dude, with canvas sides. The soldiers were seated shoulder to shoulder inside, packed in like sardines. Scout whispered urgently, "They placed us up front so they could watch. You must perform. Decide now. Do you wish to be left here with the dead Russians? You have two choices, kill or be killed." He paused, "If you do poorly here, my friend, we part company. I will not die with you."

When the fighting began, I took careful aim and laid down a line of fire all along the side of that truck, from cab to tailgate, right at the level I figured would be the middle of some one's back. And then back again. How many men did I kill emptying that one clip? No way to know, but a few minutes later, we determined that everyone in that truck was dead. I had hardly been the only one firing into that truck, but it is safe to say that at that point, I could be officially declared a killer. The fighters found a couple Soviets from another truck still alive and dowsed them down with gasoline from canisters found in one of the trucks and torched them. I can still hear the screams. You never get that stink out of your nose. I have no more to say about that.

I was a different person at that point. I felt something inside me die. It was like a connection had been unplugged. I thought at first that I could not live with this version of myself. But I did. Existence became another type of blurred reality, one day morphing into another. My actual brain shut down. I did not think. I did not reason or contemplate or engage in mental functioning of any sort. I existed. Cold, boredom, semi-sleep and raids against the Russians. I wanted to ask Scout shouldn't it make a difference that we had brought all those weapons with us? Shouldn't we get some status or consideration for that? But really, why ask questions whose answers don't matter? Scout had become distant, speaking occasionally with the fighters, but mostly withdrawing into himself. He had started out with no patience for dumb questions, so I didn't press my luck. I was just there, largely ignored by those around me. I wasn't anyone special, I wasn't even a curiosity. I held up my end, and that got me fed. I was trying to imagine how any of this was going to open up an opportunity to get out of here alive.

The routine, Dude, it was pain and hunger, mind-numbing boredom, and chewing this tar and running. Machine gun fire. The running through the hills, I describe it as putting the body on auto-pilot and letting your mind float. That is how my whole life was. You know about the lizard brain, Dude? That's what they refer to as the part of the brain that has no conscience, no emotion, just basic instincts related to survival. That's what I was going on. I let my human brain shut down. I let my actual self die away. I just acted and reacted on auto-pilot without any real thoughts being involved. I just *was*. All other reality, my past, my hopes to get out of there, everything just faded away. I was part of that group the way an ant is part of its society, just going through the motions dictated by what others around me were doing. I didn't like what I was doing, I didn't hate it. I was aware of my own existence only to the extent of knowing that I was in pain.

I don't know, Dude, maybe it was a survival skill anyone would have developed, maybe it was the tar we chewed. Maybe I am an extremely flawed individual and none of those other factors are actually relevant, but I did mass-murder on a fairly regular basis. We did not engage in combat; we were ambushers and scavengers. Sometimes we would move to a position, light up a couple trucks, and then head back without any rest, depending on whether or not there were helicopters around. Quite often we spent all night making our way to a location, only to wait around for a few hours and then head back without any action. You never knew.

I was totally absorbed in Frank's story; I could never have imagined such a thing. Just when I was on the edge of my seat, utterly enthralled with this story, utterly enthralled with his story, yard was closed for the day, and we had to return to our respective cell blocks.

Running a ticket probably sounds like a pretty sweet gig, but it is a head-ache, believe me. We make money, but we earn it. There are always guys who will insist they turned in winning tickets when they didn't. There are the gangsters who will come along and think they can do a strong-arm thing. There is no end to the idiocy in this world.

The point spread is what makes it so difficult to pick a willing ticket. It is hard enough to pick five winning teams, just going head to head, because of all the unknowns—who is injured today and not playing, what the weather decides to do, who will be taken out of the game for some reason, and so on. Add the unknowns to the point spreads, and you've got to be both very lucky and very smart to pick five winners and collect your pay off. Barking Dog had a feature that most didn't, which was called a *Push*.

With our ticket, if you pick four out of five winners, you get your money back. Guys appreciate that, and it makes us one of the most popular tickets on the yard. It is almost impossible to pick four winners;

you do that and still lose your money, you go away mad. Give a guy his dollar back and it feels like respect. From a business standpoint, the amount of money we give back pays off huge dividends.

The break in my most recent conversation wasn't too frustrating for me this time, because I saw Frank again the next morning. He probably wasn't planning to hang out, but I ran into him coming back from his med-line and waylaid him into a conversation about some innocuous thing, and maneuvered him into sitting down. Frank's not stupid, though: he knew what I wanted. With a deep sigh, he picked up right where he had left off last night.

"After this had been going on for a few months, I was in the back of a troop transport and made eye contact with one of the dead guys. He could not possibly be a day over sixteen, I thought. I looked around and thought everyone on this truck looked very, very young. What a tragedy, I remember thinking. What a stupid, meaningless, unnecessary way to die. It bothered me. How many of these kids had I killed?

I was a teen ager during the Viet Nam era. I know about mothers crying and sisters falling to pieces and families being devastated over a death in some far-off war. We grew up during the cold war, Dude, when we were taught to hate Russians—we were taught to *fear* them, but that's the same thing, isn't it? Remember being in grade school and doing those drills where you dove under your desk and all that silly shit? To prepare for a Russian attack? The godless commies. You know what, Dude? I believe that Russians love their children, too.

I don't think it was cool for me to kill so many of them. Any more than it was cool for some sniper in Southeast Asia to kill my cousin Lennie. It is always dressed up for the folks back home with speeches about patriotism and medals and flag ceremonies. It is made to sound noble and grand and wonderful and heroic, and it is only sad and pitiful. Combat death is foul and reeking and noisy. Nobody I killed died a hero's death. They were shot in the back by some asshole out on a lark.

It started bothering me. I told myself this is war, and in wars people get killed. In warfare, it isn't murder. But all that was bullshit. This wasn't war.

This was something much less honorable. I told myself that any one of them would have been delighted to kill me—that's what they were there for. The difference was that I had flown halfway around the world to be in their back yard, looking for kicks, while these kids were undoubtedly draftees. Their country was at war, and certainly back home the politicians were saying all the things ours had said during Viet Nam. By what line of reasoning was it okay for me to go over there and shoot a bunch of teen agers in the back?

Death in the movies is so sterile. Not at all like the reality. When you have a bunch of freshly killed human bodies piled up in the back of a truck, the amount of blood is unbelievable. It flows off the tailgate. The stench will turn your stomach; ripped open bowels and bladders, brain matter splattered all over. There is a sliminess to it they never capture in the movies. Violent death is ugly. Going through the pockets or salvaging clothes from those bodies is gruesome. If you can do that without barfing or having nightmares after, you aren't human.

We didn't have running water up there, Dude. I was living and fighting with men who had literally never had a bath in their lives. In the months I was there, I never washed my hands. Water was precious. It was for brewing tea and for cooking rice and couscous. I had blood under my fingernails and on my hands from scavenging in those trucks, all of us did, and we lived with it.

Frank stopped talking and sat for a long while staring at the ground. "I did a lot of killing, Dude." After another pause, "They keep changing my meds. I take the pills because, as miserable as they are, they do provide sort of a padding around my thoughts and keep the sharp edges blunted. In some ways, I am better than I was, but I think I will always be fucked up." I told Frank that I thought he was doing swell. "You have come a long way since we first spoke," I observed.

"Dude, he said, "You don't know shit about psychotropics. It is taking a herculean effort for me to sit here and talk to you. I am putting absolutely one hundred per cent of my attention and will power into staying here and being rooted in this conversation. If I let go even a little, I will drift away. Even so, I cannot exist without these drugs. I hate these meds more than God hates sin, but they protect me from the monster that is clawing away inside of me. Now that I have started, it is necessary for me to tell you this part of my story, but for now I am exhausted. It is way too early for this shit, and now you have fucked up my whole day."

As before, Frank rose to his feet without another word and ambled off in his signature wobbling gait. I am not what you would call a bleeding heart, but I will admit, my heart ached a little for Frank, for what had become of his big dream. He was really the last guy on this yard I would have imagined with a machine gun in his hands. This was quickly turning into the saddest story I had ever heard. There just didn't seem to be any winners.

I didn't see Frank all of the next day, and at about noon the day after that, I asked B-Lo if he was alright. He told me that Frank had been sleeping a lot and hadn't left the unit. "That guy is carrying a heavy load, Dude," he told me. "I don't know any specifics, but you can see it in some of those guys. I'm guessing there is something in his personal history that is not wholesome." B-Lo often speaks in understatement.

B-Lo has worked in psych for decades. His academic credentials begin and end with his prison GED. He has a perfect combination of inherent intelligence, and street smarts and yard toughness, along with just enough compassion, to make him sharper than any psychologist you are going to meet.

I have known him a long time, and his observations have always been spot-on. Over the years, I have seen him more than once take a guy on the yard who was hurting under his wing and work with him.

In the big city, that kind of counseling would run you a hundred dollars an hour. It is not a small thing to have a psych file opened up on you. B-Lo has saved any number of guys over the years from being pumped full of those awful drugs and labeled a head case. That guy is one of the unsung heroes. He has my respect.

Frank wandered back out to the yard a couple days after that. As had become his custom, he began speaking without preamble, "When I said it was necessary for me to tell you this story, I meant that. I feel compelled to get this said. I think I will be better when I do."

"I'm happy to listen, Frank," I told him.

"You're happy to listen the way a hungry wolf is happy to find a cheeseburger," he said dispassionately, "But that is okay. I don't know anyone else I would spill this to. I think," long pause, "I think I just need to find a way to say that I didn't mean it. I didn't want to hurt all those people. Dude, it just *happened*. I don't know anyone else I could say that to and not feel like an idiot. I know you can *hear* things, Dude, you get it. People tell you shit because you listen to more than the words"

I started to say something, but Frank cut me off. "Oh, shut up. God, you are such a fag sometimes. Why doesn't somebody just put you out of your misery?" I just laughed and we sat quietly for a time.

"Any of these Viet Nam vets will tell you that it is nearly impossible to bring a helicopter down with small-arms fire. Helicopter gun-ships are made to be shot at. A helicopter doesn't care about an M-16 or AK-47. Shoot at it all you want. That's shooting at them from the ground, though. In the mountains, where we were, it is sometimes possible to shoot *down* at a helicopter. They weren't prepared for that.

It didn't happen every day, but it was not unheard of for a couple of fighters to get an angle on one of those choppers and drop that sucker with just AK fire. Those were joyous occasions. These choppers—we're talking the Soviet Hind helicopter—caused us more grief than you can imagine. They move very quickly and have a kill power that is awesome to behold. Our guys weren't scared of much, but they did fear those helicopters. There are machine guns that can lay down a field of fire that puts a bullet in every square inch of a football field in a matter of seconds. They fire missiles and bombs. If they get a fix on your location in the hills they can bomb that whole hillside into rubble in no time. They have flame throwers. Almost all of our casualties came from those choppers. They were hugely feared. We feared nobody on the ground, but the faintest suggestion that one of those suckers was coming in our direction, and we scattered like roaches when the lights come on. It was infuriating to the fighters that they had such fear of these machines. I mean, these guys did not fear death; they were fanatical, single-minded killing machines. They would suck up pain and keeping on fighting if they caught a bullet or broke a bone. They could be injured and bleeding out, knowing they had seconds left to live, and put their last bit of energy into pulling the trigger one more time. They did not fear God. But they feared the Soviet MI 24 Hind Attack Helicopter; and that fear gave way to a special kind of hatred. They called them *Shaitan Arba*, which Scout had told me meant *Satan's Chariots*.

When the fighters got one of those suckers on the ground, they rejoiced like they had won the lottery. I said those machines are built with the idea that they will be shot at. They are also built with the idea that they can crash. Pilots are important assets and they are protected.

Their compartments are reinforced and padded have a complex of straps and such to hold the guy in place. The pilots themselves wore protective flight suits and helmets and whatnot. They never seemed to figure out that the worst thing that could happen to a Hind pilot up there was to survive a crash.

Those guys died a slow, painful death when the fighters got ahold of them. These guys live on hate, but what they had for those helicopter pilots was on a whole different level. Just regular Russian soldiers they actually got their hands on died painfully, but the pilots, Dude, they tortured those guys for *hours*. I can still hear the screams. What they loved in particular was when there was more than one—pilot, co-pilot, crew, whatever. That way the others could anticipate what was coming their way. They would taunt them all the way through, make them watch. I always figured they were saying things like, "See this? You're next. This is what is going to happen to you, as soon as this guy finally dies.'" It wasn't grim work, they were gleeful in it and genuinely enjoyed every second.

Any of the occasions I was there for one of these parties, it had been after our raid on a convoy. The choppers came running to the rescue and it didn't work out for them. Nobody cared—I don't think anyone noticed—that I wasn't part of it. I took that time to go through the trucks and find what I could. Food was always an issue Dude. I was so hungry most of the time; if it wasn't for the tar I would have gone crazy just from hunger. We always seemed to get enough food to keep us functioning, but never enough to satisfy. Just never *enough*. When I was out on my own going through those trucks, it was treasure hunt. I was digging through pockets that were sopping with blood and foul in ways I won't describe. The pay-off for that was that sometimes I would find something I could put in my mouth and eat. I found cigarettes and other trinkets that I'd stuff in my pack with an idea that they might at some point have value, but what I was looking for was food. By the time we left, I was bloodier than the guys who had made a day of cutting body parts off of Russian pilots.

The whole time, Dude, I was so cold. Could not get warm. Fingers and toes, mostly. My hands were like claws most of the time. To this day I have limited range of motion in my fingers. They were filthy dirty with caked on blood and grime. It was my toes more than anything, though. That first day, after we were shot down, my toes froze up within minutes when Scout and I started out. They never got warm. From there it just got colder and colder. *Pain.*

We moved around quite a lot. A few nights in this cave, the next in one several miles away. Those caves, they were all cold and drafty, but better than being in the open. Sometimes we met up with other fighters for a day or two, but it made little difference to me; I was always ignored, and lived in a sort of Twilight Zone haze. Nobody could hold a conversation with me, but for all that, I received a fair share of what food was available. When the tar was passed out I got as much as anyone else.

Frank seemed to be getting tired so I tried to give him a break by speaking to this clown Eddie who was passing by within shouting distance. Eddie is one of those guys who will talk you ear off if you give him an opening. Usually I avoid those guys, but Eddie was an interesting guy, and he could be funny, and we needed a distraction. I'd run him off if this turned out to be a bad idea. That's the thing in the joint, most of your days are spent just hanging around.

There is no real purpose to much of anything. Wherever Eddie was going, it could wait. We were as much an interesting distraction to him as he was to us.

"So, what are you crazy kids up to this fine afternoon?" Eddie said as he approached.

"What's up, Ed?" I asked.

"Hey Dude, I know you love stories, I got one for you. I been holding this in because I didn't want it to get back to the parole board. Looks like it is too late to worry about that now, so I think you will like this one." He looked at Frank, "This is a short one, okay?" Frank shrugged.

There have always been a lot of questions about why my wives kept dying off, right? People just figured there had to be something shady going on. Instead of affording me the sympathy a grieving widower should receive, people acted like I was a bad guy. I'll tell you how it came down and you tell me.

My first wife, Dude, she died from eating poison mushrooms. I was devastated. A few years went by and I was fortunate enough to find another ladylove. We were married and then a couple years later, she died. From eating poison mushrooms. I'll make a long story short here, Dude. I got married again and my third wife also died."

"Don't tell me," I deadpanned, "From eating poison mushrooms."

"No", Eddie said, "My third wife died from a skull fracture."

I bit. "Damn, man. What Happened?"

"Bitch wouldn't eat the mushrooms." Eddie said and burst out laughing

"Good bye, Eddie", I said.

"Later, Dude", he said, walking away. "Hang in there, Frank".

I had dismissed Eddie because Frank didn't seem all that amused, and I didn't need him stressing out on me. Frank surprised me by saying, "That actually was kinda funny. Eddie's okay. In small doses." I agreed.

"That dumbass joke reminds me of something that actually happened a few years back", I said. True story, no shit. I knew this guy Grant from Kalamazoo. One of the first guys I got cool with when I first came down. He was doing a little seven to fifteen for killing his wife. Went home after a couple years and I had forgotten all about him. Then I saw him on the yard one day and said, "What? You missed the food?" He told me no, he caught a manslaughter beef for killing his wife. I said, I know, I sent you home on that a long time ago. Grant gets this sheepish look and says, "I got married again." I told him he needs to stay single. They're not going to keep handing out those meatballs.

"True that," Frank opined.

In the local dialect, a meatball is a very small sentence.

"One time I was pawing through a pile of bodies and started removing the tin from some officer's shirt," Frank continued. I think he was a colonel. A real old-timer. I was suddenly struck by what a shame this was. The youngsters had begun to bother me, but now I thought of this guy. He had obviously had a long and distinguished career. Undoubtedly some heroic deeds in his history. Probably saved lives, led his men through all kinds of dangerous missions and brought them home alive. Made countless sacrifices that nobody even knew about. He had devoted his life to serving his country. A patriot. And this is how it ended. There was just no *dignity* in any of it, Dude. For us or for them. I grew up with a respect for the military and the people who protect our country. Soldiers deserve to die with dignity. They deserve to die in the process of doing something great and significant. A career soldier wants to die in combat, taking as many of the enemy with him as possible. They have a *right* to that.

They deserve a death that reflects the greatness with which they lived their lives. Not ambushed and ripped apart and splattered with raw sewage. Frank went quiet.

"'Don't get me wrong'", he continued in a low voice. "'I took his shit. I cut the patches off his shirt and removed all the shiny objects. I went through his pockets. I was in survival mode. On this day, I survived and Ivan didn't. End of story. He was an old guy," Frank continued angrily, he didn't have to be there. He could have retired a long time ago. He could have been at home, bouncing grandchildren on his knee. But no, he wanted to come to Afghanistan and try to kill me". Frank was agitated and getting loud. "Well, it didn't work out, did it, motherfucker? Got your own dumbass killed. Fuck you anyway, borsht-eating piece of shit. You should have stayed your ass at home". Frank was shouting now. "Come to Afghanistan and try to kill *me!* Yeah, how did that work out for you?" Frank was on his feet now, looking around wide-eyed. After a moment, his eyes focused and he looked at me, "And fuck you, too, Dude, you're just another jackal. You're no better than me. I'm tired of your shit too". And with that pronouncement, Frank ambled away once again.

The next time I saw B-Lo, about five or six days later, he told me that Frank was exhausted and needed sleep. "Let him rest, Dude, he needs that more than anything. You're good for him, but he has to set the pace. I imagine you are getting his story out of him—believe me, nobody else is—but let him do it his way. No pressure. For real, Dude, do not squeeze that guy." I promised B-Lo I'd respect his advice and wait for Frank to come around.

Frank was a criminal, like the rest of us, but he was always a non-violent guy. His were "Property Crimes", as opposed to "Crimes Against Persons". Frank would run through a hot credit card, but he wouldn't hurt you in the process. Compare him to these yard sharks around here, who want to rob you, and then hurt you after—because that's the fun part—and all the various predators and whack jobs walking this yard, and Frank comes out looking pretty good.

I tried to relay that to Frank the next time we spoke, which was a week or so after I'd spoken with B-Lo. Frank needed to hear that he wasn't a bad person—so my thinking went—and I tried to salve his conscience with my take on the subject. When I approached him, he looked pretty well-rested and reasonably healthy, which I took as a good sign. Maybe his meds were finally what he needed, but no more, and he was finding some peace with himself. Maybe taking some time away from me was good for him. Be that as it may, I *had* to hear the rest of his story. We made some small talk, and I launched into my prepared statements about what a nice guy he was, evidenced by how well he stacked up against his peers.

"Dude," he said, "You don't get it. I have seen the enemy. And he is me. Do you understand? That crew in Calcutta…Everything they did, I did. Sure, I hung back like a pussy when they were victimizing some miserable guy who had nothing, and thought of myself as a better person than they were. But later that night, when we sat around a club, I drank wine they bought—at least in part—with the pennies they took from that guy. How am I better?

It was the same thing in Afghanistan. The horrible things they did to those Soviet pilots. I ran and hid while all that was going on—so I was a better person? How? The guy who slowly pushed the tip of a red-hot dagger into the eye balls of a pilot was a guy I fought side by side with. How many times had I killed someone who might otherwise have killed him? I saved his life so he could go do what he did. How do I claim innocence? When we ambushed a supply truck and I carried groceries back to camp, and helped feed this guy, when I fought his enemies, when I helped create a diversion for the choppers to draw them into the trap that brought them down, I was playing a role in what they did next.

I didn't have what it took to rip their ears off with my bare hands, but I fed the guy who did. I covered his back in fire fights. I striped corpses to salvage clothes that kept him warm. So he could go out and do what he did. Just how do I declare moral superiority?

And fuck that anyway. You don't even have to get all theoretical about it. How much grief does heroin cause? I was on a mission to buy a plane load of heroin with a shipment of military hardware my crew had murdered people to acquire. If we had been successful, how many kilos of heroin would that have been? How many users would have died from o.d.? How many people would have been robbed to support the habit of junkies who became addicted from that specific shipment of heroin? How many would have committed murder over that dope? How many young girls would have ended up in prostitution because somebody tricked them into trying it? How many lives would have been shattered? And why? Because I thought it would be a neat adventure and there was a ton of money in it? Dude, I am not a good person. You know how I know? Good people don't do shit like that."

"Dude," Frank continued, "There is never a time I don't hear those pilots screaming. Their last hours on this earth were an agony. They are inside my head. You are telling me that I am not a bad guy, but they are telling me I am. That is the point of those voices…to make sure I never am able to convince myself that it wasn't me, it was someone else. They are saying, "No Frank, it was *you*. If not for you, this never would have happened. You gave them the weapons they used to bring down our choppers, *you* made it all possible. I made all those people back in those lonely, forgotten little villages in the Soviet boondocks cry themselves to sleep at night.

These people have had me on meds that leave me so drugged out, I couldn't lift a finger, but I still hear those guys. I have been knocked out, damn near dead with the heaviest psychotropic drugs manufactured, but Dude, but I always hear those guys screaming. You want to hear the clincher? You want to hear what puts a cherry on top?"

Of course I did. More than words can say; but as luck would have it, at that moment, we were interrupted by what had lately become a regular thing. Some delegation from Lansing taking a tour. A handful of people from the governor's office, along with a couple of reporters, maybe a few MSU students. Being escorted around the joint, pretending that it was about 'fact-finding" and their hour or so inside the walls would make them experts. They were trying to pretend this wasn't just a freak show excursion they were on so they would have a good story to tell at the next neighborhood pool party. As they came our way, the advance party—some low-ranking rookie cops—preceded them and ran us off from where were we were sitting. It is always important to not let the humans get too close to the exhibits—and we had to push on. By the time we found a comfortable place to relocate, yard was over and I had to let Frank go without hearing any more for today.

Hearing Frank's story was just one aspect of my life. I had a full time job, a poker game to run, joints to sell, wine to process, and my part on a ticket to hold up. The ticket was a pain, but the money was good. This is how it works: There are a dozen major tickets on the yard, ours is called Barking Dog. The ticket itself—also known as a Betting Slip—is a slip of paper two and a half inches wide by five inches long, listing all of the upcoming football games, and the odds on each. As a bettor, your job is to pick five winners. Sound easy? Try it sometime, factoring in the point spreads. Say it this way, odds favor the House. Why do guys do it? The pay-off is twenty to one. Bet a buck, win twenty. Bet five, win one hundred. And guys do win. Occasionally.

There are three owners of Barking Dog ticket. My job is to go to the library and check point spreads in the newspaper. I take notes, and then during count time, I type up about one hundred slips. My partners and I pass these out on the yard. That's my end of it. They collect slips and money from the betters and give me a copy of a master sheet. We all watch the games; we refer to it as watching our money. Afterward, we pay off any winners and then split up the profits. A winner now and then is good or business. The truth is, though, we make a killing.

When I saw Frank again, I was coming from the quartermaster. I had turned in a couple of towels and some t-shirts for new ones in return. Well, new t-shirts and less worn and stained towels. Frank was coming from the chapel. We talked about the previous night's football game the way Lions fans did that season and ended up sitting on the grass by the handball courts.

Once again, without preamble, Frank picked up exactly where he had left off, "There is a Russian word, *Mat*," Frank said quietly. "Those pilots, sometimes they would start shouting that right at the end. I thought at first it was a curse of some sort, sort of a Russian *Fuck You*, a final act of defiance, but it wasn't. These guys, though, Dude, they were tough. I mean they these were some bad-asses. You could see it in them. They were the absolute elite of the Soviet military machine and they were hard core. Think of Special Forces guys you have known. Macho motherfuckers.

Way later—I'm jumping ahead here—way later, I was back in India, and met a guy from Lithuania who spoke fluent Russian. I asked him about this word, pronounced it *m-ought*, what does it mean. He kind of smiled and asked me if I had been playing with dolls. I told him no, I don't play with dolls, what does this word mean? Know what he told me, Dude? *Mat*, means "mama" in Russian. It is the version of that word that little babies call their mothers. Like the first word you learn. Mat. *Mama.*

"These guys, Dude, these Special Forces guys, young and tough as shoe leather, and out fighting for their country, being tortured to death and in the end, when it was over, they longed with everything they had, to just be held for a moment by their mothers, to have that one fleeting comfort before they left this world. They were dying and knew it, and in excruciating pain, insane, really, from the prolonged agony, and at the very end, they screamed for mama. My God, Dude..." Frank had tears streaming down his cheeks and looked as miserable as any man I had ever seen. I handed him one of my towels and he held it to his face. And wept. With huge, deep, body wracking sobs. We sat there, Frank hunched over with is face hidden in the towel, my hand on his back and I watched the traffic around us.

You might think that in this ultra-macho environment such a thing as this would be a huge sign of weakness, or jeered at or what-ever. Not so. These guys, guys in the joint generally, know about grief. They live with it, they create it, they experience it. Look at these ghetto guys...most of them have had friends or family members affected by violence. They grew up with inadequate health care and watched people they cared about die way too young. They have witnessed their own existences slowly ooze down the sewer and have been helpless to prevent it. These guys know about grief. There was no shame in this. The few guys that noticed quickly looked away and pressed on.

Frank gradually came around and sat there staring off across the yard. After a few minutes he said quietly, "Man, fuck you, Dude." I patted him on the back and said, "I know, Frank, I know." When he spoke again, Frank said, "Anyway, one time I tried to figure it out, and I was pretty sure I spent eleven months up there in the hills, doing this shit. Later on, after I got back to the real world, I realized that it was closer to eighteen months. Seems like a lifetime.

I'm not kidding, Dude. It was like this was all I had ever known. I was in a psychological state where I wasn't even aware of myself. I was in a fog. The only thing that kept me rooted was the pain, from the cold, from the hunger, from the horrific sound of those helicopters. My whole existence was to snooze in this semi-conscious state, chew tar and run through the mountains, and then shoot up some Russians and run back. That was it. When we were inactive, I was like a robot you set on a shelf. When we were activated, I would scavenge for food. I won't even tell you about some of the stuff I ate.

One time we were running away from an ambush and one of those miserable helicopters zoomed in from nowhere. Those machine guns were awesome. I mean that in the traditional sense of the word, Dude. They were awe-inspiring. How can a single man with a single weapon chew up that much real estate and that many human bodies in just a few seconds? *Unbelievable*. We were scattered, diving behind rocks and whatever. A bunch of guys found a cave to run into; Scout was one of them. The chopper pilot saw them and eased over that way. He sort of maneuvered his chopper over and tilted sideways and they let go with the flamethrower. Those guys were roasted alive. There was no screaming or anything like you might expect. I think they died pretty much instantly. I felt more alone than I ever had in my life. Scout wasn't a warm and cuddly friend, but he spoke English. He was some-one I had known from before. Even if it had been only for a couple hours. We had gotten into this together; I had expected we'd walk out of it together.

A week or so after that, over a period of several days, there was much more helicopter activity, and the helicopters flying over us where not just the Hinds, but these enormous troop transports. It didn't take a degree in military science to understand that Ivan was putting some serious forces in the hills above us. I could see that the fighters were nervous. After a bunch of these transports had gone over, we all got some tar and a cup of hot soup and set off at a direction parallel to the hill top. We slogged along for a long time.

At this time, Dude, rations had been a bit thin for the last few days. I trucked along for a while but finally just ran out of gas. Those behind passed without even noticing me. Pretty soon, I was at the end of the column. Finally I sort of wound down and was barely moving at all. Eventually, I stumbled over something, rolled a few times, and slid downward on my back, over a cliff, straight down, feet-first, and landed in some deep snow in a more or less seated position.

See if you can get this picture. I was wearing a white, furry snow-suit I had stripped off of a dead Russian, basically sitting upright in a huge snow drift, with just my head above the snowline, at eye-level. At this point, I said, "*Fuck it*". This is where it ends. I will sit here and die. I'm ready. I'm not kidding, Dude. I was out of gas. Physically, psychologically. Spiritually. There was no will to go on. I was closer to death than I was to life anyway, and keep going for what—to continue this existence? No thank you. I'm done. The cold would take me shortly, and the sooner, the better. The effort it would have taken to climb out of that snow drift? No. The fox ain't worth the chase.

I sat there resigned to my fate when I caught a movement out of the corner of my eye. I turned my head and saw a Russian Septnaz Recon guy walk past, maybe twenty feet to my left. I was perfectly camouflaged, and he didn't see me. My first thought was, *So What?* I'm dying. Who cares how this ends? Know what clicked in my head, Dude? The reason I am alive today? The reason that man died on that mountain that day? He was *chewing* on something.

He was walking along, all casual—apparently convinced there were no insurgents anywhere around—munching on a granola bar or some such. He was *chewing*, Dude. Chewing means food.

The second thing I noticed was that he was clean. Recently shaven, crisp, new uniform, full pack. Freshly arrived from the Motherland. Carrying a full pack. I raised my AK-47 and put a bullet into the back of his head. It took a few minutes to pull myself out of that snow, but finally I made it over and ripped open that pack. Oh my God, Dude! This guy had a can of sardines! I had never been so excited in my life.

I ripped that can open and dug those things out with my bloody fingers and crammed them into my mouth. I had this guy's blood all over my fingers and didn't care. I was licking his blood off my fingers along with the oil from the fish. These were those Russian sardines with the heads on. I didn't care, I was crunching them down, and slurped down the oil left in the can. He also had some kind of weird hard cheese. I scarfed it down. I rolled him over and found a thermos of hot tea. How could life get any better? Food and a hot drink? Fuck, Dude! It was like a miracle.

Once I had taken everything off this body that was of use to me, and was just getting ready to go, I saw some movement uphill from me. Sure enough, it was another one of these guys. What I finally put together was that they had landed up in the mountains high above us and were working their way down to force us into a classic hammer and anvil maneuver. At that point I was on the extreme outside edge of that move and outside of where they actually expected to run into the enemy. These guys were probably pissed that they were missing all the action. I dropped the second guy just like I did the first. He also had food and drink, which I scarfed down without hesitation.

Before the day was over, I killed five Russians the same way. I was separated from my group and I guess the Russians just did not expect anyone to be where I was. They were just basically wandering their way down the hillside. Lying in wait, killing these guys for what they had on them, none of that meant anything to me at that point. Eating over their steaming corpses, shoving their food into my mouth with my fingers bloody from their wounds, it was nothing. I was more animal than human by that time.

In the process of all this, I was making my way downhill. Eventually, I linked up with my crew. At least I think it was my people. Who knows? They were a bunch of raggedy-looking guys with long beards.

But you know what, Dude? So was I. I started out with a beard, and I had not shaved or trimmed it up since we got shot down. I had not bathed or brushed my teeth. I was wearing ragged, bloodied clothes I had stripped off of the corpses of men who had died violently. No doubt I looked worse than many of them did. Nobody questioned my presence. I *blended*. More and more fighters were accumulating and I gradually understood that I had stumbled into a rally point. I think I recognized a few of the fighters around me but who knows?

Eventually one of the guys who appeared to be in charge was shouting and pointing and everyone was reacting, so I went where he seemed to be directing me. A few minutes later, a Russian patrol came into view. They didn't stand a chance. As soon as they were fully exposed, we opened fire and chopped them up. What was different this day was that they kept coming. From different angles and with a ferocity I had never seen. These guys were coming for us, Dude, and they were determined. They had superior firepower and training and determination.

What we had was a dug-in position, motivation, and home-field advantage. Plus, most of our guys were happy to die in combat, and our enemy's forces were draftees.

There were the dreaded helicopters, of course, but they were removed from our little battle. My impression was that we were engaged in a major offensive by the Russians to wipe us out once and for all. I have no idea how many groups like ours there were up there in those hills, but I knew there were a few. There were skirmishes going on all over the hills at that moment and apparently there just were not enough helicopters to go around. There was a prolonged fire fight, and it was touch and go for a while, but in the end, Ivan bought it. Our guys overwhelmed them and we spent the next few hours stripping corpses.

After this battle, a unique thing happened. Several trucks appeared and our guys piled in. I hadn't seen a motor vehicle since landing here. I climbed aboard with everyone else. Those around me appeared to be jubilant. They not only had just won a major battle with the Soviets, but apparently, we were getting R&R as well. A rare treat in this man's army.

As the transports made their way through the mountains, guys started to loosen up. They smiled and laughed and joked with each other. I was blown away. I had never witnessed this side of my comrades before. It was an eye-opener. I pulled out an open pack of Soviet cigarettes and handed it over to the guy across from me. He smiled broadly and took one. After he had lit it, the guy next to him gestured that he wanted one. I nodded and he smiled. This guy took one, lit it and handed the pack over to me, I gestured to him to pass them around and thus made friends with everyone in that truck. This was an unheard-of generosity. What did I care? Soviet cigarettes are for shit and I don't smoke anyway.

After about three hours, we pulled into a make-shift village. I don't know how else to describe it. It was like a whole town—fuck, I don't know how many square acres—that was 99% flea market. I'm not kidding, Dude. This whole area, as far as you could see, was a huge, outdoor market. Just stuck out here in nowhere. Why this particular spot? Who knows? There were almost no buildings. Just row after row—street after street—of people with things for sale. Pretty much everyone had an AK-47, or some other machine gun slung over a shoulder. Hundreds of vendors, Dude, selling every kind of weaponry you could imagine, but also food vendors, guys selling books, tools, canned foods, you name it. Money from a dozen different nations changed hands. At least that many languages and dialects. I wandered around for a while and watched a guy buy a chunk of roasted meat. I noticed the bill he peeled off and realized that I had one just like it in my pocket. Something I had taken from a dead Russian. I dug it out and passed it to the guy. He handed me back a piece of meat smaller than the other guy had gotten. I fixed my stare on him and he went and got a bigger piece for me. Bigger than the other guy got. The first time in my life I had ever intimidated anyone. I hadn't seen a mirror since I got here, but judging from the looks of my comrades, and all things considered, I probably presented a picture of someone you didn't want to get all riled up. I walked away gnawing on my chunk of meat.

Another vendor was selling hot tea. I watched for a while to see what it cost, and offered that amount. Can you imagine this? The guy had one cup and it was attached by a chain to the metal handle. You pay for the tea, pour it into the one cup available, drink it down and move on. You hang up the cup so the next guy can use it. Can you feature that?

I wandered around for a while, having no idea what was happening or what I was going to do next. I knew I wasn't going back up into the hills with those guys, but beyond that, my mind was blank. Then I heard the most wonderful sound. It took a minute for it to register. Two voices speaking English! Oh, my God, Dude! What a beautiful sound! I followed it to two very Anglo-looking guys standing by a Jeep. I thought at first they were Brits, but now I think they were Australian. I stood there looking at them with my mouth sort of hanging open. One of them said, "Something I can 'elp with then, Mate?" I just stared. I had forgotten how to speak, I guess. The other one said, "You alright there, Mate?" I said something, but I have no idea what. One of them said, "Crikey, that bloke is a yank!"

I think I sort of passed out, Dude, because the next thing I was aware of, one of those guys was helping me sit on a pile of cement blocks. I was aware of the two of them talking about me, but the words didn't quite register. The exchange ended up with, "Well, I'm going that way. This will be my good deed for the year."

A voice said to me, "Up on your feet with you then, Matey," and was helping me up. We walked along for a while—who knows how long and how far?—and I was aware of being passed off in the door way of a small hut; and then an ancient old woman was helping me to a narrow cot. I laid down on my back and I think lost consciousness for a while. When I opened my eyes and looked up she was coming toward me with a wicked-looking knife. I just closed my eyes. *Go ahead and kill me, then*, I thought. *Like I could give a fuck.* Right when I expected to feel the blade drag over my throat, I felt a tugging on my feet and opened my eyes enough to see that she was cutting the laces on my boots. She also cut off the layers of socks I was wearing.

I went through so much with that old woman, Dude, I don't know where to start. I was there at least three weeks. Maybe twice that. I was unconscious much of the time, in pain for all of it. I went through a period where I was sweating and shivering at the same time. I was unconscious for part of the time, but am aware of half-ways waking up at one point crying like a baby. My feet hurt so bad I couldn't stand it. The sounds in my head and the images on the silver screen in my brain were too much. The old woman would make me drink some kind of potion and then I was out. There was no point at which I was unaware of the pain in my toes.

Mostly, I slept. At various times, the old woman would help me sit up in bed and make me drink tea or slurp down some soup. Somewhere along the line I had become naked, although I have no recollection that occurrence. The first time since our plane had gone down. Any number of times she would wake me up and make me sit on the edge of the bed. She'd hold a urinal in front of me and impatiently gesture for me to let go. Then she would lay me back down and cover me up. Sometimes I would be chilled and lay there sweating and shaking so hard the bed creaked. If I had been in a hospital state-side I have no doubt I would have been declared in Critical Condition. I really was a mess.

I think I could have laid there in that hut for a long, long time, had it been left up to me. It wasn't. One morning the old woman dropped my clothes on the bed where I was sleeping. I opened my eyes and she gestured for me to get dressed. The clothes were all freshly laundered. I got dressed, because blind obedience to this old woman was now my reality.

I was made to understand that it was time for me to press on. As far as she was concerned, I was able to, and there would be no debating the issue. I can't tell you how much I didn't want to. Once I was dressed, she set my pack in front of me—it hadn't been opened—and I understood it was time to pay up. I didn't really know what I had or what would be fair, so I just dumped everything out on the floor.

I had Soviet cigarettes, some cheap East German watches, a bunch of Soviet bills and coins, and a collection of knives. Some other stuff; mostly junk. She picked up a small pistol, a couple packs of cigarettes and a few coins and nodded. I thought that was very little, but this wasn't someone you contradicted. Next thing I knew, it was being pushed out the door.

The reality around me hadn't changed much, but my perception had. I was obviously in better shape than before. I was still worn out, still in pain, and still utterly lost. I had no idea what country I was in. Still walking around with an AK-47 over my shoulder. It was like wearing glasses, Dude. You forget about it, but know when it is missing. That morning, I did as I had before, finding another tea vendor with a cup on a chain, and bought a chunk of greasy, gristly meat and walked around waiting for something to develop. There were no Aussies in sight. I wondered if those guys had actually existed.

It was probably about noon, and I watched a truck loaded with crates ease into the area and find a place to unload. A short time later, another empty truck left out the same way. I ain't so dumb, Dude. It dawned on me that there was a road there and it lead to somewhere. No concept of what be at the other end of that road, but it was movement. As long as it went downhill, I was game. I dug out a few bills, no idea how much it was or even what nationality, and positioned myself over there where anyone leaving would have to pass, and waited. Finally a raggedy old truck came along and I waved it down. By this time I was an expert at hand gestures and making myself understood without a spoken language. The driver took my money and motioned for me to get into the truck bed. Naturally, it was a rough, bumpy, torturous ride, but I was aware of the first glimmer of optimism I had experienced in a long, long time. I thought, *I. Am. Outta here.*

No way to say how many miles we bumped along that trail, but I was aware of moving downhill, so all was well. At some point, the driver passed me off to another truck—I gave the guy a couple Russian cigarette lighters and an unopened pack of cigarettes. There was some dried blood on the pack and the old man scratched it off with his thumbnail. He looked at me and said, "Rookski?" I nodded, and he smiled. This guy had one tooth and it was crooked. I had made his day, though, and got to ride in the cab. He jabbered away at me the whole trip and never seemed to notice he got no response.

Long after dark, we ended up in what I suppose passed for a village in those parts. Maybe a dozen pitiful-looking stone houses and a few out buildings. The old man pointed to a barn and waved me off. I slept that night with a roof over my head, in damp straw, snuggled up to a donkey-I think it was a donkey-for warmth. I remember thinking, when this is your idea of luxury, you know you have taken the wrong path in life. It was the single most coherent thought I'd had since the plane went down. It was the kind of thing the old me would have said.

Next morning, I was up and around and asking a familiar question, "Now what?" An old woman came out and gave me a tin can filled with some kind of soup, which I was extremely grateful for. I dug in my pack for something to give her, but she waved it off. She probably felt like she already had everything in life she needed. The old man came out and with sign language made me understand that he was heading back up the hill. If I wanted to continue down, that was the direction. I thanked him, we shook hands and parted company.

The next week or so was a replay of all that. I caught rides and ate and slept where I could. Mostly people were non-hostile. There was one guy, though, I walked up on him and he thought it was a good idea to threaten me. What an idiot. This was near a railroad crossing.

This guy had a metal bucket over an open flame. As I approached, he pulled a huge knife and started waving it at me, cursing me in some ridiculous language. I had seen this guy ahead of me and hadn't given him a thought. I was only approaching because he was in my path. I didn't come within twenty feet of this moron, but he never stopped cursing or waving that knife at me. After I passed, this guy threw a rock at me. I couldn't believe it. It hit my shoulder and it really hurt. I turned around and he spit on the ground, making some kind of gesture with his empty hand.

I couldn't afford any injuries, Dude. I had too much working against me as it was. That rock could have done real harm. I was pissed. I dropped my pack and went back toward him, and he came at me with that fucking knife. I still had my AK and swung it like a baseball bat. Caught him upside the head. I took his knife and two small coins from his pocket and then went and looked in the bucket. There were a couple inches of some kind of stew or something bubbling away. I dumped it in the snow to cool it off and then picked it up with my hands and stuffed it in my mouth. It was extremely nasty-tasting and I refuse to think about what it may have been. It was food. I ate it. As I walked past that guy on the ground, he was groaning. I stepped in the middle of his back and bounced my weight a couple times. Something snapped and crunched and I moved on without looking back. Fuck that guy, Dude. He did that to himself.

Eventually I decided to wait by the tracks for a train I could catch a ride on. It took a couple days, but I just went into snooze mode like I had learned to do up in the hills. My patience paid off, and eventually a slow-moving train eased down the tracks. As it got closer, I realized that the tops of these cars were covered with people.

I had seen this in India, Dude. If you have money, you buy a ticket and ride in the train. If not, you crawl up on the roof and take your chances. The rail road people are okay with it. You are riding at your own risk, and it is nothing to them one way or the other. I was camped out on a curve in the tracks where the train had to slow down; hopping onto the ladder and climbing to the top was no problem. I still had not bathed or tended my hair or beard. I know I looked like a wild man. And, I was carrying an AK-47. People kind of eased away from me. I asked loudly a few times, "Does anybody here speak English?" But all I got in return were blank looks.

It turned out there was a whole society on that train roof, and an etiquette everyone observed. Once people realized I wasn't there to shoot up the place and was only trying to get from Point A to Point B like everyone else, they all relaxed. At one stop, a couple of guys climbed up with bread and these pastry things, and bottled water. I flagged them down. They had zero interest in my Soviet money, but we were able to barter a few trinkets for some bread and water. I was pretty happy with what I got.

I stayed on top of that train car for a couple weeks, bartering for food when I could, asking occasionally if there were any English speakers as new riders came on board and the old ones left. I could tell by the sun that we were generally heading south, and that was good enough for me. It seemed prudent to be very observant, and in the beginning, I noticed that people reacted to my AK with respect. As in, *I respect the fact that you can kill us all in the space of a few seconds and by the looks of you, you'd probably be happy to.* Later on, it seemed more of a curiosity. There came a point that people seemed incredulous when they saw it. As in, *Really? You are just going to move around here with that thing like it's perfectly legal?* It was about the time I was noticing that phenomenon that I shouted my question about English and got a reaction from this kid, maybe ten years old. He looked startled and then quickly made his way down the line away from me. I shrugged it off and let my mind drift.

Several minutes later, I heard a voice addressing me, "Sir? May I be of some assistance to you?" I looked up to see an elderly Indian-looking guy with a bald head and round, wire rim glasses. He was about six feet tall and very skinny. I had just bought a loaf of bread and several bottles of water. I asked him and the boy to join me. "You are much too kind, Sir" he responded. He and the boy sat down. After introductions were made, and I had broken the loaf into three pieces, I said, "First and foremost, "Tell me: where am I right this minute?"

"At this precise moment, Sir, you are on the outskirts of Salong, traveling in the direction of Peshwar," he explained.

I shook my head impatiently, "What *country*," I demanded. This was where I learned that I was in Afghanistan. Up until this point, I really wasn't sure. I just knew that I was somewhere I really did not want to be. One time I had suggested to Scout he just ask one of the fighters where we were, which put a fine point on why he really did not like taking to me. Our cover story was that we had come there to join their struggle. Hard to explain that we didn't know where "there" was.

I can't remember this man's name, or the boy's, but meeting them was fortuitous. From them I learned that the area we were approaching was near an international border and carrying an automatic weapon around was dangerously illegal. It was also important that, as a foreigner—which I obviously was—all personal paperwork must be up to date and impeccable. In my case, it was non-existent. I am once again fast-forwarding and skipping a lot of story, maybe another time; if I took you through the whole trip, we would be here until Christmas. I am for now just giving you the important stuff.

My AK-47 and duffle of ammo clips was grossly illegal, but quite valuable. My new friend knew his way around. The weapon was traded for safe passage over the border, and a nice reward for him and his ward. I had enjoyed their company, and speaking English again after so long, and felt secure in the idea of having companions familiar with the lay of the land. My focus was getting back to India, though. I had to keep moving south.

My ultimate objective, of course, was to get back to Detroit, but I needed to get to friendly territory before I could do that. Afghanistan, Pakistan, that whole part of the world, you don't just walk in somewhere and announce that you are a stranded American and ask for help getting home. And what was my explanation for being there in the first place, for being penniless, for having no passport? I couldn't afford contact with anybody official. I had only made it as far as I had because of the massive population living in abject poverty, and always on the move. I was scroungy and obviously destitute and slightly unhinged. For those reasons, I did not stand out as long as I kept off the radar and stayed among my own kind.

It took several weeks to get across Pakistan, and it was much the same story as riding the train tops across Afghanistan. There were several days of rain that were particularly miserable, but I was running into people who had a smidgeon of English, and the weather was warming. A couple morons tried to rob me about half way across Pakistan. I may have killed them both, I'm not sure. Stupid people", Frank said, shaking his head. "When I gave up the AK, I picked up a fist-sized rock and slipped it into one of those heavy-duty Russian socks I still had. These guys knew I had a bag full of valuables and thought they could just take it away from me. I sort of went berserk-o with that sock, and they went over the edge. Maybe they survived, but if so, they were seriously hurt. Seriously hurt in a world where health care is non-existent for the class of people who ride on train tops. They either died instantly or died a prolonged, agonizing death. Whatever. Fuck 'em.

Anyway, all that is just *blah, blah, blah* stuff. Finally made it to Pesawanda, which is one of the crossing points from Pakistan into India. The last couple days as we were approaching, I made a point of cultivating a friendship with a couple of old timers who were from that area. I was hoping that they could take me to someone who would help me get over the border. The one guy said absolutely not when I broached the subject, and seemed frightened that such a thing was being discussed in his presence. The other one said that were the reward commensurate with the great risk, he himself would escort me over the border. We worked out a barter—which was for pretty much everything I had left—and the deal was done. It turned out to be pretty anti-climatic. We walked a couple of miles down a dusty road, and finally came to a flimsy-looking wire fence. On the other side was India. "Good luck to you, my friend," he said and walked away. All this was at a time when the political climate was friendly between the two nations and illegal border-crossing just was never an issue in that area. Getting over that fence was not a big deal.

Once in India, I felt like I was home, and an enormous weight was lifted. I was still a wreck, still living with pain in my hands and feet, and looked like a walking horror show, but I was in India. It only took a couple days to get to Delhi. Naveen was still at the same phone number. It hadn't occurred to me that my old crew would be thinking that I had ripped them off or that I would somehow be held accountable for the plane-load of weapons and/or opium.

That thought didn't enter my head until about a half hour later when they pulled to the curb in two cars and got out looking very angry. It suddenly occurred to me that placing that call was a mistake. I had the option of not revealing myself, and thought it would be a good idea not to, but at the same time, what else was I going to do?

These guys were looking all around, wondering where I was, asking each other was this a trick, and ready to give it up as a hoax when I finally spoke up. To employ a bit of understatement, my appearance had changed. It took a few minutes to convince Naveen that it really was me. "But...but what has become of you?" Naveen stammered. "What is this explanation?" I told him that our plane had been shot down and gave a brief sketch of what transpired from there. Dude, these guys were cut throats and psychopaths and never gave a shit about anyone who was not of use to them. There was no reason for them to not leave me right there as I was. They saw me as one of their own, though, and I was immediately whisked away to one of the businesses they owned. Machmood was on the phone for the entire ride across town, speaking urgently in Hindi. Naveen seemed distraught over my condition and asked endless questions, not about weapons or drugs, or the money they had never realized, but about me and how I was feeling. I told him I had been hungry and cold since I left him at the airfield, and that I was experiencing a lot of pain.

When the car stopped, we got out and went into a place that here would be called a massage parlor. This one was chosen because of the enormous hot tub. Within minutes, I was stripped and submerged in very hot scented water. There are no words, Dude. I was cold, filthy beyond description, and had not seen a razor, comb or toothbrush since leaving Delhi all those months before. Nothing in life could have felt better than that hot, bubbly water. After a couple minutes, I was joined by three beautiful girls who made a project out of bathing me, washing my hair and administering a desperately needed manicure. A huge tray or fruit and cheeses, with a bottle of wine, appeared and I was hand fed while allowing the hot bubbling water work its magic.

At some point well into the evening, a lady appeared with a basket and said that if I would be kind enough to step out of the tub, she would tend to my hair and beard. I told her that as desperately as I would like to have her do that, I wasn't coming out of that water for any reason. She said perhaps tomorrow then, and left. A couple minutes later she came back, looking somewhat shaken, and, fully dressed, got into the tub with me. Two of the naked girls got out to give her room. She cut my hair, trimmed up my beard, and left. Naveen spoke to her at the door, to which she replied, "Yes, Sir." Naveen handed her a few bills and she left, dripping water all the way. Finally, exhaustion crept up on me, and I had to get out of the water. I found my way into a soft, clean bed with silk sheets, and a soft, scented woman snuggled up on each side. I was home.

In the following days, I spent a lot of time in that hot tub. The rest of the time I was telling Naveen my story; he was fascinated, hungry for details, and wanted to hear it all. I was frightfully thin and, at the urging of everyone around me, was eating almost constantly. And sleeping. I slept long and hard every night, and took several naps during the day. Could not get warm, could not get full, and could not get enough sleep. Certainly not for lack of trying.

Naveen took me to several different doctors, also an acupuncturist, a dentist, and a renowned psychic healer. I had pills and potions and powders and new clothes and a luxurious place to live. Life was gradually getting better to the extent that regained most of the range of motion in my fingers, but still had pain in the joints. My feet started feeling better, but my toes never stopped hurting. To this day.

I had been back in Delhi for about three months, and was living in a place Naveen had secured for me. It had a giant hot tub, and all of my needs were being tended to. One day Naveen started asking me questions about Scout. I wondered why the interest, but didn't really give it a lot of thought. A week or so later, he said that he wanted me to talk to someone about Scout who had an abiding interest in what had become of him. I agreed and the next morning was introduced to a Mr. Gupta, who claimed to be Scout's uncle and employer.

The story I told was essentially true, but I exaggerated how close we had been and, for the sake of his family, also Scout's bravery and valor. There were a lot of questions, and as the conversation went on—I realized in retrospect—the questions were more and more about matters that had nothing to do with scout. I was back in my comfort zone, though, and being able to converse—it was like the lack of food and sleep, I was just happy to be able to talk and engage in conversation after being shut off from that for so long.

Indian police arrested me a few days later as an illegal alien; my visa was long expired and I had no passport. I was jailed and held without bail. After a couple days—I won't start in on what jail is in India—I had a visit from my friend Naveen, who was apologetic about bringing Mr. Gupta to see me. The request for that contact, he explained, had been made by someone much higher up in the crime underworld, and he really had no choice. Long story short, Mr. Gupta was an agent of the Indian Federal Police and had recorded our conversation. Naveen had a complex story about how he had been duped into thinking he was doing a good turn for a friend of a friend, but I saw through it all with an uncommon clarity.

Naveen was an opportunist. As a criminal, he knew that the day would come that he would need something to trade with. Maybe it was already coming down on him when I showed up.

Whatever, the story ultimately passed on wasn't about some American getting shot down and caught up in the Afghan civil war. It was a story about a bitter American ex-convict who traveled around the world to join the forces of evil in that fight.

Interpol agents took custody of me on charges of Aiding and Abetting, and Acting in Concert With, A Known Terrorist Organization.

There is a lot here I don't care to recall, and is not germane to the story at hand. Maybe I'll fill this in at a later date. I was handed over to people who were identified only as agents of the Soviet Federal Police, to be questioned and then extradited to the United States. Only I wasn't. I was taken somewhere else, and to this day, I have no idea where. Upon arrival there I started talking about my rights as an American citizen, and all kinds of idiocy like that. The whole point of holding people in those strange, far-off countries is that those legal niceties do not apply.

I started out with a slightly sanitized version of my adventures, but after getting smacked around a little—it didn't take much—I came clean and told the truth, the whole truth and nothing but the truth. I was still stuck on stupid. I figured they would see me as a sack of crap, but essentially harmless, and cut me loose. And I was wrong.

Based on what I had told Mr. Gupta, and the statements I had made since coming into Soviet custody, I was declared an Enemy Combatant, and they had carte blanche to extract information from me By Any Means Necessary. My previous explanations were deemed "confessions" of collusion with known enemies of The People of the Soviet Socialist Republics. It didn't take much tweaking of the truth to make me look really bad.

My interrogators spoke fluent English, with thick Russian accents. In the beginning, anyway. As time went on, I was convinced that I was talking to Americans. There is a difference between someone who speaks the language well and without an accent, and a native speaker of that language. Certainly there were people in the U.S. Intelligence agencies who would be interested in the information I was believed to have. How hard is it to imagine them allowing this treatment of an American citizen in exchange for information-sharing? Or maybe that's just my cynical attitude.

The Soviets wanted information, for sure, but they hated me. I was the enemy they couldn't get their hands on. I personified everything that was wrong in their world, their humiliation on the world stage that a ragged bunch of illiterate fanatics was defeating the great Soviet military machine. The same people who had mocked the U.S. for their impotence in Viet Nam now had exactly the same situation on their hands. They were furious. The objective was to get information from me, but they enjoyed hurting me in the process.

Up until this point in my life, Dude, I had never heard of the Mujahidin or those other Maoist groups fighting up there in the hills. I never heard those names spoken. They kept putting pictures in front of me and asking me to identify this guy, that guy, some other guy with a beard and turban. They had satellite photos of mountain sides and wanted to me to show them where to find the "safe houses" and what they kept referring to as "hidey holes." They were actually demanding that I cough up information like how many degrees latitude and longitude these places where. They were constantly throwing names at me, as though there had been formal introductions, and wouldn't believe I didn't know these clowns. I didn't know what they were talking about. I could not answer a single question. Remember in those old movies where there is a Nazi (or Russian, always a malevolent character) interrogator who gets in the hero's face and says, "*Ve haf ways of making you talk?*" Right? Of course, our hero never breaks. That's Hollywood, Dude. There is nobody alive who won't talk. My problem is I didn't know anything. They refused to accept that.

Obviously this was well before there was any U.S. involvement over there, but people at the top knew that one day there would be U.S. involvement. How do you infiltrate something like that? Had I had the answers they were looking for, I would have been golden. The fact that I had actually been there, had roamed those hills they could only see in satellite photos, had interacted with those people in the pictures—that was a wet dream to those people. They simply refused to accept that there was nothing there.

It got real physical, Dude, Frank said quietly. Part of the time I was strapped to a table with a blindfold over my eyes. The pain they inflicted on me was something you will never know about in your lifetime, believe me. I'm not going to say too much about all that. I remember being curled up on a cold concrete floor, whimpering, trembling, sobbing, begging for them to stop, but they didn't. Not for a long, long time.

But yeah, eventually they decided that nobody alive could endure what they were doing to me and not tell everything they knew. At that point my existence became a whole different kind of hell. Some very smart person decided that I had seen and heard more than I realized and they only need to "enhance" my memory. That's when the whole drug thing started.

It is a special kind of evil, doing that to someone. These drugs were a form of torture designed to destroy every aspect of your whole being. Had I known what was coming my way with these drugs, I would have killed myself first. If you think I am just speaking in extreme terms here to make a point, you don't get it. If I thought they were coming for me right now with one of those syringes, I would chew through the arteries in my arm and happily say good bye to all of this. I will never let them use those drugs on me again.

Did you ever do LSD Dude?" I nodded. "You know then, good acid will transport you to another reality. Much of the experience is so intense. These drugs they shot me up with were like that, but nightmarish. Absolutely horrific. Each time it went on hours; hallucinations, being in a reality terrifying and evil beyond imagining. There is no describing the awfulness of it. Being dead sounds like a pretty good alternative to all that. Anyway, one evening I was given some drugged bread and water; sleep zoomed in on me almost instantly.

I began to regain consciousness and realized that I was in an airplane. I turned my head and felt a needle stick my arm. I next woke up in the psych ward of a federal penitentiary. On my second day there, some guy in a suit told me I was being remanded to the custody of the State of Michigan, and had me sign some papers. And here I am. The end.

"Wait a minute, Frank," I said, "What are you in prison *for*? You were discharged from parole. You haven't committed any crimes here. How did you end up back in a state prison in Michigan?"

Frank gave me a sad smile, "I wondered how long it would take you to get to that question, Dude," he said. "The truth is, I don't know. I haven't asked."

"Frank," I said, getting excited, we can file a Show Cause order in Sixth District Federal Court. We can…"

Frank was shaking his head before I even got warmed up. "Do you think I don't know about Habeas Corpus, and Due Process and the 120 day rule, and yadda, yadda? Listen—One: if this is where they want me, this is where I will be. Two: I don't care. From the bottom of my heart, Dude, in all sincerity, I don't care. Right here is fine. I have no family, I have nothing to go to. I don't think I could take care of myself out there". I started to speak, but Frank cut me off again, by adding quietly, "If I am in here, I am not killing some Russian kid and turning his pockets out. In here, I am not a danger to anyone. Let it go, Dude. Seriously".

Frank withdrew deep within himself; his voice sounded like it was coming from the bottom of a well, "Tell them I'm sorry, Dude. I never meant for any of that to happen. If I had it to do over again, I would turn that AK on myself before I used it to light up that first troop transport.

I am so sorry." With those words, Frank was ambling away from me once again, the very picture of a broken man, despair coming off him in waves. A story with no winners, no redemption.

I guess I should have seen it coming. In retrospect, it was obvious. There was only one way out for Frank and sometime during that night, the voices in his head were silenced. My work detail begins before breakfast lines start, so I am out and about before pretty much anybody else. I knew immediately what had transpired during the wee hours when I saw them wheeling that gurney out of six block, sheet pulled up over the guy's face. There was no other way Frank's story could have ended.

A few days later, since he had no family to claim his body, Frank's cremated remains were deposited into a small box made of pressed cardboard and dropped into a hole on Boot Hill, an area set aside for this purpose out behind Trustee Division. A maintenance guy whipped up some Quikcrete in a bucket and dumped it over the spot; Frank's prison number was etched into it with a stick.

Had I attended Frank's interment, I would have spoken of his keen intellect, his sense of humor, his curiosity and hunger for what is over the next hill. I had known him for many years, and I never heard him wish a bad thought on anyone. My wish for Frank was that the voices he heard now where those of angels singing, that his toes were warm and toasty, and his new existence an unending adventure with a happy ending every time. Above and beyond all else, I hope Frank has found peace. Frank told me his story so I could tell the world that he was sorry. In recording his tale here, I have done my best to honor that.

Meanwhile, I just heard about an old guy in Twelve Block who transferred down from Marquette recently. I am told that he was actually born in Auschwitz, grew up in Mongolia, spent six years in the French Foreign Legion, and has a picture of himself with Nelson Mandela, taken while he was doing time in a South African prison. Now *there* is a guy with a story. I won't rest until I have heard it...

Good Night, Ruby Slippers

My name doesn't matter. If you are one of the people this is being written for, you know who I am. If you're not, who I am is of no consequence. I have been convinced by a priest who has become my spiritual advisor, confidant and confessor, to tell my story. At the end of forty-five years, I accept that there are people who deserve answers, and my prolonged silence is not only selfish, by a cruelty. There are people who know parts of this tale, but nobody has heard it all, start to finish, and there are aspects of it nobody has ever known. I will do this one time, straight through, without embellishing, editorializing, rationalizing or justifying. After this, I will not speak on it again.

This story began in Haight-Ashbury, San Francisco, in the late 1960's. When I arrived there following a four-day trip by thumb from Wisconsin, I felt for the first time in my fourteen-year existence that I was "home". I fit in, and was surrounded by people who seemed to like me fine just the way I was. I made friends, had fun, and felt more comfortable with myself than I had ever known was possible. In that, I was not unique: Haight Ashbury was Shangri-La to legions of young people marching to a different drummer.

In my case, I came from a part of Wisconsin known as Northern Michigan (In the Haight, any part of the outside world perceived as particularly Rockwellian was referred to as Wisconsin. This was not necessarily a derisive term). I am a small guy, not much over five feet tall, with "delicate" hands. Add to that that I loved rock music, and thought that hippies and Hell's Angels were just too cool, and you understand why I was a round peg in a square hole back home.

I grew up in an NRA family with brothers who played football and kicked ass. My dad's farming operation revolved around breeding beef cattle. As a breeder, he was apparently good at what he did; we had a very impressive spread and people from all over the country came to do business with us. I am using the royal "we" here. As a farm hand, I was something just short of worthless.

Nobody strained real hard to find the most diplomatic way to express that sentiment. For a breeder of champion beef, it was a particular shame to my father to have sired a runt. I didn't fit in there and nobody particularly liked me. I just knew that in San Francisco everything would be different. I was right.

During the late 1960's, the Haight-Ashbury section of San Francisco was the hub of hippy culture in America. (I detest the word "hippy"—as did all of us to whom the term was applied—and use it here only for the sake of convenience.) It really was a different world. It is easy—and I admit, not totally inaccurate—to describe it all as a culture built on sex and drugs and rock and roll, but there was so much more to it. This was a neighborhood comprised of gentle people who truly believed we are on this earth to love one another and that the highest calling in life is to live out that simple philosophy. Those who had something made sure that nobody around them went without. There were numerous organizations that fed hungry people, but more importantly, any number of individuals who made it their business on a daily basis to share what they had with street hippies and others who were just scraping by. There was the Haight-Ashbury Switchboard, where you could go and ask for a place to sleep and they would call one of their volunteers who opened their homes to street people who needed a bed for the night. There were a dozen soup kitchens, a free clinic and even a free store where you could just go in and help yourself to anything there. They received enough donations to stay in business, such as it was a business, for several years. Everywhere there was the sound of music and the smell of marijuana smoke. If someone offered to sell you some dope and you pleaded poverty, they would just give you some.

Most of the street people were panhandlers, and in Haight-Ashbury, that was a lucrative line of work. I had enough of good old Mid-Western values embedded in me that I could not bring myself to just ask strangers to give me money. It was not hard to find day labor, though, and putting in a few hours of scut work every week suited me. One day I invested my three-day earnings from cleaning squid at a Fisherman's Warf restaurant in several pounds of multi-color beads. That afternoon, after my free lunch at the Huckleberry House, I found a quiet spot in Golden Gate Park, near where I used to sleep, and set to work stringing up choker necklaces of a type that were popular at that time. That night I stood outside the Winterland Auditorium before a Jimi Hendrix concert with several dozen of these for sale. The price was one dollar each, but if you really liked one and didn't have any money, you could just have it. Some people gave me fifty cents, and that was fine, too. Twice that first night people saw that I was giving some away and paid me double just because they thought that was cool. That's how the Haight was. I traded a couple for joints and a couple more for hits of acid. It was a lucrative night. I made enough to see the concert, get stoned, share with a few panhandlers and buy my own lunch the next day.

After that first experience, I became The Necklace Guy and spent a good part of everyday stringing necklaces in the park. I loved that, as time went by, even when I didn't have them on display—I could be up in Berkeley, or way over on campus in San Francisco—people would recognize me; we would end up talking and usually smoke a joint together. Haight Ashbury was full of colorful characters. In a minor way, I was one of them.

There was a great hunger for Universal Truth in The Haight. We were a youth culture disillusioned with the world we were living in, with the values of our parents and society in general. Everybody knew somebody who had been killed in Viet Nam as well as long hairs who had been brutalized by the police, or National Guard.

It was a scary and confusing time. In our little bubble by the bay, we felt protected and took care of one another as best we could. Eastern religions were very popular and widely discussed, as was Native American spirituality and generally the idea that God was pretty wonderful, although horrendously misrepresented by the organized churches we all had grown up in. It was widely accepted that one of the short cuts to finding spiritual truth was through the judicious use of LSD.

There is no way around the fact that LSD was a big part of what Haight Ashbury was. I know it is not only fashionable but expected that one lament a history of drug use, but the truth is, I loved LSD. I had dozens of fantastic experiences with it. In that time and place, the best LSD ever manufactured was plentiful, cheap and readily available. It ranged in price from free to one dollar. The use of LSD was not just a way to get high, but a mind-expanding, psychedelic experience that truly did open doors of perception. To be on LSD was to visit an alternate reality—hence the term *trip*. Among the many aspects of the experience was a feeling of love and compassion that touched the user in such a way as to become all-consuming, even long after the drug wore off. It is not hard to understand why many people equated the use of LSD with a spiritual experience. Whether you saw it as a pathway to heaven or simply as mind candy, LSD was as much a part of Haight-Ashbury as long hair and black light posters.

LSD can also make you insane.

In the beginning, I spent my nights in San Francisco in a sleeping bag in Golden Gate Park, living out of my back pack. When weather was bad, I would check in at one of the numerous crash pads. Overall, I thought life was pretty groovy, and there wasn't much I would have changed.

There was one fly in that ointment, however, and as time went on, it became more and more of a problem. As I said, I am tiny, with light colored hair, which was now very long, sun bleached with soft golden tones and slight reddish highlights. To this point in my life, a razor had never touched my face. From earliest memory, I was described as "cute."

The State of California is home to more perverts, surely, than any other place in the universe. Perverts, at least, of the type who don't like girls, but boys they can imagine look like girls. All this was new to me because back in Wisconsin, once such people revealed themselves, they would come up missing and were never referred to again. In California, they were protected by law. I was often propositioned, sometimes several times in the same afternoon. Some of them were very insistent and intimidating. During this time, I had several different stalkers who eventually made it impossible for me to continue sleeping in the park. This was annoying and embarrassing, but in the overall party of life, not particularly a big deal.

One afternoon, I was hitchhiking over to Berkeley and hopped into a Cadillac with this guy who was dressed in a mod fashion, which I had always thought was silly.

Mod, to me, was rich people trying to relate to hippies by spending a lot of money in a boutique. He looked vaguely familiar but was friendly and I sensed no cause for alarm. He handed me a joint, and told me to go ahead and light it up. With pleasure. On the first toke, I could tell that this was something more powerful than anything I had ever experienced. I took another and my head was spinning, I said, "Wow" and the guy laughed. He said that Wow doesn't even begin to say it and that he had had his eye on me for a long time. There was more, but I faded and passed out before I had a chance to be frightened. That came later.

I woke up in a dimly lit room with a splitting headache, feeling very nauseous. After a short time, the guy came in to check on me. He was naked and was holding a tennis shoe in one hand. I struggled to get up and started to speak when he swung the shoe and slapped me across the face with it. I was sure that my head had split open. I didn't even know that such pain was possible. "You will speak only when spoken to," he informed me. From that moment forward, I existed in a nightmare. Over the next several days, I was beaten until rescued by unconsciousness, to awaken to the feeling that my skin was on fire, only to repeat the entire process again. I know that days passed, maybe weeks. I learned all the things that twisted men do to young boys. After a while the physical abuse ended, at least to the extent that it left marks, only to be replaced by a regimen of psychological torment capitalizing on humiliation.

I wish I had tales to tell of my great stoicism, and refusal onto death to capitulate. Although much of that time remains a blur, I remember cringing in fear, weeping, begging for mercy, and early on, being eager to please. Anything to stop the pain. I remember being made to grovel for a cold fast-food hamburger and a tepid glass of water and being tearfully grateful when it was finally granted. There was a time that going for several encounters with my keeper without being tortured left me feeling grateful and thinking he was not such a bad person at all.

My other life, back in Wisconsin, back in the Haight, was long forgotten; it had never been. My entire existence was, and always had been, this small windowless room, and my purpose was to perform in such a manner as to not be punished. I felt a certain pride when successful, shamed when I failed.

I was never aware of whether it was day or night, and never had any concept of the passage of days. There came a point where different men visited me in that room, and I understood that I was being rented out and that for the period of time they were there, I belonged to them. Looking back, I am amazed at the many variations on that single theme. At the time, I was only intent on being good enough to not be punished.

One day, I was cleaned up and led to another part of the house that was set up as a make shift studio and spent hours posing for two different photographers who cooed endlessly about how pretty I was and who congratulated my owner on finding such a gem. After that, these photo sessions took place several times a week, and in between times, the usual daily visitors to my room in the basement. Occasionally my caller would be one of several different women who became regulars. This should have been a relief. However, these were adult women willing pay to have their way with a young boy they knew was being held as a sex slave. They were no less twisted than their male counter parts, and tended toward sadism.

On another day, not long after that, I was taken to the studio to discover that the still cameras on tripods had been replaced with video equipment. It was a long day during which miles of pornography was shot. Different men came and went with children and women they owned. I made films with boys and girls my own age, with girls very much younger, with adult women, and with old men. And with various combinations and groups thereof.

I learned early on not to look into the eyes of the kids. Some eyes were utterly lifeless, bodies feeling nothing, going through motions to prevent brutality and hoping for nothing more in life. Some were blurred and groggy with drugs; some were screaming in agony, pleading for mercy, imploring me to somehow help them. It is my great shame that my strongest feeling about all this was that they would do something to screw up the shoot and that I would be punished for it. Throughout all of it, I had no real conscious thought. I did not like any of it, I did not hate any of it. What I was doing assured that I was not beaten and I was fed with degree of regularity. At some point it was discovered that a few shots of whiskey and some marijuana made the performers more relaxed which resulted in a better film. I was pitifully grateful for that.

Just as all this became routine, a woman was brought in one day with a makeup kit, and spent some time working on my face. She told me several times that I was "a star". I didn't understand at first that I was looking into a mirror when she was done. The face of a very pretty young girl was looking back at me. I was dressed up in girls' clothes and could certainly pass scrutiny anywhere in the world. There was about me nothing whatsoever masculine. With the nails of my long, narrow fingers painted pink, a delicate gold necklace and a pearl ring, the transformation was complete.

Me, as a girl in appearance about thirteen years of age, opened a whole new universe of possibilities in terms of movie making. I was indifferent. The only real thought in my head was please don't hurt me and thank for not hurting me. Beyond that, I was an automaton. I functioned. I did not think. I do not know, and cannot guess, how many miles of film was shot, or how many different partners I was paired up with. When my work for the day was done, the day, and everyone in it was forgotten.

All that changed one day, and I felt my first real emotion when I was put together with a girl I recognized from the Haight. I had seen her around, but we had never spoken. She had a tan complexion, long raven hair and violent eyes. Her eyes were not just blue, but actually a brilliant shining violent. We made a film the pretense of which was two young lesbian lovers, only to discover one was actually a boy who disguised himself as a girl for a chance to get into bed with the other. At some point, there was an equipment malfunction so it was short day. We were alone for several moments and I became aware, for the first time since my capture, of enormous shame. I looked at her and said quietly, "I'm sorry. You know. About that." Indicating the bed. She replied dully, "That's okay, I wasn't there." I knew exactly what she meant. For much of the time I had been in captivity I hadn't been there either. Just before she left, she whispered, "My name is Celine."

Afterward, I lay on my mattress whispered the name to myself Celine. Celine. I now remembered, she used to sing. A voice as pretty as her eyes. She was on the stage a lot with various local bands and sat with a group of her friends in the park, singing and laughing. I used to see her with an enormous woven basket filled with sandwiches and fruit, passing it out to street people. Celine. Celine from Haight-Ashbury. I've got to get out of here.

I knew that escape was impossible. And would be fruitless in any event. There was no place to hide, and just thinking about it would get me hurt. Thinking these thoughts terrified me to the point that I whimpered in fear of being found out. These were not thoughts I was allowed to have. Something had awakened, though, and I could not go back to being utterly mindless. I pledged to act on any opportunity that came along. With that thought, firmly implanted in my subconscious, I dismissed it and forced my waking mind back to blank.

There was never any actual conversation with me beyond telling me what to do, berating me, reminding me that I was not missing because nobody even knew that I existed, but somehow, I garnered the idea that I was not by any means the first to have been taken by the Cadillac man. I had the distinct impression that the thing with the photos and then the films was something new. The film operation was expanding and getting more sophisticated every day. The combination of Celine and I left our owners giddy. They were widely praised and envied in their circles for having found such beauties. My cross-gender versatility made me the catch of a lifetime.

As the film business grew more involved, there were occasional forays out of the house which is how I learned that we were in San Diego. Several times they had Celine and I together on a secluded stretch of beach; sometimes in Balboa Park or other local outdoor areas. We were never allowed to carry on a conversation, but we communicated with our eyes and knew the day would come that we would escape. The one thing I knew for sure was that I loved this girl and that the pain of the whippings and more creative torments I had endured paled next to the pain of contemplating her suffering. I knew I would go through it all a thousand times if necessary to win her freedom.

Three different times, the Cadillac man took me to pick up Celine and her keeper and then drop them off on the way back. I knew where she lived and how to get there. I filed that information away.

The man who kept me carried a small pistol behind his belt buckle which sometimes become uncomfortable while driving or otherwise sitting for extended period of time. Sometimes he would shift it to a more comfortable position. One afternoon we all went to the beach, but had to cancel the shoot because it was too breezy and sand was getting into the camera equipment. After dropping the others off, we returned to where we lived and entered through the kitchen door. He slipped the pistol out from his waistband and set it down to pull his sweater over his head. Without any actual thought, I picked it up, held it to the back of his head and pulled the trigger. He fell face forward to the floor, spasmed once, and became very still. I looked at the small toy-like gun and whispered, "Wow."

I realized for the first time that this was actually a very large house and took time to explore. I knew that if I found any other adults there, I would shoot them as unhesitatingly as I had him. In one room, I found photographic equipment and boxes filled with negatives, prints and reels of film. In another I found a small suitcase containing neat bundles of money. There were some twenties, but mostly fifties and hundreds. I also discovered a collection of records and the nicest stereo system I had ever seen. All of this, along with his collection of jewelry, and miscellaneous things lying around that caught my eye, I loaded into his Cadillac in the attached garage. This required a dozen or more trips, each time stepping over that body in the kitchen, forever frozen halfway through pulling that sweater over his head. I felt nothing for him. There was no hate, no feelings one way or the other about ending his existence. In the room was a table and chairs, a toaster, and a body. They were all inanimate objects about which it did not occur to me to have any feelings.

On this particular day, I had been dressed in lavender hip hugger bell bottoms and a white silk tank top. My role of the day that of a pretty young boy rather than a girl. After loading the car, I found where "my" clothes were kept, and dressed in my most feminine outfit, carefully applying my make up as I had been taught, choosing tasteful accessories. In the bottom of the makeup case, I discovered a collection of photographs from which I realized the room I had lived in had at least one hidden camera. And that the men and women who had visited me there, as they say now days, had been "caught on video". There was also an address book filled with names and phone numbers, many of which had stars or coded figures next to them. On my last trip through the kitchen, I stuffed the book and pictures down the front of his pants, and assumed that when the police performed a more thorough search of the premises even more would turn up.

By the time I pulled out of the garage, it was dark enough that, especially with the tinted windshield, it would be unlikely anyone would notice that a very young girl was driving this caddy. It took less than twenty minutes to drive to the town house where Celine lived.

The door was answered by that man who had done such terrible things to that beautiful girl. He was astonished to see me there alone. I told him that there was trouble and that he was parking the car and told me to come on ahead. He let me in and as soon as the door closed behind us, I lifted the gun and shot him through the face. At that point, for the first time in many months, I left my emotions run free.

I let go a primal scream and shouted, "How do you like being dead, you son of pig!" With every bit of strength in me, I kicked his ribs and heard them snap. I kicked over and over again until I was physically spent and gasping for breath. When I finally stopped, I looked up to see Celine dressed in a sheer pink teddy and fish net stockings, her hands over her face, and a look of horror in her eyes. I said her name and she looked away from that thing on the floor and at me for a long, confused moment, and then burst out crying. She collapsed on the floor and wept with huge, body-wracking sobs. I was confused, not understanding this at all, until I knelt down to help her up and she threw her arms around me whispering, "Thank you, oh thank you" over and over again.

While Celine got herself composed and changed into blue jeans, I went through the place picking out things I thought could be useful to us, including a couple heavy gold Rolex watches and three very beautiful guitars.

There was a substantial amount of cash, several pounds of marijuana and over a half pound of heroin. He had maintained a well-stocked bar, every item of which was loaded into the caddy. Celine gathered up all of the outfits from Victoria's Secret and Fredrick's of Hollywood and shredded them with a razor blade. We found a collection of photographs, which she went through using a paper punch to remove her face from any that included her. These were left in plain view next to the body. Less than an hour after I first knocked on the door, we were driving across San Diego, flowing signs toward highway 101. No discussion necessary. There was only one place to go. Haight Ashbury. Home.

As soon as we were well clear of the city of San Diego, Celine asked me to pull off the highway in the next town because she had to make a stop. When I hesitated, she said, "Please. It's important." I took the Escondido exit and pulled into a service station where Celine asked for directions to the nearest Catholic Church and asked me to take her there. On the way, she explained that when this evil began she had promised the Holy Mother that as soon as she was delivered, she would immediately go to a church and pray a Rosary in thanksgiving for her deliverance. This was Greek to me but I understood that it was important to her. When we arrived at the church, she insisted that I accompany her.

I had never been in a Catholic church before and was awed by its majesty and the sense of solemnity. Celine lit candles for St. Jude and St. Teresa and thanked them for protecting her sanity while she was in the clutches of the Evil One. I sat in a front row pew while she kneeled at the communion rail fingering her rosary beads, occasionally crossing herself, sometimes with head bowed and eyes closed and sometimes looking with adoration upon the depictions of the Sacred Heart of Jesus and the Immaculate Heart of Mary. This was a peaceful interlude. I would have been content to set there for hours.

As we drove up the coast, she told me that she had been "stolen" after having been lured to what supposed to have been a singing audition. She told me that the first time we met, she had known that I would somehow play a role in her escape, and that she had given me her name so that I could pray for her as she was praying for me. Celine was very matter of fact about her spiritual life and assumed everybody else was as well. To her, it was not a question of faith, or believing, but simple reality. One would never ask, do you believe that water is wet and rocks are hard? Do you have you have faith that birds fly and fish swim? This was the way that Celine knew that God so loved the world that he sent his only begotten Son, that his Holy Virgin Mother watched over all God's children and smiled on those who lived according to her son's teachings, and that all the angels and saints in heaven were rooting for us to succeed, and wept when we suffered. Celine knew this this the way anyone knows that night is dark and lemons are tart. This is just the way it is.

As though she was sure it was a concern of mine, she assured me that she had prayed for their souls. I knew who "they" were. She seemed perplexed by by response. "But of course we must pray for the evil, how else will God ever win them back?" She went on the explain, as though speaking to a five-year-old, that all of existence is a struggle between Good and Evil. When a good person dies, they are joyfully welcomed home to their eternal reward. When a bad person dies, the angels weep, because it is a victory for The Evil One and there is no chance that God can recover their souls. That is where we come in. If we petition for them, it can make a difference. There followed an explanation about the Hierarchy of the Saints and some other Catholic stuff I couldn't really follow. I just told her I'd have to think on all that. Personally, I was happy with the idea that they were burning in hell.

Upon arriving in the Haight, we piled all our belongings in a motel room a and parked the caddy with the keys on it over in the Fillmore where it was sure to be stolen with a quickness, and returned to our motel. That night we drank rum and coke and wept in one another's arms until we finally collapsed. It had been a long and draining day; we slept for nearly ten hours, our first order of business the next day was to find an apartment. Neither of us felt like contacting old friends or going to our favorite spots. Celine got a newspaper and spent almost two hours on the phone calling number after number and finally announced that she thought she had found what we were looking for. We took a cab to a building on Gate Street, close to the heart of Haight Ashbury. The apartment was a third-floor walkup with dormer windows that looked out onto the neighborhood that we both loved so much. It was a building with security doors that required a key to enter from the street and visitors had to be buzzed in. Neither of us would have been comfortable with less.

Celine was a couple of years older than me and much more knowledgeable about these things than I was. She handled dealing with the building manager, who was skeptical about renting to two such young girls. Celine asked, in a manner both naïve and innocent—as though this thought had just occurred to her and she was genuinely curious about the answer—"would it make a difference if I gave you two hundred dollars? The manager paused for a long moment, giving the matter serious consideration and seemed surprised to hear himself answer, "Well, yes, I guess it would". We were moved in by noon. We had a kitchen, living room, two bedrooms and a bath. Getting everything situated was an all-day process. That night we drank more rum and again slept long and hard.

After breakfast the first day in our new apartment, Celine said we had to deal with the box of photographs, negatives and reels of film I had found in the house in San Diego. I hadn't dared start a fire there and there had been no way to dispose of them since, so we still had them. Celine set a votive candle in large serving bowl beneath an open window. One by one, she removed the pictures and made several piles. In all, it appeared there were about three dozen minors. She set aside at least two shots of each that most clearly showed their faces. Over each and every one, she crossed herself and said a short, heartfelt prayer. These went into an envelope with a note that said Please help these children. They are being held in slavery in San Diego. A second stack showed most clearly the adults, male and female who were engaged with them. Both stacks were packaged up and sent to the San Francisco office of the FBI. The rest we went through one by one. Celine prayed and then set it to flame in the serving bowl. She told me that the wisp of white smoke being drawn out the window was the evil spirit being exorcised and reduced to nothingness. The reels of film we discovered were mostly of us; those that weren't involved people who were also included in the photos we were sending the FBI. We spent three hours going through them a foot at a time with pinking shears and paper punch. The confetti that was left found its way into the Bay Area sewer system. Afterward, we drank wine and smoked marijuana and lay in one another's arms for hours without speaking.

When we went out, it was only for short periods of time, and we avoided old friends. I never set foot outside except in girls' clothes and make up. Celine didn't question this. I never questioned it myself, which is a testament to how traumatized I actually was. There is in me not a single gay molecule. I have never had any desire to "be pretty." It was only much later on that I realized this matter of dress was a type of hiding place. This was the "not-me" me. As long as nobody knew who I was or where I was, they couldn't find me. If they couldn't find me, they couldn't hurt me.

Our occasional forays out into the world were not pleasant experiences. We were both scared of people and regarded most "citizens" —non-hippies—with great trepidation. We usually walked arm in arm or held hands.

Even in our apartment, it was seldom we were not touching one another. We had gotten into the habit of sitting side by side, watching the street life outside our window. This was very peaceful and we both felt like we were still a part of the neighborhood without having to expose ourselves to people. When we weren't holding hands, we often sat barefoot and made sure our toes touched. There was always contact.

In the beginning, we sometimes did not leave the apartment for days on end. Sometimes we would just lay still for hours, just holding one another. Sometimes we would cry together—for ourselves, for each other, in grief for what was lost, and always for those less fortunate than ourselves who remained the property of evil men. Sometimes the mental anguish was overwhelming and relieved only with the alcohol and marijuana we had brought with us. This usage was more medicinal than recreational.

As scary as the outside world was, Celine insisted that we go to mass every Sunday morning. I enjoyed the feeling of the church and didn't mind. The real treat, though, was that I got to hear Celine sing. Such a beautiful voice that people turned their heads to see where it was coming from.

We also attended the daily early morning masses or communion services that were sparsely attended and very peaceful. A turning point came one morning at a 5:00 am communion service when a nun named Sister Agnes, who had known Celine before (In our world, "before" always meant before San Diego) came over and gave Celine a powerful hug and made her promise to stop by "the Center" one day soon. Celine promised, which meant she absolutely would do it.

The Center referred to was a safe house for women in distress, located over near the university. I was amazed to learn that Sister Agnes had a PhD in psychology and lectured at various colleges and universities when she wasn't running the women's center or running around involved with the dozen other projects she had involvement in. I didn't know nuns could do all that.

I rode the trolley with Celine later that afternoon and rode back home alone. I was the first time I had been out alone since our return to the Haight and I was very uneasy. Back at the apartment I sat straight-backed in a kitchen chair staring a clock until it was time for me to meet Celine for her trip back home.

It was immediately obvious that her visit with the sister had done Celine a lot of good. She seemed more relaxed and was more talkative than she had been before. For all the time we spent together, up to this point, we had not engaged in a lot of conversation. During the ride home, Celine told me about an organization called HAND—Haigh-Ashbury Neighborhood Development, which she wanted to become involved with. She also told me that Sr. Agnes knew a little bit about San Diego and that she was encouraging Celine to talk it out with her. I was amazed that she was able to talk about it, but understood how it could do her some good to do so.

It soon became routine that Celine would spend a part of every day with the ladies at the center, many of whom had a long history of terrible abuse. She was quickly returning to what I imagined was the person she used to be. It was painfully obvious that I was stuck in an unhealthy place. One day she told me it was time to come out of hiding and that she wanted me to come help with some renovation work HAND was doing for a downtown shelter. With much loving encouragement from Celine, I left the apartment the next day looking pretty much like any other teen age male. I felt naked and vulnerable and was sure everyone was staring at me. Celine held my arm and spoke to me in soothing, encouraging tones without which I would have turned tail and run.

At the project, I was introduced to Tim, a long-time Haight Asbury resident who made his living renovating kitchens. He asked me to help him with some kitchen counters he was installing. He told me that he had been looking for an apprentice and that if we worked well together, I would end up learning some valuable skills. Celine nodded and I agreed. Tim had several boxes of miscellaneous bits and pieces of tiles left over from numerous different jobs. Our trick was to piece these various sizes, shapes and colors together in a mosaic that would look good as a kitchen counter. As it turned out, I was a natural. I have always had some inherent artistic ability and from early childhood, was a jig saw puzzle junkie. Everybody was impressed with the pattern I laid out with these pieces of tile, which made me in inordinately proud. Tim taught me how to set and grout them in place and

I became totally engrossed in the doing of it. Finally, Celine came and told me that we had to leave soon or we would miss the last trolley run of the night. As much as I hated to stop what I was doing, the prospect of walking home in the dark was entirely too frightening.

We could afford to take a cab, but that meant getting into a car, in the dark, with a man we didn't know. We walked hand in hand to the trolley stop.

Everything changed after that. I never wore girls' clothes again; after a few weeks and without comment, Celine donated my old wardrobe to the Women's Center. Tim was impressed with my natural aptitude and the single-minded purpose with which I tackled any job.

After working with me on several volunteer projects, he asked if I would like to work for him full time; minimum wage, but a full apprenticeship. Of course I would.

Celine and I fell into a routine much like married couples anywhere. We joked about "becoming normal." Every workday morning, we parted company at the Trolley Stop near our building, she off to the university and I to my job with Tim. We would meet "back at the ranch" for dinner and discuss our day. Celine had learned about "Volunteer Rockers" at the hospital—people who came in to spend a few hours a day holding babies and rocking them to sleep. Many of these were babies abandoned at birth or born to drug addicted mothers. These children needed as much extra love as it was possible to receive and Celine was the answer to that need. She wanted nothing so much as to be a mother, but owing to something that appened when she was a young girl, had been told that it would never happen. These abandoned babies became her children and she spent every possible moment holding, touching, stroking and praying over them.

We had no compunction about living on the money we had brought with us from San Diego. It takes money to live. Celine missed feeding people on the street but did not feel up to having that kind of contact with strangers any more. She somehow learned about a deli downtown owned and operated by a couple who were Auschwitz survivors.

It became one of her daily stops to spend money there and have food parcels anonymously delivered to various shelters and needy people she knew of. One Rolex watch was donated through an intermediary to the church, which raffled it off as part of a fund-raising effort for one of Sister Agnes's undertakings. We donated the movie-making equipment to a group of artists connected with Feminist Studies at UC Berkeley who were endeavoring to document and expose—and thereby shame the politicians into cracking down on—women being exploited by pimps and pornographers. One night on 60 Minutes we saw a story about a woman who had given cameras to a bunch of homeless children in Calcutta and taught them photography. She was hoping to repeat the project in Bangkok. We sent her our collection of professional cameras, tripods, and several hundred rolls of film.

We never missed an opportunity to give away something we had brought with is from San Diego. None of it was ever missed. To the observer, we were every day Haight-Ashbury people, but we still kept to ourselves much of the time and jealously guarded the sanctuary of our apartment. We would help someone find a place to stay, provide them a meal, even put them up in a hotel, but nobody could stay over with us. We were not a crash pad. It was seldom that we had company and even then, we felt better when they left. We needed space and time to ourselves. Sunday was always our day to be together and decompress. After returning from early mass, we disconnected the buzzer from the street door and spent as much time as necessary working together preparing an elaborate Sunday dinner.

Our Sundays became days that we talked for hours, sang along with Beatle records, played silly games we made up ourselves and made each other laugh. Sometimes we got high, sometimes not. We talked, we touched, we held each other and life was good.

I learned that the woman I loved was actually full blooded Cajun French and had made her way to San Francisco from the very heart of Louisiana Cajun country. So Cajun was her upbringing that English was actually a second language to her. Much of her childhood was a sad story, though, and that was a topic she discussed only with Sister Agnes. I was grateful that she never shared the worst of it with me; what little I knew broke my heart.

Celine was healing, but still suffered from terrifying nightmares, from which she would awaken in tears. She did not recount them to me, but I knew. I was the one person in her life that truly did understand. Through it all it her Catholic faith sustained her, gave her strength and great optimism about the future. Where I had come from, religious people were Baptists and Pentecostals. They raged on about hellfire and brimstone and generally made religion very unappealing and uncomfortable to me. The religion Celine presented to me was a beautiful thing.

I began attending Catechism classes and was confirmed Roman Catholic in a ceremony with Sister Agnes as my sponsor. It was a proud moment for me and extremely meaningful to Celine that we could now take communion together.

My greatest pleasure during that time was listening to Celine sing. Such pure, beautiful music. She loved to sing and I loved to listen. She had sung on stage many times before San Diego and was beginning to be known as an outstanding talent. If things had been different, she certainly would have gone far. Now, even though she still sang, there was no desire to be on stage, with so many people she didn't know looking at her. For the same reasons, we never went to concerts or attended gatherings that involved large groups of people. There were several Bay Area bands—Lamb, Hot Tuna, Small Faces, Beautiful Day—we were both big fans of. For reasons we never understood, these people were never "discovered". They often played concerts in the park and other small local venues we were comfortable enough attending.

We gradually began spending more Saturdays in Golden Gate, listening to bands and visiting with friends. There were always guitars and tambourines and songs to sing.

Working with Tim, I began meeting people and making friends of my own. They were all hippies, but different than those I had known previously. These were people with a sense of responsibility, who worked for a living and did not spend the largest part of each day hanging around getting high. Most of these were in some way involved in construction. I got to be friends with a carpenter who invited me to work out with him at a gym downtown after work.

Weightlifting was something I had never considered before, but loved immediately. Over time, less time than I had expected, I developed thick, rounded shoulders and had muscles piling up everywhere. I was astonished at the difference it made in my over-all appearance. While all this was evolving, my complexion grew somewhat ruddy and, long overdue, my beard finally grew in. It was reddish and fuzzy at first, but finally stiffened up to where it looked like a real beard. I wore it trimmed short and neat most of the time. That whole "cute" look was a thing of the past. With my muscles, long hair and beard, a guy at the gym once told me I looked like a biker, only smaller. I laughed and felt hugely com-plimented, delighted that he hadn't said, "you look like a girl." I started working out on the heavy bag with some kick boxing moves another friend taught me and began to see a Me that I had never imagined. It was pretty cool.

In our personal lives, Celine and I continued to heal and prosper and grow. This world we both loved so dearly, however, was in sad decline. If we were naive about anything, it was that Haight Ashbury would exist forever. How could it not? So many vibrant, alive, car-ing young people all in one place sharing so much love—how could such a thing just fade away? Who would ever want to leave here? But people did. Bill Graham closed the Fillmore West Auditorium, and The Family Dog was boarded up shortly thereafter. HAND lost their funding and so did the Switchboard. The Huckleberry House locked their doors and pretty soon there was no place for the street people to sleep and meals were scarce.

It seemed that every week friends stopped by with their VW buses packed up, to give us their new address at a commune in Colorado, a loft in East L.A., a beach front tribe in Mexico, or just some place back in Wisconsin. It was sad to watch the slow death of Haight-Ashbury. The street people were longer smiling hippies hugging strangers and wishing everybody a nice day, but psychos and speed freaks and long haired junkies with battle scars and jailhouse tattoos. Those gentle people with flowers in their hair, eager to share their meager wealth had simply disappeared; for the first time in my memory, people were being mugged on the street and there were more sirens in the night than there was rock & roll music. Still, Celine and I were Haight-Ashbury people. This was home and we were sure it would get better. We were willing to wait it out.

One night I returned home and found Celine in her favorite rocking chair, beaming. In her arms was a tiny baby girl. "Isn't she beautiful?" she whispered. It took numerous attempts and much probing for me to get an explanation. Finally, Celine explained that the baby was given to her my its mother because she—the mom—was not able to care for her properly. She knew that Celine would care for the child and bring her up right. She spoke in an awed voice, never taking her eyes off the child in her arms, "I am this beautiful baby girl's mother."

I can see the resemblance," I said. Except, of course, that the baby was black. In spite of, or maybe because of, the rough road much of her life had been, Celine was uncommonly down to earth and practical. In most things. In the matter of this child, however, she was absolutely goofy. As she sat there cooing and baby-talking, I noticed that the child had a deformity in her left hand. The hand was snarled-looking with short, twisted fingers. There was nothing healthy-looking in her over-all appearance. I knew enough to tread lightly, and only asked if the child would be needing any special care or medical attention we should be concerned about.

"This baby will be just fine," Celine assured me. "All she needs is a mother's love," and that topic was closed. "Her name is Josephine," She informed me a few minutes later. "She is named after a great-grandmother who was an beautiful human being. She is called Josie."

Josie it was, and from that moment forward, our lives revolved around this child. Celine was in Seventh Heaven. She had a baby to call her own and all was right with the world. Celine referred to it as an adoption, but I was worried that a few of the important legal niceties had been sidestepped.

As time went on, Celine needed more and more money, "For our daughter," she would always say. I assumed that the child had endless medical needs and said nothing as our savings dwindled to nothing. I worked as many hours as I could to keep up with rent and groceries, but money was quickly becoming an issue.

We were in agreement that heroin was evil, and had never contemplated selling any of the half pound we had brought with us from San Diego.

However, I had read an article in High Times magazine about treating mediocre marijuana with heroin to turn it into super weed. This was in the era when most marijuana came from Mexico and much of it was mediocre at best. Much coveted and sought after was the weed being brought home by soldiers returning from Southeast Asia. That pot was to Mexican what Kool Ade was to moonshine whiskey. I bought a kilo of third-rate California ditch weed and followed the easy step by step instructions in the magazine and it worked as advertised. I rolled up a huge pile of very skinny joints and began marketing them as killer Viet Namese weed. Nobody had ever gotten so stoned on such small joints before; I sold out quickly and everyone who tried it clamored for more. I made a tremendous amount of money, but there never seemed to be enough. I actually did feel guilty flim-flaming people who trusted me, but rationalized it by telling myself that they wanted to get high and were happy with what they got. No harm, no foul.

A very strange thing happened with that little girl, who became healthier and happier under Celine's constant ministrations. I gradually came to view her the same way Celine did. I had never in my life given a moment's thought to having a child. I never longed to be a dad. But now I was one and it was profound. I grew to love that girl as much as Celine did and was proud to refer to her as my daughter. We were our own little family. I had never experienced such deep and wonderful feelings before. We lived in a place where people were already experimenting with new definitions of "family" and we did not stand out as an oddity. I couldn't imagine anything more wonderful or fulfilling. It was difficult to leave in the morning and I hurried home after work to spend time with my wife and daughter. When Celine taught Josie to say "Daddy" I thought I would burst with pride.

One night I came home from work to be confronted in our doorway by an extremely sleazy looking pimp and a pitiful wrung out junkie whore. For the sake of simplicity, I will synopsize what happened next. Through her screaming and dramatics, and his threatening and posturing, I was made to understand that they were claiming rightful ownership of my daughter and were demanding an absurd amount of money to go away and leave us alone. It turned physical and both of them ended up getting punched out.

The police arrived just as things were winding down. Both of my confronters were found to be in possession of illegal drugs and he was carrying a switchblade knife. I was not frisked. They were both arrested for the drugs and weapons, as well as disturbing the peace; I was allowed to go on about my business. Throughout the whole police intervention, the junkie (I would use her name here if I knew it) was screaming about her baby being inside this building, but the cops didn't hear a word of it. She was stoned, a known street walker and black. When the guy with her spoke up, the cop handling him "accidentally" cracked his head against the car door while pushing him into the back seat. Life in the big city.

Now I understood where all our money had been going. Upstairs Celine confessed to everything I had surmised. I was, and remain, astounded that she was able to be so deceptive with me about our child. She had always been absolutely above-board and scrupulously honest in every aspect of her life. At the same time, though, having a baby was more important to her than anything. It was the one thing that could override her common sense and commitment to her Christian ethics. I lay awake long into the night trying to figure a way to make this work.

I went to work as usual the next morning, but had a call before noon from a lady who lived in our building. She advised me to get home as quickly as possible. I arrived to find Celine utterly distraught. It shames me to admit it, but I was glad I wasn't there when the Child Protective Services people wrestled Josie from Celine's arms and carried her away. To witness the aftermath was traumatic enough. Celine was inconsolable.

I was not surprised to learn that even a visit with Josie was out of the question. She was gone; there was nothing we could do about it, and nothing to fill the void left in our lives. Celine didn't eat; she curled up in a ball and wept silently. She lay still as a corpse, utterly without sound or movement, with a steady stream of tears. She gradually went limp and did almost nothing but sleep. All of our savings had been depleted by that time so I had to keep working. There were several different friends who spent as much time with her as possible. As time went on, more than one expressed concern that she might never recover and was in real danger of starving herself to death. In desperation, I tracked down Sister Agnes and asked for her intervention.

Sister came to the apartment that night with another nun, Sister Anna, who sat talking with me while Sister Agnes was in the bedroom with Celine. After about forty-five minutes she came back out. I noticed that she had an empty baby food jar and was relieved that Celine had taken in some sustenance. Sister told me that the road ahead would be long and difficult and asked if I was up for it. The question startled me. Of course I would be there for Celine. What else would I do?

The Sisters came and went after that, always giving me encouragement and advice on the best thing I could do for Celine's recovery.

Our friends were beautiful people who never wavered in their support and willingness to help out. It was very much a team effort, and even though the others saw great progress when they got Celine to eat a bit, to me the Celine I knew had not been in evidence for a long time. Everyone assured me that she would be back.

Nobody seemed to realize that I had lost a daughter too.

One evening after Sister Agnes had been in with Celine with about half an hour, Celine screamed with an intense and awful emotion, "THEY. TOOK. MY. *BAY-BEE!*" This was followed by a deep, unrestrained sobbing that was excruciating to hear. Sister Anna noted my stricken expression, patted my hand and smiled grimly, "Now the healing can begin," she said.

And it did. Begin, that is. The following Sunday, Celine began attending mass again, but did not sing. Other routine activities followed. It was progress. She wasn't the old Celine yet, but it was progress. It seemed a huge victory when she washed her hair and brushed it out the way she used to. I began seeing more and more small traces of the strong and optimistic woman I knew her to be.

We had a visit one night from some old friends who had fled the city months earlier. They were living in a commune in the hills a couple hours south of San Francisco near Santa Clara. The life they described sounded idyllic. It immediately occurred to me that a change of that sort might be just the thing Celine needed. By the end of the evening, it was decided. I called in to work the next morning, told a bunch of lies, and set to work packing the van. We headed out before noon.

Peaceable Kingdom was a 350 acre spread in the Santa Cruz mountain range in northern California. When we arrived, it was populated by approximately thirty-five hippies ranging in age from young teen agers to several adults in their 50's. The numbers were constantly fluctuating; wandering gypsies came and went, "permanent" residents would suddenly leave without warning. Frank Zappa once described us as a general of transients, and he was right. We defined it as freedom, but that was simply making a virtue of being irresponsible. For so many of us in this subculture, there was no work ethic, no desire to sink roots, no drive to accomplish. Live For Today, Tomorrow May Never Come.

It was for that reason that most communes failed. Sustained devotion to hard work was anathema to our credo. Also, it is impossible to accomplish much of anything when constantly stoned. As so many of us were. Peaceable Kingdom—P-Kay—was more successful than most. It had been founded by a young couple who had inherited a large sum of money, then sunk it into their dream of founding a self-sustaining artist's community. Its inception was unique in that it was not done on a shoe string with the idea that All You Need Is Love. They were discriminate about who moved in as a permanent resident. You had to bring something to the table, along with a willingnes to work and contribute to the overall functioning of the place. As such things go, P-Kay was functioning rather well.

For all that, though, this was several dozen hippies living in their own little world. Do Your Own Thing was still the general operating philosophy. People may have put in the requisite number of hours tending the gardens or taking care of the animals, but they did so stoned.

Marijuana, homemade wine, and psychedelic drugs were as much a part of the everyday diet as were the organic vegetables. There were a number of artists in residence who were there for the sake of their art, and were very serious about it, but at the end of the day, this was another bubble where people lived for sex and drugs and rock and roll.

Celine and I had smoked our share of pot and had certainly indulged in psychedelics while we were in the Haight, but oddly enough, when life became unbearable for Celine and she was comatose with depression, she never indulged at all. When she didn't, I didn't. It wouldn't have seemed right. By the time we moved to the commune, we had pretty much drifted away from the idea of getting high. It wasn't something we ever discussed or gave any thought to, we just gradually grew into a place where getting high was no longer a part of our lives.

From the beginning, I was uncomfortable about the youngsters at P-Kay. There was a collection of young girls—I guessed them to be between thirteen and fifteen, give or take. They were all dopers. Several were pregnant, for the others it was just a matter of time. I was also uneasy about the children. Hippy kids are born into a world where there are no rules. Blame it on my mid-western roots—I believed that children need some kind of structure and they don't need to live in an environment where clothing is optional and there are brightly colored pills are left lying around everywhere.

My contribution to the community, and the real reason for our invitation, had to do with my wood working skills. By this time I was an accomplished cabinet maker and all around carpenter. Celine was well known and much loved and would be welcomed anywhere; that she wasted no time organizing and operating a day care center was a bonus nobody had anticipated. The parents were delighted to bring their kids to Celine every morning, and she was delighted to have them.

Daycare allowed the parents to go about their business without the little ones being constantly under foot. As much as these people did genuinely love their children, it was understood that they were better off not being around much of what was the daily routine. Quite often Cline would have a group of kids well into the evening. More often than not, when I went past her building, I could hear them singing. With any group, regardless of size, or median age, Celine would immediately instigate a sing-along. Without exception, the kids loved it.

Because of the timing of our arrival, a cabin on the edge of the compound was available to us. The location was perfect for our needs. It was largely hidden from view by a huge barn and a copse of evergreen trees. We had no desire to live in the Big House, an enormous Victorian which was a bee hive with all the activity day and night. There was other housing available on P-Kay, but we felt fortunate to have secured the degree of privacy our little cabin afforded us.

Celine was given a building, formerly a tractor barn, to transform into an area for her kids. My first weeks there were divided between upgrading and renovating our cabin and transforming Celine's barn into an appropriate day care center. Having children to care for was the therapy Celine needed. The teen age girls were drawn to her and became willing assistants just to stay in her orbit.

Caring for those children was a two-edged sword, as it turned out. She invested so much of herself in each one, and every time a mother casually strolled in to announce, "Yeah, we were just talking about some friends in Oregon (or Greenwich Village or Van Couver, whatever) and decided, hey, why not? So, we're gonna split..." it struck Celine like a physical blow. She had the others to sustain her but in terms of her recovery, it was often two steps forward and one step back.

Without us saying anything, it somehow was understood that people should not feel free to drop in on us unannounced without a specific reason. That was highly unusual for this time and place. Everything was always very open, very casual, very free. Celine and I needed time to ourselves, and people seemed to understand that.

In our time together, we spent many hours just holding each other, not speaking, but communicating nonetheless, gradually healing the scars from San Diego. We never recovered from our deep and abiding distrust of strangers. We were both uncomfortable with the idea of eating or drinking something we did not see prepared or come directly from its source. It was so easy for someone to slip something in your food and we both lived with a dread of waking up in a locked base-ment room somewhere.

For myself, I was happy to be living in the country, doing work I enjoyed and was good at. Once all the many and long-overdue repairs were completed, we mapped out a number of new projects I could lead the way on. It was gratifying to look around the place and see what a difference I had made. Things were really shaping up.

One of the artists, a sculptor, started a daily yoga class and Celine got involved with it. Almost immediately, she was totally enthralled with it. Her morning and evening Hatha Yoga routines became very important to her and were showing immediate benefits. I was amazed to see the difference just a couple weeks of yoga made in her life. Her muscles began to tone up, her posture improved, she had a healthy glow I had never seen before. She was also more relaxed and centered than I had ever seen her. It was really quite remarkable. She told me at one point that she could feel her insides healing. When Celine spoke of her insides, she was referring to that part of her that had been damaged in childhood and left her unable to bear children. Such notions always saddened me; Celine so desperately wanted to be a mother, and often latched onto the thinnest of omens to believe she was now able.

I did not encourage such thinking.

After we had been there about three weeks, an aspiring actor who has some skills as a stone mason came to live at P-Kay. We worked together on several projects and he turned out to be a really decent guy. He had three years of Tae Kwan Do experience and asked me to start sparring with him. Which I was happy to do. He was also a huge proponent of yoga and encouraged me to join the group Celine was a part of. Very soon, I began every morning with an hour of yoga and every afternoon with a couple hours of martial arts. During the rest of the day, I was outdoors, doing physical work that I enjoyed doing, and generally getting healthier every day. I liked most of the people around me well enough and don't think I had ever been so content with life in general.

One of my favorite activities at P-Kay was Campfire. There was no actual schedule to it, just an announcement a couple times a week that it was on. Usually the whole community would turn out. With the signature campfire as the backdrop, we would sometimes just sing songs; usually a couple different poets would get up and read their latest work. Sometimes an actor or two would enact a scene, either an original work or something from a famous movie. Sometimes people would just get up and express some thought that was on their minds. It was always a good time and I enjoyed immensely.

One of the projects I was most eager to tackle was a solar powered outdoor shower. Day One on that project, I looked up to see a car with Indiana plates pull into the driveway with a Costa Mesa County sheriff immediately behind. Bernie and Anita came out of the Big House and spoke with them in the driveway. From my vantage point I couldn't hear what was said, but could see that see that the sheriff was speaking in a very no-nonsense manner and that Bernie and Anita were feeling very intimidated. Finally, Anita—with the demeanor of a dog walking with his tail tucked—went into the house and came back out with a sullen teen age girl in tow. The girl's mother, already unhappy about the situation in general, was even less happy to see that her very young daughter was about to become a mother herself. After some harsh words to the sheriff about what he allowed to go on right under his nose, to Bernie and Anita for "aiding and abetting," and a few choice words to the rest of us vermin in general, mom spun off in a cloud of dust, prodigal daughter in tow. The sheriff stood and took a long look around, an expression on his face reflecting something several stages beyond disgust. One of my workers commented philosophically, "Nothing good will come of this."

The story I got later was that this little cupcake had run away from home a year or so earlier, along with a cousin and a friend from school. Along the way, the others had turned themselves in to juvenile authorities and been shipped back home. One or both had spilled the beans about P-Kay being a safe haven for run-aways, which had culminated in today's little drama.

Apparently, Anita and Bernie had been contacted about this girl on more than one occasion and had lied about her being at P-Kay. The next thirty-six hours passed with great tension in the air. A couple of long-time residents who had warrants pending, one of them a draft dodger, lit out within an hour of the sheriff's visit. I set to work preparing a contingency plan in case the worst thing happened.

The worst thing happened the following afternoon. I was out working on my shower and heard Celine call my name. From her tone, I knew it was trouble. I came around the corner of the barn to see three California Highway Patrol cars and a grey van with tinted windows. People who could be from no other agency than the one who had snatched up little Josie were grabbing kids, terrified and screaming, and stuffing them into the van. Bernie and Anita were being led out of house in handcuffs. I held Celine back as she tried to run to the children's defense, carried her to our van and pushed her in. I drove straight into the woods, leaving all of our personal possessions behind.

Most of the day before I had spent with a machete and chain saw, roughing out a path from our cabin to an old fire road back in the woods. It needed much more attention than it got. Almost immediately, both side mirrors were snapped off and the windshield on Celine's side was smashed in. I kept inching forward, fearing nothing more than to end up in the clutches of the California police. I had no idea what would happen in that event, but I knew that Celine and I would be separated, with no idea how we would get back together afterward. I was ready to fight any fight to keep us together.

Any number of times, I had to stop and back up to find a way between two trees or around some obstacles in our path. The undercarriage was scraping the ground much of the time and I feared the oil pan would be ripped open. Both headlights were smashed and the radiator was seriously damaged by the time we reached the fire road. It was marginally better, but hadn't been maintained in many years and was rough and strewn with deadfall and debris. Throughout all of this, Celine was silent. I knew that was a bad sign, but I needed to concentrate entirely on what I was doing.

It took several hours to find an actual road. Amazingly, our little VW bus was still running, albeit in a rough, stuttering manner, without lights and dripping vital fluids every step of the way. Staying to secondary roads, I worked my way as close to San Francisco as I could. We had used savings to keep up the rent on our apartment so we had someplace to go to.

It was well after dark when we reached the junction with Highway 101. I sat there pondering just what to do, trying to think of some lie I could tell the highway patrol when they pulled us over, when Celine spoke up for the first time, "Go ahead, we'll be okay." I looked at her, waiting for more.

Sounding wrung out and defeated, she informed me that The Virgin had relayed to her that we were to go forward boldly and we would be under her protection. Feeling somewhat less confident than Celine, I pulled out onto Highway 101, heading for home, keeping as far to the right side of the pavement as I could. About three hours later I pulled into a parking spot behind our building, having come to the attention of no police agency. Celine looked at me, utterly dejected, "All those beautiful babies," she said. "I'll never see any of them again." There was nothing to say to that. I helped her inside and we fell into an exhausted sleep. Early the next morning I gave a neighbor a couple of my Viet Namese joints to help me push the van over a few streets over from our home. We parked it on Clayborn Street, stripped off the plates and left the keys in the ignition. It was stolen within two hours.

Predictably, Celine fell into a depression, although it was not nearly as all-consuming and destructive as what we went through with the loss of Josie. As often as possible I accompanied her on her visits to the Sister. Sister Anna and I began talking more and more and as time went on, I began to think of her as a close personal friend. She seemed to like me and be truly interested in all that was going on in my life. With extreme subtly, without any clue that it was happening, she somehow planted the seed that I should call home and tell my mother that I was okay. I was a little mystified as to how all that evolved, since making such a call had never been a part of my thinking. I had left that world behind and as far as I was concerned, good riddance.

Even so, one evening while Celine was hidden away in the depths of the ladies' center, I found my way down to the Haight-Ashbury Switchboard and asked to use a phone. They always had phones available to anyone who wanted to call the folks back home, wherever that was. I was immediately struck by how excited my mom seemed to be hearing from me. She kept asking if I was okay, did I need anything, and other endless questions about my life. At one point, she stopped and asked quietly, "Do you ever think about coming home?" I replied simply, "I am home."

She let it go at that. The conversation picked up from there and eventually I relaxed enough to start talking, and ended up saying much more than I would ever have thought possible. Excluding San Diego, I told her pretty much the whole story. I was aware of sniffling on the other end. After I finally wound down, there was a long pause and I heard my mother whisper, "Oh my God." She made me promise to call again and I knew I would.

"You have a mother?" Celie was astonished and incredulous. "You have a nice mother and you don't even talk to her?" She couldn't have been more bewildered. Nice Mother was a term Celine used to differentiate those from the other kind. In Celine World, a Nice Mother was an object of adoration and not to be taken lightly. I had never spoken of my family at all. Celine didn't speak of her's either, not with me anyway. We both just left that topic alone.

Now she was excited and fascinated with the idea that I had a Nice Mother and she wouldn't let it go. She peppered me with endless questions about my mother, my aunts, life in Michigan, and I began to feel a bit harassed about it. Finally, in exasperation, I suggested she call herself and get it all from the source. She was caught up short. Her eyes got big; "I can do that?" she asked, as though such a privilege was beyond imagining.

As we walked down to the Switch board, she was like a kid going to buy a pony. "What will I say?" she asked me, "What if she doesn't like me…What should I say if she asks me…maybe she blames me for you not going home…are you sure this is okay…?" and on and on. It was a relief to get there and put the phone in her hand. I was confident she could handle it from there and went back outside. Through the window, I watched as she progressed through her initial meekness, to more relaxed chatting, through a period of weepiness, to giggling, and back and forth. A couple friends came by and we sat on the curb drinking wine in a sack and talking until she came back out. She was quiet and pensive on the walk home. I waited until we reached our building to ask what she was thinking. In a voice tight with emotion, she said quietly, "She told me I could call her 'Mom'." As I left for work the next morning, Celine told me, "Your mother is nothing less than a saint and I will be very hurt if you are not nice to her every day of your life from this day forward."

About five weeks later, I got off the trolley car coming from work and found myself face to face with my parents for the first time since I had left home without warning. I was carrying two bags of groceries and was so was relieved of the awkwardness of how to greet them. I simply said, "Hey". My mom said, "Hey yourself." My dad immediately launched into a painful explanation about a last-minute invitation from the Cattlemen's Association to a seminar in Reno, and since San Francisco is so close, my mother insisted they hop over...all designed to dispel any notion that they would travel across the country to track me down after I ran out on them the way I did. I buzzed Celine and told her we had company and we headed up.

The moment she opened the door, Celine squealed and flew into my mother's arms. They hugged and got weepy and carried on so long that it got uncomfortable for my dad and I just standing there. I motioned him to a chair in the living room and grabbed us a couple beers from the fridge. I asked about the farm and we made small talk while the women folk prepared a meal in the kitchen, each one talking a mile a minute. The atmosphere calmed down and got more comfortable as the evening wore on. We had dinner and talked and began seeing each other in a new light. As it was getting late and about time to call it a night, my dad nodded at my hands, callused and shop-worn, and said, "Working man's hands." I shrugged, "I try to stay busy," I said. He nodded in response to that.

To the uninitiated, that exchange would appear to be of no real substance. If you are from the rural mid-west, however, you know that volumes had been spoken. Where I come from, the Working Man is the salt of the earth. The Working Man built this country. He is the paragon of quiet strength and integrity. He will give you an honest day's labor for a fair wage because that's the deal, and that is how a man cares for his family. A man works with is hands, answers when Uncle Sam calls—that is a man who deserves respect. My dad acknowledged me as a member of that fraternity, and my modest response was the appropriate one. I was forgiven and welcome to come back home was the message.

It turned out that Celine and my mother had had numerous conversations since that first night at the Switchboard. Celine had no idea they would be visiting, but recognized her immediately from having spoken to her on the phone. Apparently quite a lot had been said about me, my work ethic, my church attendance, and other matters significant in that strange world I grew up in. After their visit Celine was convinced that northern Michigan was the most wonderful place in the world, although leaving Haight-Ashbury was still an incomprehensible notion for either of us.

It was into the third month after we left Peaceable Kingdom—we never heard how that drama played out—when Celine greeted me with a big announcement, "I am with child" she declared formally. She read the expression on my face and immediately set to reassuring me that it would be okay. The Holy Virgin had told her she would have a successful pregnancy and that all would be well.

Celine was in a state of ecstasy, and couldn't stop babbling about plans to be made, names to mull over, people who must be notified, where to shop for baby clothes, and on and on. She paced, she giggled, carrying on about grandchildren, choosing and discarding possible names, fretting over their education, declaring she wanted enough children to start her own commune. It was deep into the night before she calmed down enough for us to settle into our comfortable chairs by the window and focus on matters that must now be addressed. We spoke long and seriously and ultimately reached conclusions that a week earlier would I have been unthinkable, but now were the only thing that made sense.

I made my way down to the Switchboard and placed a collect call to Michigan. I wonder how many calls were placed from California during that era that began with these words: "Mom? I'd like to come home." There was great melancholy in facing the fact that even in its best times, The Haight was not a great place to raise children.

A third-floor walk-up, in an inner-city slum was not the best place for a pregnant lady to find her way into motherhood. Celine was adamant that this child, and the ones to follow, grow up with grandparents and aunts and uncles and be able to play outdoors and never have to be scared. I could hardly argue that.

And it was not like we were leaving the Haight-Ashbury we had loved. It was still a sad decision and if not for Celine's pregnancy, we would probably still be there today. My mother and I had a long and emotional conversation. I put Celine on and she spoke for what seemed hours, alternately talking, crying, giggling, sniffling, and ultimately strengthening a bond that was to evolve into a deep and abiding friendship.

We paid cash next day for the standard-issue WW minibus and spent a day making rounds and saying goodbye. By unspoken agreement, we gave away what remained of the possessions we had brought with us from San Diego, although I did keep one item that was hidden away in a tool box.

Tim was overwhelmed and embarrassingly grateful to receive the custom-made Fender acoustic/electric guitar. The Les Paul went to my work out partner at the gym and Celine gave the Martin twelve string to a self-proclaimed "radical lesbian" friend in Berkeley we were both sure was the next Joni Mitchell. The jewelry was distributed to shelters and lesser items to hungry friends who would translate it into rent money or groceries. What small amount of marijuana and liquor that were left was handed out to neighbors in the building. As an expectant mother, Celine had become an absolute purist and I was not comfortable with carrying contraband cross-country. Neither of us had a license.

We said our good bye to Haight-Ashbury early one chilly, foggy Saturday morning with a slow drive past all of the spots that had meaning to us, across the bridge for one last cruise up and down Telegraph Avenue in Berkeley and then out onto the highway for a straight-though drive into a new beginning for us both.

We eased up the driveway of my parents' home to see my mother waiting on the front porch. Before the van came to a full stop, Celine was out the door, flying up the steps, she and my mother embracing like twins separated at birth. My father, of course, was out working. It was my job to go to him. We got off to an awkward, uncomfortable start, but I grabbed a bale of hay and joined him in the afternoon feeding. Being willing to jump into hard work forgives a lot of sins in America's heartland.

And, of course everybody loved Celine. It is said that pregnant women have a certain glow. Celine had started out with a glow. Now she could be light house beacon on the darkest, stormiest night of the century. The idea of "family' was important to her and now she had one. Even the most strightlaced and uptight of neighbors and relatives who stopped by to check out "the Prodigal Son and his pregnant hippy girlfriend" came away agreeing that "that is one special girl."

By this time, long hair on men was not the same outrage it had been several years earlier. Except in Northern Michigan.

It is not good to stand out in any way in these parts and even without the hair, I had pretty emphatically distinguished myself as different.

During those first few weeks several of the area bullies felt called up on to give me special attention. These were red neck sluggers and brawlers, though, and I had picked up a few big-city tricks in the gym that they just had no way of dealing with. I was still a small guy and got touched up a bit, but nobody had their way with just smacking me around, and nary a one of them came back for seconds.

Out of respect for the Wisconsinites, Celine and I agreed to sleep in separate beds until we were married. I was assigned a basement nook, Celine a room in the attic. Some of the kin folk were uncomfortable about having to enter a Catholic church to for the wedding, but the reception was a blow out. As a couple we were a different kind of duck as they say in those parts, but owing to Celine's natural charisma and innocent piety – and the fact that I seemed to be comporting myself in a respectable manner, in a shorter time than I would have thought possible, we were sincerely welcomed into a community that is slow to assimilate outsiders. In the beginning, there had been some talk about me going back to school but that was, at best, silly. If I hadn't quite fit in before, I was now in a different universe than others my age. One after noon I sat in the Tastee Freeze with some guys I had grown up with. While one was excitedly carrying on about copping a feel in the movie theater last week, I was distracted with thoughts of my wife's pregnancy. Another was fretting about Mary Lou being mad at him for sitting next to Sally Jo in study hall as I made a mental note to follow up with that insurance agent about which health plan we would go with for the baby. While they lamented their meager allowances, I was calculating, groceries, utilities and rent. It was a delightful surprise that I had learned much more from Tim than I realized and gradually built a reputation as skilled craftsman who "does good work" –high praise indeed in the heartland.

When the first winter storm of the season blew in, Celine went bananas. She excitedly woke me up at dawn, demanding that I show her how to make a snowman. She was sure snow would taste like ice cream and could not resist running out into it in slippers and a nightie. She informed me in terms that would accept no argument that we would spend the day making snow angels, sledding, tobogganing, ice skating and making a snow fort. She could not comprehend that I did not share her excitement and stared at me in disbelief when I explained that you cannot build snowmen or make snow angels in the course of a blizzard, the lakes hadn't frozen solid yet so ice skating was out of the question for at least another month or two, and the hills had not built up enough for toboggans or sleds. She seemed inclined to argue until I reminded her that she did not have ice skates and we did not own a sled or toboggan. Shortly after stores opened that morning, however, we were proud owners of all of the above.

As Christmas approached, Celine was beside herself, determined to have a real family Christmas. There was a large, long unused equipment building on the property between my parent's place and ours. We secured permission to use it and spent every spare moment in November and December cleaning and preparing it. We hauled couple hundred bales of hay down from my dad's barn and stacked up around the walls, held in place with 2 X 2 laths for insulation, and covered that with red material. We trudged deep into the Woods and felled a huge Christmas tree which we hauled back with a neighbor's John Deere. Celine spent entire days on the phone with relatives and friends from the church, taking copious notes on who would be there, what dish they would bring for the buffet, how many children there would be and all their ages; she tracked down chairs, tables, T. V. trays, punch bowls, plates, silver ware, three gas ranges and other fixtures we jury-rigged into a pretty respectable make-shift kitchen.

We bought tons of trinkets, small toys and candy and divided them into piles, one each for the youngsters expected to be attending and piles of more adult novelties for the grown folk. Celine sat up long into the night sewing stockings and affixing a name to each, which were filled with those goodies and hung all over the realistic-looking plastic and cardboard fireplace now adorning one end of the building. On Christmas eve, we went to mass and then spent the rest of the night garnishing the enormous fir tree. Celine marveled that she would soon be an actual mother and that we would be our very own family and that she couldn't imagine being happier.

The big day came off without a hitch. Norman Rockwell could not have orchestrated it better. There was a light snowfall, the temperature was mild, with no wind. We had a full house, an abundance of food and everyone appeared to be having a great time. Celine, naturally, rounded up all the children and soon had a choir filling the house with song. It was infectious and soon pretty much everyone joined in. No way could it have been a better day.

Celine had no doubt from the beginning that she was carrying a daughter. She gradually swelled large enough for twins and had trouble walking. In the days just prior to her due date she informed me that she would like to name the baby Ruby Rae. Ruby for a "good witch" who had been particularly kind to her in childhood and Rae, which was my mother's middle name. I told her I thought that was a splendid name that any little girl would be proud to carry.

Ruby Rae entered this world one snowy January night not long after and I was there to meet her at the gate. Before she drew her first breath, I said, "Well, hello there, little Ruby Slippers, welcome to the world." I don't know what made me say "Ruby Slippers" but for some reason, that name stuck and she was called that more than anything else. My mom knitted her some little booties with shiny red yarn and red rhinestones so that she actually had a pair of ruby slippers to wear. We had great fun with that.

You have never seen a woman more euphoric than Celine was after Ruby came into the world. She finally had her very own baby. She was surrounded by loving family and all of her dreams were coming true. I was ten feet tall and couldn't stop smiling.

Celine informed her daughter several times a day that "Your name is Ruby Rae and I am your mother." Never was a child more loved, cuddled, or cooed over. No little girl was ever the subject of more rosaries, novenas, chaplets or appeals for intercessions on her behalf. Celine did the math and figured exactly how many babies she could produce if she stayed fertile until she was fifty and was momentarily stunned into stupefied silence when told that doctors will not administer fertility drugs to otherwise healthy women just because they want to have as many babies as possible at one time. "But," she stammered, disbelieving, "I am a mother," as though that clarification would make all the difference. "This is what I do."

Based on her own experience and that of other's she knew, Celine was convinced that doing Hatha Yoga was the best way to return her working parts to their best possible condition after giving birth and to prepare herself for her next pregnancy. As torturous as it was to be separated from her daughter for two hours at a stretch, she enrolled in a Yoga class at the community college about fifteen miles away. Since relatives all but came to blows over who would watch over Ruby Slippers during that time, there was never a baby-sitter shortage. One particular Saturday, even I was granted that privilege. I was doing some work rebuilding the roof over our front porch. Before she left, Celine came out and gave me a comprehensive course on baby-care and a list of emergency phone numbers and left the monitor so I would know when the sleeping baby awoke from her nap. Celine guiltily confessed that she wanted to take an extra hour this day for something that had to do with singing with a group on campus. I told her I would be here, don't worry about it, go— happy that she was enjoying life. I was doing some extra fancy work on the soffit of this roof and entirely lost track of time. It was nearly two hours later before I went in to check on Ruby Slippers. I had carried an arm load of scrap material around to the back of the house and went in through that door so I didn't smell the gas at first.

I wish I could say that our daughter looked like a little angel fast asleep having peaceful dreams with puppy dogs and butterflies. She did not. Her silky golden skin was the color of cold oatmeal. Her eyelids were half opened and those sparkling blue irises, now turned up and very dull. Her little tongue was a sickly blue color. I braced myself against the door frame until my head cleared and then went into the kitchen to turn off the gas. I sat with Ruby for a few minutes and then went into the basement to retrieve that one item I saved from San Diego.

The house we lived in had been a "starter home" for any number of relatives over the past few generations. All had fancied themselves handymen. Much of the carpentry, wiring, plumbing, etc. had been rebuilt, repaired and tweaked by God-only-knows how many repairmen. This was true of our gas range. It worked well enough, but you had to relight the pilot every time it was turned on. It was therefore necessary to turn a switch in the back each time to turn off the gas flow. Celine's sense of smell was compromised due to having her nose broken when she was younger; she often she forgot to turn he gas off and didn't notice as the fumes accumulated in the room.

In all the time we had been together, Celine and I never had an argument or said an angry or unkind word to one another. That blissful record was shattered shortly after moving into that little house. Over that damn stove. One day I snapped at her, "Damn it Celine, if you can't turn the thing off, don't touch it at all. Do you want to kill us all?" Of course, it was an enormous big deal that I had spoken to her like that, but I didn't apologize. It didn't matter, though; she never did master the process of turning that stove off.

Celine was surprised when I met her coming out the door of the music room on the campus. I told her that my mother was staying with the baby and that I had something special arranged. She was somewhat uneasy from the vibes she was picking up from me, but I asked her to trust me and, of course, she did. With a touching childlike innocence.

I drove us to a Catholic church not far from the school and asked to see a priest. I told Celine it was important to make a "good confession"—a term that refers to approaching this sacrament with particular solemnity and sincerity so as to realize the greatest benefit from it. Driving home we recited a rosary together and sang the Chaplet of Divine Mercy. With perfect timing, that concluded just as we pulled into our driveway.

I opened the door for Celine to enter the house ahead of me, pulled the pistol from my pocket and shot her through the back of her head. I caught her lifeless body before it hit the floor.

Never again. Never again will my Celine suffer heartache in this world. I laid her on our bed and tucked Ruby Slippers under her arm and sat there with them until long after sun down. After lighting a candle for them, I sheared off all my hair and then walked down to my parents' house to explain in a very few sentences what had happened. People who knew us well understood but had trouble forgiving me. Our Catholic friends appreciated the significance of how I orchestrated the last hour of Celine's life on earth, but had grown to think of her as one of their own and agreed that it was a good thing for me to be in jail.

The police and court officials were furious that, after making one brief statement, I refused to acknowledge their importance by being interrogated or cooperating with their circus. I would not meet with the attorney appointed to defend me. After several weeks in jail, the court handed down a life sentence, and I was immediately transferred to the prison at Jackson. I have been here ever since. I will be here until the day I die.

This institution is my monastery, my life an on-going penance. Early on I secured a job in the critical care wing of the hospital here, which is the final stop for any DOC inmates suffering AIDS, terminal cancer, or the ravages of old age. I do the work nobody else will. I massage swollen feet, empty bed pans, clean oozing, ulcerated sores and change wet, foul smelling bandages. Several times each day I give sponge baths and change filthy sheets. It is a common occurrence to have bed pans flung at me. I eat only the meals provided by the facility, abstaining from meat, desert, butter or added seasonings; I fast two days a week. I own no clothing other than state-issue, my sack cloth, and have no personal possessions. My Bible, my only reading material, and my rosary beads are borrowed from the Catholic Chaplain's office.

As I understand it—owing to my many years on the job and the nature of my work—I am one of the highest paid inmates in the system. Every month I sign this amount over to the chaplain and he donates it to a charity that aids abused children. There is a notarized form in the mail office up front instructing that any incoming mail arriving for me be returned to sender or destroyed. I do not watch television or listen to the radio or engage in leisure time activities.

I allow myself no luxuries, adhering as closely as possible to the standards of penitents of antiquity. It's a Catholic thing.

There is no justification morally, legally, nor in the Catholic Code of Canon Law for the actions I took, and I have never sought to justify them. Yet, if there is a God in heaven—and surely there is—then my beloved Celine most certainly exists in a state of celestial bliss.

Every night in the dark confines of my cell, as I settle in for the night, I take warm comfort replaying in my mind's eye the image of Celine stepping over to the other side and being greeted by her own daughter. I imagine them playing together in fields of flowers, laughing and singing; always singing.

In the wee hours before sleep takes me, I speak to them both and know they hear me. "Good night, Celine. I love you still.

And good night to you, my precious Ruby Slippers."

Albert

Marquette Prison
June 4, Evening

Hey Dude…

Great to hear from you, and to know that all is well down your way. It remains winter up here in the Polar Ice Cap. I'm not even kidding. There are still mounds of snow, and sometimes when the wind comes in off Lake Superior, temperatures dip down to zero and below. I know you guys are enjoying summer weather down there. Lucky you.

The exploits you asked about are much more involved than you realize. I can't write it all in one sitting, and to do it justice, I must start at the beginning. I may send this off a chunk at a time. It could take a while. Neither of us is going anywhere anytime soon, so I might as well do this right.

Actually, the very beginning of all this was an armed robbery in Benton Harbor that went terribly wrong. Dear god. I wish that hadn't happened. Crimes that involve fire arms…bad business, Dude. I'll say this, though: I'm done with it. I have hung up my guns. I can't say too much about that fiasco, but I will say I needed to find a new zip code and had heard good things about Austin, Texas. Winter was setting in, and I thought, hey, why not? My take-away from the aforementioned Benton Harbor nightmare provided me with a little traveling money and not much beyond that. This chick I knew from Dowagiac ran me down to Chicago and I caught a bus from there to Austin. Stop me before I get started. I get to talking about Austin and people ask if I am on the Chamber of Commerce or something. Love that town, Dude. What a great place. I was lucky enough to be there before the yuppie invasion. Let me just say this and I'll get on with it: You could be on a city bus or in the grocery store check-out line, whatever, and people would be having the I Love Austin conversation, talking about how glad they were that they moved here and how much they love Austin, and yadda, yadda. I was one of them. Good old Austin. Since then, of course—ain't that the way of it? —the Austin everybody moved there to experience is gone because everybody moved there to be part of the experience and that destroyed it all.

Okay, so, I made the mistake of letting someone in Michigan know where I was, and naturally, as soon as they were in a crack, that information became a bargaining chip and I got ratted out. I was living under some pretty sketchy ID at the time so I didn't drive or try to do anything fancy. Had a little job in a shop that sold organic vegetables and candles. Hipster clientele; paid less than minimum wage, but they hired without a background check and I got tons of good food as a bennie and it was fun to work there. It wasn't like a job at all. Local paper declared it The Number One Spot In Austin For People Watching. That kind of place. So, one day I come back to my rented room to hear from the neighbors that I just missed all the excitement. The local police had raided—apparently in a very impressive fashion— and hauled away the guy who lived down the hall from me. Something about a fugitive warrant from Michigan. He left protesting loudly, insisting they had the wrong guy. Coincidentally, he looked a lot like me. I wasted about five minutes gathering up the few possessions I didn't want to leave behind and boogied out to the Greydog. (which is how the locals refer to Greyhound Bus Lines).

Here's the thing about being wanted by John Law: you have to careful, of course, but really, once you are out there in the mix, what are they going to do? Are there not about a million people walking around everywhere you go? I had been frugal with the small amount of money I had, and it didn't cost much to get to San Antone. That same day I rented another small room and there you go. As much as it hurt—and it did hurt, believe me—it took a lot of years to grow that hair—I shaved my head and took to wearing shades all the time. I had a short neat beard, which I committed to letting go wild. If I got busted on that outstanding warrant, it wasn't going to be because someone recognized me.

San Antonio doesn't get the same hype as Austin, but let me tell you, S.A. has a lot to say for itself. It's about three times the size of Austin, and again, don't let me get started. For a city that size, San Antonio is great town. I loved it there. It's everything you could want in a city, and as a bonus—it's summer year-round! I mean, what do you want? Anyway, I'll stop myself. I tend to carry on about cities I have loved. There are a few of them, but all that is a different conversation.

Okay, so I'm down in San Antonio and trying to be cool and low-key. Seriously, seriously could not afford any heat. I lucked into a job with a landscaping company. It didn't pay very well because there were so many illegals doing that kind of work and they worked cheap. The guy I worked for loved Mexicans as workers—and he did treat his workers well—but he wanted bi-lingual white guys as crew bosses. I spent a couple of my younger years in a Spanish-speaking foster home and can get along okay conversationally. I was paid essentially the same as the illegals, but he let me sleep in the shop, which was a huge plus. It saved me a bundle. Rent is not even cheap down that way.

The headquarters of this landscaping outfit was a huge pole barn on the west side. There were tons of equipment in there, but also an old cab-over camper, which became my new digs. The interior was in pretty good shape and I was content. I had a bed and a little stove for making coffee and simple meals. There was a table with bench seats. I ran an extension cord in through the bathroom window, which gave me radio and TV. It was actually pretty swell.

When I got this job, I was grateful for it. The heat was two steps behind me, and I needed exactly what I had. I did the job and played the role for several months. The guy I worked for was okay, the work was outdoors and the kind of thing I really don't mind so much. In the beginning, anyway. I should have been thinking about making a career of it, but I started getting restless.

The thing about a job is, it just really eats into your day. There were so many cool things going on around me, and I was too tired and too broke to make the rounds. Every work day ended dirty and sweaty. I was sunburned, and more than anything, hey, I was missing all the fun. All these places downtown trying to out-Happy Hour each other. Chi-Chi's had One Dollar pitchers of kick ass Margaritas, with a free buffet, another place always had live music, and free shots with every $2.00 pitcher of draft beer. All kinds of stuff. There were bands playing everywhere. It was all just a huge party. All those secretaries unwinding after a tough day on the job....

It wasn't all party stuff, but neat things would be going on over at the university, different exhibits and programs, plays, concerts. They built a Sea World while I was there. Interesting things. All of the above: things you don't want to do alone, and can't do looking like I was looking. At one point during this period, I remember marveling at folks who have jobs and do all the right things for decades on end. I was sure they are better off than people like me, but, really, if there was a pill you could take to become normal, I'm pretty sure I would run from it.

I had a very small circle of acquaintances, but I did know a guy who sold marijuana, and I was a regular. When I say, I knew a guy, what I mean to say is I knew an ass-clown I wanted to sock in the mouth every time I was near him, but he sold a nice bag of good weed at a reasonable price, and I like marijuana. Business is business. He never did anything that made me want to sock him, he was just an idiot and I didn't like him. For one thing, he called himself Billie Joe, and tried too hard to present himself as genuine country and talked like comic book hillbilly. You've known posers. Don't you just want to smack those people?

One neat thing about going over to Billy Joe's place was getting to see Julie Patchouli. Patchouli, like the incense. She was this really fun hippie chick who was seriously out of place with this hockey puck and I didn't get it. Julie Patchouli was cute and funny and dressed in all these wild 60's era clothes—think of Janis Joplin on the Pearl album—and wore tons of jewelry and always made me laugh. She flirted with me a little every time I came around, but you could see Billie Joe didn't like it so it was always brief.

Certainly I had thoughts of stealing her away, but hey, I live in a freaking barn and come back to it every night with dirt packed under my fingernails. What's my pitch going to be—let me take you away from all this; I can get you a job laying sod with people who don't speak English?

One Friday—payday—I stopped by Billie Joe's to replenish my stash and when he left the room to measure out what I asked for, Julie Patchouli got real serious and rushed over to whisper in my ear I should meet her at Selena's Bridge on the Riverwalk Sunday at 1:00. She might be late, but wait. *Please!* She bounced back over to the other side of the room, singing along with the radio, making up silly lyrics of her own to the tune.

I didn't give Julie Patchouli any real response. First and foremost, I was all about remaining low-key and off the radar. My shit detector was telling me there was drama on the horizon with this chick. Did I need that? No, I did not. Did I meet her on the River Walk at 1:00 Sunday? You bet your ass I did. Are you kidding me?

Having mentioned the River Walk a couple times, let me just paint a quick picture. This is my favorite part of San Antonio. Probably everyone's favorite thing in S.A. It is so cool.

The Riverwalk is a riverfront park about fifteen miles long, five miles of it right through downtown. Each side is lined with restaurants, shops, and bars. There are tables with umbrellas everywhere, or benches where you can sit in the sun or under cypress trees. You've never seen so many flowers. Occasionally a pontoon boat with a Mariachi band playing slowing drifts by. Really beautiful; it's hard to believe it's real. Selena's Bridge is the unofficial name for a stone arch bridge a few blocks off Cabot Street. It's called that because the famous We Did It! scene in her movie that was shot there. There is also a scene in Miss Congeniality shot along the Riverwalk. Watch for those movies and you'll see what I am talking about.

I don't mind telling you I was excited about this meeting. The corners I had been painting myself into for the last few years had left my confidence shaken. On top of that, how you gonna meet chicks when you work yourself silly every day and come home exhausted every night—and home is a pole barn full of landscaping equipment? Seriously. I was ready for a girlfriend and I liked Julie Patchouli.

I was waiting at a table in a comfy little spot right on the water, with shade, surrounded by flowers that had the air perfumed. There was a band playing near-by and it really was idyllic. Julie Patchouli bounced up about ten minutes late and immediately ordered a pitcher of margaritas. Dude, the girl was *on*; she talked non-stop and was so interesting and funny and entertaining, I couldn't help thinking, man, what a joy would it be to live with this chick. She wasn't just funny, she was clever, funny with a really intelligent edge to it. This wasn't some 60's burnout. The girl had it going on. We hit the bottom of the first pitcher before I could let go of my concerns of what this was about, and just let myself enjoy it. Most fun I'd had in a while.

We sat there all afternoon, talking and laughing. Julie Patchouli had this cigarette holder-looking thing that you could slide a joint inside of and smoke it in public without anybody realizing what was going on. We made use of that dandy little device throughout the afternoon, the margaritas kept coming, as well as several plates of really scrumptious munchies. I remember that time as one of the most pleasant afternoons ever. I had lived with a lot of stress for the last couple years, hadn't had a lot of fun, and sure hadn't let go and laughed and just felt good like this in forever. What a treat.

I gotta admit, it got pretty silly there for a while. I wasn't used to drinking like that. Anyone paying attention would have known we were wasted, but we weren't rowdy or obnoxious. Mostly just laughing. Have you ever laughed so long and so hard that your sides ached? I mean, it got painful, laughing so hard. Julie Patchouli just got more and more animated. After a while neither of us could really speak a coherent sentence, but whatever we slurred out to each other was still hilarious.

We sat there having our own little party until close to 5:30, when Julie Patchouli said she needed to get rolling. She flagged down our waiter and slipped him a couple twenties. "This one is on me," she said and actually gave me a wink. "You'll get the next one. I really have to run. Thanks for your company. It was fun." (At least I think that was what she said. Her speech was somewhat impaired, as was my ability to comprehend simple sentences.) And then she was gone.

Okay. What just happened, right? I had gone down to the Riverwalk wondering just how this chick was thinking to use me, what kind of foolishness was she was hoping to get me caught up in, what massive drama was going to play out there under the Texas sun…and what? She underwrote the best time I remember having in, well, seriously, in forever. I'm telling you, years later, that afternoon with Julie Patchouli stands out in my mind as something really special. Man, I needed that.

But life goes on. Monday morning, it was back to the weekly grind. The following Friday afternoon I was back to see Billy Joe. In the few seconds he was out of the room, Julie Patchouli asked me if we could meet again the following Tuesday, whenever I got out of work. "Brackenridge Park, 5:00," I whispered, and suddenly Billie Joe was right there. He must have had the small amount I wanted already measured out and within reach in his back room. He saw Julie Patchouli standing next to me and instantly overtaken by a dark, suspicious aura that was all-consuming.

"I'll tell you what, Billie Joe," I said quickly, "Seeing you every Friday afternoon is the highlight of my week. "I don't know many people, but I know the *right* people!"

This was the friendliest I had ever been to Billie Joe and just like that, he lit up and forgot everything else. He said something moronic, and I laughed and kept up the charade for another minute or two. I'd always been stand-offish and a bit chilly with this guy because I saw no reason to pretend. We did business, period. He obviously had a real need to be liked. This lad is not well-adjusted, I thought as I walked away. I had a whole new sympathy for what Julie Patchouli was dealing with.

Dude, this is the most typing I have done since I quit doing research in the law library. I've barely scratched the surface. It is going to take a while to get this story to you. I'll get back on it as soon as I can. Later, man...

Marquette Prison
Thursday, June 11

Hey Dude...

Expected to get back on this before now, but it has been easy to procrastinate. This is dredging up some stuff and I haven't even gotten started. This is kind of like having a loose tooth you can't stop wiggling back and forth. Uncomfortable, and gratifying at the same time. Haven't done much writing about those days, but you sure have me thinking about them...

Anyway, Julie Patchouli. The following Tuesday, I got away from the job early, which was unheard of. You not only don't leave before quitting time, you work right up to when the second hand comes around and it is officially four o'clock. Then you wrap up and start loading up the tools and such. This is a big outfit, though. There were several crews out that day and the big boss left me in charge of the site I was working. I slipped one of my workers a couple bucks and told everyone he was in charge, and caught the city bus back to the west side.

I had rigged up a shower, which was no more than a garden hose slung over a rafter with an old sprinkler head duct-taped on the end. It worked. Leaving the job site early gave me time to get cleaned up and into my best clothes before setting out. I caught a lucky break coming out of the barn; a supplier we dealt with regularly was just leaving the office. I knew his greenhouse was just off the McAllister Freeway and I asked him for a lift; he told me hop in and that got me all the way to Tuleta, where I caught the Alpine bus and was bam, I was there.

Brackenridge Park. Migod, Dude, how do you not love this city? The big attraction here, of course, is the sunken Japanese gardens, which are beautiful in a story book way. You just can't quite believe it is real. Like at the Riverwalk, you can completely lose sight of the fact that you are in a major American city. I stood there for a while, just absorbing the vibe, and suddenly Julie Patchouli was by my side and all was right with the world.

I'll spare you the gooey details. We had a great time. At first, we just strolled along the walkways, over the stone arch bridges, loving the exotic plants and the koi ponds. There is a Japanese pavilion out on a little island. We watched the waterfall—a sixty-foot waterfall into a bamboo thicket—from where we were sitting, embracing the moment. A quiet time, not talking much. We finally made our way over to the Jingu House restaurant. We drank warm rice wine and ate delicious food. "This is the second story-book experience I have had with you," I told Julie Patchouli.

"I'm glad you're enjoying it," she said simply.

"I would enjoy it more if I understood. That's really detracting from the experience," I told her.

"Fair enough," she said, "and I apologize for dragging it out for so long. I didn't mean to; I've just been enjoying the moment."

You see what I mean, Dude, about this being a classy chick? If she had come back with some crap like What? What are you talking about? Like I was supposed to drag it out of her, or believe she was just head over heels about me, that would have spoiled everything. There was no bullshit to this girl, though.

"I am stuck in a really crappy situation," Julie Patchouli began. "I know you wonder what I am doing with a wanna-be like Billie Joe." She paused and smiled tentatively, "At least, I hope you are wondering. All I can tell you is that he has changed dramatically from the person he was when we first met. We came out of a small town in northern Louisiana, and back then Billie Joe —he was just Bill back then—was an alright guy. What we had in common was that we were both going crazy in that hole-in-the-wall town. Do you know that song by Mo Bandy? She sang a few lines, *Nobody gets off in this town/old folks here wear all frowns/Let me see if I can set the scene/ it's a one-dog town and that dog's old and mean/we've got a stop light, but it's always green/ nobody gets off in this town...*I swear to God, they wrote that about the town we are from. You get the picture.

Billy Joe and I were both outcasts, damned with the worst attribute a mean-spirited small-minded small town can bestow: Bad Attitude. Meaning, no respect for authority, no school spirit, probably not even good Christians. Serious stuff. We were both seen as rebels in a world where conformity and respect for authority is equated with the highest of virtues. You have to be from such a place to really get it. Anyway, of course we found one another. Mostly we were buds, but early on we did fool around some." She shrugged. "We had to break out."

"I'll go into the Reader's Digest Condensed Version mode here. I had a Ford Mustang my older sister had given me when she got married, but very little cash. Billie Joe had been working at the grain elevator for a year or so and had been smart enough to bank his pay checks. We pooled our resources and headed out for Austin with the idea of getting jobs and starting a new life. In the beginning, it was great. We rented a house on Baylor Street in Clarksville, and things started coming together.

We both got jobs right away. Clarksville is a unique neighborhood, full of huge old trees, neat little houses that people took pride in and kept looking nice. It was close to downtown and Town Lake, but was its own little entity right there in Central Austin. Clarksville was mostly young adults, people our age, and they were cool. Some were university students, some had young children. In the evenings, people congregated in back yards, tipped back a few Lone Stars, and just enjoyed one another's company. Smart, funny people just enjoying life. It was so unlike where we had come from; I could not have been happier.

"Being around cool people was a mind-blower for Billie Joe. He kept trying on different personas, trying to find an identity people around us would think was cool. He tried being an intellectual—around people who were the real deal, you understand. He went through a horrible period where he was an inner-city hip-hop figure, talking like a ghetto rat, with his pants hanging off his ass. I was so embarrassed. He went through several transformations and wouldn't accept any advice on the matter. He made such an ass of himself. It cost me friends, since people saw us as a couple. I was saving up my money toward getting a place of my own.

"As part of his effort to be a cool guy, Billie Joe decided to become a weed dealer. He had gotten a job with a roofing crew and some of those guys were pretty rough. I never got the whole story, but I have no doubt it was as simple as them seeing what a goof-ball this guy was and they decided to work him. Billy Joe came home one night with a grocery bag full of marijuana and news that he had quit his job. He was pretty sure that our neighbors would buy him out instantly; he never caught on that they saw him as an obnoxious asshole and they wanted nothing to do with him. He spent his days begging people to buy some pot from him while I went to work and paid all the bills and kept us going. I promoted the idea that he should get his job back and try to sell weed on the side. That was out of the question. He had convinced himself he was a player and players don't hold down nine-to-fives.

"Again, I don't want to relive the whole sordid tale, and you don't need to hear it. It turned out that Billy Joe had gotten this weed on credit and couldn't pay for it when payment was due. They added usurious interest to the amount owed; eventually he got beat up pretty seriously, and a couple guys came by the house and threatened me, just for good measure. I was freaking terrified.

Long story short, all my savings and the money I brought in that didn't go to paying bills and groceries, went to keeping him out of trouble. My Mustang ended up going to pay off the balance of his debt, which started out being a fraction of the value of that car.

I broke in, "You seem too smart to have bought into all this," I observed. "You had wheels and a job. You had friends. Why didn't you get out?"

"Yeah, crap. I know," she said dejectedly. "Let's set up a game board and let people buy guesses as to how many times I asked myself that question. What can I say? His mother is the sweetest lady I have ever known. His sister was a close friend growing up. We were buds back home in a world where nobody wanted anything to do with either of us. We started this adventure together. I just kept hoping I could fix it. Sure, given a chance at a do-over..." I nodded, and she continued, "At this point right now, I'm mad. I've got an investment here. Billie Joe owes me. He has to make this right.

Anyway, one night Billie Joe rushed into the house and told me we were moving and grab whatever I want to take with me, we had to go right now. I refused. He was frantic; I mean really scared. He promised to get my Mustang back, made all kinds of promises, begging, pleading, demanding, saying whatever he thought might work, but *we have got to go.* I said, 'you go, I like it here.' He reminded me of the guys who had threatened me. They will be back, he said. You have no choice. In the end, I left with him.

I grabbed a few things and we were out of there. Billie Joe had a car out front and I didn't even ask where he had gotten it. He was so nervous I thought he would wet his pants. We ended up in a motel in San Antonio. He signed us in and came out of his pocket with a knot of cash like a softball. When he brought our things into the room, there were three large bags—you know those paper grocery bags with the little rope handles? —filled with marijuana. Several kilos in each. Omigod, Billie Joe, what have you done?

Billie Joe never gave Julie Patchouli the whole story, but obviously, he had ripped somebody off. And then ran down the road to San Antonio. I would have gone farther, but as we have established, Billie Joe was a knucklehead.

Dude—it is way past my bed time. I gotta crash. I think this will go out in tomorrow's mail, and you will get further installments as I crank them out. Later, Bro…

Southern Michigan State Prison
Wednesday, June 21

Hey A.B:

I received the first installment of Julie Patchouli, and have actually read it a couple times. I appreciate you going to the trouble. Thanks for sharing, as they say. What a great cast of characters. I can easily visualize you in this scenario; always knew you were a survivor. Later, man…

Marquette Prison
Thursday, July 1

Hey Dude…

Things remain slow up this way. The big news is that all of the snow is
gone. It is still a good idea to carry a jacket out to yard because it can get
chilly if the clouds roll in, but for now the weather is pretty nice. They
say actual summer is supposed to fall on a week end this year, so we have
that going for us. I have started back with more of The Story. Fortunately, I kept a copy of my last letter so I would know where I left off…

"Whatever Billie Joe did to get that money and that weed, it
changed him," Julie Patchouli continued, "He was never silly again
after that and could go dark when he was drinking.

He settled on an identity—Pure Country—since that is cool in
Texas—and went to gradually building up a circle of people he would
sell small amounts of reefer to. He was making that stash last, selling
it in a way as to get the highest profit. The old Billie Joe would have
been trying to sling kilos, to show everybody what a big shot he was.
This was a more serious Billie Joe. He did some wheeling and dealing.
I never knew the details, but he would come home with all kinds of
bling he had picked up somewhere, bags of pills, powders, more pot,
all kinds of stuff.

"I'm pretty sure he was dealing in stolen property and other crimes
also; selling weed is lucrative, but he was handling way too much
money for just that. He was always carrying boxes of stuff in and out
of the house. It didn't take long, with the money he had stolen—I
never knew how much that was—and the money he was bringing in,
and Billie Joe was driving a new three-quarter ton Dodge Ram with
all kinds of features; he owned more pairs of boots and cowboy hats

and Texas t-shirts than an army of good ole boys could wear in a year. His closet was full of pearl button shirts and boot cut Levis. Okay, Big Guy, what about my Mustang? Again, I'll make a long story short—we went 'round and round about this for weeks—there was always some reason he couldn't get my car back or provide a replacement. It was impossible for various reasons for him to give me any money. He became belligerent and ornery as a default position. It had been a long, long time since there was any intimacy between us, but he became jealous and suspicious and possessive.

"My one option is to go crawling back home." She shook her head emphatically, "Can't do it. No, he is going to make it right for that Mustang. The rest of it I will chalk up to my own poor judgement in hooking up with this loser. It takes money to live and Billie Joe spent all my money back in Austin and put me in jeopardy with these thugs he went in debt to. I am not leaving empty-handed.

I've started grabbing a pinch of weed out of any bags left unattended, and building up my own stash. I can occasionally sell small amounts to people who come by when he isn't there. Eventually I accumulated a couple hundred dollars. Slow going. My bigger challenge has been to get away from him for a few hours at a time. Crap, the stories I have had to make up and the slipping and sliding. I can't believe I got myself into a situation like this. Bottom line: I want out."

"That's where I come in," I said dryly. Obviously, there was a reason for all this, but it kinda hurt to have it out there like that. It felt like she was saying, I wouldn't give you the time of day if I didn't have a use for you.

"Listen, I have been living like this for months. A lot of guys come and go, dealing with Billie Joe. If I was just looking for someone to use, I could have been gone long ago. What I see in you is a kindred spirit."

I put on an expression that said, *don't patronize me*, and she quickly added, very serious now, "You are not all that inscrutable; it's all over you. You are not a guy who works like a rented slave and sleeps in a barn without compelling reasons. You're hiding from your own monsters. I'm saying let's combine forces and break out. You need it, I need it. I need money to make a new start. I only want what is fair, and he is not in a mind to be fair. Whatever your issues, I assume a fist full of cash will go a long way toward resolving them."

At that point, we were strolling along a cobble stone walkway around a koi pond, heading for the exit. I knew I was in; I just didn't want to seem easy. I was still dealing with the Benton Harbor thing in my head, "I don't do violence," I said quietly.

She stopped abruptly. "Oh my god!" She said. "Is that what you think? I don't want to *hurt* him. I want what is right. I want a new start. I want to get away from this stupid man. I don't need revenge. I need *out.*"

Finally, I said, "Okay, let's figure out the details." She flagged down a cab and told the driver to drop us at a cantina downtown. We got there and ordered a couple Dos Exes beers. No pot, no tequila. This was business. The challenge was that Billie Joe had a secure vault built into the house they were renting. He had paid a couple guys come in and weld a solid steel frame into the closet, and attached a steel security door. Inside the closet was a heavy-duty safe. Julie Patchouli assumed I knew how to use a cutting torch. She was right. The problem with cutting torches, I explained, is that they don't work like in the movies.

Also, those things get hot, and that kind of cutting throws off sparks; there is a very real possibility of setting the whole place on fire. We'd have to rent one and a rig like we'd need would be heavy and clunky, and how would we transport it? There was a danger of the cutting flame burning up whatever was in the safe before we even got to it. There had to be a better way. We sat quietly for a while, Julie Patchouli seemed disheartened and depressed by what I had said. I sat thinking and came up with two questions.

"It is unthinkable this clown doesn't own guns," I said. She told me he had several but, oddly enough, he wasn't really a gun guy, like you might think, and he didn't carry. Julie Patchouli didn't know guns and couldn't tell me much about them, so I asked her when there would be a time that I could get in there and look at them. I'd also needed to look at the safe situation. She said that would take some study and we left it at that for the time being.

My other question went to the guys he was hiding from in Austin. She didn't know if he had ripped off the same guys he got the dope from originally, but that was the only thing that made sense. She thought one guy was called Morgan and it seemed she had heard the name Brody. I filed that away.

We called it a night. Julie Patchouli paid for our drinks and gave me twenty bucks for a cab. My first impulse, of course, was to pocket the twenty and try to get home by bus, but then I said, screw it, I'm tired of living like that. That feeling spilled over and, from that point forward, I hated my job. I resented sleeping in a barn and I was not pleasant to be around. It was time for a change. A plan, such as it was, began to jell in my mind.

When we met at a downtown cantina a few days later, Julie Patchouli was rushed and nervous. "Get me into that house where I can look at the situation," I told her. We'll go from there." We sat for a while, sipping our beers, and finally she told me to come over the next night about six o'clock. She would make sure the coast was clear.

Julie Patchouli met me at the door the next night as I arrived. "Billie Joe is here, but he is fast asleep. He won't bother anyone." I looked at her skeptically, "He took a bunch of valium," she added.

I stepped into the living room and there was Billie Joe, sprawled in an easy chair, head on chest, drooling onto a spiffy new Willie Nelson t-shirt. I didn't ask how she got the V's into him. I didn't care. At that point, I was all business. He didn't look as though he would be alert right away, so I ignored him and let Julie Patchouli show me to the closet Billie Joe had reinforced. I could see immediately that this was first rate professional work. Billy Joe at least had sense enough to hire the best.

Breaking into this thing would be a major undertaking which would involve some serious equipment, a lot of noise, and way more time than I wanted to spend committing a felony. As I had to remind Julie Patchouli—even though Billie Joe is an asshole, even though the contents of this vault are illegal items, even though he owes you money, peeling a safe in a private home is actually a crime, and you can go to jail for it.

Tearing this thing apart was out of the question, although I wasn't ready to blow it off. We just need a different approach, I told her. I looked at the gun collection. There were two pistols, two shotguns—a pretty nice Ithaca twelve-gauge pump in a custom case and a sawed-off 410 snake charmer, and a .30-30 hunting rifle. One of the pistols was a .38 Special with a box of shells. I knew instantly what I was going to do. I put a few shells in my pocket.

"Billie Joe is going to open this safe for us," I said. "Figure out when you want to do this. I'll need that .38. I don't want to take it with me, but I'll need it when I come through the door. Can you make that happen?

She suddenly looked frightened and started to speak. I cut her off. "Your end of this effort is to set up a time when no one else will be around, and have that piece where I can put my hand on it when I come through the door. Put it in the mail box out front, under a magazine on the coffee table, whatever. From there, you are a victim, just like Billie Joe. Play that role and you will be okay. The less I tell you about what I am going to do, the better you will be able to play your part. In the end, expect to be kidnapped.

There is an office in the front corner of the pole barn I lived in, with a sliding glass window on the interior side. I can slide that window open and crawl in over the desk and get to the phone in there. It is awkward and painful on my knees and not something I do often. I gave Julie Patchouli the number. Do not call just to chat. Only call well outside of business hours. Never call and ask for me or to leave a message. It's not that kind of operation. When you call, let it ring for a long time. Now that this was a Go, I was all the way no-nonsense. There was no more tee-hee, ha-ha. This was business. She nodded nervously and I left without further conversation.

The call came shortly after 6:00 am two days later. "This Thursday afternoon about 4:30. The gun will be between the cushions on the couch" Julie Patchouli was whispering frantically. "Ask for an eighth-ounce, so he will have to go in the back room and split up a quarter. That's it," she finished and hung up. That's it? Okay, that's it, then.

The following Thursday afternoon, I strolled up and knocked on Billie Joe's front door as I had many times before. "Yo, Billie Joe, my man," I opened, feeling foolish, but I knew he liked that kind of smack. "Zup?" I asked. Predictably, Billie Joe was delighted with my greeting and invited me in. I wondered, How is it that no one has ripped him off before now? I stepped into the living room and told him I needed an eighth ounce of his best weed for now, but I had a party to go to and there would be a couple old boys there who were serious about their smoke. They were flying in from Chicago and wouldn't try bring-ing anything on a plane. If they liked what I had, they would want at least an oh-zee each, and would it be okay if I brought them over? Billy Joe ate it up like candy. He was visibly excited and told me, "Hold on," and ran off into his stash room.

As soon as he was through the door, I went to the couch and the .38 was right where it was supposed to be. Julie Patchouli was in the kitchen, looking at me with a frightened expression. Billie Joe came back with a baggie in his hand and a big smile on his stupid face. He started to say something and I pointed that pistol right between his baby blues from about ten feet away. "Freeze, right there," I told him. "Do not speak. Do not move." I looked at Julie Patchouli. "You! Get out here!" I shouted. Julie Patchouli came into the room and said, "Please don't..."

"Shut up!" I screamed. "Don't talk, either of you. Do as you are told." Julie Patchouli was utterly terrified. "Anybody speaks out of turn, I shoot. Understood?" They both nodded. I pulled a roll of duct tape from my pocket and tossed it to Julie Patchouli. "Tape him to that chair." Billie Joe stood there looking stupefied. "Sit down or I will sit you down!" I growled. He stood there staring off glassy-eyed;

Julie Patchouli helped him into an armchair and proceeded to tape his wrists and elbows to the chair arms and then his ankles to the legs.

As this was going on, I watched Billie Joe catch up. He gradually came to terms with the reality of his situation. I pointed the gun at Julie Patchouli, sit, I commanded. She took a seat to the left and behind Billie Joe, where he could not see her. "This is what is going to happen," I explained, "You will give me the key to that vault and tell me the combination to the safe inside. If not, I put a bullet into Little Miss Sunshine's kneecap; you can listen to her scream for a while and then you will tell me. I looked Billie Joe in the eye. "Talk." He shook his head.

Heaving a deep sigh, I opened the cylinder of the .38 and dumped the shells on the floor. I pulled a shell from my pocket and inserted it into a chamber. Without asking a question, I spun the cylinder and pointed the gun at Julie Patchouli. Click. Julie Patchouli gasped. "Where is the key to that door?" Billie Joe shook his head. I spun the cylinder and pulled the trigger. Billy Joe shook his head each time. Julie Patchouli was stunned. She flinched and squealed each time I pulled the trigger, but her expression went from *Really?!?* when he wouldn't answer my first question, to disbelief, to horror, to anger, to outrage to something I couldn't quite identify, but knew was one of those things that fall under Hell hath no fury… "Billie Joe, how many times do you think this hammer will drop on an empty chamber? I asked. He scrunched his eyes closed and shook his head.

Now I was worried. I had not expected he would call my bluff. I was feeling the stress. Julie Patchouli started to say something but I shook my head. It finally struck me; I went into the room where his other guns were, and came back with the snake charmer.

"I misread you, Billie Joe, but here's the deal." I broke the .410 open and inserted a shell. "At this point, I have to get out of town. We can't pretend this never happened. If I go away broke, I will go away with blood on my hands. I am all done playing with you. I pushed the barrel into his crotch, clicked the hammer back and said, "I will count to five and then pull the trigger. Talk or don't." I started counting quickly, with no pause in between, "one, two, three, four…"

"Okay!" Billie Joe shouted. "Okay!!"

"Play time is over," I said, "Say it right now, or I shoot!"

"In my boot!" he whimpered. "The key is in my left boot!" As I was jerking it off his foot, he added frantically, "the heel is hollow, twist it!"

I twisted the heel and sure enough, it slid open and there was a key inside. I took it to the closet door and was in like Flynn. "Talk to me, Billie Joe," I said. He knew what I wanted. He was defeated, and knew he had no win. Through tears, he recited the combination to the safe in the closet. It opened, pretty as you please.

I have never seen the likes of it. Inside this safe were stacks of cash, piles of jewelry, pills, baggies of—what? Cocaine, heroin, crank? Didn't matter, it was all money. There was about six and a half keys of marijuana. This was by far the sweetest score of my criminal career. Billie Joe had it going on.

All of it went into my gym bag and then I was back out in the living room. Julie Patchouli was sitting where I left her, looking stunned and bewildered. "Time to roll," I said. She didn't acknowledge me, but walked around in front of Billie Joe and looked him in the eye. "You low-life piece of shit." She said in the coldest voice I had ever heard spoken. "You would have let him kill me." Billie Joe's mouth was moving, but he wasn't producing any words. "After all I did, after all I gave up for you…and I stopped liking you a long time ago." Billie Joe couldn't make eye contact. After a long pause, she hauled off and slapped that old boy so hard—crack!—the whole left side of his face turned beet-red and his upper lip was instantly swollen.

"Go grab anything you want to take with you", I told Julie Patchouli. "I need to have a word with Bill." I had to physically pull her away and set her in motion. If I hadn't been there, she might have beat him to death.

"Here's the deal, Billie Joe," I told him, then paused. "You need a cigarette?" There was a pack of Marlboros on the table by his chair. Billie Joe nodded dumbly. "I lit up a smoke for him and placed it between his lips. He sucked at it hungrily. "I'm leaving here with your money and your drugs. I'm taking your truck. You will not report the truck stolen or come looking for us. That is our agreement.

If I ever have reason think you have violated our agreement, I will contact Morgan and Brody up in Austin, and give them not only your contact information, but also the names and addresses of everyone you love back in Louisiana. You know I can do it. His eyes got big and I knew this was an effective threat. "Start over. This kind of shit happens to players all the time. Suck it up and get on with your life.

And listen to me, you will not slander Julie Patchouli to the folks back home; she has not, and will not, bad-mouth you to them." At the risk of sounding hokey—but look who I was dealing with—I added, what happens in Texas stays in Texas. Agreed? Let this be over, move on from here, and all will be well. Got it?" Again, he nodded dumbly.

I gathered up the guns and a few other items that caught my eye and carried them out to the truck. He had an impressive collection of boots: Tony Lamas, Ariats, Naconas; these didn't come from Cheap Charlie's Discount Boot Emporium. This was quality merchandise. There was a pair of Lucchese I fell in love with. Normally, I would have put those on and loaded up the rest. I don't know, I just wasn't feeling it. I grabbed a couple cases of expensive liquor, but otherwise didn't take much out of the house.

I got Julie Patchouli into the truck and, as casually as possible, pulled out and headed for the highway. She seemed to be in a state of shock; enough so that I was a bit worried. "Listen to me…" I started.

Julie Patchouli cut me off, "Let me out up here." Her eyes were wide open and glassy. Oh shit, just the kind of drama I didn't need. She started babbling, and I realized that she was having trouble processing the fact that Billie Joe was willing to let her be knee-capped, and on top of that, I was just casually spinning that .38 cylinder and pointing it at her as I pulled the trigger. Nothing in her reality had pre-pared her for the intensity of what she had just experienced. The girl was overwhelmed and really getting agitated so I pulled over to where there were trees close to the edge of the street. I eased over and parked near enough to one that she couldn't open her door.

I took a .38 shell from my pocket and bit down on the slug with my front teeth, wiggling it back and forth until it detached. "Look," I told her, "It's empty. I broke these apart last night and emptied out the gunpowder. Blank cartridges. For effect. I scared you back there. I'm sorry. I thought it was necessary. You know the term Shock and Awe. I needed Billie Joe to buy my bluff. Otherwise, my only recourse would have been violence and I didn't want to go there. She calmed down half a degree, but was still really upset. "Listen," I told her, "This is a success story. We won. We have the money, we have the dope. You are rid of Billie Joe. You are a free woman. You can buy a new Mustang, you can rent a house in Clarksville. You can do what you want to do. This is a happy time. Be happy."

It was a gradual process, but we were under the shade of a huge old Live Oak, in a relatively secluded area, so there was time. I watched her eyes as she gradually eased into her new reality. "Do you under-stand? We did it. Just what you have been wanting. You are free. We can go look at Mustangs this afternoon."

She didn't say anything, but did seem to be getting a grip on her-self. Finally, she drew in a long breath and slowly let it go. She blinked a few times and said simply, "Okay."

I hopped out of the cab and reached behind the seat for the duf-fle I had stuffed there when we came out of the house. I pulled out a bottle of Crown Royal and handed it to her. She didn't need any prompting to crack it open and take a sip. While she was busy with that, I fired up a joint and handed it to her. "This is purely medicinal," I said. That got a chuckle and I knew we were back on track. I left her with the medications and headed out for the highway. Next stop, All City Landscaping.

We arrived at the shop and I opened up the big garage door and backed in to the cab-over. "You need to hop out and help me get into position," I told her. She did and it didn't take long to get the camper loaded and strapped down, and then we were headed for the highway.

"Did we just steal a camper?" Julie Patchouli asked, still sipping the blended whiskey as I got up to speed on the 410 Loop Highway, Westbound.

I gave her a look and said, "We're just on a crime spree, aren't we"? Julie Patchouli giggled. I added, "Would you like to count the money?" She said she would like that very much.

I was driving just to be driving, with no particular destination in mind. Julie Patchouli had a fist full of cash and counted out some amount, "This is my Mustang," she said, stuffing the bills into her shirt. She counted some more. "This is what I had saved up that went to keep Billie Joe from getting beat up a second time." That likewise went into the shirt. "This is his part of the rent and other expenses I paid in full, while he was out being a *playa*." Finally, she held up a five-dollar bill, "This is for the lunch I bought him at Mac-Donald's in Round Rock one day when I know he had money in his pocket." Another deep breath, "Okay," She said, "Billie Joe's debt is paid in full."

"I'm so happy for the both of you," I said, trying to sound facetious and peeved, even though I was tickled. "Is there anything left over for the hired help?" The old Julie Patchouli was back and I felt great. The pep talk I had given her an hour earlier started to seep in on me. This was a win. A damn nice score right at a time in my life when I needed one. Sweet!

Julie Patchouli looked into the duffle again, "Yeah, there are some nickels and pennies wedged in the crack." She pulled out a couple stacks of bills and riffled the corners. I saw a bunch of 100's and 50's flash by. "I told you, I just want what's fair. He owed me. That account is paid in full; now I can forget that dingle berry, and get on with my life. The rest is yours and you are welcome to it." Just a quick glance over that way told me I was getting way more money than she had claimed for herself. "I would like to call one of these keys my very own," she added, indicating a fat kilo wrapped in plastic and sealed with packaging tape, "and tuck it away somewhere." How could I object?

There was a bunch of money in there beyond what she had just flashed on me, plus I had the truck, the drugs, the guns, he jewelry, and the camper. I had woke up that morning with seventeen dollars and a bus token. I was all smiles.

Julie Patchouli found KZEP on the radio and we just cruised for a while. I was enjoying the feel of my new truck and the idea of having some real money in my pocket; Julie Patchouli was lost in her own thoughts. Eventually I swung off onto the Bandera road in the direction of Kerrville. We had discussed several different ideas during those hours in the Japanese Gardens and the Riverwalk, but all that was feel-good talk. We both liked the idea of going totally gypsy and just seeing the country. Now that we had everything we needed to do that, in style and indefinitely, that idea had less appeal. I was still wanted in Michigan and I was now driving a stolen truck with no driver's license. Julie Patchouli maintained the fantasy of renting a house in Clarksville and returning to that wonderful situation she had known there, but was smart enough to know that never works. Thomas Wolfe said it best, You can't go home again, and nobody needed to remind her that Morgan and his crew were still in Austin.

That's it for now, Dude. Getting this on paper has been an enormous job. We are still a long way from the end. I need to chill for a while. Gimme some space here...

AB

Southern Michigan State Prison
Monday, July 9

Yo AB…

Hey, I know how draining this kind of thing can be. Don't forget, I'm
the story guy. I'm won't squeeze you for more than you are comfortable with. Take the time you need to process this and get the right size
with it. As you said in the beginning, neither of us is going anywhere
soon. Hang in there…

Marquette Prison
Tuesday, August 14

Okay, picking up where I left off…

We came upon an inviting spot and I pulled over and indicated the
Crown Royal bottle. She handed it to me and I treated myself to a
nice, smooth pull. Good stuff. Julie Patchouli lit up the joint she had
put out half way through earlier and handed it to me. After I let out a
good toke and looked at her she just said, "I don't know. What do you
want to do?" I shrugged.

   Taking the joint back, she hit it and finally said, "There is an option
I never mentioned before. I thought it might be too corny for you, but
maybe not. I personally am liking it more and more." She proceeded
to tell me a story about a good friend in Austin who had taken her
a couple times to her visit parent's ranch out in the hill country. She
loved it there. It was idyllic; there were a few horses and some dairy
goats. They had yard birds and a flock of geese that lived on a little
pond. They owned a few hundred acres, much of it wooded. When
things with Billie Joe were at their worst, her friend had offered her a
job on the ranch.

Her parents were elderly and Mother was in failing health. She needed a personal assistant. Their operation was a fraction of what it once was, and they were fine with that, but despaired of giving up the last few animals and her mother's beloved gardens. At the same time, they valued their independence above all else and had great reservations about someone moving in to take care of them.

Julie Patchouli had been offered room and board and a stipend to live in and take care of things on a trial basis. Nobody was totally comfortable with the idea. "This camper," she said, "addresses the biggest issue. We could live on the river, and I could spend as much or as little time in the house as necessary. You could do the animals and gardens. We'd be off the grid, and—as far as I'm concerned—in Shangri-La. What do you think, Cowboy?"

I understood the attraction, but hey, I am a product of the inner city. I like pool halls and night clubs and after-hours gambling joints. What I knew about animals was that they usually smelled bad and some of them will eat you.

On the other hand, I wasn't fully confident that Billie Joe was capable of following directions, or sticking to agreements made while taped in a chair with a shotgun jammed into his tender areas. I was driving a stolen vehicle without a license, and that put me one traffic stop away from disaster. The idea of being off the grid was attractive, but the selling point was living in the camper with Julie Patchouli.

I started the truck up, "Give me directions," I told her. Less than two hours later we turned into a very long drive that led to a house almost a quarter mile off the road out in rural Llano County.

The homestead was all very neat, if you looked at it through the eyes of usta-be. It was obvious that this spread once could have graced the cover of Better Homes and Gardens. That touch of elegance was still evident, that look that said someone had spent many loving hours of pampering and fretting over these gardens. Now they were looking overgrown and shabby. There was a hinge on one of the shed doors that needed to be tightened up. There were a few spots that could use a little touch-up with paint. Julie Patchouli went to the door while I waited in the truck, studying the grounds with a critical eye. I was surprised at how much of the whole landscaping thing I had absorbed over the past months. The more I looked, the more I saw opportunities for improvement.

Half an hour later, Julie Patchouli returned from the house. "We're in." she said. "There is a spot down by the river where we can camp. You do the outside work, I'm the inside help. We are being paid with room and board, and Jake is going to have someone come over and dig a pit to build an outhouse over." She seemed very pleased.

"You drive a hard bargain," I observed.

"I just *look like* a little sissy girl," she sniffed.

The spot she directed me to was secluded and well away from the house; it was ideal for a camp site. I built a little fire and we munched on stale sandwiches I had in the camper. Later on we shared a joint and sipped mixed drinks while watching one of those sun downs the hill country is famous for. Bed time came shortly thereafter; it had been a full day and we were both exhausted. I marvel now that there was no awkwardness or hesitation when we went inside. I stripped down to my boxers and slid between the sheets, Julie Patchouli followed me in just panties and snuggled up. We were instantly out for the count and slept like that until the early morning sun attacked my eyes and my stirring woke her. "I've got to get Evelyn up and running," she said, "and get some breakfast going. I'll bring you out something shortly."

And, yes, after that our relationship did become intimate, as they say, and, delightfully, we were very much on the same wavelength. No details will be forthcoming. I will just say, *I had much to be grateful for*, and leave it at that.

Armed with a cup of instant coffee, I went outside to study the surroundings, which looked better and better with each passing moment. I found a comfortable spot and just sat there studying the vista, getting enthused about the possibilities. After a time, Julie Patchouli sat and handed me a covered plate.

Under the foil were fried eggs, biscuits and gravy, sausage links and grits. She read my expression. "Country folk take breakfast seriously," she said. While we are here, I will be preparing their meals. What they eat, we eat."

"I could get used to this," I said. After breakfast, we took a tour of the outbuildings and found all the tools necessary to clear the area around our camp site. I found an old porch swing. It was covered in dust and needed a bit of repair, but before the day was over, that puppy was hanging from a tree branch in our yard.

Julie Patchouli walked me through the care and feeding of the various livestock. She was from town, such as it was, but all of her kinfolk were country and she had spent enough of her younger days on farms to know the basics. Mostly the animals took care of themselves. I had to make sure there was always water available to them and we wrote on the feed bags how much they were supposed to get on a daily basis. All of the pens were overdue for cleaning and that became a priority. "Nothing is urgent," Julie Patchouli said, "They will be happy to see gradual progress. Once everything is caught up, it will take very little effort to keep things looking nice. I'll help with the outside work. I enjoy gardens and animals."

And so it was. That afternoon I mucked out the horse stalls, and added that to an already-existing compost heap. I put down fresh straw for bedding and then went out to find that Julie Patchouli had been on a weeding and pruning frenzy. We declared an end to our work day. It had gotten pretty hot and we decided to find out how skinny dipping in the Colorado River would feel. (Answer: It feels nice. It feels very nice.)

That became our routine and I was in bliss. I put in a few hours a day working with the animals, touching up the vegetable and ornamental gardens, and doing light repairs. I found that I enjoyed the work and was gratified to see the place gradually getting spruced up. It was an accomplishment, and I was proud of us.

… I'll admit it, Dude, up to this point in my life, I didn't have much to be proud of. I have made some miscalculations. Never mind my crappy-ass childhood—a story you will never hear—just look at the last few years before I ended up on this ranch.

I was on probation for two years and they rode me hard—weekly drug tests, I had to maintain perfect job attendance, weekly group counseling, and GED study. They took most of my pay for supervision fees, court costs, and restitution; the P.O. was constantly checking on me at work and knocking on my door at the boarding house. I had a 10:00 curfew and didn't dare miss it. I spent six weeks in Wayne County Jail in Detroit before they gave me the probation, so I knew what I had to look forward to if I got PV'd. That kept me honest. Wayne County Jail is a horror show.

Just a few weeks after that highly unpleasant experience wrapped up, I caught a felony in Kalamazoo County—broke into a pharmacy— Bam! Six years and some change in prison, where I met you. I had an eighteen-month parole and violated after thirteen months testing dirty for marijuana and amphetamines. That had me back in the joint for just under two years. Back out on parole for nine months and that awful thing in Benton Harbor. After that, almost a year in Austin, not miserable, but not great. It was okay, but frustrating and a dead-end rut. Lost what little I had there and went down to San Antonio. Again, not just utterly awful, but no joy. I was working hard, and didn't have much to show for it. I'm not trying to break your heart, I'm just painting a picture. I have been fucking up for a long time. A shrink once told me that I was my own worst enemy and I think he nailed it. I had not built a happy or meaningful life for myself. Now I was living in a camper on the Colorado River and life was good. Who saw that coming?

Since I mentioned it, let me go off on a side tangent here. That mandatory GED study? There was a nice lady there, actually a nun, who took an interest in me. The first person in my life to ever suggest that I wasn't intellectually inferior. She told me I had a lot of inherent abilities and should consider journalism or some other profession where I could write. Nicest person I ever knew; her confidence in me made me want to do well with my GED, and made me really work at it, rather than just go through the motions to satisfy the probation people. She got me to reading books, which I was surprised to realize I really loved. To this day, I am never not into a book. I kicked butt on the GED, and the sister was so proud of me. Later, when I went to prison they had college classes and that was my thing. I think the probation people put that GED requirement on me just to make my life miserable, but the joke is on them. I actually smartened up to a significant degree. Anyway...

Take all that and then look at me now, on this ranch. One day I was sitting there on the riverbank, a fishing line in the water, Julie Patchouli was nearby, singing one of her songs to some little animal, and I thought, this is what it is like to be happy. It was a first for me and I gotta tell you, it felt good.

One thing I didn't see coming was the relationship that developed with the livestock. At first the horses were big, skittish animals that I found intimidating. I was terrified one would step on my foot. As time went by and we got to know one another, I began to appreciate the beauty, the grace, the majesty (how often do you get to use that word in a sentence?) of these creatures.

I spent a lot of time grooming and talking to them. I gathered up crab apples in the woods that Julie Patchouli hand-fed to them. After a while, when I went into the barn, they would all rush over and want to nuzzle my neck, rub against me and talk to me in that language they have. Horses can make you feel special, Dude, I kid you not. I miss those guys.

Just a note about horse grooming. Julie Patchouli had some familiarity with farm animals in general, but we both studied from a book she found in the house and I am confident that we got it right. These guys would have been okay with a lot less, but you could see they loved grooming and appreciated the extra attention we gave them. I came to enjoy it too.

We found everything we needed in the tack room: dandy brush, metal curry comb, rubber curry comb, water brush, mane brush, hoof picks, sponges to clean around the eyes and nostrils. We checked them regularly for ticks and bot flies, kept their hooves clean and docked their tails. It was a big job, and way more than anyone could reasonably have expected at the wage we were being paid (ha-ha), but you've heard the expression, a *labor of love?* That's what this was. Once you have been loved by an animal, Dude, well, you see a lot of things in life differently. I'll leave it at that.

That experience spilled over to the other animals. There are different kinds of goats; what we had were Nubians. Dairy goats. Those are the kind with the droop-down ears. Really nice looking animals, very mellow. Especially the kids.

Those little guys are so cute. Nubians are extremely playful. It's like watching a playground full of children. Each one had its own personality. They were always so happy to see me coming, you could tell they had talked it over and decided I was just the coolest guy ever. I loved them right back, I can tell you.

Those ornery-ass geese, always hissing at me and complaining about something. I didn't take it personal. The ducks were affectionate, in their way; chickens were brainless, but they meant no harm. Man, I miss all those little guys. I always had someone to talk to.

Dude, all this has left me really nostalgic. I'm a little wrung out. More later...

AB

Jackson Prison
Friday, July 22

Hey AB...

I literally laughed out loud reading about our experiences with animals, as though I could never understand. Did you forget who you are talking to?

Did you forget how I got this dumbass nickname hung on me? Man, what I would give to smell the inside of a horse barn or get on my knees in a vegetable garden, and get my fingers in the dirt. You're right—how many guys on the yard would understand that?

Can't wait for the next installment!

Dude

Marquette Prison
Wednesday, August 4

Dude:

Oh yeah, I did forget. You are a genuine country boy. That is so rare that it is easy to forget. And yeah, I'd pay money just to smell the inside of a horse barn right now. Anyway, back to business. I'm picking up right where I left off last time…

Our routine became to do the outside chores in the mornings, before the day heated up. After lunch, Julie Patchouli and I would sit around our camp site, just enjoying the beauty of it. We spent a lot of time in the river. Over time, it got better and better. I had cleared out a nice area and transplanted quite a lot of landscaping down there. Julie Patchouli added all these hippy touches—sea shells, colored glass, feathers, wind chimes, all kinds of things hanging from the trees; painted rocks, bird feeders everywhere that were always occupied. You've never seen so many humming birds, Dude.

Julie patchouli taught me how to fish in the river. Another new experience. Fishing is one of those things—like golf—that have always been a puzzlement to me. I'd hear folks talking about it, see it on TV, and I'd think, *what am I missing? Where is the kick?* I won't carry on too much; suffice it to say, I get it now. I get the attraction of fishing. I was not-so-gradually becoming *country*. Nothing in me was longing for the city. Live in an apartment? Have people all around me all the time? Traffic?

Are you kidding? Give up this for that? Yeah, right. We sometimes marveled over the fact that we could get on this river in front of us and float downstream to a spot within walking distance of her home in Clarksville. Two completely different realities.

I knew I had totally gone native when I went out fishing one morning while Julie Patchouli was up at the house. I pulled a couple catfish out of the water and took them home. Within a few minutes, I had them gutted and filleted, and sizzling in a cast iron frying pan over an open fire. That kind of thing had become routine and I thought nothing of it. Julie Patchouli showed up right on cue with some scrambled eggs and fresh goat milk. You can't buy a breakfast like that anywhere in America, Dude. I remember thinking, *how does life get better than this?*

There were plenty of days when I didn't bother getting dressed at all except when I went up to tend to the animals, and then it was just pulling on a pair of shorts. Back at our place, why bother? It was always warm out and we were both in and out of the river several times every day. There was an endless supply of marijuana. All our needs were being met and it was so freaking peaceful. I never knew life could be so mellow.

You know my name is Albert. I have always gone by my intials, A.B. From the *go*, Julie Patchouli called me Alberto. That tickled me so much, I can't tell you. I have used that since then, but it sounded different coming from her. *Alberto*. Makes me smile every time I remember her voice saying that name.

One day Julie Patchouli's friend, JoEllen, came to visit from Austin. There was good news and bad news. JoEllen was ecstatic about the way we had rehabilitated the old homestead, and the condition of the animals. She knew Julie Patchouli and had trusted her to do a good job, but what she found was way above and beyond. Mother and Daddy loved Julie Patchouli and couldn't imagine life without her.

JoEllen was tickled about the little homestead we had created for ourselves on the riverbank.

The bad news was that JoEllen was one of four siblings. The others had decided to involve themselves in their parent's affairs and even though details were sparse, it was generally accepted that nothing good would come of it.

The sibs were all professional people, living respectable lives off in suburbia, whereas JoEllen had always been a free spirit and the black sheep of the family. Even though we had been there for months at this point, one of them had recently learned that JoEllen had couple of her reprobate friends—*who we know nothing about*—camped out on the river and looking after the old folks. This had escalated to a crisis in the family. A delegation would be arriving soon.

Kenneth pulled up a few days later. He was a big guy, but with that soft, pale, office-worker look about him. He walked around the place in slacks and wing tip shoes. He was obviously looking for something to be outraged about, but had grown up here and knew what he was looking at. He couldn't find anything to work with.

Looking around the grounds there was nothing to complain about, but looking at us, well, certain kinds of people could find fault. When you saw Julie Patchouli, you'd automatically think *hippy girl*, which I think most people found cute and endearing. Not everybody can make that look work, but Julie Patchouli pulled it off. It wasn't just a look, it was who she was. Kenneth, unfortunately, appeared to be one of those people who saw the 60's as the single most dreadful and shameful era in world history. And to look at me...well, I wasn't fit for polite company, as they say down home. I had stopped shaving my head a few months earlier and now my hair just looked shabby and unkept, like I was way, way overdue for a haircut. My beard was out of control. I seriously looked like I would be right at home living under a bridge and eating rats.

Julie Patchouli told me that Evelyn had given him an earful when Kenneth expressed his discontent about current arrangements. Jake asked him if he or one of the other kids would move out here and do our jobs if he ran us off. That cooled his jets, but that didn't mean all was well. Kenneth stayed overnight and next morning began promoting the idea that Mother needed to be in a Constant Care Facility. Of course, she was opposed to that, but Julie Patchouli conceded Evelyn was pretty weak and feeble, and Jake didn't have a lot of punch left in him. All we could do was ride it out.

Then Kenneth was gone, but his ghost haunted our paradise. I began talking about waterfront property in Michigan where there are thousands of lakes and rivers. We had a wad of cash to work with. Maybe find a like-minded couple to go in on it with us. Maybe even a small commune-type thing. What we had here could be re-created with a little effort. Julie Patchouli was non-committal.

Between them, Julie Patchouli and JoEllen called different people they knew and established that Billie Joe was adhering to the agreement I had laid down for him. He blew off the truck and picked up from where we left him. Apparently, he had another stash somewhere and our rip didn't leave him devastated. JoEllen added that the rumor was Billie Joe had hooked up with a couple hard cases he met dealing drugs and had branched out into an occasional armed robbery. I asked Julie Patchouli if she was going to visit him in prison. She agreed that prison seemed inevitable for the boy. Suddenly she said, "Oh my God! JoEllen told me that Morgan and a couple of his guys were all up at Huntsville now. What if Billie Joe ends up there with them?"

I shrugged, "Actions have consequences."

Life went on and Kenneth faded to an uncomfortable dark cloud off on the horizon, like if your doctor said, "Well, that's something we'll certainly keep an eye on…" It took some of the wonderfulness out of our situation, and stimulated both of us to think in terms of where we would land next. Julie Patchouli was committed to caring for Evelyn, whom she had grown to love, as long as possible.

One day I found an old rope in one of the outbuildings and carried it down to the river. This thing was over two inches thick and long enough for the idea that immediately jumped into my mind. It was a huge job, but after I tied it around my waist and climbed up to the top of an enormous Cypress on the river edge and got it tied to a sturdy branch, I was able to slide down into the water and carry it over to the bank. With a running start, I could swing out over the deepest part of the river and let go; it was a good thirty-foot drop. Cool! I was having big fun with that, bare-assed, of course, and looked up to see Kenneth standing on the riverbank. Ever have someone look at you like you were something they had to scrap off the bottom of their shoe? I had the impression that he wanted to talk to me so I held up one finger and swam over to where I had a pair of cut-offs on the opposite bank. When I was presentable, Kenneth informed me that his nephew Robert would be moving out to the ranch, "to keep an eye things."

"Is there anything in particular you think needs closer scrutiny?" I asked.

"Robert will provide a family presence," he responded.

"What does that have to do with me?" I wanted to know.

"Regard Robert as my representative, "Kenneth instructed. "Consider what Robert says as coming from me."

"Okay," I said conversationally, "but who the fuck are you?" I let Kenneth choke on that until he began to stammer out a response, and then cut him off, "I ask because I work for Jake and Evelyn, and until one of them says otherwise, what you have to say don't mean shit to me."

Kenneth stood there staring at me, stunned and lost for a response. I am guessing he wasn't used to people talking to him like that. I let my shorts drop to the ground. "If you'll excuse me, Kenneth, I said formally, "this conversation is over and I will return to my business. Good day, Sir." I casually walked over and dove into the river.

When I looked up, Kenneth was walking, rather stiffly, back toward the house. Had I thought there was even the remotest possibility it could make a difference, I would have tried to talk to Kenneth, but as Dylan said, *you don't need a weatherman to know which way the wind is blowing...*

I told myself, this isn't The End, but I can see it from here. Those were the days, Dude. I'd have been happy to stay there forever. More later....

Alberto.

Marquette Prison
Wednesday, August 9

This project has become an obsession. When I'm not doing it, I'm thinking about it. What have you gotten me into?

Julie Patchouli told me later that Robert was a student at UT Austin; the Student Advisory Council had suggested Robert take a semester off, to re-evaluate his academic goals. I've listened to enough bureaucratic double-speak to understand that Robert was a fuck-up. "And this is who is going to supervise us?" Apparently, the sibs had decided that a "family presence" was necessary and nobody wanted the job. Parking Robert out here conveniently answered the question of what to do with him.

Life went on. My way of dealing with all this was do my best to not think about it. There seemed no doubt that our days here were numbered, but I had a truck, I had a camper and hadn't even touched the money we took from Billy Joe. I wasn't desperate about not leaving here. I just seriously did not want to.

The count-down clock began ticking a couple weeks later when I went into the horse barn to tend to my buddies' grooming needs and came face to face with a clean cut, rather dorky-looking individual wearing creased slacks (what was it with these people?) and a shirt with an alligator applique. "Who are you?" I asked, knowing the answer, but offended that he was petting one of my horses.

"I'm Robert," he said, stepping over and offering me his hand. I shook it. Why not? This guy hadn't done anything to me. "Uncle Kenneth said you would be expecting me."

"So you got kicked out of school," I said in response. "How does Uncle Kenneth feel about that?"

"Technically, not kicked out, just invited to take some time off to contemplate whether or not UT is a good fit for me. I expect that when next semester begins, I will be allowed back on academic probation and afforded the opportunity to establish that the break was good for me and that I am returning as a squared-away lad, ready to pursue academic excellence. Uncle Kenneth, by the way, is *disappointed*."

I couldn't help it, I kinda liked the guy. That might be over-stated, but I did not dislike him. He had an irreverence that struck a chord with me. He knew it was all bullshit and he was willing to push the envelope.

"You must be that awful man who lives down by the river," he continued. "I have heard conflicting assessments of your general character and worth as a human being."

"I'm guessing that Uncle Kenneth's version is the less flattering," I ventured.

"He doesn't like you," Robert offered conversationally.

"You speak fluent understatement, Robert."

"That I do, my friend. That I do. That aside, I am intrigued by Aunt JoEllen's description of your encampment. I'd love to see it." I motioned him to follow me.

I showed Robert around the area and he was duly impressed. I can't explain it; the guy was just likeable. I handed him a Lone Star and we both sat on lounge chairs on the riverbank. Robert said all of the appropriate things about what a comfortable little "retreat"—his word—we had carved out for ourselves here and I fired up a joint. Shortly thereafter, we were buds.

Robert told me it was his job to report to Uncle Kenneth regularly and keep him abreast of the debauchery and shenanigans going on here and determine how his parents were being abused and taken advantage of by the two reprobates camped out by the water.

"Well, there will be plenty to report, Robert, because we are out of control out here.

"I have a sense," he said, "that all is chaos and madness. Uncle K, however, will hear none of that from me. Running you off would mean that I would be saddled with all the chores you are obviously performing flawlessly. To put a fine point on it, I don't want your job."

"What do you want, Robert? I asked.

He seemed surprised by the question. "Why, *this*, of course. I want to sit on the riverbank and smoke marijuana and consume alcoholic beverages. This particular proclivity of mine is the very reason that some highly educated people at the University of Texas suggested it might be advantageous for me to examine my priorities and determine if my future actually was tied to academia. In Austin, my foot-lose and fancy-free inclinations were inhibited by social norms. Out here, I can embrace my inner hedonist."

Robert drew a deep breath through his nose and looked around. "In short, Dear Albert, I don't want your job. I want your lifestyle. That is something we can *share*, is it not?

I poured the last quarter of my warm Lone Star down my throat, "Welcome to the neighborhood," I said. We shook on it.

Robert decided on a site down from us that was blocked from our view by trees and undergrowth. Closer than I hoped for, but at least out of sight from our location. I was expecting him to show up with a load of brand new LL Bean camping gear and pitch a tent. How naïve of me. The same crew that had built our outhouse showed up one morning with chainsaws and a Bobcat bulldozer to create a road to Robert's campsite. A number of huge old trees were slaughtered and reduced to kindling, and an area near the riverbank was graded for the 18 X 20' cabin that was later brought in on a flatbed truck. Julie Patchouli wept.

It got worse. The next Friday afternoon, a couple dozen of Robert's closest friends showed up and the party began immediately. That night we lay in bed listening to the blaring music, the hollering, girls shrieking and laughing and there was no more living in denial. Our paradise was lost. The next morning, we awoke to massive litter—beer cans, potato chip bags, condom wrappers, cigarette butts, etc. everywhere—and very unpleasant evidence that the merry-makers had felt free to use our outhouse.

Of course, it was time to go, but Julie Patchouli didn't want to leave Evelyn. Kenneth was just standing by waiting for that excuse to park her in a facility somewhere. I hated the feeling of helplessness, and grieved with Julie Patchouli over what was happening. The younger me might have gone to war with the intruders, but there was obviously no win in that.

Robert came over later on and asked me to sell him some marijuana. I had plenty, so why not? Pretty soon I was the go-to guy. They didn't seem to care that I was charging outrageous prices. I had forgotten the pills and powders we had confiscated from Billie Joe, since Julie Patchouli and I had no interest in them. Much of it I couldn't even identify. Robert and his crew recognized it all immediately. I had several baggies of pills I would leave out when selling some weed. Occasionally one of them would ask, "how much are these?"

I'd just shrug and say, "same price you were paying in Austin." I'm pretty sure nobody caught on that I was bluffing my way through because I was amazed at how much these things sold for. If they had laid down half as much I would have been happy. I was delighted to be getting rid of that stuff, and loved that the bucks just kept rolling in.

Not everyone was as likable as Robert, and after a while, he was only okay in small doses. His shtick could get old. There were a couple others who had no problem letting me know they saw me through Kenneth's eyes. Overall, start to finish, I really didn't like any of them, but didn't find it necessary to make a big deal out of it. I mostly just sat back and watched. One in particular—I kid you not—was called Biff. Can you seriously believe that? *Biff.* He was built like a linebacker and was obviously used to having his own way. I fantasized about him drowning in the river. I also wanted his truck tires. One day Biff saw fit to tease me about my tires, and pointed out the spiffy B.F. Goodrich R17's on his truck. Close to $2,000 worth of rubber, wrapped around D67 milled black satin Gladiator rims that cost way more than the tires themselves. I coveted Biff's tires. I needed new ones and his were nice. It would be a joy of stick it to him.

Julie Patchouli didn't just cook and clean. She took care of Evelyn, including bathing her. She shampooed her hair and spent time brushing it out. She sat by Evelyn's bed for hours, reading to her, sometimes just holding her hand, quietly singing her little songs, or just sharing the solitude. Jake mostly could care for himself, but it was obvious his clock was running down.

Julie Patchouli came dragging in one night looking utterly distraught. She had been growing more and more despondent by the day over what was happening to our home, but this was something else. She was finally able to tell me that Evelyn had had a stroke, and it really did not look good for her. Whatever happened next, they were going to take her away. She had spoken with JoEllen and it was understood, the time had come. We could deprive Kenneth the joy of throwing us out by leaving on our own.

Early next morning came news that Evelyn had died in her sleep and Jake suffered a massive coronary upon hearing the news. It would be a double funeral. Two days later I took Julie Patchouli in to the funeral home to pay her respects. I was waiting outside in my truck, head back and eyes closed, when there was a knock on my window. I opened my eyes to see a very well dressed, fiftyish woman looking at me intently. I dropped my window and she said, "I just wanted to thank you for all you did on my parent's farm. Especially in caring for those animals. It meant so much to them.

My mother loved her flower beds and it warmed her heart to be able to look out at them, immaculate and beautiful even when she could no longer work them herself. You have given much for little in return. God bless you for that," she said and then walked away before I could respond.

That was nice, I thought. It didn't mean we weren't being evicted, but I was touched by it nonetheless. Julie Patchouli came out a short time later and told me that the funeral was scheduled for Thursday morning, but she had said her good byes and that was it for her. She proposed that we say good bye to our home at the same time that same day. That worked for me.

As luck would have it, Robert's friends had been planning a trip to Kerrville for the famous annual music festival there on that day and around nine o'clock they all piled into the biggest vehicles they had between them and were out of our hair. We took time to walk around the grounds one last time, say tearful farewells to the animals and hug a few of our favorite trees. Julie Patchouli wanted to go sit in Evelyn's room for a spell and I headed back to the riverfront.

It took only a few minutes to jack Biff's truck up and remove the tires. Putting them on my truck was enormously gratifying, as was replacing them with my baldies. I wondered how long it would take him to realize what had happened, and was sorry I couldn't be there to see the look on his face.

I had been talking endlessly about Michigan in recent days and had the route planned out in my mind. Our last night in the river, Julie Patchouli asked, "You don't mind making a stop in Austin on the way? I need to meet JoEllen at Whole Foods." It was a bit out of the way, but what did I care? I told her *no prob* and went back to whatever I was babbling about.

The buildup to our departure was so drug out and drama-laden that the actual leaving was anti-climactic. Austin was just under two hours out. We listened to *Morning Edition* on KUT and didn't talk much. I saw JoEllen as soon as we pulled into the Whole Foods parking lot. I told Julie Patchouli I was going to run in and use the restroom.

When I came back out, JoEllen was putting Julie Patchouli's suitcase into the back of her van. I could see the rest of her stuff was already in there. I stood in shock, staring dumbly.

Julie Patchouli walked up to me with a sad smile and teary eyes and put a finger to my lips to keep me from speaking. "I will be forever grateful to you for helping me escape from Billy Joe and being a part of what have been the most wonderful months of my life. Now it is time for a new beginning." She put a hand to her heart, "You will always be here; I will always remember you with joy and thanksgiving, and will always, deeply and sincerely, be wishing the best for you, Alberto." She went up on her toes, kissed me lightly in the lips and then was walking away.

I was dumbfounded. Stupefied. *Did not* see that one coming. The girl never deceived me or misrepresented her intentions. She just let me believe the fantasy I created I in my own mind. Had I known what was happening, the intervening time would have been torture. I said nothing, and made myself turn back to my truck, as opposed to standing there like an idiot staring at them driving off into the distance.

I won't say much about what that moment was for me, Dude, but will just leave it at this: I was in pain. And was for a long time thereafter. Enough said. I pulled out onto Lamar Boulevard, hung a left on Keonig Lane, and left again at the I-35 onramp. I had come to love Texas, Dude, but Michigan is home, and on this day, my destination.

Dude, you wrote asking why I was back in the joint, and forty pages later, you are still wondering…and what does any of this has to do with that? Maybe nothing. Maybe all my stories from now on begin in that time because I am so much a different person today. Maybe I just needed to tell this tale, and who else would I ever unload all this on?

Whatever, this has left me exhausted and emotionally drained. We'll call this the end of Part One. Someday—and it might be a while—I will be up to writing Part Two. You'll know that time has come when you hear from me again.

Happy Labor Day

Alberto

Marquette Prison
December 13

Hey Dude…

I'm back. I know, it's been a while. Writing—and re-living—all that about Julie Patchouli left me drained and dredged up a lot of memories I have been dealing with since my last installment of this tale. On some level, I'm sure it is somehow therapeutic to get all of this out and re-examine it from the distance of the time that has passed. On another level, it has not been easy. I miss that girl. I miss the life we had. Writing about it is a stark reminder of what I have lost.

Anyway, I'm back in the saddle, and picking up where I left off last time…

Driving up I-35 out of Austin, I was in a state of shock. My world was shattered. My mind sort of went into a blank mode where I didn't think about anything, and I was in Oklahoma before I was very much aware of my surroundings. First thing that really made an impression was that I was hungry. Pulling off the highway into a shopping center to buy some munchies for the road I saw a young couple trying to hitch-hike and looking very dejected. They were holding up a sign, but I assumed whatever it said wouldn't be enough to overcome all they had working against them. I'm pretty sure Ardmore, Oklahoma is not the ideal location for a black guy and a white chick traveling together to hitch a ride.

I tossed my purchases into the camper and swung around to pick them up. You have never seen two people more grateful for a lift. I could tell by the look of them that they had traveled a hard road. We chatted a bit and I got a pretty good vibe from them, so I pulled off into a BBQ joint a couple miles down the highway. They gave each other a concerned glance and I said, "Don't worry, this comes with the ride." They looked at me like I had just floated down on a cloud and had a halo. Julie Patchouli remained uppermost in my mind; I couldn't help thinking how much she would approve of what I was doing.

After they wolfed down their food, I learned that this happy couple was heading for Chicago. They had started out from Pismo Beach, California, traveling with friends. The friendship became strained and finally frazzled somewhere near Amarillo, where they were left roadside. Nearly penniless, but determined to get home, they had soldiered on, and now here I was like the answer to a prayer. I told them that I was going to Michigan, and if they wanted to drive, I would get them home. Of course, they jumped at the offer. I gave Lydia a fifty-dollar bill for gas and meals. The tank was almost full, although mileage on this beast, especially carrying the camper, was pretty lousy. I told them pull into any drive-through when they were hungry, buy gas when it gets low, and don't bother me until that money runs out. They seemed a little bewildered by it all, but were certainly agreeable.

I was happy to help these two out, but the larger point was that I needed to get drunk and I wanted to get where I was going. Riding in the camper gave me the opportunity to do both. As referenced earlier in this saga, I am a fan of strong drink. I'm not stupid about it, though. My idea of getting high is to have a couple shots of Tequila, or some such, and smoke a joint. I don't over-indulge in the alcohol because, for me, that ruins the high. I never, *ever* just drink until I am blotto. Until that moment. Getting rip-roaring drunk, falling down, barfing, acting stupid, all of that and more was not just my journey, but my destination. How else could I deal with the loss of Julie Patchouli?

The next couple days remain a blur. Occasionally J.T. or Lydia would tell me they needed more money for gas and I would give it to them. Somewhere along the line, one of them told me they were utterly exhausted and wanted to pull into a rest area and catch a few Z's. I gave them money for a motel. Meanwhile, I got drunk, raved, howled at the moon, sang along with oldies on the radio, and passed out. I woke up feeling wretched. When we crossed the Minnesota line, I pretty much had it out of my system, and asked them to pull into the next truck stop we came across. Once there, I paid for three showers and bought some aspirin.

We had a sit-down meal in the restaurant there and talked for a while. I had a real dinner of basic down-home comfort food—meatloaf, mashed potatoes and gravy, green beans—and that went a long way to making me feel somewhat human again. J.T. and Lydia were actually pretty decent people. It occurred to me to appreciate that they had not ripped me off. It was certainly there for the doing. They were so grateful to have connected with me in their moment of extreme need, it never occurred to them that they were heaven-sent to me. I not only needed some alone time to drink that girl off my mind, but hey, I still was without valid I.D. Every second I was behind the wheel, I was running a risk.

We ate and talked and it was all very comfortable. I don't recall the specifics of that conversation but I recall it as a pleasant interlude and I enjoyed their company. I bought a map and contemplated the best way to get these love birds home. It turned out that they lived way out near Winnetka. My proposition to them originally included me taking them to their front door. Looking at this map, I dreaded doing so. This was a heavy-traffic time of day, I had never driven in Chicago before, it was way out of my way, and I just really didn't want to veer off in that direction. Finally I proposed instead that I drop them at the nearest bus stop and give them a hundred bucks each as a parting gift. They were good with that. "If you don't mind me asking," Lydia asked tentatively, "what do you do for a living?"

"I usta be a criminal," I said, realizing the truth of it as I was saying words, "but I recently retired." Lydia said, "Oh," and J.T. nodded as if he has assumed the criminal part. We said our good byes a short time later.

I took highway 80 over to South Bend, veered north, and made my way, finally, up to Grand Rapids. On one level, it was stupid for me to be in Michigan. I had absconded from parole, and was still wanted in connection with the Benton Harbor thing. On the other hand, this was home and I knew a couple of no-bullshit guys in G.R. My biggest concern was getting I.D. and some paperwork for the truck. I was pretty sure they could help me get hooked up.

It took some doing but I finally connected with my friend Steve. It was great to see him. We met in Jackson eons ago and did some years together. I always liked Steve because he was *real*; he was smart and he was tough. Steve was old-school in a way that is uncommon these days. I told him I was looking for I.D. to make me legal, and paperwork to make the truck legal. I assumed he would know someone, and I was right. Within 48 hours, I had everything I had come looking for, including a title and insurance on the truck. Money Talks.

It was great to see him again and connect with a couple other old friends, but I wasn't into it. I was still in a bad place over Julie Patchouli and realized that I didn't have much in common with those guys anymore. I was no longer enamored of big city nightlife or the constant talk of different ways to make a quick buck. I didn't want to be there with them. I wanted to be on the river with someone else.

Five days after I rolled into Grand Rapids, I headed out again on Highway 131 North; less than four hours later, marveling at the magnificence of the Mackinaw Bridge. After crossing it and continuing north until sundown, I slept in my camper in a roadside rest area. Next morning, I called a real estate agent at a number displayed on a nearby billboard. She told me there were several parcels on the St. Mary's River in my price range and in an amazingly short period of time, I was the proud owner of one of them.

It was a beautiful, elevated spot with a breathtaking view, black bears and bald eagles were a common sight. Two hundred feet away, on the opposite bank, was Ontario, Canada. I found an ideal location for my camper and took it off the truck. In the coming weeks, I built a frame around it preparatory to winter blowing in.

For the next several weeks, Dude, I worked like a man possessed. Pretty much sun up to sundown—clearing brush, trimming trees, establishing a driveway, building a deck on the riverbank I could fish from, just making the place my own. I borrowed some of Julie Patchouli's ideas about dressing up the trees with various ornaments and worked up an area for next spring's garden. When the temperatures dropped, I attached translucent fiberglass panels to the 2 x 4 frame around the camper and basically was living inside a greenhouse. Winter can be brutal in the north country, but I stayed pretty toasty. The small propane stove kept the camper warm enough in normal circumstances, and with the greenhouse built around it, I had no heating problems even during those stretches of sub-zero temperatures.

I had been out there for a few months before finally venturing into town with the idea of socializing. The seclusion and hard work had been therapeutic—and productive—but now it was time to re-join the human race. Yoopers—people in the U.P.—really are a people apart, and proud of it. I knew I had stepped into a different culture; there was nothing subtle about it. It was different, but people were friendly and welcoming once they realized I was harmless, and wasn't one of those outsiders who look down on them or saw the locals as "quaint." The easiest way to describe Yoopers is to say watch the movie *Fargo*. I know—that's not in the U.P.—but that is how Yoopers talk and they are essentially the same folks.

Jobs are scarce in that part of that world and I was lucky to land one working as kitchen help in a nearby hospital. It was minimum wage, but I liked my co-workers, and the job was enjoyable. Meals were included, and in the evening, there were usually left-overs to take home. Along with fishing and occasionally dropping a deer with the hunting rifle Billie Joe had given me, my groceries were covered. I didn't have much, but I didn't need much.

After work one Friday, I was introduced to contra dancing, which is rather like square dance, but way cooler and you don't have to dress up for it. I loved it immediately. Contra dancing was very popular locally and there were dances every week end. My third or fourth time there, I spoke with a nurse I had seen around the hospital but had never approached. I was delighted beyond all reason when she told me her name was Rosemary. I took it as a good omen that her name was a type of incense.

It was a long, cold winter and I sometimes wondered why I hadn't found a spot on a river in that magical land down south where it is summer year-round. Probably a common thought in those parts, but then spring came, and all was well. I put in a lot of hours working on my place and gradually becoming a real Yooper.

Rosemary and I began "keeping company" as they say; it was very slow-going, but nice. She was a local girl who had gone to college in Sault Ste. Marie and had really never left the U.P. She had no desire to do so. "Where would I go?" she asked. "And why? This is home." (*That's* a true-blue Yooper.) Rosemary's story was an old one: she had married young and it went bad quickly. In her case, Mr. Wonderful turned out to be a very bad man, who did a lot of damage to a lot of people, but especially his young wife. He eventually ended up with a long prison sentence and her emotional recovery was a slow process. I was willing to be patient and give her all the space she needed to decide about me. That approach was working well until I was arrested on my outstanding warrants.

Nobody had mentioned that a serious background check was standard operating procedure when working in a hospital. My I.D. was pretty good, but a question arose, and everything gradually unraveled from there. Apparently a red flag popped up somewhere in the process; it took a while for it all to come apart, but come apart it did. I wrote Rosemary from the county jail, and got a couple lines back asking me to not write again.

From the local jail, I was transferred to Benton Harbor to face those charges, but enough time had gone by that they really didn't have a prosecutable case. One witness had moved without leaving a forward, another was no longer certain of important details. There was no video, they had no finger prints. It was a case where they knew it was me, but just had nothing to work with. Eventually charges were dismissed. That situation remains heavy on my conscience, and that is no small thing, but I will never serve time for it.

All that leaves is parole violation. I have nineteen months remaining on that old sentence. They can make me do every day of it, and send me off scot-free at the end, or release me before that and have me back on parole and under supervision for a while. No idea which way that will swing, although it is more likely—based on the way things usually work in the system—that they will release me on parole.

Another nineteen months of my life down the tubes is no joke, but I can take that hit if it comes to that. However much more time I do, I know that will be the end of it. I am done with all this madness, and will never commit another criminal act. I own that property on the St. Mary's and still have some cash buried out there from the Billie Joe thing. I'll be all right. The good news is that a couple weeks ago I sent my copy of this very long letter to Rosemary and got back a card with a request to receive any further installments. That gave me a lift.

So…all those weeks ago when you wrote and asked what was the story behind the story with me being back in the joint? This is your answer. I spoke with you days before I went home just a few years ago. My life experiences since then have left me a totally different person. I have had some victories. I have loved—and been loved by—a beautiful woman. I have found value and joy in things I once would have made light of. I have sat on a riverbank with a kid goat in my lap, it's head on my shoulder, and been mesmerized by a beautiful sunset. I have found reason to value my existence, and for the first time ever, Dude, I am confident of a bright and rosy future.

I wish you the same.

Alberto

My Summer Vacation

My name is Sonny. I rob banks. It's what I do.

People are impressed when they learn that I did my first (of many) bank robbery at the age of fourteen, although it seems a bit grandiose to refer to that escapade as a bank robbery. The world is full of people who come up with ideas just like mine, but never act on them. Those people are dreamers. Me, I'm more of a doer.

During this time, Aunt Jane's pickles was a major employer of high school kids in the area. They paid sixty cents a bucket for picking cucumbers. In reality, that was a pretty decent wage. If you were there to make money, and went down each row picking with both hands, you could fill a bucket in no time. It adds up quickly. When I took off on my sting ray that Saturday morning, I told Mom I was off to meet the truck that picked up workers at the grain elevators downtown for a day of pickle picking.

Instead, I rode down to the park, stashed my bike and retrieved the essentials for my morning's work from my back pack. I had one of my sister's old wigs, which had long ago been relegated to the kid's room for Halloween, dress-up, and what have you. I tucked in my t-shirt and pulled on a grossly over-sized sweatshirt. My ensemble was completed with this ridiculous hat that was a very *in* item with twelve-year-old girls that summer—kind of a sailor hat that pulled down over the eyes with a strip of tinted vinyl in front that acted as sunglasses. I have no doubt that I looked very much like a twelve-year-old girl as I strolled into the bank with hat on over my blonde wig and that baggie sweatshirt.

Once through the door, I didn't hesitate. I headed straight for an untended teller's window and hopped up on the counter. I leaned over and began scooping hand fulls of cash from the drawer and stuffing them down the front of my shirt. There were several bank patrons; they were staring at me with perplexed expressions, like they couldn't quite comprehend what they were seeing. I kept at it until I was down to grabbing the nickles and dimes. Finally, a guy in a suit came out of one of the offices and shouted, "Hey!" I hopped down, sprinted across the lobby, through the door and across the parking lot, across the firehouse lawn, through the cemetery and into the park, back to my bike. Nobody had followed me. Within seconds, the hat and wig were stuffed down into a trashcan, the money was transferred to my backpack along with the sweatshirt and I was peddling back downtown in a leisurely fashion.

The scene around the bank was absolute chaos. Some Barney Fife deputy was standing outside the front door with his pistol in a two-handed grip, looking around wide-eyed.

Both of the County cars were there, lights flashing, and a State Police car was zooming in from the post just north of town with sirens screaming and lights flashing.

The crowd assembling outside was trembling with excitement. Rumors were already circulating about armed men in masks holding hostages and all manner of drama. I watched the show for a while and then mosied on home.

I had picked this particular Saturday because the whole fam was to be off at some big-deal church function for the day and I would have the house to myself. (Had it not been for my job, I would have been forced to endure this affair also. But—as important as it is to nurture the immortal soul—a honest day's labor for a fair wage is a sacred thing in itself, which provided the escape clause I needed. Thank you, Aunt Jane.)

Safely hidden away in my bedroom, I dumped my haul on a blanket on the floor. I had never seen so much money in my life.

I counted it three times and ended up with hugely different totals each time. Finally, I concentrated on building little stacks of $100.00 each. These I double and triple checked. The quarters and dimes were built into stacks of $2.00 each. Using this approach, along with pencil and paper, I was able to determine that my haul amounted to $1, 647.85. (One thousand, six hundred and forty-seven American dollars. With an eight-five cent kicker.) That was damn near a million bucks! I was pretty sure I had at least half the money in the world right here in front of me.

My next question was, "Now what?" It wasn't like my family was so prosperous, or so unaware of my doings, that I could just start showing up with shiny new possessions without anybody taking notice. Strange as it may seem, the money wasn't really the point, and I hadn't given it a lot of thought. The doing of it was the point. The money itself was more a really swell fringe benefit.

One thing I knew I wanted was to get laid. In the big city, a guy with a pocket fill of cash could have accomplished that goal in relatively short order. In my circumstances, though, it was a challenge. I set my sights on my best friend Dib's sister Rita.

Dibs and his mom were working at the pickle station that summer; Dibs as a picker, his mom in the office. The little sister was dropped off on the way somewhere and picked up again after work. Rita stayed home, did the housework, and had dinner started when they came through the door. An ideal arrangement for my purposes.

The morning after my big score I took off—ostensibly to pick pickles—and did a little shopping. I went into several different stores making small purchases at each, accumulating the fixings for a truly outstanding pizza, and a six pack of RC Cola.

Each store I went into, people were buzzing about the big robbery. Without exception, everything I heard said was grossly inaccurate. I gave a high school kid two bucks to run me out to Dibs' place and pretended to be surprised when Rita told me he was working. I told her I was trying to hide from my mom for the day and she invited me in.

Don't misunderstand. My mother is an exquisite human being. That's the problem. When your family is evangelical, you mom is Aunt Bea, and everything is so freaking wholesome, you need to break out sometimes. Dib's mom was cool. She used to work in a bar. She let him have Playboys and everything. Their house was not utterly immaculate, and everything was not in its assigned place at all times. There were usually dishes in the sink. It was comfortable. They felt sorry for me and I was always welcome there.

I had known Rita literally all my life and regarded her as a kid sister, but something interesting had developed since last summer and I was beginning to see her in a whole different light. Rita was a little chubby, although she had become delightfully curvaceous. She had kind of kinky hair and a scratchy voice and she laughed too loud. At the same time, she was cute and funny and I really liked her a lot.

That first day I helped her with the housework, we fixed the pizza and just sort of lounged around for the afternoon. It was cozy. I could tell that she enjoyed it too, so I ventured to suggest that we do it again tomorrow. She thought that was a splendid idea.

That quickly became our routine and as the days went on, our meals became more and more elaborate. That pizza was replaced with filet minion, jumbo shrimp, prime rib, and fresh Maine lobster. With all the appropriate fixings, of course. It was into the third week before we did the deed.

I have to admit, that first go-round was pretty amateurish and not so gratifying for either of us; when it was over we both looked at each other and burst out laughing. I'll say this for us, though: neither of us were quitters. We hung in there and over a period of time, I think we got it pretty well figured out.

Throughout this time, nobody knew our secret. It was assumed that I was out picking pickles and nobody suspected that Rita did not spend her days alone. At the end of every week, I would flash some money around at home and humbly accept the praise I received for my outstanding work ethic. I hung out with Dibs some evenings and on weekends, like always; I'd see Rita and we'd kid around like we always had. Nobody suspected a thing.

It was great, but all good things must come to an end. What was cool about us is that we didn't have that clingy, desperate can't-live without-your-touch thing going on.

We both knew that when it was over, it was over. We didn't even try to figure out a way to keep it going. The summer came to an end and with it our foray into domestic bliss.

Our last day together, I confessed that when I had showed up there that first day, my intentions, as they say, were not honorable. "Gee," she deadpanned, "I hadn't guessed".

On my way out the door, I handed her a one-hundred-dollar bill, which she calmly accepted with a quiet "thanks," folded into quarters and slipped into her back pocket. Throughout the summer, I had brought her little gifts, small things that wouldn't raise any eyebrows— a couple different record albums, a few little trinkets I knew she'd enjoy—which she accepted gracefully. She never questioned how I financed the lavish meals or any of the rest of it. "It is important," I told her, "that nobody know where that came from."

"I know where it came from, "she said. From the expression in her eyes, I knew she had figured it out. "Don't worry, I'll never tell". After a long pause, I kissed her on the forehead, turned and left.

Life took us down separate paths after that and other things filled the space she and Dibs had once occupied. A few years later, he was killed in Viet Nam, and I have never seen Rita since.

She ended up marrying some really square guy with an office job; she is doing the responsible suburban soccer mom thing now and is apparently quite content. True to her word, she never told, not even after the bank offered a substantial reward for information.

During the summer of 1967, I became a millionaire, ate a lot of good food and learned some important life lessons I didn't realize until much later. I think of Rita often, and every time the thought causes a little twinge in my heart. She was my first love and remains the classiest chick I have ever known.

Sonny II
(Sequel to "My Summer Vacation")

*A*fter that first robbery, I was hooked. I liked money. I liked the possibilities it opened up in life. I loved the feeling of accomplishment and was thrilled by the knowledge that there is *Nothing To It But To Do It*. That first little sting whetted my appetite. I set my sights higher.

From earliest memory, I had been stymied by the harsh reality that I was just a kid. That was the brick wall my grand aspirations always ran into. I cannot remember a time I wasn't frustrated that I wasn't older and freer to carry out my big ideas. Years are centuries when you are a kid. Had I been a man of the world and knew people outside of that one-horse town I was stuck in—or at least had a drivers' license— my second robbery surely would have had a happier ending.

I had some cousins who lived on a dairy farm a couple miles outside of town. They were a few years older than me, and I had trouble getting them to take me seriously. I knew that they had broken into a couple of business and it was no secret they would walk off with anything that wasn't nailed down.

They were somewhat lacking in imagination, but I knew they were ballsy enough to pull this thing off and if they tried to cheat me out of my end of it, I could fall back on that standard favorite of outlaws everywhere: *I'll tell your mom.*

It was an uphill battle, but once I got them to focus and hear me out, I started to feel pretty good about our prospects. There wasn't a point at which a light bulb actually went off over their heads, but they did gradually stop wising-cracking and start asking intelligent questions. When they started making suggestions of their own, I knew they were in. It's like I said before, we walked through each stage step by step and each step was doable. We could take off this bank. Once these old boys started visualizing bundles of hundred dollar bills (which in their minds translated into shiny new convertibles and playmates in bikinis crawling all over them) we had some serious conversations and started putting together a time table.

My crew, such as it was, consisted of my cousin Larry, who was eighteen. He was a big boy and strong as a young bull elephant, as farm boys tend to be. Larry quit school at sixteen with a plan to make his fortune working for Oldsmobile. Sounds short-sighted now, but back in those days, guys actually went that route and did okay.

Larry's timing was off and the golden era of making big bucks on the assembly line came to a sad and screeching halt shortly after he signed on. Going back to high school was out of the question. He was now a permanent hand on his dad's—my Uncle Dan's—dairy farm. He was frustrated and dreamed of bigger and better.

There was also Darryl. He was twenty-two and currently living with his folks following two years in the Army and a failed marriage, and after a horrendous beating (from a fight he started) in Biloxi, Mississippi that left him hospitalized and in need of reconstructive surgery. Darryl was quiet in an eerie way and probably half crazy.

And then there was Darryl's ex brother in law—"Call me J.C."— who was twenty-six. His name was Julius Charles and if you called him Julia Childs, he would punch you out. He didn't care if you were only fourteen.

He had been a bully, and a braggart and an obnoxious ass-clown all his life and showed no indication of growing out of it. He always called me "Squirt" and tried to vote me out, even though it was my plan we were working with and he had come in late. He was used to having his own way in such things but had no answer when Darryl asked, "How are we going to do this with some snot-nose kid know-ing about it, and mad at us too, if he is not a part of it?" J.C. finally relented with, "Okay, Squirt, you're in; just stay out of my way." What-ever the hell that meant.

We wasted a lot of time with inconsequential peripheral issues, and J.C. laying down the law about how things would go, how we would divide the money, and blah, blah, blah. When it came to the actual plan, though, we stuck pretty close to my original. It didn't bother me to pretend that it was all J.C.'s brainchild. I just wanted to see that child born.

The big day finally arrived. Larry and Darryl—again, as farm boys tend to—had a comfortable relationship with large machinery. Larry and I started the day bright and early with a visit to the county road commission. I shimmied up a drainpipe to a third-floor landing and put my elbow through the window, unlocked that puppy, and crawled in.

Sounds like a move you'd see on the silver screen, doesn't it? It wasn't quite that smooth. A climb like that is hard work and after you get a few feet off the ground, it's scary. Those things are not made for climbing on and I ended up with a cut on my elbow that should have gotten stitches. Once in, I bandaged my arm with a handful of Kleenexes and a roll of scotch tape from some secretary's desk, and ran down stairs and let Larry in.

He used an office phone to call Darryl and tell him to come on. Shortly thereafter, we drove away in two ten-ton trucks with enormous steel snow plow blades in front. These we drove to the recycling plant.

J.C. had once worked at Area Farraday Recycling and this was the reason he had been brought in. Being J.C., he had made copies of all the keys in the place before he was fired. He had bragged about this to Larry and Darryl and they were impressed with his initiative and criminal instincts. My question, which went unanswered but not unpunished, was, "So what? What are you going to go back and steal out of a recycling plant?" As it turned out, months later I answered my own question.

When we arrived with the trucks, J.C. opened the loading bay doors and we backed in. J.C. actually did have a pretty respectable working knowledge of the place. I filled a ten-gallon bucket with diesel fuel and set it in the center of one of the truck beds. Darryl tossed me a roll of dynamite fuse he had swiped out of his dad's tool shed.

I tied a weight around one end and dropped it in the bucket. We left about a ten-foot tail of it hanging out the back of the truck and repeated this operation on the other truck. Next, the trucks were backed up under a chute that poured in a heaping load of pellets made from old truck tires. We then backed that joker up to huge spout which spewed forth massive amounts of recycled cooking oil. How much oil? I don't know. A lot. One heck of a lot. The smell was extremely unpleasant. Our next stop was the local high school.

Our new high school was a very big deal. What was referred to as 'the old school' had continued to operate many years after being condemned. The locals watched their kids play basketball in the same gym they had played in and it was old in their day. They joked about being able to turn on a light in the attic and see it in the basement. This was not a prosperous community and rising funds for this school was a long, drawn out process.

The new school was set well back from the road and somewhat outside the town proper. Our point of interest was the metal and auto shops. They both had huge bay doors similar to the ones at the recycling plant. The shops were on the back side of the school and faced into a wooded area. When the snow blades hit them, those suckers gave way like they were aluminum foil.

Darryl and I hopped out and went to work while Larry and JC were busy in the shop next door.

I grabbed a couple of huge shop fans and turned them on full blast, aiming them at the back of the truck.

Meanwhile Darryl was busy smashing out windows and doors with a sledge hammer to assure good air flow. At one point, he let out a huge rebel war whoop, which was answered by Larry, busy down the hall with the same task. Having the time of their lives. To them, the day was already a success; if it all ended right here, they would go home happy. I just shook my head. I wanted to make a cutting comment about their lack of professionalism, but it really was kind of funny. We stretched out the dynamite fuses, lit them and then headed into the woods.

J.C.'s car was parked right where it was supposed to be. So far, these guys had done everything they were supposed to and I have to admit, I was impressed. The smallest thing going sideways could have queered the whole deal. We made our way to J.C.'s newly painted car and drove downtown.

The new paint job was just one of many uphill battles I had to fight against this moron to bring this day's events to fruition. JC's plan was to steal two cars for this operation. After wasting several days with them kicking the logistics of that around, I finally spoke up, "*Or,*" I said loudly enough to be heard. They finally wound down and looked at me.

"Instead of committing a couple of extra felonies and having to hide two stolen cars from the cops and the rest of the world, we could just swipe a set of license plates, paint your car with white wash and call it good. A quick presto-change-o of plates, a hop, skip and zip through the carwash, and bam—howyadoin."

J.C. hated me most when I was right and he was wrong, but especially when I talked all jazzy like that. Which, of course, is why I couldn't resist. It was the only way I had to jab back at all the mean-spirited crap he sent my way. His face-saving out was to declare that since I was Mr. Big Shot and had all the answers, it would be my job to get the plates and paint and make it happen. "You want to run this outfit so bad, Squirt, start by running *that.*

Rather than fight another battle with this Neanderthal, I snuck out late that night, tossed a couple Big Macs to the dog inside and crawled over the fence in the local junk yard. I found plates that would work almost immediately and was home within an hour. The paint I bought with my own money and did a slap-dash job on JC's Buick the night before we set out. BFD.

We were sitting in a parking space downtown near the bank with all eyes focused on the skyline toward the north-east corner of town.

To all appearances, it was a bright, sunny day with nothing to mar the beautiful blue sky. As the minutes ticked by, I began to feel a little sick. After containing himself much longer than I would have guessed possible, J.C. began expressing his inability to deal with delayed gratification and frustration by cussing and fussing and carrying on in manner than suggested someone in this car was about to take the ass whipping of his life. Just when he had built up a semi-psychotic head of steam, Larry said quietly, "We got smoke."

Indeed we did. It had taken a bit longer than anticipated for the fuses to burn down to the diesel fuel and get the rubber pellets burning in that lovely, smoky way they have, but happen it did. With the shop fans feeding oxygen and directing the smoke, there was a huge, rapidly expanding cloud forming over that end of town which to me spoke of something Biblical. This was an ugly, black, roiling, pulsating, angry-looking cloud, growing larger by the moment. The reek of it was evident to us downtown and we were upwind.

Within moments, the whistle shrieked to life at the volunteer fire department a block away from where we were parked.

The town came to life, everybody heading in the direction of that oily, greasy-looking cloud of smoke. From our perspective, we could look toward the State Police post a couple miles out of town and see two of their cars screaming toward us. True to the script, they turned off on a side road that lead from the highway over to the school. Straight ahead of us we could see the county sheriff's department and watched their cars tear out toward the school. Not to be outdone, the city police were on their tails, lights flashing and sirens shrieking. Within minutes, we were sitting in a ghost town, with the local constabulary all accounted for. Simplicity itself. From the time I got out of bed that morning, everything had come off like clockwork.

I later learned that the smoke billowing out of those shops was so thick and the fire so hot, the fire trucks could not get within a hundred yards. As a bonus, the school building itself was in flames. The horrendous stink of it was overwhelming to the point that people several miles downwind evacuated their homes for the day.

Clothes hanging out to dry had be washed and rewashed for the smell and soot. Farm animals were protesting loudly in their pens.

As a diversionary tactic to occupy everyone's attention, it was a beautiful thing—although I am quick to admit, a bit overdone. I had no idea what a huge thing I was setting in motion.

We all had those over-the-head Halloween masks—Darryl as a pirate, J.C. Frankenstein, and Larry a gorilla. I was Tweedy Bird. From that point it was supposed to go just as you have seen a hundred times in the movies. We filed through the door in our masks to a bank lobby where you could hear crickets chirping. There was one teller, filing her nails, and someone making coffee in a side office. After I had robbed this same bank less than a year earlier, their insurance carrier insisted they hire an armed security guard. By the time that demand was actualized, the security guard turned out to be the bank president's retired father in law who spent his days snoozing in an easy chair by the door. J.C. was carrying a sawed-off shot gun and swung it like Casey at the Bat up against the old man's head—totally, *totally* unnecessary—and snatched his pistol. He began waving his gun around shouting at the two women in a cracked and strained voice that sounded more hysterical than threatening. Not at all the plan.

The stunned teller seemed more perplexed than intimidated. I was seriously worried that this idiot was actually going to shoot somebody. Darryl was nearest me; I looked at him and snapped, "Take control of that!"

Darryl turned to J.C. and shouted "Hey!" His voice was so loud, and so commanding, that J.C. stopped and looked at him dumbly. "Get your shit together and take care of your business!" Darryl hissed through his mask. He sounded scary. J.C. immediately calmed down, ran around the counter and began emptying cash drawers into a bag. The teller by now was petrified and just stood staring wide-eyed around her. I could see J.C.'s intent as he worked his way toward her.

"Darryl!" I said and nodded in that direction. He looked up and read the same thing I did.

"Don't you hit her", he shouted, dropping his bag and walking toward J.C. "Don't you hit that lady." J.C. was already holding the shot gun as though he were ready to swing it. He shifted it a bit so that his finger was on the trigger and turned it so that it was almost pointing at Darryl.

They stared daggers at each other for a few long moments, and then J.C. snorted a fake laugh and said, "Sorry. I didn't know this was your mother," and backed down. We emptied out all the cash drawers and grabbed what money there was in the vault, the door to which was left hanging conveniently open on Saturday mornings. On my way out, I grabbed a big bag of quarters and dimes sitting on a cart near the vault door. Change is money, too.

You can't imagine the thrill. Robbing a bank is an experience everyone should have at least once in their lives. I would do it for free. I cannot imagine that combat, or drugs, or skydiving or any of the other things people do for kicks can begin to equal the adrenaline rush of robbing a bank. As a pretty nice bennie, in the end, you have a big pile of cash money you get to call your very own. A classic win-win.

We ran out to the car and Darryl stood in front of the drivers' door so J.C. couldn't get in. "Give me the keys" he demanded.

"My car, I drive," J.C. shot back.

Larry spoke up, "Can we have this pissing contest some other time?"

Darryl didn't move. "I'm driving." Again with the staring contest. The clock was ticking and I was about to set off on foot when Darryl continued, "You're an idiot and I don't trust you. I'm driving."

Larry said, "J.C., give him the keys so we can out of here. You boys can get out the tape measure when we get home." Finally, J.C. slapped the keys into Darryl's hand and we got into the car.

Darryl started it up and eased away from the curb, driving non-chalantly along our prearranged route. I had a sense that everyone else in the car was sharing my vision of J.C. behind the wheel, squealing tires, car fishtailing down the street, swerving over the sidewalk, drawing the attention of anyone not at the fire. Nobody spoke. We should have been giddy, but tensions in the car were running high. J.C. was indeed an idiot, and Darryl really was a little crazy. Adrenalin was pumping and everybody had a gun. We had a formula brewing here that could lead to problems none of us needed.

A couple miles out of town, Darryl turned off onto a two-track that bisected our neighbor's corn field. About a half-mile in, a small creek traversed the property. We pulled up next to it and everyone went to work. My job was to remove the bogus license plates and dispose of them.

I pulled a shovel from the trunk, buried the plates about four feet deep, along with the masks, and then rolled a huge rock over on top. J.C.'s original plates were there where I had left them the night before and quickly snapped into place. Meanwhile the others were tossing buckets of water at the car and scrubbing it with brushes. The water-soluble paint disappeared.

Ten minutes after we turned off the black top, we were back on it in a whole different car, driving at the speed limit toward Larry and Darryl's house.

Back at the house, we dumped all the money out on the living room floor, and it was a beautiful thing. The sight of it broke the tension and there was a substantial amount of whooping and hollering and back-slapping until J.C. noticed the bag of change. He suddenly switched gears and started a tirade about how stupid I was and my pettiness could have jeopardized the whole operation and all kinds of general rot.

Everybody there understood that the whole tantrum, roughly translated, actually meant, *"Darryl really punked me out back there. I need to reestablish my credentials as a tough guy."* He wound all that up with the idea that since I loved nickels and dimes so much, that could just be my take. Chump change for a chump, and what does a snot-nose kid need with real money anyway.

He was getting himself all worked up with that notion when Larry quietly informed him on a tone that shut him up that I would get my fair share. J.C. Mumbled," Fine, whatever." That was the end of the conversation, but I had no illusions about it being the end of J.C.s' intention to cut my throat if he could.

Once we settled down to serious money counting, I put the trickiest part of my plan into effect. When nobody was looking, I pulled out a fifth of Old Grandad I had prepared earlier, and said, "I think a celebratory toast is in order." I pretended to take a big slug, and made a show of coughing and gagging. Predictably, J.C. snatched it away from me, making much of my being under aged and all his usual tripe. They went to passing the bottle around, each one passing it over my head.

I made eye contact with Larry and Darryl, they both just shrugged. They weren't going to make a full-time job out of coming to my defense. After a few minutes, I mumbled, "Oh shit," and laid down next to the sofa. They all got a huge laugh out of that.

I pretended to be passed out, biding my time, while the others started counting out the money. I had put a supreme effort into finding some roofies, but this was the boondocks and I was a kid. I settled for mashing up a dozen Benadryl and a few Valium and putting those in the whiskey.

I had hoped for something more dramatic as result. It appeared that they were drunker than they should have been from that amount of whiskey, but nobody was snoozing yet and it was getting increasingly difficult to lay still.

At one point, J.C. threw the bag of coins at me and said, "Here's your lunch money, Sleeping Beauty," and even Darryl laughed. What can you expect, I thought. This is the Big League. It's like they say, *If you can't run with the big dogs, stay on the porch.*"

I almost laughed out loud myself over the predictability of it. An argument broke out over the actual count, the way it was being split and whether or not J.C. was entitled to extra because it was his car. Three drunks with guns arguing over a pile of stolen money. Lovely. None of them seeing it as the greatest windfall that would ever come their way and being happy with what they had. Not for the first time, I damned the luck that made J.C. a part of this.

The argument calmed down after Larry remembered that his dad had some Wild Turkey stashed away and went to retrieve it. Soon they were seriously slurring their words and obviously winding down. The Benadryl and Valium finally catching up. About half way through the Wild Turkey, things got quiet in the room. I was about to sit up when I heard some movement behind me and kept still to see how it played out.

When I heard the bag of change being picked up, the whole picture appeared in my mind's eye like I was watching it on the silver screen.

J.C. had only pretended to be as drunk as the others and had just waited for them to pass out. He wasn't just looking to double-cross me, he wanted the entire take—even the dimes and quarters—and was on is way out the door with it. As soon as the door closed behind him, I ran and got my Uncle Dan's shot gun from the rack in the mud room.

J.C. had parked his Buick inside a small one-car garage when we drove in earlier. I heard the car just as I came out the back door. I stood with the shot gun to my shoulder, aimed directly where his face would be when he backed out, and waited. And waited. Finally, I crept over and peered through a small side window. J.C. was sitting behind the wheel, head back, snoring lightly. I went in, gathered up most of the money from the front seat, and left. I closed the garage door behind me. After I got to the house, I stopped and thought about it and decided it wasn't a good fit. I went back to the garage and already the small building was cloudy with exhaust fumes. I reached in and turned off the ignition.

The world certainly would have been a better place if I had just gone on about my business—but hey, why cross that line if you don't have to?

Inside, I split the money as best I could. I am not good with large numbers and was under a lot of stress—I really wanted to get out of there—but did my level best to make sure the brothers got their share. (Fuck J.C.) I scribbled out a quick note to Darryl explaining what J.C. had tried to do (blaming him for the drugged whiskey) and told him where their money was stashed. I stuffed that in his shirt pocket and then buried the money under a big pile of corn silage in the cow barn.

I counted out twenty-five hundred for my pocket, and buried the rest of mine in a spot where I was confident it would remain safe until I found my way back to this neighborhood. The one thing I knew for sure was that I needed to disappear.

I had given this matter much thought. Accepting that I was just a kid, and factoring that in, I knew I couldn't go roaming around the wide world with massive amounts of money. I had paid my sister $7.35 (that girl drives a hard bargain) to sew a concealed pocket into the lining of my leather jacket. Two thousand dollars went in there, the other five hundred in my pockets. One hundred in each pocket, one hundred in my wallet.

My cousin Augie, the youngest of that clan—and a pretty decent guy—had a 350 Honda with saddle bags. I packed a few belongings into the saddle bags and at the last second, went back and got the bag of coins.

I had left them on the seat next to J.C., loving the image of him waking up and gradually realizing that this was his cut. Then I thought, quarters and dimes are money too, and fuck J.C. Those are *my* quarters and dimes.

I knew some guys from a church camp I had been forced to attend who I thought of as kindred spirits. They now had a huge house in

Oklahoma City, to which I had an open invitation. That seemed far enough away for my purposes. I had always loved motorcycles and thought there was no such thing as getting enough. I envied those guys who did cross-county trips and basically lived on their machines. How does it get cooler than that? If you have ever asked yourself that philosophical question, here is a little exercise for you: Get out on the highway on two wheels, open that puppy up to sixty and hold it there for ten hours. At that point, if you are anything like me, you will reevaluate just how cool all that really is.

At the end of ten hours, I was ready to say "Uncle!" I was contemplating dumping the bike and catching a Greyhound.

By this time, though, it was late at night and I was far from a city big enough to have buses coming and going at all hours. I found out that checking into a motel looking like a fifteen-year-old, with no ID, is impossible. Exhausted, hungry and grappling with the nagging thought that I might not be quite as clever as I had thought, I ended up sleeping behind the dumpster at a 24-hour Shell station somewhere inside the Missouri state line. At dawn, I woke from a fitful, uncomfortable sleep, made breakfast of a couple Snickers bars, bought a tank of gas and got back on the road.

After a couple hours, I pulled off at another service station, in Joplin, Missouri, to ask directions to a Greyhound stop and use the restroom. Returning to the Honda, I realized that I was under the intense scrutiny of a local county deputy sheriff who could have been sent down from Central Casting.

I had never thought of Missouri as hillbilly country, but this old boy could have stepped onto the set of Hee Haw and fit right in. He sauntered toward me, pulling his belt up over his huge belly and said, "Is this heya yore motor- sicle, boy? I told him it was. "You look awful young to own a pretty blue machine like this. Yore daddy buy this for yew?" He was having huge fun and I knew he was toying with me, but what could I do?

I told him about working on my dad's farm and saving up my money for three years so I could get this as soon as I turned sixteen, hoping that chatting it up with him would help. He may have been a hayseed, but he knew from the word *go* that there was something wrong with this picture. "You a long way from home with a Michigan plate on this shiny new scooter," he observed. I told him I bought it used from a dealership in St. Louis, who had taken it as a trade-in just the day before. The conversation got friendly from there and he ended up saying, "Okay, Son, you have yoreself a good day and take it easy out there. Its real easy to get hurt on one of these things. They don't call them "murdercycles" for nothing." I assured him I'd be careful and wished him a good day.

Just as he was walking away and I gave a big mental "Whew!" he turned around said, "Well, you know, just so I can say I'm doin' my job and all—my boss is a real ball-buster—let's go through the formalities, and you can be on yore way. Just let me take a quick glance at yore license and registration, and I kin git home to my dinner. Might as well take a peek at your Proof of Insurance, too, as long as we're right here." It all went downhill from there.

When I feigned perplexity that I couldn't find my license in my pockets, he offered, "Well, lemme hep you look.

Mebbie it's in this this here saddle bag", and popped open the top of the one nearest him. With a grin that reminded me of crocodiles I had seen at Nature World, he asked, "You a coin collector, boy? Seems to me you got a lotta silver heya. All bundled up nice and neat in this here bag with a bank logo on the side. What a purdy bag.

Where does a fellah get a bag like this, innyway? I'd like to git one fer my missis, I do believe she'd get a kick out of that. Cat got yo tongue, boy?"

I stood and gave him my famous blank look and he finally said, "You need to say somethin' to make me feel good about you, boy, or yore young ass is gone ta be under arrest here and I mean right sudden." A few short moments later, I was handcuffed in the back of a police car.

At the jail, I maintained my blank stance. I thought, "What can they do to me?" There was no aspect of talking to them that would work to my favor. No lie I could tell that could not be tracked down and disproven. I decided to just go with passive resistance and see where it lead. I figured at worst I would end up in some juvenile facility somewhere and those are notoriously easy to slip out of. They had my five hundred dollars, and I had a receipt to prove it, but I didn't think anyone had found the two grand in my jacket. All things considered, I felt pretty good about my prospects.

The jail I was in was too small to have a juvenile wing, and as a minor I had to be kept separate from the adult offenders. The solution for this was to give me a huge cell—which normally would have held a dozen or more inmates—to myself. I had a television and plenty of reading material. The food wasn't nearly as bad as you might think. After the first few weeks, I was thinking I could do this indefinitely.

My balloon burst one quiet afternoon when the deputy who arrested me sauntered in and leaned against the bars to my cell. "You think you pretty clever, don't you, little Yankee boy?" he asked. I ignored him. "Sittin' here takin' advantage of our taxpayers feedin' you and keeping you in a warm bed at night. Still don't wanna talk? Guess whut? It don't matter no mo'. You got found out. Go on and pretend you don't heya me talkin' to yew boy, but I bet yore young ass will heya this: They's some folks from Michigan on the way here right this minute, even as we speak, and they mighty unhappy with yore young ass, you betcha.

They don't think yo act is funny at all. Not a-tall. Go wan an' laugh that one off, that's what you do" I didn't flinch, but my insides clenched. Damn! *Damnation!* He mentioned the specific county in Michigan, so they knew. How did they know? I did not sleep well that night.

When I continued to ignore him, he muttered, "I bet yore mama real proud of yew; I jes bet she is" Low blow, even for a red neck cop.

About mid-morning the next day, a court appointed attorney came to see me. Up until this point, I had refused to tell him anything. I was hugely relieved that he was there on this day, though. When I came into the room he laughed, "You look like you might be a little more open to conversation this morning", he observed.

"This whole thing of me being so amusing to all of ya'all is getting a bit stale," I told him. "Can you just tell me what my situation is?"

He did; my situation was that my cousin Augie had reported his motorcycle stolen, which for some reason surprised me. That information connected with the information put out there by the locals in Missouri, and, well, there you go. I told him I wanted to fight extradition. Again with the laugh. "You have been watching too much television. There is no fighting extradition. You are going back to Michigan to face the music. And for what it's worth, I think that is the best thing that could happen."

I told him it was a great feeling to know that I had a dedicated member of the Missouri bar going all out on my behalf. He took more umbrage to that than I had expected and leaned over the table with a very serious expression on his face. "Let me tell you something, young man," he began. "Actions have consequences.

That's life, and nowhere is it written that my job is to make sure that rule does not apply to you. My job is to see to it that your rights have not been violated. They have not been and they will not be. Extradition law is the most cut and dried law on the books. If you are the person named on an arrest warrant issued by the proper authorities in the State of Michigan, you *will* be extradited. Period. That is the law. And as far as that goes, you can't fight shit anyway. You are a juvenile. Even if there was a way to fight extradition—and there isn't—that way would not be open to you. You have been working the system here thinking you are going to out-smart everyone and walk away from here laughing, but reality has caught to you and you have just a few hours to grow up and start taking responsibility for your actions. You committed a man-sized crime and you need to man up and deal with it. Do you understand me, boy?"

I asked him if he practiced that speech in front of a mirror and he went away mad, but I felt like crap. I knew he was talking sense, but

I wasn't ready to face what was ahead of me. I just wanted to get to Oklahoma City and hide from all my problems.

Late the following afternoon two deputies from back home arrived to fetch me back.

I had made myself feel somewhat better overnight by practicing the argument that all they had on me was borrowing my cousin's motorcycle without permission. It was all a huge misunderstanding and I would apologize profusely. As far as all that change in Augie's saddle bags, well, I don't know where he got all that. I should have checked the saddle bags before setting out. My bad.

I knew both of the deputies. One used to go out with my older sister in high school. The other one was a volunteer football coach for a couple years after he graduated. I knew that in our present circumstances they couldn't be friendly toward me, but I was unprepared for their overt hostility.

I don't think I had ever used the word "loathing" in a sentence before, but that was the word that came to mind when I was trying to decipher the vibes these two were putting off. *Disappointment*, sure—a very adult position as they both knew me as a pretty decent kid from a really good family; *severe disapproval*, if they assumed I was part of the robbery, of course; some degree of disgust, even, if they believed I had turned my back on my upbringing and shamed my family, fair enough.

But, but *loathing*, and a barely concealed anger along with a very real sense that they seriously wanted to knock me around for a while before throwing me in the back of their transport car. I looked at the one who used to go out with my sister and said, "Hey Reggie. Long time, no see."

He gave me a stone-faced look and told me to use the rest room now because there would be no stopping along the way. End of conversation. On the highway, they turned on their flashers, set the cruise control at 90 and set off for home sweet home. There was no conversation and, as advertised, no bathroom breaks. Everybody there gave me the same treatment when I got to the county jail.

The next day I was taken to court for an arraignment, which was postponed, but the judge did appoint a lawyer. I got the story from him later that day. It left me feeling small, and, I have to admit it, ashamed of myself. I knew that people were proud of that new school, but I didn't get how emotional it was. I learned that there were people who actually stood watching that fire and wept. People who had worked for years trying to bring it all together and had finally succeeded in giving our little community something to be proud of. They saw that school as hope for their children's future, that they would get good educations and go on to a bigger and better life than they themselves had had.

That school said that we were not just some little no-account bunch of rubes out here in Nowhereville.

We had us a school to rival any in the region and we were damn proud of it.

The damage done was way, *way* beyond what I had contemplated. The school's insurance deductible was in the six figures. They couldn't afford anything fancier. Everything in the shops was destroyed. The fire had burned so hot that the structural integrity of the building was compromised and that whole end of the school was shut down. There was no part of the school unaffected. They reckoned they would never get that horrid smell out completely. The gym floor was warped and peeled, the whole thing needed to be rebuilt and refinished. State inspectors said *No Way* would the cafeteria be allowed to serve meals until a long list demands had been met. The farthest nooks and crannies in the building were caked with grimy, oily soot that didn't let go easily. All of the machines in the typewriter room were caked with the awful soot from that fire.

Likewise, the band instruments. There were a couple of volunteers who came in and took each one apart, cleaned and oiled them, and reassembled them one by one.

There were volunteers arriving in groups with buckets and scrub brushes, literally scrubbing the floors on their knees to remove the residue of that fire. All of the local groups—Jaycees, Eagles, the IOOF, all the church lady groups—coordinated together to organize fund raisers to help rehab the school. That school was the legacy our parent's generation passed on to their children and grandchildren in hopes that they would have a better life. And then I burned it down so that I could rob the local bank of their life savings while they were distracted by the fire. I had never felt lower.

It didn't end there. The old man J.C. had cracked in the head with his sawed-off never really recovered. He was actually in a coma for several days, from which he gradually emerged with an array of physical and psychological issues he was expected to never recover from.

Firefighters at the school had developed COPD and other related health issues from working in that smoke without the proper breathing equipment. The list went on. Lawyers from all over the state were lobbying everyone who was downwind of the fire to sue for all kinds of real and imaged damages. There were so many aspects to this thing—each and every one utterly wretched—that I never could have imagined.

I'm not even going to touch on what this did to my family. Actions have consequences, the man said. True that.

First thing my court appointed lawyer said was that I deserved to be chained to a wall and be kicked in my ass every day for the rest of my life. Once again, I was left with the suspicion that my legal defense might be lacking. There was more bad news. My cousin Darryl was found slumped over the wheel of his brand-new Delta 88 outside a whorehouse in Niagara Falls, New York, with a .38 slug in his brain. There was no trace of any money on his person, in the pretty red car, or in the motel room he had rented two days earlier.

I was sick. Darryl was an alright guy. I always felt kind of sorry for him. It seemed like he couldn't get a break in life. He was just always somewhat out of step and had a sadness about him that made you want to do something to ease his burden. After he got beat up so bad down in Mississippi that time, he was even worse off than ever and never really got over it. I can't remember seeing him smile. He wasn't a bad guy; I never understood why he attracted so much hard luck and trouble. I had hoped having a big chunk of cash would help.

That murder was mean enough and cowardly enough to have been J.C.'s work, although I had never thought of him as actually homicidal. I guess being humiliated by Darryl during the robbery, and ending up with no money from the take could have pushed him to it. Another consequence that never occurred to me. If J.C. did do that, he got away with it. When he showed up back in town a week or so later, the cops already had suspicions about him and hauled him in just to see what they could sweat out of him.

Almost immediately, he told it all. His version of events put absolutely all of the blame squarely on me. In J.C.'s telling of it, I was the devil and he was a victim. He vehemently denied involvement in Darryl's murder, while suggesting they take a close look at me for that, but could offer no alibi for himself during that time frame. Based on information garnered from J.C., Larry was arrested and also came clean.

Larry did me a solid, though. I think he appreciated the idea that I made sure he and Darryl got their slice of the pie. Obviously I could have walked off with all of it, but I did right by the brothers and now he was sending it back to me. He took pains to minimize my involvement and recounted numerous examples of J.C. bullying me. He told how all along J.C. insisted that all I should get was the quarters and dimes and how he had tossed the bag at me while I was sleeping and said that was my cut. He had no knowledge of me getting anything other than that. There was no evidence anywhere that I got anything beyond that, and he made them acknowledge that. The cops didn't like me and wanted to accept J.C.'s story, but Larry's story made more sense.

When they asked J.C. about the discrepancies, he admitted that what Larry said was true, but that he was just kidding about all that and be wasn't bullying me, he just had poor people skills and played too rough sometimes. He sounded mealy mouth and pathetic even to those who wanted to side with him.

The insiders—cops, lawyers, court people—were able to piece together a fairly accurate account of what had transpired and they had a pretty concise picture of J.C. Those people were a small minority, though; to the public at large I was a monster.

I attribute that largely to the local news media. In reality, the story of a fifteen-year-old master mind operating a "bank robbery ring" was just too sexy to pass up. I was told they had never sold as many papers. Their manufactured stories about me were breaking all sales records. They didn't even have to lie, they just had to print J.C.'s confession and later interviews with him and follow up with all kinds of editorials and vaguely related stories.

They ran a piece by a prominent child psychologist about recognizing the signs of psychopathology in children right next to my picture. That kind of thing. The public ate it up. When they reported Darryl's murder in a story side by side with yet another story about me, noting that it took place during the time I was "missing", the locals went bananas. Everybody pretended they didn't know that I was "missing" in a jail in Joplin, Missouri. People like to make believe they are skeptics, but they believe what they are told to believe. If they read it in the newspaper, it is true.

The old boys who owned and operated the court system—like their counterparts in every court house in the country—were ultimately politicians. They were voted into office, or came in on the coattails of someone who was, and depended on the good opinion of voters for their paycheck. To them I was an opportunity. They disliked me personally—something about my attitude in regard to public servants—so it was easy for them to get on that bandwagon. If the voting public needed to see me as the personification of all evil on earth, then so be it. This whole dog and pony show was literally the crime of the century in this little hole in the wall and everyone clamored to make the most of it. The old *Tough on Crime* position seemed to be the favored approach. I didn't stand a chance.

Don't misunderstand; I'm not claiming actual innocence here. I'm not saying they were too hard on me. I don't offer it as a defense to say I had no idea what I was doing or any awareness of the possible ramifications of the actions I took. I didn't intend to hurt all those people. I'm sorry that I did. I am not expressing self-pity here. I am expressing my repugnance for those hyenas who exploited the situation for their own personal gain, somehow making themselves morally superior to me in the process. My disgust for all those small town hot shots who were so giddy over the opportunity to use me for their self-promotion knows no bounds.

Anyway, when the final clown car was put away the last balloon popped and all the confetti all swept up, the Court went with what they knew from the git-go was the one and only option available to them. They sentenced me to be confined to a to a juvenile facility until my eighteenth birthday.

A bit more than two and a half years. No joke, but really, a gift from heaven. My two remaining co-defendants would have happily traded places with me.

Larry got a break in that the teller who had been in the bank that morning thought it was him who had stopped J.C. from clocking her with the shot gun.

Considering the damage J.C. had done to the old man, this was no small thing. Larry also had no arrest history and was widely known as a hardworking guy who was easily influenced; he was seen as having been taken advantage of and pulled off onto the wrong track.

At the same time, however, this was a serious crime with multiple victims and an attached homicide. Larry was sentenced to twenty-five to fifty years in federal prison with credit for time served in the county jail and a note to the Federal Board of Pardons and Parole that the court would not object to his early release if that august body saw fit to recommend such. Twenty-five years is a big number, but that was for public consumption and to benefit the judge's reelection campaign. With the way the federal system works, all things considered, smart money said he'd probably do about five years, maybe less.

J. C's lawyer had a much tougher time of it. There wasn't much you could say for the boy. He was what he was and there was little mystery to it. His lawyer carried on way too long about how J.C. had cooperated with the police, and that his cooperation lead to the arrest of other perpetrators in this heinous crime. It all fell flat.

Any sympathy he may have garnered was neutralized when a spokesman for the family of the security guard re-defined J.C.'s "cooperation" as a "cowardly act of ratting out his friends and co-conspirators in hopes of circumventing justice." He was able to say things no lawyer would have been allowed to regarding J.C.'s involvement in Darryl's murder. Ultimately J.C. received a life sentence and was transferred to the federal prison at Milan within forty eight hours. His file had a note attached saying there had been widespread media coverage of his *cooperation with police* and that he may be seen as a police informant by other inmates and in need of protective custody.

Meanwhile, I—the Master Mind and driving force behind this outrage—was being sent off to a "boy's home" for mere thirty-four months. It rankled in some quarters. What joy they would have experienced, though, to have a real understanding of what that facility was.

J.W. Franklin School was a nightmare. All my imaginings of what I was heading into were so far off the mark as to not be in the same universe with reality. Most mistaken by far was my fantasy of how easy it was to escape from a juvenile facility. The biggest break I got (aside from my sentence) was that I was dressed out in my own clothes for transport to Franklin. I wore my leather jacket—with the concealed $2,000.00—and was allowed to keep it.

J.W. Franklin Facility features what is called "open housing" which is newspeak for barracks.

The noise settled down to a moderate roar sometime during the wee hours for a very short time. At all other times, it was deafening. These clowns didn't talk, they yelled. They slammed drawers and doors. Radios were always on maximum volume. Any way one can possibly make noise they exploited to the fullest. They loved and seemed to thrive on noise and chaos. Everything was filthy and smelled of the damp mustiness of unwashed bedding and unwashed bodies.

There is zero privacy any time of the day or night. In the communal bathroom, toilets are separated by plywood panels four feet high—the width of a sheet of plywood. Showers are plumbing fixtures that hang from the ceiling and spray straight down. The water is always ultra-hot and blasting, adjusted so that it strikes like pins and needles. All of this is absolutely in the open surrounded by a six-inch-high border to direct runoff water to a drain. The food was atrocious.

But never mind that. What made Franklin miserable—as is the case in any lock-up—was the inmates. Overwhelmingly inner-city, illiterate, uncivilized, brain dead, violent and with bad teeth. It was truly staggering how savage these individuals were. Almost without exception, they were incarcerated for crimes of mindless violence. Some were violent sex crimes, some were violent robberies, some were just random assaults.

They seemed to believe the highest calling in life was to hurt someone. They didn't appear to care who. Anytime of the night or day you could look around and see a fight in progress. It was commonplace to see someone pick up an object and smash someone else in the face with it. Explanations for such assaults could be "I didn't like the way that fool looked at me," to "I never did like that sucker." And that's not to mention the gang warfare.

The protocol for gang members was that whenever you see someone of a rival gang, you attack—without hesitation, without any actual provocation, without fear of consequences, with whatever you can pick up, with your fists if nothing else. Absolute insanity. I asked one of those guys once what that was all about, like, what is *the point* of all that. He acted like I had just asked him to decipher the theory of nuclear fusion. I don't think any of those clowns knew the "why" of it beyond the idea that "this is what we *do*." I didn't see much of a future for any of them.

My reputation had preceded me to this little corner of Paradise, which was a double-edged sword. Everybody knew that I had been involved in an actual bank robbery and that most of the money had not been recovered. The population was about evenly split: One half wanted to be my best bud and hope to find out where my money was stashed, and the other half wanted to rip the information out of me. This was not just the inmate population, but also much of staff.

Staff tended toward being friendly and solicitous rather than threatening and intimidating. As such things tend to do in jail, my fortune was grossly over estimated. Word was that it was at least a million dollars, and probably more. The details were exaggerated also; the story most commonly repeated involved a running gun battle with the cops and a professional hit on one of my partners after the fact. I was extremely high profile. I chatted up a couple gang guys; they kept an eye on me and ran off anyone who approached looking to put the squeeze on me. I knew that someday there would be a bill to pay there, but I was just living day to day. It worked out, but I couldn't imagine doing almost two and a half years like this. I kept my eyes open for any crack I could wriggle through.

The staff people who were friendly toward me kept finding ways to get me alone and try to have serious conversations with me. There were different approaches...

"You know, Son, if you need someone to talk to..." "Obviously you are a cut above the average guy around here, maybe I can get you a job over in my department...If there is ever anything special you need that isn't on the approved commissary list, come and talk to me..." It never ended. I trusted them less than I did these guys in the barracks.

One day I was summoned to the Superindent's office, which is something that never happens. He was a large man with a Teddy Roosevelt mustache. He told me that he had some staff people on the way over for a little pow wow and told me that much of what he was going to say was codswallop (*codswallop?*) but for my own good, he expected me to go along with it. "Let's not you and I get off on the wrong foot, okay, Son?"

About that time several department heads arrived and we all took a seat. The Super went into a drawn-out speech about the attention I had been getting from certain staff people, "It is not necessary to mention names, that is not what this is about," he assured everyone.

"But I want you all to know that I have had several extensive conversations with the Michigan State Police, the FBI, and certain county officials who have informed me that most of the money from that robbery has been recovered; most of the rest of it is believed to have been frittered away by his—pointing at me—adult codefendants. All this young man ever realized for his efforts in that famous robbery was a bag of quarters and dimes. And even that was recovered and returned to the Treasury Department.

In short, ladies and gentlemen, there is no Lost Dutchman's Mine." This got a bunch of confused looks. The Super looked peeved. You could tell he really liked that line. "There is no hidden stash of bank loot" He clarified. Do you have anything to add, Son?" he asked me. All eyes came my way.

"All of that is true, "I said. "I don't know where all these stories came from. I have never claimed to have any money stashed away. I rode away on my cousin's motorcycle with a bag of quarters and dimes and the cops in Missouri took that. All I got out of that robbery is a lot of grief," I concluded.

"From the horse's mouth," the Super wrapped up. "Please, I'm asking you as a favor to me, *please* go back and repeat this conversation to as many of your subordinates and co-workers as possible. Dismissed."

After they left, he put his hand on my arm and said, "You did well, Son. I know there is still a substantial amount of money unaccounted for. Maybe you have it, maybe not. Not my concern. I have an institution to run and I needed to put all that treasure-hunting to bed. Stick with that story and we won't have any problems, okay?" I agreed that we didn't want any problems and was sent back to the barracks.

Of all the people I got special attention from, the one that most concerned me was Knuckles.

Knuckles was a maintenance worker for the facility and was said to have the longest seniority of all the employees. Knuckles was a strange looking little man, probably five foot seven with a hunched appearance. He was sort of bow-legged and his arms were too long. Knuckles had thick black hair with grey streaks. Even though his body appeared to be somewhat deformed, he gave the impression of being abnormally strong. His real oddity, and the origin of his name, however, was his hands. This man had enormous hands. They looked to be nearly twice the normal size. I often felt him looking at me. Finally, one day a couple weeks after my meeting in the Super's office, he made his approach.

"I'm not stupid," he said by way of introduction. "And I know disinformation when I hear it. You have a big knot of cash hidden away somewhere." It was not a question. You are not a regular dummy, playing it close to the vest, playing these idiot bangers against each other for protection. I asked him where we were going with this. You've got style, kid, I'll give you that." I asked him where we were going with this.

"I'm telling you why I trust you," he said. "Why do you care? Because I am the guy who can walk you out that front gate."

"Say more," I said. There wasn't much more to say, really. I wanted out of there, he wanted my money. I told him I had eighty-eight thousand dollars, but it was a number I grabbed out of thin air. I didn't count it like that when I made the split. I'd pick up a hand full of bundles and split it two ways: three bundles of twenties here, a bundle of fifties and one bundle of tens there, six bundles of tens in this pile, and so on. As far as an actual tally, it never happened. The feds were throwing all kinds of numbers around, but nobody knew for sure.

One of the interesting aspects of bank robbery that they do not teach in high school civics class is that everybody is motivated to lie. If your bank is robbed, that means any amount of money missing can be ascribed to the robbers. You can walk into your own vault and stuff whatever is left into your pockets and who will know or care? The robbers took it. If you have been embezzling, the slate is wiped clean, and shortages are blamed on the robbers. Made some bad investments? Juggle the books a little to call that money cash, and boom, it never happened.

Banks are insured, and like any other insurance settlement, bankers do their damnedest to scam their insurance company for a fatter check.

Police and prosecutors exaggerate the numbers because the bigger the number, the bigger a crime they solved and get to use for their own aggrandizement. Finally, the thief is always going to lie. To his friends and those he wants to impress, he will inflate the number. In other circumstances, he will lie the other way. Eight-eight grand seemed like a nice round figure for my purposes in this conversation. " "Closer to one hundred and thirty-five thousand", Knuckles said, "I already told you, I'm not stupid. I did my homework on this. But what's few grand between friends?"

"We're friends now are we?" I asked.

"Enough playing footsie," Knuckles snapped, instantly angry. "You want out of this motherfucker or not?"

"Yeah", I said, "I want out. Are you asking as a friend or as a guy who wants all my money"?

He chuckled, "Like I said, you got style. The truth is, I *am* your friend, that's why I only want *half* of your money. We both know you'd turn it all over, but I'm not greedy. And let's stop talking baby-talk.

"Fine," I said. "You are welcome to half. How soon can we leave?"

The delightful answer to that question was "Right now." And just like that, I was gone.

Probably the oldest trick in prison movies. The old hide-in-the-laundry-cart move. And there I was, in the back of a ten-ton truck with the facility name on the side, and half a ton of damp, smelly laundry piled on top of me. It was extremely gross.

At Franklin, as in other joints, inmates turn in their laundry in mesh bags with a tie around the tops. These bags are tossed into carts that are then rolled to a staging area and loaded onto trucks. Those trucks then carry it to a central laundry. There are different sized carts that serve different purposes. I was in the bottom of the largest cart, which was placed in the part of the truck bed farthest from the gate. To find me, the searchers would have to remove every cart, and dig through a lot of very nasty laundry bags. It just wasn't going to happen.

Inmates don't escape like this for real because these trucks are locked shut when loaded and unlocked when they are safely inside the receiving institution. What are you going to do—escape into another joint? In this case, Knuckles was the guy with the keys. I felt the truck stop at the entrance and could hear voices, and then we were on the highway.

Knuckles had explained that the institution's laundry was delivered to the state prison in Jackson every Tuesday afternoon and picked up every Thursday morning. He had been making this run every week for over twenty years. Normally trucks leaving through that gate were inspected pretty thoroughly, but he had been doing this for so long, and most people he worked with were so lazy, that now they just waved him through. He told me that his employment record was unblemished and nobody ever really paid him no mind.

He had been putting off his retirement just waiting for someone like me to come along. We were the answer to each other's prayers.

After riding in that miserable truck for about forty-five minutes we stopped and I heard the back gate roll up. It seemed to take forever for Knuckles to dig me out. He got me out on the road and pointed to a farm house across a field from where we were standing. Go over to that house and wait for me. If you are not there when I get back, I will kill everybody in your family."

He took a folded piece of paper from his pocket and read off my parents address and said the names of everybody that lived in that house. "I told you, I'm not stupid. I'm going to deliver this truck and you *will* be here when I get back." I started to say something and he barked, "Don't!" Don't say it.

Just do as your told and we'll part company like gentlemen." And then he was off. What else could I do?

I walked over to the farm house and waited for him.

He had crossed a line, though, and I knew I would have no problem sticking it to him if the opportunity arose. I would be looking for that opportunity.

The farmhouse was empty and abandoned. To pass the time I explored the house and outbuildings. I found nothing of particular interest. Which is to say, I couldn't find anything to use as a weapon. I wanted something I could conceal, like a pitchfork tine or some such thing. I had a bad feeling about the way this thing with Knuckles was going and thought I'd feel better with a little equalizer close at hand.

I was actually better off without it. When Knuckles came back the first thing he wanted to do was frisk me. When I resisted that idea, he pulled a gun and told me he wasn't going to ask again. I let him feel me up while he held the pistol against my side. "Does this mean we aren't friends anymore?" He said he was just making sure. I started to speak again and he told me to shut up. He seemed pretty emphatic about it. (What's that old expression—*Out of the frying pan and into the fire?*)

Knuckles had a van outside and told me to get in it. He wanted to know where the money was stashed and I gave him a location in the county I was from, assuming he would know—he not being stupid and all—where I was from. He demanded specifics and I told him that was impossible.

I said I could go right to it because I knew the area, which was in the woods of a farm where I used to play as a kid. You had to go down a path and turn off where there is a chink in the river and where my cousin Bobby shot a deer when he was twelve. I don't even know the name of the road it's on, I just know how to get there. I know how to get through those woods, but I don't know how on earth to describe that to somebody. Knuckles was getting very agitated.

And I was getting increasingly nervous. I had assumed he just intended to take all the money and leave me high and dry. That assessment now seemed optimistic. I think the plan here was for me to be found in the same condition as my cousin Darryl. As I was pondering this unpleasant reality, I noticed that there was no door handle on my side. "Hey Knuck," said in a friendly town, "like maybe could have an actual conversation like friends do on a long drive in the night, "You know that guy over in Dorm B with the…"

"I told you to shut up!" Knuckles screamed. Then he was off on a tear telling me I better not be thinking about double crossing him and he wasn't stupid, if I was one of those guys who thought he was stupid, he would show me a thing or two, he'd done it before, and he was off to the races. This guy was a genuine psycho. I noticed his huge hands were griping the wheel like he wanted to pinch it in half and he was sweating profusely. Maybe it was setting in on him what a serious crime he had committed carrying me out of Franklin and he was thinking the suspicion would fall on him, I told myself, stretching for a reasonable explanation for this erratic behavior. Whatever dialog he had going on in is head was doing a number on him because he was getting more and more jumpy by the minute. It was getting less and less likely we would part company as gentlemen do. I made one more attempt to say something to calm him down when that huge right mitt flew off the steering wheel and smacked me across the face. It was like running into a brick wall.

Now I was officially scared. My nose was bleeding like a facet and Knuckles was carrying on about something else. His ranting took on a different timber and he seemed to be off on a whole new subject. Through the fog in my recently addled head I understood that the big guy had just realized that he was low on gas. He got enough of a grip on himself to remind me that I was a fugitive from justice and he had a gun. At any point he could claim that I escaped from the school and he had captured me and was taking me back. Anybody would believe that. He advised me to just sit still and play it cool because I couldn't get out my side and he was going to be over there on his side pumping gas and it would be a real shame if he had to shoot me when I tried to escape again. He was deep into a role, like he was auditioning for a play, talking more to himself than to me. He told me get into the back of the van, leaned in and pointed that .38 at me with the reminder. "I can shoot you any time and no one will say I was wrong. Think of that before you try something slick."

We pulled into a service station and I knew my opportunity as soon as I saw it. There was an elderly couple in a Cadillac Seville at the pumps next to us. I smeared blood on the window and wrote HELP ME in it with my finger. By waving my hands back and forth, I finally caught the old guy's attention, but he seemed to think it was a prank. I could hear Knuckles slide the gas nozzle in so I knew he was at the back of the van and couldn't see me. I got back up front and rolled down my window and got his wife's attention. My bloody face got the reaction from her I was hoping for. In a stage whisper, I said, "He's got a gun!"

A few quick words between them and the Caddie peeled out. My heart sank, but then I realized that it just swerved around to the front of the station. They both went in.

I could see them talking to the guy behind the counter. He handed his phone to the lady and reached under the counter. I couldn't tell for sure, but it looked like he had a pistol in his hand as he drew it back.

He came out of the station walking toward Knuckles as though he fantasized about such an encounter every day. When he was within 20 feet of the van, I dove out the window. I heard Knuckles shout "Hey!" and another voice holler, "Sir! Drop your weapon. Now!" I was out the window and sprinting toward the carwash at the back of the lot, just to put something between Knuckles and me (and the cops who would soon be arriving). I heard three gunshots.

No way to know for sure, but it sounded to me like there were two different guns talking.

Luck was with me. As I came around the corner of the car wash, there was a guy who had just pulled his still-dripping car up near the rest rooms and was getting out. I was sprinting full tilt and didn't slow down. I dropped a shoulder and rammed into this poor schmuck full force. He sprawled, his car keys flew and I scooped them up, was behind the wheel and peeling out before his head began to clear.

I didn't even look over in the direction of Knuckles' van, but peeled out into the night. That stolen car carried me to Kalamazoo, where I left it with a full tank of gas—the least I could do, I thought—about six blocks from the Greyhound station. Those nice people took me the rest of the way to Oklahoma City.

Oak City turned out to be a bust. At church camp I had a lot in common with these guys because we were all misfits. In the free world, though, we were on different wavelengths. Their idea of having fun and being outrageous was to get drunk and make lewd comments to women on the sidewalk downtown. They'd go to the mall and tell teen age girls what a treat they could have if they weren't jail bait. What a bunch of morons. Fortunately for me, I was wearing my magic leather jacket and could pull solutions from the secret pocket sis had sewn in for me.

I had no ID and needed to be careful, but was able to break away from those clowns long enough to meet some people on my own. About the third week there, I got invited to visit a commune in the Rocky Mountains of Colorado. That visit turned into a two and a half year stay and I spent that time smoking weed, gardening, and walking around naked much of the time. I often thought, *this is better than JW Franklin.*

One time I thought, *I wonder whatever happened to Knuckles.* And then I thought, *No, I don't. I don't give a rat's ass what happened to Knuckles.*

The law has no answer for a guy like me. When I turned eighteen, I was free. They couldn't stick me back in a juvenile facility because I wasn't a juvenile. They couldn't send me to an adult prison because I had no adult convictions. Double jeopardy laws prevented them from re-trying me in adult court. I became a free citizen at the age of eighteen, just about the time I felt like I was outgrowing the commune. I wrote the county court back home for a copy of my birth certificate, with no reservations about giving them my actual address. I got a Colorado driver's license, and set out to see the world.

I'd had it in mind all along to find a way redeem myself with my family. They didn't deserve all the crappiness I had brought their way. I thought seriously about joining the army, which is always a hit with folks in the heartland. In the end, I settled into an artist's community in New Mexico, got a PELL grant and part time job and took classes in American History so I could tell the folks back home I was studying to be a teacher. Mostly just biding my time.

Papers back there made much of the idea that I had once again beat the system, which gave them an excuse to run the entire series of stories again and get everyone all riled up one more time.

They created such a toxic environment for me, I didn't dare go anywhere near the old homestead. I was willing to be patient, though. Life was pleasant, and that money wasn't going anywhere.

At the conclusion of my second semester of college, things seemed quiet enough on the Homefront that I should be able to slip into town, meet with the fam, show off my report cards, and go dig up my money. I thought that, because life is usually that simple and things normally go that smoothly. And it did for a couple days. Sunday dinner with the old folks, me saying all the appropriate things, they in turn considering the possibility that I had grown out of my youthful rambunctiousness. I drove past my Uncle Dan's farm and at a glance could see that the area where my money was buried remained undisturbed.

To this point, my cousin Larry was the only one who knew that I'd had a chunk of that money in my possession at one time, and he hadn't said a word.

I was pretty sure he had a stash, too, because it would have taken some serious effort to just blow all the money that was unaccounted for when he was arrested. I hoped he had a little nest egg to come home to.

After I had been in town a few days, I ran into some old friends who insisted we make the rounds. Why not? We stopped by and dropped in on people I'd been cool with in high school, most of them married now, many with a kid or two. Some in college. It was pretty neat to see the old crowd again. None of these people hated me for burning their school down.

A couple did see fit to mention that the place still smells funny, but it was all friendly and joking around. Later on, we hit a couple bars. I was getting tired and just about to wrap things up when we were leaving a dive called Mr. Friendly's. I stepped outside and came face to face with Mr. Julius Charles himself. In the flesh. Imagine my surprise.

J.C. let go a primal growl, his face contorted with a deeply-felt hatred and he went berserk. Without hesitation, he lit into me with fists flying, and believe me, they were landing. He tagged me a good six or eight times before I could lift my hands up to block them. I fell backward over the curb.

The way I fell left a parking meter and fire hydrant between us so I had two or three seconds—significant time in a situation like this—to reach around for something to work with. A lesson learned at J.W. Franklin. As luck would have it, there were several chunks of concrete that had broken loose from the curb within reach. I grabbed one and flung it as hard as I could at J.C. as he made his approach to kick me. That concrete thunked him in the forehead and he staggered back a few steps—right into the path of an oncoming car and the end of his existence on this planet.

My mission on this trip had been to mend fences with my family and show them that I was no longer the burner-down-of-schools or the robber-of-lifesavings of my misspent youth, but a mature and responsible young man ready to go forth and make an honest contribution to the world I live in. Then I got into a drunken brawl outside a sleazy bar six miles from their front door and killed a guy I had robbed a bank with when I was in Jr. High. I wasn't going to be able to hang a Mission Accomplished banner on this one.

The explanation for J.C.'s presence went back to that guy who spoke on behalf of the security guard's family. Since he was not an officer of the court and was only there delivering a Victim Impact Statement, the court had given him leeway to speak his piece. Way too much, according to the Sixth Circuit Federal Court of Appeals.

Tying J.C. to Darryl's murder when that was not supported by the evidence was certain to have made an impact on the jury, and therefore tainted the proceedings, they declared. They further declared those proceedings null and void and sent the matter back for retrial. At that point, J.C. was on the same legal status he'd been on when he was first arrested, and the court set a bond. Somehow, he came up with a substantial amount of cash, (think about that for a moment) and viola—there he was heading into Mr. Friendly's.

I was arrested and charged with first degree murder, which, of course, was absurd. There were numerous witnesses to the event and they all told the story the way it happened. The court would not reduce the charge or offer the jury an option to choose a lesser charge. I was planning to grab that money on my way out of town and hadn't gone near it yet, so I was essentially broke and ended up in court with another good old boy court-appointed lawyer. It just kept getting better.

In the matter of J.C.'s demise, all the evidence from the original fire and bank robbery was paraded in front of the jury, the fact that I was incarcerated for only a few months, that this was the second homicide tied to that crime, and on and on, and the jury, who remembered my name well from before, was seething in their seats.

There was no question in any quarter that I would be convicted and sentenced to Natural Life in prison. The sentence means just that. Incarcerated for the remainder of your natural life on this earth.

Just as proceedings were winding down, I caught an amazing break. A fancy big city lawyer—Mr. Kelly Arthur Madigan III—came to visit me in the county. He instructed me to call him Kelly and explained that my parents had mortgaged their home to hire him and he was confident he could do something about the charges against me.

I was really touched. It never occurred to me to ask my folks for that kind of help. I could hardly bare to face them.

Obviously, I was grossly over-charged and obviously, my court-appointed attorney was grossly incompetent. He was dismissed and Kelly filed a bunch of motions that really caused a lot of excitement in local legal circles. The trial was put on hold for a couple days while the judge and prosecutors tried to sift through them. The strategy was to overwhelm them with paperwork. The Court had to respond to everything filed and it was an enormous job.

After they had a few days to really appreciate the job in front of them, my team would step in and say, Hey, all we want are reduced charges.

Reduce the charge to Manslaughter and give the jury an option to dismiss entirely, and we will withdraw the motions.

It should have worked. Instead, the prosecutor found some money in the budget to hire a couple legal-eagles to come in and work on those motions exclusively. Naturally, the judge denied them all. We knew he would, but the denials had to come in the form of lucid, cogent legal arguments.

Kelly wasn't done. He told me that his motions weren't all just smoke and mirrors. He had filed for some perfectly legitimate requests. The judge's denial of everything, plus his insistence that I be over-charged gave my team plenty of ammunition to file for an Emergency Consideration hearing in the Court of Appeals.

To not get bogged down in a lot of legalese, I'll suffice it to say when the local prosecutor showed up to make oral arguments before that august body, he was scolded like a bratty child. There were some choice comments for the judge also. This kind of thing is by far the worst nightmare any lower court judge or prosecutor can face. It is rare for the justices to be so expressive, but they weren't holding back. They declared that I was obviously over-charged and ordered that First-Degree Murder be taken off the table entirely. I could be charged only with crimes whose definition fit the facts on record. The judge and prosecutor were thoroughly cowed by this rebuke from the higher court. When my trial resumed, there were new jury instructions. They were given the option of finding me guilty of Manslaughter—which carries a maximum sentence of 15 years—or the lesser included offense of Involuntary Manslaughter or Not Guilty.

Kelly made a valiant effort, beseeching the jury to consider only the facts of the crime, and not their feelings about me personally. It was well done, but in a small town full of small-minded and angry people, there was little chance of a break. As far as they were concerned, by getting that Appeals Court ruling, I had yet again beat the system. They weren't going to go easy. I was found guilty of Manslaughter with recommendations for the maximum sentence, which is 12 ½ to 15 years.

Kelly wasn't going for it. He requested a conference with the judge and prosecutor in chambers, and gave them copies of the appeal he would file that day if I was sentenced to anything beyond 3 to 15. The appeal detailed all of the shenanigans perpetrated thus far, and concentrated on the idea that there should have been a change of venue, due to the obvious bias against me.

He assured them this paperwork would be filed with the same higher court justices who had so recently slapped them down in public. They both blanched.

Every day people have no idea. In law, as in politics, the real stuff goes on behind the scenes. Court room procedures are there for public consumption. We may as well have had rehearsals to make sure everybody played their roles properly and got their lines straight.

In the end, I agreed to accept five to fifteen years without a fuss, as long as that was the end of it and they didn't try to influence the parole board against me or interfere with any Good Time credits I may accumulate. In all reality—judging it strictly as a matter of law—I should never have been charged with a crime, and this was grossly unfair. At the same time, I was guilty of causing no end of grief for more people than I would ever know. I was sick at heart about my cousin Darryl. I might be able to get a favorable ruling in the Appeals Court, but that would send my parents even deeper into debt. Five to fifteen was the best deal I was going to get so I rolled with it.

I am currently housed in Kinross Correctional Facility, in Michigan's Upper Peninsula. I can tell you without any qualms that this is so many times better than J.W. Franklin that I want to shout for joy occasionally.

Not that this is that much fun, but I have known worse, and I know this is temporary. It will feel good to walk out of this sucker.

Meanwhile, I am doing the standard jail thing of weight-lifting, jogging and studying real estate law via correspondence course. According to informed sources, I have somewhere north of one hundred thousand American dollars hidden away on my Uncle Dan's farm. I want to be able to put it to good use when I leave here.

Once again, my reputation as a bank robber has proceeded me and once again, it is exaggerated. Apparently, everybody thinks about banks—after all, that's where the money is. I've had any number of guys approach me with stories about banks they have had their eyes on, seeking my advice, hoping we could partner up out there at some time in the future. Mostly I tell them I am retired.

There's this kid from Alpena, though, whose wife is a teller at a fairly large savings and loan and full of fascinating bits of inside information. We have had some conversations. I haven't made any commitment to this couple, but I have given them a lot of thought. When the time comes, maybe we can work something out.

Because hey—I rob banks. It's what I do.

T.J.'s Story

"**M**an, you don't know, Dude," T.J. began. "It's tough out there. Parole is impossible. The whole system is designed for failure. I just couldn't get anything going. Nobody would work with me, and the people I should have been able to count on all cut my throat. I couldn't catch a break. Seriously, man, I didn't stand a chance."

T.J. was my next-door neighbor in Eight Block for several years and we got to be okay. Normally, he is exactly the kind of guy I have a low tolerance for. Over a period of time, though, I decided he wasn't evil so much as stupid. I kinda felt sorry for him. He paroled out last winter and now, in early spring, he was back. I met him with the same line I always used with these guys, "What? You missed the food?"

"It's not like that, Dude," T.J. insisted. "I'm not one of those losers who *want* to come back. I was out there scuffling and grinding, trying to pull something together and get on my feet.

Against all odds, against absolutely everything and everybody in the world fighting against me, I was actually starting to pull something together. I just couldn't catch a break. I wouldn't be here at all if that skunk I married hadn't gone to my P.O. with her big *boo hoo* story. I guess she got comfortable with me gone and decided that she wanted to go back to being single. Why not? Life is easy for a hoe."

I could already see where this was going and I really didn't want to play. This was the point I would usually end a conversation, but it was a nice day to sit out in the sun, and, I don't know, over the years he had grown on me. I was willing to lend a sympathetic ear. Life is hard for these guys who honestly just don't get it. I did not see a productive and meaningful future for the guy.

"First of all, don't ever think you can make it out there without cheddar. Money is everything. Naturally, nobody would help me out with what I needed. Everybody was pleading poverty, but they seemed to be doing okay to me.

I'm trying to get my ole lady back out on the street, but her and my Moms have become besties while I was gone, and they are sharing a house. Moms is telling me lay off, the girl don't wanna hoe no more, she don't have to. Part of staying at the crib is I can't dog her about catching tricks. What kind of shit is that Dude? I mean, she's *my wife*, and my mama is making up rules for us to live by? What did they care? They had everything they needed, including all kinds of luxury items that didn't come cheap. Ax someone to help a brother get on his feet? You'd think I was talking about an organ transplant.

T.J. was still a young man, in his late 20's. He was somewhat shy of six feet tall, medium build. He usually has a neat appearance and isn't particularly loud—which is a thing with me—for a guy as dumb as he is. That bothers me because I have sensed over the years that there is intelligence in the guy, but he is just stuck on stupid. I think that if he developed a new perspective on life, he could do okay.

T.J. reminds me of that great line Walter Mondale used a few years back talking about Ronald Reagan—*"It's not what he doesn't know that bothers me, it's what he knows for sure that just ain't so."*

"Meanwhile", he continued, "my faggot P.O. was squeezing me about getting some kind of bullshit job. Yeah, right. I'm really gonna walk out of here and start flipping burgers or mopping floors for minimum wage. You bet. Work like a slave and make just enough to pay rent on some flea bag hole in the wall and live on Ramen Noodles. I don't think so.

Someone told me about this place online where you can buy college degrees that will fool anyone.

Plus, there is a number people can call and they will verify that the thing is real. Having the right paperwork is everything. I don't mind having a job, but I'm not going to be Steppen Fetchet. Dude, I don't do manual labor. Forget that. I sweat in the gym, not making someone else rich. Naturally you need a credit card to order one of these diplomas, and naturally nobody I knew had one. Or so they claimed. Sure, you can order with a debit card. Problem there, you gotta *buy* those things, and that goes back to the root problem. I didn't have any freaking money. Plus, these diplomas ain't cheap. If someone would have just ordered one of these things for me, I would have been golden. Flash that puppy in front of someone and sweet talk my way into one of those jobs you can just bluff your way through. How many people with those degrees are just educated fools? Sit behind a desk and talk on a phone or something; I can do that. You got 30 days from when you order on a credit card it until the bill comes due; plenty of time for me to make it right. Would somebody look out for me and trust me for a month to come up with it? Yeah, right. I guess my word ain't shit. It became clear that I couldn't count on anyone and would have to do things the hard way.

First lucky thing that happened to me was when I went in to report to my faggot P.O., I run into this clown I was in the county with on my last bit. He was dealing with the same crap I was and was pretty fed up with it all. Just like me. We put our heads together and figured out that our only option in life was armed robbery. What else could we do, Dude? Seriously. I'm kind of scared of doing stick-ups, but you know the expression, *desperate times call for desperate measures.* You know what else they say: *Armed robbery equals instant cash.*" T.J. looked at me sheepishly. "Actually, nobody says that. I just made it up. It's true, though, right?" I slowly nodded in the affirmative, as though I was pondering the wisdom of that statement.

This idiot, Carlyle, had a pistol—okay, it was a starter pistol, but it looked real and that's all that counts. He went to telling me about this bridal shop downtown. Everything in that joint looked expensive and everybody works there is either female or gay. None of them will want any trouble.

I'm not so stupid, Dude, I put thought into this. We got one small pistol between two guys and there might be a bunch of people in there. We had to take control of the situation right from the *Go*. You ever see how the SWAT team comes into a place? All yelling and breaking things? Shock and Awe.

Make people understand *right now* who is in charge. That's how we went in. Carlyle was waving the gun around, screaming for everyone to get down, and I was throwing things around, knocking over displays, creating a ruckus, yelling at people to get on the floor. Mostly they did, but, of course, there had to be one guy who thought he would save the day and try to slip into a side room. I had to bust him upside the head with a stupid-ass cupid statue that was on the counter there. Fag went down and laid real still, blood gushing out of his ears. I told him, 'Why you make me do that? How stupid are you?' All he had to do was get on the floor and be quiet for a couple minutes. *Fool.* T.J. looked at me again, his frustration apparent. You know what I'm saying, Dude?"

"Guy made you crack his head with a chunk of plaster," I said dryly.

"'Zackly," he said, "So next, we got the manager and she is play-acting like she can't get the cash register open, so Carlyle had to kidney punch the bitch, just to get her attention. She pretended to be really hurt and fell on the floor doing this thing like a fish out of water. I ax her, 'What is wrong with you people? Why you *wanna* get hurt? You can see we're serious, why not make it easy on yourselfs?' Finally one of those gay boys that works there said he would open the thing up.

I grabbed him by his hair and pulled him over to the counter. The drawer pops open and all I see is credit card slips. I'm about to bust this fairy's face and he knew it. All of a sudden, he is babbling about they don't take cash. All of their transactions—*transactions*, Dude, they don't make sales, that do *transactions*—are done by credit. Why even have a cash register? They were just begging for someone to come in and rip them off. Probably hoping for it so they can stick it to their insurance company.

Anyway, Carlyle says he's not about to leave empty-handed and goes around dumping out purses, and snatching jewelry. I still had this sissy by the hair and told him I would smash his face into the counter if he didn't produce some cash right frickin' now. He believed me and said there was a petty cash box in the office. I drug him in there and went into a desk drawer and came out with this metal box. Didn't even have a lock on it. Seriously, who does that if they don't *want* to get robbed? I cracked his head against the wall and he fell down whimpering. Trying to make me feel sorry for him. I *had* to do that, Dude. How I'm gonna let someone disrespect me like that in the middle of a robbery? He knew that money was in the office when he was carrying about their cashless *transactions*. Punk woulda played fair, he wouldnta got hurt. Maybe the lesson did him good. I went into his pockets while he was laying there sniffling and found a nice little knot of cash in a money clip. All the cheddar I got in the office I stuffed down the front of my pants and told Carlyle there was nothing in back but more credit card slips.

Carlyle had some old woman's purse and was stuffing everything he got from the people on the floor into it. Right then, I see the price tags hanging on these gowns and I'm like, *For Real?* Dude, those dresses were costing in the high hundreds and even thousands of dollars. Can you believe that?

I hollered at Carlyle and showed him what I was looking at and he had the same thought I did—these dresses were the money, forget everything else. We set to gathering up armloads of them and were getting ready to run out the back of the place when I look over and see this zip damn fool I had left on the office floor kind of scrunched under the desk, talking on his phone. I couldn't believe it. This moron was begging me to stomp the life out of him. All we wanted was some cheddar, dresses, whatever. We didn't go in there to hurt people, but they kept provoking it. Why are people like that, Dude? I kicked the phone out of his hand, well, into his face, but he deserved it, and we headed out the back. We can hear sirens and they are coming this way. Fortunately, Carlyle knew this part of downtown, and knew where to slip and slide and get out of sight.

Okay, Dude, so now we are running down Montgomery Avenue in the middle of the afternoon, both of us got arms full of wedding gowns. We didn't go unnoticed. I was two steps behind Carlyle, ducking and dodging, up and down allies, across parking lots, through abandoned buildings, and after a few blocks, Dude, I'm outta gas. I tell Carlyle, hold on, man. I'm puffing for breath, about to fall out. Carlyle says, come on, man, there is a spot up ahead…which turns out to be a couple more blocks. I was *dying*, Dude.

Carlyle leads me to an old school bus parked in a rickety, falling-down garage way off in Nowhere. His big idea is to stash the dresses here and split up. We'll come back for them later. That made sense because, hey, we're running around downtown Detroit bear-hugging a bunch of wedding gowns."

T.J. paused to flag down a guy passing by, and bummed a cigarette. Those two had a lot in common and had to kick it for a few minutes. I didn't mind.

It became apparent that this guy didn't realize T.J. had gone home and come back. He was just assuming he hadn't seen him lately. I was contemplating T.J.'s story so far and was a little surprised by how easily that violence had come to him. I guess I never knew that about T.J..

"Okay, He continued. "Do you have the picture, Dude? The dresses are all in the back of the bus and Carlyle is talking about we split up, catch a ride, whatever, meet somewhere tomorrow and get these suckers back to the hood and see about slinging them. He's hoping I don't ask—fat chance—I say, Good plan…what about all the cash and jewelry from the people on the floor? Half of that is mine, right? Carlyle say, yeah, right, right. Of course, we in this together. We leaving that here, too. He shows me where the purse is stashed under the pile of dresses. We can hear sirens and I'm a nervous wreck. Carlyle is talking about people who saw us run by with the dresses knew we were dirty, and are probably flagging the cops down right now and pointing out where we went. We need to get in the wind. He's taking sense, so I go east, he goes west.

I don't have to take you through this whole long, drawn out story, Dude. You know what happened. I caught a downtown bus, went about two miles out on Gratiot. I couldn't stop thinking about that purse with the cash and jewelry. I got off that bus and caught one back. I head back over to that garage and—big surprise—there are no dresses, no purse full of cash. I couldn't believe it. Carlyle made off with everything. How did he move all those dresses? I don't know, but like I said, this was his hood. He probably ran over to some homie with a ride and they packed all that stuff up. Just that quick. That was cold, Dude. Seriously cut throat. You just can't trust anybody. You'd think a brother would learn. I was way, way over on the other side of town from where I was staying. If I hadn't had that money stuffed in my drawers, I would have been stranded way off in BFE.

There is no excuse or a guy like Carlyle, Dude. I put my life on the line in that robbery. I deserved my fair share. I *needed* it. He knew that. That was just about the dirtiest thing anybody ever did to me. That hurt, man. How can somebody just do that? Walk away with my money like it's nothing. Cold blooded.

Now I was back where I started from. With nothing. I got a few bucks from that rip, but not enough to write home about. My so-called wife was useless at this point. Just when I needed her to hold up her end. Never trust a woman, Dude. Seriously. When we first hooked up, she was a star, out there grabbing the green. That few years I was away, she got lazy and totally lost focus. I suddenly deserved zero respect. I told you before she was a hoe. I gotta tell you, there is more to that than you would think. It's profession, like any other. My girl was a real, live hustler; she could get out there and just grab money out of the air. We were living large. I was the brains of the outfit. Then I went

away and she lost all her motivation. I was having trouble getting her
back on track.

Anyway, this thing with Carlyle kinda took it out of me, Dude. I
knew that guy was gone; I didn't even bother looking for his ass. I laid
around my mama's house for a stretch, smoking weed and working on
40-ouncers, trying to get past it.

Finally, another break comes my way, through—of all people—
that supposta-to-be hoe, supposta-be wife of mine. I overhear her
and a couple of her hoe friends talking about this sucker in the hood
who is selling crack out of an abandoned house just two streets over.
I know this fool, and I know that whatever he got, I can take. Don't
look at me like that, Dude, I needed that shit more than he did. His
old lady was still out there taking care of business. I told you, the
people I got in my corner—big laugh—I can't do anything legit. I
have to do it rough.

Like I said before, Dude, I ain't so stupid. Those crackheads out
there? You gotta watch those cut throats—rip your ass off in a heartbeat. Guys run crack houses know that and go to work with a pistol
in one hand. When they on the job is when they most dangerous.
I ain't looking to get my ass shot. What I got going for me is that
I know where this clown *lives*. Right? These crackheads coming to
his dope house know squat about him, so he feels safe when he anywhere else.

I'll make a long story short here, Dude and take you up to the
interesting part. Took me over a week to scope everything out. I spent
that time slipping and sliding, ducking and dodging, finding out what
I needed to know.

Bottom line, I catch this hot shot drug dealer dragging his dumb
ass home in the wee hours and crack his dome right outside is back
door. Right when he was tired and beat and thought he could finally
let his guard down. Got twenty-five $10.00 rocks and a pistol. Nice
score. No cash—and believe me, I looked everywhere cash might have
been—real up close and personal—you unnerstand. I guess one of his

partners carried the money off at night. Whatever. I finally had a little something to work with. Not a lot, but *something*. Right?

Took ten of those rocks next day and slung 'em in about fifteen minutes in a park downtown. Bought a pretty decent jacket, and got a huge break while I was in the store. Goof turned his back for a second and I kicked of the raggedy-ass shoes I was wearing and slipped on a nice-looking pair of gators.

Really nice shoes, Dude. With those and the jacket, I was on my way to looking respectable. Stopped into a Goodwill store for a shirt. The jacket and shoes made it look better than it was, but it was coming together.

The new clothes made me start feeling good about myself and I headed back to my mama's crib with a spring in my step.

By the time I got there, I decided I was done playing around with this lazy-ass bitch supposta be out turning tricks. I took control of the situation and bought my pimp hand down. Had to be careful to not mark her up, but, believe me, I laid down the law. Bitch went to work. I walked her down to Woodward, and five minutes after we got down there, I watched her hop in a car. Things were finally looking up.

While Bernice was taking care of business, I headed back to my mama's to get the rest of my rocks. Dude, I was sick what happened next. Why can't I catch a break?

While I was out earlier, my mama found them rocks and smoked 'em up with a couple of her dope fiend neighbors. Do you hear me Dude? My mama smoked up my rocks! Do you know how hard it was for me to not smoke them up myself? I got what you call *self-discipline*, Dude. I can put off my own good time in order to reach a bigger goal a few steps down the road. That's how you succeed in this world. I worked hard for those rocks, and I *needed* that money.

I got in Mama's face and ax her how she gonna come up with a hunnert and fitty bucks to straighten me out on these rocks and she's screaming about my lazy ass laying around her house, mawing down on her groceries and dogging her best friend—talking about *my* hoe wife. It was too much, Dude. Next thing, I'm pistol whipping this loud-mouth bitch all over the kitchen. She been disrespecting me since I got off the bus and never would help me out with a loan. She needed to get her head straightened out. I left her there thinking about how *wrong* she was and headed downtown to get some cash from Bernice.

I get downtown, and Bernice is nowhere in sight. I say, *Cool, she out takin' care of biz.* I hang around waiting for someone to drop her ass off, and after about a half hour, I'm getting edgy. Dude, I went into a bar, and there this bitch is sitting, drinking with a group of her hoe friends. *Laughing,* just having big fun.

I pull up and demand my money. Bitch says, "*Your* money? *Fool!,* this is *my* money!" Naturally they all got a huge laugh out of that. Seriously, Dude, what could I do *but* pistol whip this hoe? Come on, man. State I was in, she just in there drinking up all my cheddar? Who wouldn'ta checked off? Wrong is wrong, man, and this bitch was all the way wrong.

I didn't think this was the kind of bar where people wanna jump into your mix like they all John Wayne or some damn body. I gave those fucks way too much credit for having enough class to mind their own; shee-it, these heroes was on me like white on rice. I didn't stand a chance.

Next thing you know, I was on my way to jail, my new jacket all ripped up, those new shoes all scuffed up and ruined. I was raggedy as a Chinese chicken. Someone in the bar picked up my pistol, so that was gone, too. I had nothing, Dude.

Okay, so now I'm in Wayne County Jail and there is only one person I can call to put up my bail, and you know who that is. All my life, whatever else is going on, Moms would come down and bail me out. This time, though? Yeah, right. I get my one phone call and Moms is carrying on about I crossed a line and blah, blah, blah. On top of that, she and her best friend go down and give my fag P.O. an earful. Only thing beat me back here was the headlights on the bus.

All I was looking for from the time I got out, Dude, was an even break. Just one fair shot at getting on my feet. Lost everything I worked so hard for, people who could have helped me out all hate me now for trying to make something of myself. I never had a chance, man. I was just born under a bad sign. I ask you, Dude, seriously—why does everything always happen to *me*?

-XXX-

Life Happens

*M*y friend Ronnie set his face on fire few weeks ago. I suppose it had to happen. He has been having a lot of asteroid trouble. A couple days after the incident, I was informed that arrangements had been made for me to visit him on the third floor of The 700 Club.

The 700 Club is the latest multi-million-dollar investment Michigan taxpayers have made in their Department of Corrections. It is an entirely self-contained psych facility which serves the system as a whole. Instead of each institution having its own psych services, anyone who needs that kind of attention is now sent here. Residents of The 700 Club do not mingle in general population; they have their own Health Care, Food Service, and fenced-in yard area. They do not use the regular visiting room; their visitors are brought over to them. This is a very high-security area with no blind spots. There are cameras *everywhere*. For reasons apparent only to some bureaucrat in Lansing, this unit was christened with the puzzling moniker 700 Building. From Day One, however, nobody—including the doctors and staff who work there—has ever referred to it as anything other than The 700 Club.

Third floor is actually a mini hospital designed to meet the needs of psych patients. Ronnie was admitted here because of the nature of his injuries. Where he would go next was still up in the air. I used to work in the old psych unit, back when they still had inmate nurses.

They don't need us anymore, though, because the care of psych cases now falls under the appellation Better Living Through Chemistry.

Back in the old days, it took a battalion of pretty serious individuals to keep order in a psych unit. The operating philosophy was, *Nobody is so crazy they don't understand a beat-down.* Then the suits realized that once you get those guys wiped out on psychotropic drugs, your great grandmother can manage them all from her wheelchair. You can always spot someone on psychotropics—he has this zombie look about him and is doing the trademark Thorazine Shuffle. The drug of choice these days seems to be Prolixin. Jailers love this stuff. Toss a thimbleful of Prolixin into a hurricane, and within minutes it won't be able to blow out a candle.

When I got up to Ronnie's room, I saw they had him in with this kid Kevin I knew from my days as a nurse. Kevin had long psych history. He was hospitalized now with a broken leg that needed to be kept in traction. There was probably a story to that, but I wasn't up to hearing it. Kevin did this thing called "association". You could be having a normal conversation with him and then he would seize on one word and run with it. It didn't even have to be in context. For example, one day I saw a book on his bed and told him, "That is some of the best science fiction I have ever read." Kevin said, "Red! Blue, yellow, pink, orange, purple..."off and running, all rapid-fire, back to back, and on and on. He didn't stop with the easy ones, either. Pretty soon he was down to burnt sienna, golden umber, ocher, amber, puce...It went on for a while. It could be any subject. If he stayed calm these outbursts were rare, but any degree of stress and he was off to the races.

Anybody who has any kind of mental disorder is referred to as a "bug". This term is applied across the board, from the individual who just a little quirky—*that guy is a straight-up bug!* —to a raging psychopathic maniac. Out of a population of five thousand, there are several hundred bugs who line up at the infirmary window when "Med Lines" are announced over the P.A. Some of them show up once a day for a little something to help them deal with anxiety and unwind enough to sleep at night. Some of them are there four times a day for meds that would slow a strapping young Tyrannosaurus Rex down to a crawl. Those who require meds that leave them incapacitated are admitted to the 700 Club.

I was sitting there looking at Ronnie's face and it wasn't pretty. His forehead and cheeks were pretty well toasted, and hair on the sides of his face had been singed away. His ears looked like someone had gone over them with a blow torch. I will be surprised if he ever has eyebrows again, but, fortunately, it doesn't look like he damaged his eyes. In any event, his days of being referred to as a good-looking clean-cut boy-next-door type are over.

Ronnie has fallen much further than most of us. Not long ago, he had the world on a string. He grew up in one of those Norman Rockwell homes in the Upper Peninsula, not far from the Wisconsin border. He had been an honor student, all-around athlete, and for four years, captain of the football team. His childhood sweetheart, Mary Beth, was class Valedictorian, state champion baton twirler or some such thing, and—of course—the prettiest and most popular girl in town. Ronnie and Mary Beth seemed destined for a life of wholesome bliss. They set off to university with plans to put off marriage until after graduation and then take turns putting each other through grad school.

Life in the big city was a whole new reality. Back home Ronnie was a big fish in a small pond. Now he found himself just one of hundreds of good-looking athletic types who excel at everything they do. On the gridiron, he had to work his heart black and blue just to make the team. Giving 110%, he was seen as someone to keep an eye on, who might develop into a player of significance someday.

The two beds in Ronnie's room were separated by a curtain, which was supposed to offer some semblance of privacy. I was sitting on a folding chair at the end of Ronnie's bed, in no hurry to wake him up. I had no idea where the conversation would go, and I was apprehensive about his immediate future.

While I was contemplating this, several visitors filed in on Kevin's side of the curtain. His whole body tightened up and I knew things were about to get real silly. As soon as everyone got situated, the one I had pegged as the source of Kevin's discomfort—a big guy with Retired Military written all over him—informed Kevin that it was time to get himself squared away. "Squared!" Kevin shouted, "Rectangle, parallelogram, oval, triangle, pentagram…"

It's not like Ronnie was a scrub when he started playing college ball. He just wasn't real, real special. If you follow the game, though, you would have heard his name. It occurred to him for the first time that maybe he wasn't a shoo-in for the pros and that rocked his world.

When Ronnie came shuffling out of Receiving that day, clutching his bedroll and looking for all the world like some kind of refugee in his brand-new state issue clothes two sizes too big, he was really a pitiful sight. He was lost and confused, a day-old lamb in a world of jackals. Lucky for him, I was the first person he ran into. I took him under my wing and helped him get situated. Ever after that, he was like a kid brother. Over the next several months, I heard his whole life story, including the sad tale of how he ended up here.

If being away from home for the first time ever was a tough transition for Ronnie, Mary Beth was exhilarated. Back home, from earliest memory, she was always Ronnie's Girl. Life on that particular pedestal meant that all the other guys regarded her as they would a married woman. She had always accepted that as her identity and had never questioned it. The campus crowd had a whole different perspective. Mary Beth was a beautiful girl, and had that wholesome, slightly naïve country-girl thing going on at the same time. She immediately started getting all kinds of attention she had never experienced before. Early on, she decided it was not a bad thing.

I think if anybody had been paying attention, they would have seen Ronnie slipping. His whole shot—his scholarship, the love of his life, his chance at making the pros—he'd always taken it for granted, but suddenly nothing seemed certain. He was unprepared for how rough the game was at that level. Those boys play hard out there. It's no joke to have some raging 300-pound hulk get a good running start and then slam into your blind side. Take a few of those hits Saturday afternoon and then show up for practice Monday morning to find out you are the only one not wiped out. Your confidence can take a hit. It didn't take long for someone to pull Ronnie off to the side and explain how it was that no one else was feeling any pain.

I had a flirtation with performance-enhancing drugs back in my muscle-head days, but they scared me to death and I didn't use them for long. Believe me, though, I get the attraction. Muscle mass packs on like magic and recovery time is cut down to almost nothing. The particular juice I was on was mild as such things go, but I was already nervous about it when Lyle Alzado convinced me to cut it loose.

If you are not a fan of pro football, let me just recap that sad story for you. Lyle Alzado was one of the toughest hombres to ever play the game. I mean, he was a beast. He finally got too old for it and retired. Shortly thereafter, news broke that his brain was full of cancerous tumors and then, boom, he was dead. Just like that. The steroids he was using sometimes had that unfortunate side effect. Turns out, that was the same juice Ronnie got started on.

When Kevin finally ran out of geometrical formations—which, believe me, took a while—he began whining to his mother about the job he had been assigned to in the housing unit. In the wing he lived on, it was mandatory for everyone to have a job. None were very demanding. A typical job would be to sweep a ten-foot hallway every morning with a push broom, or empty two waste baskets. These tasks were perceived by the in-patients as enormous and onerous undertakings, and protesting the injustice of it never ended. Kevin had been assigned to fold ten sheets in the unit laundry three times a week. His punishment for failure was loss of TV room for that day. He was distraught about missing Judge Judy on those days, to which his mother had some sage advice, "Well, fold your sheets, then, Son."

"Sohlzenetsen! Aleksandr Isayevic Sohlzenetsen! Petr Aleekseviv Kropotkin! Mikhail Yurievich Lermontof! Vladimir Vladimirovich Mayakovski, Anton Pavlovic Chekov…"

A casual observer might think Kevin is a scholar of Russian literature, but it is likely he knows little or nothing about any of it. In the course of his life, he has heard those names and they all went into a file somewhere in his brain waiting for someone to push the right button. He probably has dozens or even hundreds of such files just waiting to be tapped. The "read out" is actually a type of seizure. Afterward, if you ask him Chekov's middle name, he probably wouldn't understand the question, much less know the answer.

Every once in a while, someone would make a crack about me being Ronnie's baby sitter or some such. Pissed me off. It wasn't like that. There was just this child like thing about him. He stuck pretty close to me, not because he was scared the way a weak person is in the joint, but because he was just lost. He just seemed slightly confused most of the time. He was a good dude, and I didn't mind having him around. There was a blind faith and a *need* on his part that made me realize I had a huge responsibility there.

That was brought home to me one day on the yard when we walked into a shake down and it looked bad for me there for a minute. That summer there was way too much dope on the yard—something new they were calling Cracker Jacks—and therefore, way too much violence. Stabbings were up like 500% and the administration was always looking for new and creative ways to root out drugs and weapons.

Right when all of this was at its worst, I was having a beef with some wanna-be tough guy over in Four Block, and was carrying a knife in my belt. My experience in the joint has been that usually just having a weapon is enough. Flash it on the idiot and let him know you are ready to jump ugly and usually the matter will resolve itself. I hadn't said anything to Ronnie about it because I didn't want him involved any kind of way. So, we were walking the yard one day and came around that corner over by the paint shop and bam!—we were suddenly in this gauntlet of yard cops. They had a bunch of us surrounded and were herding us into an area where a couple other cops were going over everyone with hand-held metal detectors. All I could do was play it out, but I was sweating bullets.

The process was excruciating. I kept looking around for a chance to drop this thing on the ground and kick it away from me, but these cops were all eyes. They got to the guy in front of me and when the wand passed over the front of his waist, the alarm started buzzing. The cop just about jumped out of his skin. Old boy told them, hey, chill. It's my belt buckle. He raised his shirt and sure enough, there was a big, silver rodeo buckle. The cop told him to beat feet. Then he was waving that thing over me. It went off in the same spot. The cop looked at me and said, "Belt Buckle?" I nodded and he told me to beat it.

When we got away from there, I laughed and lifted my shirt to show Ronnie what I had there. His mouth dropped open and all the color drained from his face. I had to help him over to a bench to sit down. He was actually trembling. When he could finally speak, Ronnie whispered, "What if you got *caught?*" I told him I'd rather have the cops catch me with it than have some idiot catch me without it. "Dude, what would I *do*? He whimpered. Part of the administration's no-nonsense approach to getting weapons off the yard was that anybody caught in possession of one immediately got slammed with 12 months in segregation, with a transfer to Marquette at the end of it. Ronnie demanded I promise him I would never carry it again. He was so stressed, I finally gave in and promised, but I was lying. I knew that if the situation called for it, I'd do what I had to do.

There are basically two kinds of bugs. There are those who came into the system that way. Most of them probably came into the world normal enough, but somewhere along the line decided to destroy their brains with drugs and alcohol. The other group is made up of those who made it here more or less in charge of their faculties, but crumbled under the stress of living in this insanity.

Kevin had a drug history, but his situation was unique. He told me once in a lucid moment that he had grown up with the image of God as an old man sitting up in the clouds, manipulating his every more with a joy stick. That really bothered him so he got into the habit of doing all kinds of unpredictable things, knowing that these at least were his own independent actions. Like, he would be walking along and suddenly, without warning, would jump up into the air, run twenty feet to the side, drop and roll over a few times and then howl at the sky. Being from a strict Pentecostal family, he couldn't tell anyone he was trying to break out of God's control, so he just said he didn't know why he did that stuff—it just happened. The more attention he got for it, the more he did it. His parents ended up taking him all over the country, consulting with all kinds of specialists, undergoing the latest space age testing and treatments. This was a fun game and he really got into it. Taking all those pretty pills and capsules was just part of it. Some of them actually made him feel pretty good. By the time he got old enough to decide he didn't want to be a crazy person, he had become a crazy person.

That's the thing about psychotropic drugs. They make you manageable by turning your brain to mush. You can always spot one of those guys on meds, they walk like they are pulling their feet out of deep mud with every step and tend to carry their hands waist-high. That's the Thorazine Shuffle. Their attention span measures in seconds. When you see that, it's time to say *"Adios,"* because even in the rare instances somebody gets off these drugs, the person they used to be no longer exists.

You might think that conversations with Ronnie would revolve around football and jock stuff, but you'd be wrong. What Ronnie longed for and talked about endlessly was his dad's farm. He wanted to go home and work up the soil for his mom's flower bed like he did every spring so she could enjoy it every time she looked out the kitchen window. He wanted to take care of the animals and break a sweat throwing hay bales and fret over whether there would be enough rain to bring in the soy beans. Mostly, he just wanted to be there.

All the cows had names and one Christmas Ronnie bought a bunch of those little personalized license plates like kids put on their bicycles and hung them around the cow's necks. His mom had sent him the pictures they took that day out there in the snow and these were his most prized possessions.

Kevin calmed down and was engaging in passably rational conversation when one of those Pentecostals was moved to lay on hands and go to calling on *Geezus*, insisting this was *The One Way*, when Kevin erupted with "One way! Throughway! Two way! Subway! Waterway! Rail Way! High Way..."

If you didn't take time to get to know him, you could assume Ronnie had lost all contact with reality. Most of the time, though, he had a pretty good grip on things. You just had to understand there was some brain damage in there. Sometimes his thinking was a little screwy and he could get spacey when he was tired. There were some blank spots in his memory banks, and there were a dozen or so words he had all twisted up and it could take some ciphering to figure out what he meant. One of those words was *steroids*; he always said *asteroids*.

Take a guy already considered a bug and listen to him explain how asteroids have damaged his brain, and there you go. Ronnie told me once that the asteroids had burned holes in his brain, and that was how I had visualized it—like his brain was made of cheese and someone dropped some red-hot embers in there.

This idiot biker named Spider Webb—I happen to know that his name is Theodore, but if you are a biker and your last name is Webb, what else are you going call yourself? —convinced Ronnie that he could plug up the holes in his brain by stuffing baby marshmallows up there. He got real cute about it, talking about how the ancient Egyptians used to pull people's brains out through their nostrils and that's why people snort dope, because it is a direct pathway to the brain, and all manner of rot. Thought he was pretty funny. I walked up on Ronnie and he was packing these little marshmallows up his nose with a pencil. I had to talk to him for a long time to get him to dig them back out. He said he just wanted to get better.

Shortly after that, a couple Mexican bangers beat the snot out of Spider Webb following a prolonged and impassioned argument over the age-old question of who was hotter—Jan or Marsha Brady? (If ever asked, I will say Jan. I see where voting for Marsha got Spider Webb).

The one guy, Chuy, got busted for that and ended up doing ninety days in the hole. A couple different times, I sent him over cigarettes and magazines. He never knew where that stuff came from. I see him occasionally, but I've never mentioned it. I'm not trying to make new friends; I just thought of that as my little contribution to a job well done.

The hell of it is that Ronnie has no real recollection of that whole thing with the fire that got him here. There seems to be little question that he started it, but the whys and wherefores of it all are pretty hazy to him. Nobody really cared about the details anyway. What mattered was that a frat house went up in flames and some fresh-faced kids from good families got hurt, a few of them pretty seriously. Ronnie's only explanation had to do with asteroids.

Just as Kevin was winding down a recitation of all the planets and their moons, a cop came down and told his visitors it was time to wrap it up. They looked relieved. As soon as things quieted down, Ronnie opened his eyes. "Hey Dude," he said and smiled.

"Hey, Roast Beef," I said. The story behind that tells you something about how Ronnie's mind works. Or doesn't. The guy's initials are R.B. when he played ball. He was a Running Back. It was a natural for me to call him R.B. from the beginning. The guys he met through me called him that. One day I introduced him to my friend Dutch. Dutch misunderstood and called him CT. Ronnie said no, Arby, like the sandwich. Dutch asked him how so, and Ronnie went to carrying on about this roast beef sandwich place that he really liked. Dutch just shook his head and walked away. After that I went back to just calling him Ronnie.

He sat up in bed and started telling about this idea to ask his dad about maybe getting a few dairy goats, you know, as an experiment, see how they do. "Ronnie, how did you come to set your face on fire?" I interrupted.

He signed deeply. "I really screwed up this time, didn't I? Dude, it just made so much sense at the time. I thought I was really onto something." We danced around it for a while, and finally Ronnie asked me if I remembered reading Stephan King's *The Tommyknockers*. I did. "Okay, you know the part where the guy was obsessed with his computer and was always at it and they come into the room one day and find him there, and his eyeballs are gone, and there are wires going from inside his head directly to the monitor. Remember that? Okay, now think of Arnold Swartzenegger in *Total Recall*. You know they did this thing where they would implant memories inside your brain and you would have that as your reality. Right?

What Ronnie had done, drawing on those two references, was try to impress his dad's farm into his brain in such a way that it would become his permanent reality, and he would just be there all the time. He had stripped the insulation from an extension cord, and wrapped the bare wires around the bows of his metal frame glasses. He popped the lenses out and taped a picture of he and Mary Beth on the farm in happier days across the front. Then he put the glasses on. And plugged them in.

It took three weeks to get permission to see Ronnie again. He was still in the 700 Club, but now in the residential wing. From the paperwork I received, I saw he was on Alert Status, meaning any time of day or night if he waved down an officer and said he was feeling "funny", they would immediately summon a psych nurse.

There was a button next to the gate on the 700 Club yard, which I had to press to get someone to bring Ronnie out and let me into the yard area. He was looking pretty disheveled, and it took me a few minutes to re-button his shirt, straighten his collar, and get his shoes tied so we could take a little stroll. We set off for a bench about 20 feet away. That walk turned out to be an enormous undertaking for him. With each step, it was like he was pulling his feet out of sucking mud, and he was doing this thing with his hands like Grandpa McCoy. He talked a bit but it was hard for him to focus, and he tended to drifted off in the middle of sentences. We sat there for a while, watching the pigeons come and go. It was peaceful and he seemed to enjoy being outdoors. His burns had some kind of ointment smeared over them; some of them seemed to be oozing, but looked to be healing well enough.

After a while I walked him back to his gate and buzzed for the officer to come fetch him. I had brought along a bag of beef jerky and these cinnamon candies he liked, and a bunch of other junk. I was busy stuffing it all in his pockets, trying to conceal everything so that he could make it back to his cell without someone taking it all away from him. The whole time I was telling him just be cool, try to get some rest, and he was going to be alright, just hang in there. Once I had him all situated, I leaned on that buzzer for the third time and looked up to see a single tear running down his cheek. "What happened to me, Dude?" His voice was utterly forlorn.

The officer had arrived and opened the gate. I stepped through, faced him, and with my arms spread wide, I shrugged, "Life, Ronnie. That's all."

"Life happens," he agreed.

"All over the place," was all I could do for a response. I turned and started walking.

"Dude?"

I stopped and looked back. "You'll come see me again? Won't you?

"Sure I will, Ronnie. You just concentrate on getting your strength back and I'll see you again as soon as I can swing it. Promise."

I could feel Ronnie's eyes on my back as I walked away. This was the second time I had made Ronnie a promise I knew was a lie. This time, he knew it too.

-XXX-

Cloud Nine

"I've killed two people, Dude," Nine began, "within less than two weeks. Once with a kitchen knife, once with a switchblade. In each case, it was an accident, slash, self-defense. In each case, I was the victim." Nine paused to draw on a joint. "If that sounds self-serving and contradictory, let me add this: I am not a violent person, and I am not a sociopath. And I have not the least twinge of conscience over either."

I raised an eyebrow skeptically. "I know, right?" Nine responded, "What a crock. It's impossible that all these statements could be true at once. Let's revisit that question when you hear the whole tale."

That was as good a hook as I had ever heard. I tried not to show it, but he had me. This, I had to hear.

Another toke on the joint, "this is a story I have never told before. Any half-assed attorney—hell, any first-year law student—could get an acquittal on the facts of the matter, but I'm happy it never came to that." He shrugged, "it's been long enough now that I'm not worried about charges, so screw it."

Nine, an aging hippie pot dealer, had tracked me down the day before and said he had a story for me. This was a first. Normally I hear about people and have to wring their story out of them. Like a true pot head, Nine knew where the good dope was, and figured out the best way to get the best deal. I wasn't mad at him. What he was proposing essentially was if I get him high and he would talk to me. We had a lengthy conversation on the topic and I let him know I wouldn't be scammed. Don't even waste my time with something you made up or a story you heard somewhere. I conveyed that I was not particularly interested and was mostly annoyed at his hubris in approaching me. He had let slip enough details, though, that I was hooked, and I secretly admired his resourcefulness. We met on my favorite bench in Peckerwood Park; I passed him a fat joint and surprised him with a jar of hooch. After a time, he leaned back with his eyes closed and sighed deeply, his body visibly relaxing. Finally, "thank you, man." I waited.

"Back in the 60's", Nine began, "well, let's just say, I was there. Those were the days. I was lucky enough to live in Ann Arbor for the best part of it. Actually, I was all over. That's what we did, right? Hippies were always on the move. Zappa nailed it, we were a generation of transients. If you couldn't afford your own VW bus, you thumbed it. I don't know how many thousands of miles I hitched, Ann Arbor to Berkeley several times, once from Salem, Oregon, to Daytona for Bike Week. Down to Mexico, a couple trips into Canada. Always on the go. I was crazy because Ann Arbor was just about the coolest place in the universe back then. I could be in Haight-Ashbury or Greenwich Village and mention Ann Arbor and people would say, 'far out, I heard it's really happening there…' I loved Ann Arbor, but felt compelled to *go*. Had a lot of great experiences along the way. Had a few bummers, too. People who weren't a part of the whole 60's thing could never possibly understand.

"Anyway…back then—this is something incomprehensible to those of subsequent generations—a lot of people were just *nice*. People were generous and compassionate and cared about other people. I'm talking about people who weren't hippies, just everyday people; it was 'in' back then to just be nice. That's why hitch-hiking was so easy.

More often than not, when I caught a ride and in the ensuing conversation told the about how many miles I had covered and say I was sleeping outside, etc., people would want to feed me, maybe hand me a couple bucks when I got out of the car. It was the world we lived in. That's why my defenses were down when that predator picked me up outside of Providence, Rhode Island.

I had been to an outdoor concert in Pennsylvania, of all places. It was kind of far out because coming out of Lewisburg, PA , heading for NYC, I got picked up by this chick who was actually married to the sax player in Sly and the Family Stone. Sly had headlined the concert I just left. She was full of stories. We did a couple doobies and had a great time for a couple hundred miles. Sometimes a ride could be huge fun. I told her that I was headed for New York City—I had people in Greenwich Village and really loved going there. We were both pretty lit up and sometimes the finer points of communication suffer for that. She had picked me up on Highway 476, heading East, and I told her I wanted to hop out when we hit 380, which goes into NYC. She thought I said 280, which veers up north and out into strange and hostile regions. When she pulled over and told me this was my spot, I didn't question it. Ten minutes later I realized where I was. No place you want to hitch hike through, I can tell you that. The whole thing I just said about people being nice? Yeah, in your more rednecky and hillbilly-ish areas? Scratch that. Different vibe all together.

After that, rides got scarce. I ended up on a secondary highway, which is always a mistake. I gathered that I was generally facing Boston and I had people there, so I figured, why not? You've heard the cliché, *it's about the journey as much as the destination.* From Boston to New York is three or four hours on the train, which is so cheap and efficient it doesn't even make sense to hitch-hike it. Anyway, from there rides were just short hops and those weren't exactly coming back to back.

It was a nightmare, Dude. This was mid-August; the heat and humidity was off the charts. There was no shade near the road. I stood out there baking in the sun, sweaty, head achy, dizzy much of the time, feeling worse by the minute. I straightened myself up as much as possible, hair tied back, shirt tucked in, hoping to not scare the locals. At night I tried to sleep under the stars, on hard, bumpy ground with bugs crawling all over me; sweaty, itchy, utterly miserable. Add to that dehydration, and extreme hunger. Those days seemed endless and remain a blur. After moving along one short bump at a time, I finally drug my sorry ass into the suburbs of Providence, Rhode Island."

I had seen Nine around, of course. More often than not guys are known by nick names, or at most, by their last name. I know a handful of guys whose nick name is actually a number. Nine was generally well thought of and well liked. He minded his own business, never tried to scam anyone and had never been suspected of repeating things he should have kept to himself. This was our first actual conversation, but right away I felt comfortable with him, and sensed a genuineness that is lacking in many of our contemporaries.

"When I hit the city limits," he continued, "I was exhausted; filthy, hungry, desperate for things to look up. While walking along a sidewalk, heading toward the ocean, this really clean cut guy in a Lincoln Continental pulled over. By this time, I'd had enough experience in life that I recognized the type instantly. Like I said, though, I was tired and really hungry. Normally these guys wanted to feed you and be super friendly and afterward ease into their move. At that point you can say *Hey, I didn't realize that's what this was about. That's not my thing, man. I thought that meal was just a friendly offer...*

Nine, of course, is a nickname. His real name is Cloud Nine.

In many ways, Nine is a cliché. He's maybe 5'11", skinny, long hair, shot through with grey now, with an outrageous walrus mustache. On his right forearm is a peace sign tattoo with a marijuana leaf growing through it. On the other forearm, a big *Woodstock, '69*. His other tats were the Zig Zag Man, the Do Dah Man, and over his heart, King and Queen of hearts. The King is Jimi Henrix and the queen is Janis Joplin. On his right wrist is a cloud with a sunrise coming up behind with the words, Cloud Nine under it. It's actually really cute. (An adjective I don't get to use often when discussing guys in the joint.) All his tats are top notch professional work.

Over the years, I have picked up some interesting things about guys in the joint; there are things we all have in common, even guys that are so different on the surface. Nine is an intelligent guy, and rarest of creatures on this yard—he actually has several years of university education. He doesn't realize, though, how much he has told me about himself. First and foremost, that even as a teenager, he was a player, a con man, and manipulator. He would surely be startled to hear those labels applied to himself, but even at a tender young age, he automatically recognized this guy as a mark and was willing to play dumb, even flirt a little, say what he needed to get a meal.

Nine continued, "So this guy opens with, 'hey man, you really look tired, can I give you a lift somewhere?' "These guys, it was always, "*Hey, Man,*" showing that they spoke the lingo, they were *hip.* I hopped in and told him I was trying to make my way to the Salvation Army, see if I could get a meal. He tells me, sure, no problem, although the Sally Ann is way over on the other side of town. I'm pretty sure he just drove around aimlessly for the next little while, to give us time to chat and become best friends. He finally says, "Well, hey, I live near here, why not we stop in at my place and I'll fry us up both a couple burgers?" I'd much rather have stopped in at some retail establishment, but man, I was *tired,* Dude, and I was hungry. I said, 'sure, whatever'.

I wasn't surprised that he had a really swell townhouse on the ocean, in Little Compton, out on Goosewing Beach. Those guys always seemed to have money. We ended up having cheeseburgers and chips with beer. We sat on the floor at an oversized coffee table, like it was made as a dining table for people who like to sit on the floor to eat. It probably made him feel like a 'hep cat'. After stuffing my stomach and tipping down a couple beers, I was nodding out, man. I just needed sleep. This guy, Garry—with two R's—he laughed and told me I might as well crawl into bed. There was a spare bedroom.

There are alarms going off in my head, and I didn't like any of my immediate options in life. I wasn't just tired, Dude, I was sleep-deprived. That's a real thing. It is illegal under the Geneva Convention to intentionally inflict that on POW's. It is considered a form of torture. I traveled with a sleeping bag but rarely used it. There was almost always some place to crash. Seven days and nights I was outside. On the best night of it I might have dozed on and off for three hours. Then spent most of the next day standing in the sun trying to catch rides that turned out to be going down the road just a few miles. All that time living on stale snacks and whatever I could scrounge up to eat. A few days of that, I was a little loopy. By the end of a week, I was a wreck—weak, spacy, mentally scrambled, and just so *desperately* needed sleep and nutrition. Not to mention a bath; at that point so dirty and grimy, I was ashamed of myself. There was somewhere in me a small voice telling me that I was exercising poor judgement, but Dude, if you have never experienced that kind of exhaustion, you just don't know how distorted your thinking can become.

I finally said "what I'd really like to do is take a shower, if that is okay". He said, "great, and while you are in there, I'll run your clothes through the wash". Another necessity, believe me. Okay, so I stripped down in the bathroom, tossed my clothes out and locked the door. Boy, did that shower hit the spot. Ever been there? Where you are so filthy and funky that a hot shower is just bliss? I was ripe, man. I treated myself to a long, hot shower, and at the end, turned on cold water as long as I could stand it to wake myself up and started thinking I'd get my clothes, say thanks for dinner and head out.

I found this big, fluffy robe on the inside of the bathroom door and put it on. I felt ridiculous, but hey, I had no clothes at the moment. I went out to fetch my back pack, but Garry told me he had taken the liberty of getting all my clothes together to make it a full load, and everything was in the dryer. As much as my small wardrobe needed laundering, this really bothered me, but hey, what could I do? I checked, and everything was just too damp to put on, so I sat on the couch.

Then there was a glass of beer in my hand. Why not? Of course, the beer instantly nullified the effects of my cold shower and next thing I knew, Garry was shaking my shoulder, waking me up and telling me to go ahead and take the guest bedroom and he would see me in the morning. I was too tired to think. I carried my beer glass to the kitchen sink and when I set it down, noticed a steak knife there on the counter. I slipped it into the pocket of this robe with some vague thought that if he got aggressive with me, I would pull it on him, let him know I was serious. I headed to the bedroom, wrapped in this big drag queen robe, climbed between the sheets and was instantly dead to the world.

I have no concept of how long I'd been asleep when my eyes popped open and I realized that Garry was in the bed with me, his arm over my waist. *Spooning* me. I started to move and suddenly his other arm was around my throat. His lips were on my ear, telling me to relax. I tried to move, but the arm across my throat squeezed down; I didn't have a chance of getting away. Dude, I was a kid. I didn't weigh a buck thirty-five soaking wet with rocks in my pockets. This guy was fifteen years older, way bigger, way stronger, and with a serious tactical advantage. I was freaking out. There was still a sheet between us when all this came down. I am guessing he didn't realize that until it got to this point.

Dude, the guy was poking me, you understand…poke, poke, poke, the sheet was between us, but just toying with me. I couldn't see anything, but I understood what it was that was jabbing at me. With his lips on my ear, he whispered that he was going to pull that sheet away, and I should just relax. This next part, Dude, I don't know how to explain, there was no thinking on my part. Nothing. I had no idea what happened until it was over, and even then, I was utterly dumbfounded. While he was tugging at that sheet, his arm across my throat loosened up slightly and all in one motion, that steak knife was in my hand, I was rolling over toward him and pushing that knife up under his rib cage, my palm following through so that the end of the knife went all the way in. I mean that knife disappeared. He let go of me then.

I was suddenly on the floor, sitting with my back against the wall, looking at this guy who had an expression of absolute surprise on his face. His eyes were wide open and he was making sounds like he was choking, gasping for breath at the same time. There was blood bubbling out of his mouth and then he was still. When this guy died, his eyes were wide open. Gradually, they closed part way and it was creepy as hell. He was looking at me, Dude, from the other side. If it hadn't been for that, I probably would have sat there for a long, long time, just staring off into space. I had to get away from those eyes, though. I got up, turned on a bedside lamp and walked around the foot of the bed. Dude, those eyes followed me. No matter where I went, the eyes followed me. Freaked me the fuck out, I shit you not. One of the pillows was on the floor; I picked it up, and tossed it from across the room, trying to land it on his face to cover those eyes. It landed and sort of rolled off. I went into the master bedroom and got more pillows and went back. Standing as far from the bed as possible, I tried to throw one over to cover his face, to cover those eyes. Another miss. The third one did it.

"Nine," I interrupted, "what was up with the pillows? Why pillows?"

"Truthfully, I don't know, Nine continued. "I needed to cover those eyes, but hey, there were towels, blankets, rugs, various articles of clothing, all kinds of stuff in the apartment. Why was I concentrating on covering his eyes with a frickin' pillow? Why is a pillow the thing you use to cover a dead guy's face? Did I mention that I was a little wigged out here? Does any of what I was doing have to make logical sense? To me in that moment, the only thing that would work was a pillow. The other weird thing is, once his eyes were covered, I relaxed. I mean, I was just suddenly stress-free, nonchalant, thinking in rational, down-to-earth terms. I was telling myself to get my clothes from the dryer, get dressed, gather up whatever I could use from the apartment, try to wipe out my finger prints and so on. Getting my clothes from the dryer, this thought entered my head: *I just killed a man and I am remarkably calm and collected. I am not freaked out on any level. What's up with that? How can this be?* As a flower child—meaning a person utterly committed to peace and love—I know all that is a punch line these days but I was a true believer—*how can this not be utterly mind-blowing for me? Why isn't there some kind of reaction on my part?* It was a puzzlement. After getting my clothes from the dryer, I was dressed and heading toward the bathroom and suddenly had a devastating cramp in my stomach. I mean—*Dude!*—I was bent over with my hands around my middle, this powerful claw squeezing my gut. It was excruciating, and had me frozen, my mouth open, I couldn't make a sound or draw a breath. I stood there like that for maybe 30 seconds and then all of a sudden, whoosh!—my bowels emptied like someone kicked over a bucket of water. Or, raw sewage, more to the point. I don't want to be too graphic here, but I want you to understand. This was completely liquid, oily, greasy, and the reek of it was like nothing I have ever encountered anywhere. I made my way back to the shower and turned the water on, and undressed as it ran over me. I did my best to rinse my clothes and then tossed them out onto the bathroom floor. I don't know how many times I soaped up and rinsed off under scalding hot water, but still didn't feel clean when I was finally done. I gathered up my wet stuff in a plastic bag and dressed in my other pair of jeans. The clothes in the trash bag were destined for the nearest dumpster.

It was much later—I mean years later—that I realized that whole thing was the reaction I was wondering why I didn't have. The psyche works in strange and mysterious ways. In my case, the freak-out was expressed physically instead of psychologically. Who knows why?

I did a quick run-through of apartment for stuff that would be useful on the road, and came across a pearl-handled switchblade in a dresser drawer. That went into my pocket, along with some jewelry, a small amount of cash, and some other small articles that would fit into a backpack. Then there was nothing to do but split. I turned up the AC to high, hoping it would help keep the smell down, and high-tailed it out of there. I still wanted to get to New York, but I had friends over in Cambridge, Mass, and made that my short-term destination. Being somewhere else right then seemed like a really good idea."

As I was saying before, Nine told his story the way guys in the joint do…it was filled with, *suddenly there was a beer in my hand*. What did that mean? Did it appear by magic? Did the guy tell him, go ahead and get yourself a beer? Did someone offer it and he accepted? My point is, there are a lot of ways to end up with a beer in your hand, but the one he chose is utterly passive. The beer was suddenly there. The beer *happened* to him. There was nothing he could do about it. And at that point, what else could he do but drink it down? He knew he was tired and he knew that a beer would make him sleepy, but it all happened to him, so he is not responsible for whatever events followed his having that beer. Ergo, he is a victim. Another person might have said, "I made the mistake of having a beer, and in my condition, it just knocked me out," but that would mean he was responsible for his actions and what grew out of those actions.

"I didn't want to be seen walking away from this place," Nine continued. "In the end, my only real option was to take his car put some real estate between me and *there*. I drove down to Boston in less than two hours and left the Lincoln parked with the keys in it near the Charles River Esplanade. Cambridge is just across the river; I connected with my people, got stoned—man, did I need that—and tried to forget about what had just happened.

Angela Davis was speaking on the Harvard campus the next night and I was excited about that. My friends there were both students. Bobby was at MIT and Roberta was journalism major at Radcliff. That's right, Robert and Roberta, Bobby and Bobbi. Neither of them was amused by the obvious Bobbsie Twins reference and liked me because I never made it. I also got points from Roberta for not referring to Radcliff as a "girl's school". Radcliff is a Women's College. That kind of thing was serious business with Roberta. She was part of a feminist group known as *Cell 16*. Those chicks were no-nonsense. She was cool though; worked at a place that counseled guys in how to avoid the draft and had founded a group that that provided free breakfast for school kids. Anyway, we had some time to kill and were downtown, in the Central Square area, walking along Mass Ave. when this kid stepped out and asked if we were looking for some weed. *But of course.* He told me that he had some for sale and that it was like nothing we had ever smoked before.

I have to tell you about this guy, because I remember him so clearly even now. This kinda goes to what I was saying earlier about the times we lived in back then. I think especially for those of us who were on the move all the time. Life was full of amazing experiences. I hesitate to mention this guy's most outstanding feature, but as long as I am spilling...this kid was uncommonly good looking. Just a really, really nice looking guy—I'd guess between 16 and 18 years old—something *angelic* in his features which seemed to be somewhat Asiatic. He had the most amazing afro I have ever seen. It was enormous. Anyway, I asked what was unique about his weed and he told me it was *silly* weed—pronounced *silliweed*—and that it came from Ghana, in Africa. We talked for a while and just kind of connected.

We ended up going into a coffee shop and talked for a long time. Then it was a choice of going to this guy's house or seeing Angela Davis. As much as I wanted to check out this silliweed, it was a no-brainer for me. He drew us a map to his place and we parted company.

Angela Davis is mostly a name from history now, except for those of us stuck in that era. Some white folks remember when she was in the news, but just shrug if you mention the name. *BFD.* Most of these black guys don't understand what she was about. They think she was Black Nationalist or just one more radical out there demanding equality. Some of them get rowdy if you tell them she was communist. That word is used so much as an insult or to denigrate someone's position. Even back then, a lot of people didn't get it. She just wasn't preaching communism or calling for a communist revolution. Her political persuasion, though, was communist. Angela Davis was a communist. She was a member of Che-Lumumba, which was an all-black branch of the Communist Party, USA, while she was at Brandeis. She joined the black panthers, but was first and foremost dedicated to Che-Lumumba. The concept of communism has become so bastardized… anyway, that's a conversation we should have sometime.

This particular night she opened up with, *"We have to talk about liberating minds as well as liberating society."* She talked a lot about prison that night. I remember this line in particular, *"Jails and prisons are designed break human beings, to convert the population into specimens in a zoo—obedient to our keepers, but dangerous to each other."* Did she nail it, Dude? My all-time favorite was this, *'I am no longer accepting the things I cannot change. I am changing the things I cannot accept.'* Great stuff, no? It was a good talk. She spoke for over an hour. I was so glad I didn't miss it.

Okay, I'm off-track. You gotta hear about the silliweed, though, man. This was too far-out. We followed the directions Spencer had given us and ended up way off in BFE. This house was huge. And ancient. It made me think of the Addams Family. As we approached, the door opened and this black guy stepped out, maybe in his 70's, reminded me of Scat Man Carruthers, actually. This guy was dressed in formalwear. I don't mean he was wearing a nice suit; I mean, formal, as in black tie and tails. He was carrying a top hat, although I don't think he ever put it on. He smiled and said, "You must be Spenser's new friends!" as though he was absolutely delighted with the idea. "You are welcome here," he said, "Come in, come in." Inside the house was like a museum. Stuff everywhere.

We were shown to seats in the living room. There was shelf on the wall, maybe six feet off the floor, and it was filled with dolls. Several dozen, it was hard to tell, but they were magnificent. Obviously handmade. I mean, Dude, the detail in each one. Just extraordinary. Each face was unique, hand painted, with individual hairstyles. Some had little hats. All of their outfits were amazing. Hand stitched, tailored to each one. Intricately detailed. The whole room was full of stuff on shelves, in glass cases, sitting on pedestals. Not all of it was as amazing as the dolls, but it was all just really neat stuff.

The guy, we never got a name, started talking about these people he knew who had hiked across the Himalayan mountains in the dead of winter. It was a fascinating tale. I wish I could recall it word for word for you. He wrapped that up with, "but that's not what you're here for, you folks are interested in Silliweed." He pointed to an ornate cigarette box on one of the coffee tables and said, "Help yourselves." That box was filled with hand-rolled joints; we took two and split them between us.

In one corner, there was a hexagonal glass case, maybe four feet in diameter. It gave the impression of coming up through the floor and going through the ceiling into the upstairs. I wanted to go up and check. Inside was a fairy garden, filled with intricate miniature people and fantasy creatures. It had stairways going up the sides of the mountains, waterfalls, living plants, so much going on, I felt like I could spend days studying it trying to absorb it all. I can tell you this: if I had the option of shrinking down to size and in living in that little world, I'd go in a heartbeat. It was the most beautiful place I've ever seen. There were also a couple of regular aquariums. One was, I'm guessing, about 300 gallons, with lights that cast the water a soft shade of light blue throughout. It was filled with jellyfish. If that doesn't sound special, you are missing something. It was so peaceful and serene with those guys just sort of flowing around in there. Beautiful. There was so much to see, but hey, by this time, I had a serious buzz going and had to sit down. I returned to my over-stuffed chair and took a deep breath and let it out slowly. I was *high*, Dude. High, in the traditional meaning of the word. Just blissed out. I thought, *what's so silly about this?*

"I sat there with my eyes closed, just enjoying this wonderful sensation and felt myself slowly rising into the air. Dude, I've been buzzed before. This did not wig me out. It was a really nice effect. Then I was sort of sailing through the air. Really cool. I opened my eyes and I was across the room from where I had been sitting, staring into the eyes of a Rock Fish, if you know your tropicals. I had seen this salt water tank earlier but never got to it. This was a huge tank, with a big chunk of coral in the bottom and just a few fish, including a giant Plecosto-mus. Very clean, very, very cool. This fish and I looked deep into each other's eyes for what seemed a long time and then I was walking back toward my chair, but from a completely different direction than where the aquarium was. I sat down and said, "Wow".

The old man laughed and said, "Wow, indeed, my young friend." He started talking to me and I was cracking up laughing, I mean laughing in a way that literally made my ribs hurt. Nothing in life had ever been so funny. I have no idea now what he said.

"Nine," I interrupted. "Where are we going?" This was turning into just another stoner story, and I have heard enough of those over the years. I've lived a few of them myself. These kinds of stories are a dime a dozen.

"Yeah, sorry, I got sidetracked. This place is a story worth hearing, though. I'll run it past you some time. Let me just wrap this up." He paused to light a Kool. "From the time I sat down from looking at the Rock Fish until we left, there were a dozen really far out adventures in that house. At one point I sat back down and closed my eyes again. I snoozed out; my next awareness was this really severe Chinese woman standing over me saying, "*You go now!*" I opened my eyes and was blinking, looking around. Bobby and Bobbie were across the room, both of them obviously just waking up. '*You go now!*' Really shrill. It seemed like a good idea to split.

As we were walking away, Roberta said, 'I really wanted to ask about copping some of that weed.' I did too, but we were all seriously intimidated by the Chinese woman.

It was weird. After that night, I was *tired*, in a way that new to me. Just weary. I wanted to go home. Greenwich Village was closer, though, and my peeps there were the kind of people you want to be with in a crisis. Pushing that knife all the way into that guy, it kinda fucked with my head, no matter how stoned I got. I *wanted* to go home, but I was *drawn* to NYC.

The trip was uneventful; I got off the train a couple miles from Man-hattan, and stuck my thumb out. Got picked up almost immediately. I got lucky with this ride; a couple from Arizona who wanted to be able to tell the folks back home they had visited Greenwich Village. Normally I resented such people—come on, man, this is a neighborhood, not a freaking zoo—but these folks were nice in an innocent way, so I indulged them. Besides, they smoked a joint with me—just to show how cool they actually were—and it got me a ride pretty much to my doorstep. They wanted to see the Fillmore East and where Abby Hoffman used to live and that was an easy one. I've only walked past Abby's place a thousand times—30 St. Mark's Place. The Fillmore East is right around the corner; if I told you the concerts I've seen at Fillmore East—not to mention the Fillmore West in San Francisco—you'd think I was just going down a list of everybody who rocked it back then. Anyway, I had them drop me off at the Second Street Deli—best bagels in the universe, I always stop in when I am in the Village—and right in the neighborhood.

It was getting on to evening, and I was just strolling along, enjoying my buzz when suddenly—*pow!*, out of nowhere, this explosion in the middle of my chest. I was stunned. Man, it hurt. I was staggered backward and suddenly there is a hand at my throat, pushing me up against the wall of an apartment building. There was an angry face demanding money from me. What? *What is happening?* I was in pain, but mostly, just confused. Scattered. I couldn't focus or grasp what was happening. Next thing, *pow*, again, this time a punch to the side of the head and as I was falling, this guy pushed me into an ally there and I went down hard. There was a tattoo on his shoulder, *Angelo!* Dude, I was laying on my back in this ally, dizzy, terrified—I admit it—I had never even been in a fight. I was not equipped for this this. So I'm looking up at this guy and was struck by the idea that he wasn't huge. Intimidating as hell, but not a big guy. You could see he was wiry, though. Angelo was maybe five foot ten, slender. He was dark skinned, black hair, greasy, a 50's look about him. He was wearing a sleeveless t-shirt and back jeans, and some wicked looking stompers. He was shouting at me, "You think I'm playing, bitch? Give me your fucking money!" Dude, I didn't *have* any money. I remember laying there wishing I did, wishing I wasn't too fucked up to apologize for being broke. I wanted to promise that I would go get some money and bring it back to him. I'm not even kidding you, Dude, if he had said, *yeah go get some money and bring it back*, I would have. I was freaking *terrified*, man.

I couldn't even speak. He reached down with both hands, grabbed my shirt front and slung me deeper into the ally. The end was blocked off. Someone—I assume Angelo—had pushed the building's dumpsters across to block the way. Who does that, Dude? He just set up a trap and waited for someone soft-looking to come along to start punching on. To this day, that is utterly mind-boggling to me. How can someone be like that? How can that be what gives you joy in life?

At this point I was up against the wall and he was coming toward me, walking slowly, loving every second of it. I'm sure the money was secondary. I dug deep into my pocket to show I was trying to cooperate and found the switchblade I had picked up down in Goosewing. I pulled it out and flicked it open. I was holding it straight out in front of me, like a magic wand or something, *pointing* it at the guy.

He stopped in his tracks and laughed, "Oh, you a badass now? You gotta cut me?" He was genuinely amused. He came up on me, throwing punches, but pulling them, showing me he can slip past that knife and tag me a dozen different ways. I backed up and started sort of waving the knife around in front of me. Finally, I saw a round-house left coming at me and I could see he wasn't going to pull it. I ducked under it and swung the knife at the same time. I felt it make contact and leaned into it. Just like in Goosewing, that blade found a soft spot and went all the way in. And just like before, I was utterly stunned. I had a knife in my hand, but nowhere in my mind was the thought, "I am going to stab this guy". This time I pulled it back out. That took the fight out of him.

Angelo staggered back and was leaning against the opposite wall. He was bleeding profusely and seemed shocked, but also angry. Mostly angry. He was leaning back, holding his side, cursing and telling me all the things he was going to do to me. I had to get past him to get to the mouth of the ally. If I could have spoken, I would have apologized. I was thinking something along the lines of, *he was beating on me before and didn't even know me; now I have made him mad, how much worse is it going to be now?* He was talking about beating my face into the street and pushing himself away from the wall, like he was coming for me. I snatched up a brick out of the pile of rubble and slung it. Cracked him right in the forehead. That sat him down. Now he was just cursing me, and now he had two things to be mad at me about. I was utterly desperate, Dude, terrified, freaking out; I snatched up another brick and started to throw it and he sort of started whimpering. That brought me up short. He wrapped both hands around his head and said, "No, stop, that's too much. It's too much…" I dropped the brick and ran.

Dude, that haunts me to this day. *"That's too much…"* Too much, as in, too much pay-back—this is way more than I did to you? Or, too much as in, this is more than I can take? Too much to bear? Or what? "That's too much! "I've never forgotten that. Nine shook his head slowly a few times, "I wish I could," he added quietly.

"You already know the punch-line. Word on the street next day is that this guy Angelo had been found dead in an ally off 4th street. Beaten and stabbed, they said." Once again, it time to split.

I made my way out to the highway and got on I-80. Caught a ride with a trucker who took me all the way to Butler, Pennsylvania, and ten minutes after I got out, these two biker dudes picked me up. They were coming out of Jersey, heading to Saginaw. They were wiped out and told me that if I would drive and chip in for gas, they'd take me to my front door in Michigan. *Hell yeah!* They were all about driving straight through and I was good with that. From the conversation, I gathered that they had some legal problems, and that the car might have been hot. They were in a hurry to get where they were going, but I couldn't tell if it was about that or if they were seriously running from whatever they had left behind them. I didn't care either way. I had a ride all the way home. I was all smiles.

We did stop for a spell in Cleveland for the one guy to enjoy a quickie with this chick he used to be hooked up with. That gave me the opportunity for a short nap, which I needed. Then we were on the road again. Next thing you know, I'm strolling down Washtenaw Avenue, happy to be home.

"Dude, killing those guys does not make me a *killer*. Not having a conscience problem over it does not make me a psycho sociopath," Nine insisted argumentatively. "What was I *supposed* to do?"

Nine was stoned enough that his guard was down and in his eyes, I saw a man tormented. He wasn't demanding answers from me, he was trying to convince himself.

So many guys on this yard, with so many issues. Right and wrong, good and bad, sin and virtue. Abstract notions, all way above my pay grade. I looked him in the eye, "Nine, you are okay in my book. Don't ever let *anyone* convince you that you are *wrong* for protecting yourself. Your first and foremost job in life is to take care of *You.*

Cloud Nine stood slowly, stretched his back and said quietly, "Thanks for the buzz. Someday I'll tell you more about the Silly House. No charge." With that, he turned and strolled away, a man whose conscience was eating him alive, who was tormented by the notion that he couldn't feel remorse.

The only thing I know for sure was that I wouldn't rest until I learned more about that silly house out there north of Cambridge, Mass. For the moment, though…A friend of mine was molested by a particularly odious predator when he was a youngster. We learned recently that that creep had been convicted on a number of charges for similar aberrant behavior. He was scheduled to arrive here this afternoon. There will be a welcoming committee. I think I will mosey on over and see how that scenario plays itself out. There might be a story there…

The Cracker Jack Man

I can't imagine how you heard that old story about the cackles, but yeah, that was me. At this stage of the game, what's the point of denying it? I don't usually tell prison stories, but hey, you want cackles, I'll give you cackles.

These "local color" stories are hard to tell because there is so much background you need to understand for it to make any sense. As far as the joint goes, I will be the first inmate ever to give people the straight poop. Like I said, what do I care? First of all, take everything you know for sure about prison—everything you have read, seen in a movie or generally accept as a given. Bunch it all up together in your mind and hit the Delete key. Everything You Know Is Wrong.

Prison populations are made up of goofs, geeks, dope fiends, and psychopaths. There is nobody here for doing something clever and there is no honor among thieves. That thing in the movies when someone is found to be informant and is butchered on the spot? Give me a break. If there is a stabbing on the yard, the real danger is that you will be trampled by the stampede to see who can get to the captain and be the first to tell. When you see on the news that some crackhead has beat his great-grandmother to death for the change in her pockets or some atrocious sex crime involving children—hey, those are the people you will meet in prison. Those dashing, devilishly clever criminals you see on the silver screen are actors.

This little tale takes place in Jackson prison, a small village surrounded by brick walls. This institution is comprised of "inside the walls" and Trustee Division. T.D. is composed of The Blocks—two regular cell blocks outside of the walls—and five farms that are located several miles from the main prison. TD is the place to be. Guys out there can get all kinds of stuff, even liquor. Hell, you can just up and walk away of you want to. On one of those farms, they raise chickens, which provide eggs and Sunday dinner or the whole enchilada. Guys in TD come inside for medical, dental and other things TD isn't equipped to handle.

So one day I am over in the infirmary and see this kid who was recently transferred to TD and ended up on the chicken farm. He was loving it. He went to telling me about this stuff they call "cackles," which is an additive they mixed into the chicken feed to make the egg shells tougher and reduce breakage in transport. Somebody got the bright idea to mix a spoonful of this in a cup of coffee and drink it. (You really gotta wonder, don't you?) Turns out, this stuff will make you high as a witch doctor. Kinda guy I was in those days, my immediate response was, "Gimme some." The kid told me he had a homeboy out there who was a truck driver and delivered supplies to where I work, and he would send me some through him.

I was assigned to grounds maintenance at the time. All of the fertilizers, poisons, gas for the mowers, and so forth was stored outside the walls for security reasons and brought inside in small amounts, as needed. I'm looking for this dude to slip me an envelope or somesuch with a couple shots in it so I can cop a buzz and go on about my business. I'm telling you, I almost freaked when we were unloading our supplies and the guy slaps a twenty-five-pound bag and says, "This is from Packy."

The grounds maintenance building is called the "yard shack'" although it is actually a very large building filled with all kinds of junk. There must be a hundred or so bags of different things laying around, been there for years. It was easy to just stash my bag in the mess. I scooped up a coffee cup full to take back to my cell and tried a spoon. I gotta tell ya, it was okay. Sorta like speed, but it made your face feel all fuzzy and set off this vibrating sensation all over. Not bad at all, really.

I flagged down a couple of the regulars and turned them on to a shot, and pretty soon everyone was clamoring for more. Within an hour, a spoon was selling for five bucks and there was no keeping up with demand.

The language in prison is really interesting. Someone should do a study. For no reason I can imagine, this stuff was immediately being referred to as "cracker crumbs." Several other names came into use, but the most widely-used label eventually became Cracker Jacks. A five-dollar package was a "sack."

Cracker Jacks was an overnight sensation. Nobody knew I had twenty-five pounds of it. I had three homeboys I was tight with and I provided them all with an eight-ounce scoop for a hundred bucks each, which allowed them to get zipped (and stay that way) and make a few bucks at the same time. Once they got rolling, they were coming to me several times a day for re-ups, and had a network of guys working under them.

In the meantime, I was busy selling five dollar sacks as fast as I could put them together. As far as anyone knew, I was just one of many out there slinging sacks of this stuff.

Pretty soon, I got more money than I have ever had in my life. Institutional money is called "script" and made in the form of poker chips in the denominations of quarters, dimes, and dollars. I had seven large coffee cans of dollars. I had over one hundred cartons of cigarettes under my bunk, and twelve really nice leather coats. I had guitars, radios, jewelry, canned food and munchies that wouldn't quit. There were five different guys holding stuff for me in their cells. I paid them for their services and also told them go ahead and chow down on the groceries, but don't hit me too hard on the other stuff. In this situation it is understood—the guy is gonna steal a little or he is gonna steal a lot. As long as no one disappeared with everything I left with him, I was happy. I never knew how much of my stuff these guys helped themselves to because I didn't keep track. What did I care? It was all gravy.

I had stuff stashed all over the yard shack, and gave away tons of groceries and such to these old heads who had nothing. All this, and I had barely made a dent in my stash. Absolutely everybody in town was buzzing on this junk. You never seen such happy maniacs.

If you are familiar with the convict mentality, you know what happened next. Not to put too fine a point on it: Everything turned to shit. Instead of just mixing up a spoonful and quietly enjoying the pleasant sensation, these goofs went to mixing like ten spoons at a time.

Some of them were mixing Cracker Jacks with valium, a mix referred to as a "CJ and V." There were others mixing it with the traditional institutional favorite, fermented anything. Heroin addicts at that time were shooting a concoction of Talwin and Valium (known as Teddys and Bettys), which provides a rush similar to heroin. Their new thing was to drink a Mintzes Mixer (named for Warden Mintzes)— a Cracker Jacks and hooch cocktail—followed up by shooting some Teddys and Bettys. And who knew what the hell else? All of a sudden, those knuckleheads were dropping like flies. It all went off the Stupidity Index one Sunday when three guys died and nine were in the psych unit under heavy sedation. They carried a van load of bozos down to U of M hospital for kidney dialysis, and I don't know how many turned yellow and learned that, for all intents and purposes, they no longer had a functioning liver.

While all this is going on, one of my partners got beat up and robbed in a blind spot over behind the kitchen. He was so busted up, he has never recovered all the sight in his right eye. Over a few teaspoons of this junk that makes eggs more transportable. Next thing you know, some guy gets stabbed over a spoon; another guy, for criminy sake, mainlines some of this crap and spends the last five minutes of his life screaming in agony and vomiting blood. It gets stupider by the day.

I cut off the source, but by this time there was so much in circulation, the supply continued throughout the week. As it began getting scarce, the violence increased. These idiots were killing each other over this stuff. Do you understand what I am telling you? You got a spoonful of chicken feed additive that makes you high, and someone will jam a screwdriver through your heart and take it. What's wrong with this picture?

By this time, the administration is frantic. They don't know what the hell is going on. They lock down the whole joint and bring in cops from other institutions, as well as State Police sniff dogs, to do an inch-by-inch, fine-tooth-comb search of the entire facility and everyone in it. It took a large truck to haul off all the weapons they found; you'd be amazed at all the other weird stuff that turned up (that's another story in itself, believe me), but as I could've told them, they found zip regarding cracker jacks. They don't even know what they're looking for.

I was ready at that point to never come within a country mile of that stuff again. Or at least for a long time. As far as I was concerned, I had enough to live like a king for the next couple years, and if the need arose, I could always very quietly put a few sacks out to a selected clientele without raising a ruckus. Life is never that simple in jail. One of the clowns I put to work got involved with these bad dudes slinging heroin. In the end—even with as much money we were making, you understand—he somehow owes them a small fortune. I got him begging me to come up with some more or these guys will kill him. (I know these guys. This is a serious threat.) This other goofball went bananas with a couple bookies and he ended up in debt for a king's ransom. All of a sudden, he's making sounds that suggest his only way out may to be roll over on me. I gave both of them twelve ounces to get straight and made them understand this was The End. They turned this over to the people they owed, who immediately sacked it and picked up where we left off. A spoon is about one gram; there are twenty-eight grams in an ounce. I just put a fresh twenty-four ounces out there. You do the math.

At this point, we got a full-blown crisis. The guys selling this stuff don't care about squat except getting as rich as possible before it all plays out. They started cutting the stuff to stretch it, and didn't care what they cut it with. Rat poison was no different than powdered sugar. It was time to get out of Dodge. I put in a request to transfer to Marquette, which is way the hell and gone up in the Upper Peninsula. That was a radical step. Nobody wants to go to Marquette. Transfer there is usually for disciplinary reasons. As prisons go, that one ain't much fun. I gave the classification clerk my best leather jacket and two cartons of Pall Malls to make sure it happened. I was scheduled for the next bus.

There is quite a lot of "green money"—regular U.S. currency—in circulation in Jackson, although it is contraband and will be confiscated if found. Green money is quite valuable. Think about it. There is only so much you can do with script. Green money you can make deals with cops to bring you stuff in, send it home, hire a lawyer, etc. I was paying top dollar for all the green I could get my hands on and sending it out to a Christian girl I knew who offered to open a bank account and deposit it for me. The leather coats went out to different people as gifts; liquidating my assets became a full-time job.

I made a deal with this old Arab guy who wanted to buy a hundred cartons of cigarettes for ten-dollars each.

I had done business with him in the past and I knew he was straight, so I gave him the cigarettes. He was on his way to the telephone to call his wife and tell her where to send my money, when these three dope fiends blindsided the old guy and robbed him. He made it to the infirmary, but died later that night. Later, Ali. Good bye, thousand bucks. A couple days before the Marquette transfer, there was a major shakedown in Eight Block. Three cops shook down my cell and had a field day.

Any amount of script over ninety-five dollars is considered contraband. They counted out ninety-five of them jokers and left me a receipt for the other seven hundred and seventy. There are also limits on clothing, cassette tapes and the like. Any jewelry, other than a wedding band with no stone and a watch valued under fifty dollars, is contraband. The guys holding the loot for me were likewise hit hard. Say it this way, I lost a lot of stuff. Those rules are designed to discourage the kind of hustling that results in the kind of wealth I had accumulated. The kind of wealth I had accumulated indicated I was involved with something not entirely kosher. If I hadn't already been classified for Marquette, I could, at that point, have reasonably expected to be sent to Marquette.

The losses didn't really bother me because, hey, I'm the Cracker Jacks Man. My last day there, I scooped up seven pounds of that stuff and stashed it away in my property. The remainder stayed right where it was. Chances are good I'll be back this way before all is said and done. That was money in the bank.

After arriving in Marquette, I got with a couple old heads I knew and ran the situation down on them. My proposition is this: you guys hold on to this stuff, get high as much as you want, but don't sell any. You want something from the commissary, let me know, and I've got you covered. Let me be the one and only person here selling this stuff so I can keep things quiet and under control. I'll do this in such a way that outside of a chosen few, no one will even know this stuff is in town.

Nothing is ever that simple in jail. Turns out the one guy was a real goof. He couldn't resist the chance to make a buck and play the role of drug kingpin. He had the smallest amount, which was sixteen ounces in a Jergen's lotion bottle, but hey, do the math. That's a bunch of dope. He ounced it out and it was gone by the time I knew anything. Next thing you know, the yard looks like gladiator school and the administration is freaking. I'll say this for myself: I'm always thinking. This brainstorm hit me like the solution to all my earthly problems.

I stopped the captain and told him to put me together with the deputy warden, and I can solve all this Cracker Jacks foolishness before lunch. Ten minutes later I was sitting across the desk from The Man, who said only, "I'm all ears". My rap was simple. Cracker Jacks is in Marquette; none of us wants a repeat of what happened in Jackson.

I am in a unique position to stop it. I will bring to you, and place on your desk, every last crumb of that stuff that exists in this institution—and I can promise you we're talking no less than six pounds—and guarantee you that it will not resurface. I will give up no names or any other information, but I will stop this scourge once and for all. In a very deadpan voice, the dep responded, "And all this you will do as a service to humanity".

"No," I responded, "All this I will do for a parole."

The dep flipped open my file and went over my particulars. They ain't pretty. It's the damnedest thing, really. On paper, I look like a real desperado, but in reality, I'm not such a bad guy. I mean, I'm not dangerous, and there is a long list of people I won't steal from. Those who know me say I am generous to a fault, and I can be a million laughs. Right now I am doing thirty-five years for a bank robbery in which gunfire was exchanged with the police. That is what is known as "aggravating circumstances." They get aggravated when you have a Hollywood-style shootout with the cops in downtown traffic. What can I say? I was scared. Nobody got hurt.

I also have a juvenile record for fleeing and eluding police in a stolen vehicle and escaping from a detention facility in Kentucky. I have adult arrests for cocaine (twice), and this really unpleasant thing that had to do with a piece of jewelry they found on me that was last seen on a corpse in a funeral home. Aggravated circumstances, roughly translated means, *This clown gets no breaks.* The dep looked at me over the top of his glasses and said, "A parole. You're a comedian, right?" I asked him if he thought all those corpses littering the yard downstate were a skit from Saturday Night Live. He said he would get back with me.

I left out of there really depressed. That guy treated me like I was some kind of chump, just when I was feeling clever about myself. "Don't call me, I'll call you." Right.

I spent the rest of the week laying in my cell, not thinking about anything, just chilling out. The yard was in chaos. That sixteen ounces of cackles had those fools going berserk. When I heard that this kid from Grand Rapids had died, I was just sick. I did time with his dad back when we were both in juvie; he gave me my first tattoo. I gathered up every last crumb of that stuff that was still stashed away and flushed it into nonexistence. Gone forever. Good riddance. *Finis.*

Bright and early the next morning, I was summoned to the deputy's office. He gave me a cup of coffee and sat me down. "Well," he said, " it took some doing, but word came this morning directly from the governor's office: I am ordered to get that stuff off the yard. If you can hold up your end of it, we can start processing your release papers. How much of that stuff can you bring me?"

That was nineteen years ago. I've been here in Marquette ever since. When I couldn't deliver, they took a closer look at me and found out about all the money and stuff that was confiscated from me down in Jackson. The coincidence that Cracker Jacks showed up in Marquette about the same time as I did was not overlooked. They confiscated everything I had except a toothbrush and a bar of soap and gave me a statement saying this was "suspected drug proceeds" and would be returned if their investigation cleared me. I don't know how much of an investigation there was, but apparently, I was never cleared.

The girl I sent all those hundred-dollar bills to moved without leaving a forward. Things got tight there for me for a while. I don't brood on stuff like that. I figger, that's life. You got your ups and you got your downs. I have been through a hundred scams and hustles since then. Right now I'm thinking, I know this guy who works in the treatment plant out in T.D. here. I figure I can tie a line to a handball and flush that sucker; he can fish it out on that end, attach a package of dope and I can haul it back in. I can cop a buzz, maybe make a few bucks...

About Phil Lippert

*P*hil Lippert was sentenced to life in prison, convicted as an accessory to murder at the age of seventeen in a case of betrayal, sexual intrigue, secret double-crossing, and lies by authorities. After serving nearly three decades in Michigan's notoriously brutal walled prison at Jackson, he escaped and lived quietly in Texas and Mexico for more than five years before recapture. In prison he earned his associate's degree from Jackson Community and nearly completed a bachelor's degree in psych and social science from Spring Arbor. He spent much of his prison time penning stories (literally) and working with Sister Patricia Schnapp's writing and social-issues classes out of Siena Heights University. Phil served 42 years in all before completing parole. He lives in Michigan with his wife, Cynthia.

Fresh Ink Group
Independent Multi-media Publisher

Fresh Ink Group / Push Pull Press

&

Hardcovers
Softcovers
All Ebook Platforms
Audiobooks
Worldwide Distribution

&

Indie Author Services
Book Development, Editing, Proofing
Graphic/Cover Design
Video/Trailer Production
Website Creation
Social Media Management
Writing Contests
Writers' Blogs
Podcasts

&

Authors
Editors
Artists
Experts
Professionals

&

FreshInkGroup.com
info@FreshInkGroup.com
Twitter: @FreshInkGroup
Facebook.com/FreshInkGroup
LinkedIn: Fresh Ink Group

Fresh Ink Group
FreshInkGroup.com

If you ever find yourself on the Strange Hwy—don't turn around. Don't panic. Just. Keep. Going. You never know what you'll find.

You'll see magic at the fingertips of an autistic young man; a teen girl's afternoon, lifetime of loss; a winged man, an angel? Demon—? Mother's recognition, peace to daughter; Danny's death, stifled secrets; black man's music, guitar transforms boy; dead brother, open confession; first love, supernatural? —family becomes whole!

You can exit the Strange Hwy, and come back any time you want.

See, now you know the way in, don't be a stranger.

Fresh Ink Group
FreshInkGroup.com

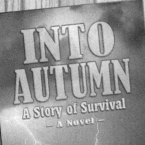

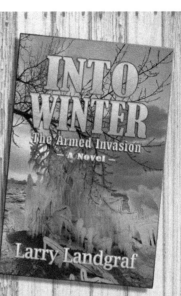
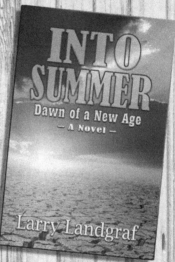

Four Seasons Series
Larry Landgraf

What drives a man to spend 26 years performing night after night? To persevere through a stifling tour bus, bad food, strange women, flared tempers, a plane nearly blown from the sky? Just how did that troubled military brat with a dream claw his way from dirt-floor dive-bar shows to the world's biggest stages? Aviator, author, and Country Music Hall of Fame drummer Mark Herndon lived that dream with one of the most popular and celebrated bands of all time. He learned some hard lessons about people and life, the music industry, the accolades and awards, how easy it is to lose it all . . . and how hard it is to survive, to embrace sobriety, to live even one more day.

Herndon's poignant memoir offers a tale at once cautionary and inspirational, delightful and heartbreaking, funny yet deeply personal. From innocence to rebellion to acceptance, can a man still flourish when the spotlight dims? Are true forgiveness, redemption, and serenity even possible when the powerful say everything you achieved somehow doesn't even count? That you're not who you and everyone who matters thought you were?

Mark Herndon refuses to slow down. So look back, look ahead, and join him on the trip. He's taking The High Road.

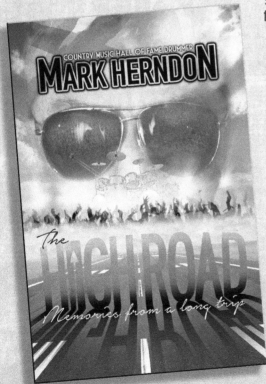

Fresh Ink Group
FreshInkGroup.com

CPSIA information can be obtained
at www.ICGtesting.com
Printed in the USA
BVHW060501070721
611241BV00016B/887